My Angel

by

Christine Young

ISBN: 978-1-62420-620-7

Cover Artist: Genene Valleau

Printed in the United States of America

Dedication

To Sharon Morris:
I couldn't have done it without you.
You taught me, encouraged me, made me frustrated and sometimes
confused, but you always supported my efforts.
Thank you.

Chapter One

Denver, 1893

A polished azure sky looked down on a day that vacillated between winter and spring--a day unable to make up its mind. Cool breezes lifted Angela Chamberlain's brand-new canary yellow skirt off the moisture-laden sidewalk. A blazing hot sun dried the puddles in the street left over from last night's deluge.

Unlike the day, Angela had no trouble making up her mind. Angela knew what she wanted out of life. She touched one finger to the sapphire earrings adorning her newly pierced ears.

She wanted adventure.

She had a terrible craving to see the world--to climb to the top of the Eiffel Tower, to walk the Great Wall of China. She yearned to fly in a hot-air balloon high above the earth, or ride in a gondola in Venice. She wanted to fall in love with a man who was as brave and smart as her father and as dangerous as Devil Blackmoor.

Angela's wish list had no end.

Instead of adventure and romance, in three short weeks she'd be enrolled in Miss Somebody's finishing school for young ladies, where knowing which fork to use was more important than riding with the wind on her favorite horse, Kangee. A place where changing one's clothes three times or more each day was common practice.

Two days ago she'd told her father she didn't want to go.

And two days ago her father had told her she would learn to appreciate the schooling and that she was a very lucky young woman. He'd also promised her a trip to the continent for a graduation present.

A graduation present! She wanted to yell at him, but wisely kept her mouth shut. She wanted to travel now. Today. But more than anything, she didn't want to be confined to the stuffy drawing rooms in the East. Just like her father, she needed freedom. But her father meant to take the choice from her.

To gossip and chatter with rich society women was not her destiny. To know which wine was served with fish would not make her happy. This was his dream for her. Sam Chamberlain needed to look to his own heart and remember the choices he had made twenty-five years ago.

Her destiny was out there somewhere, waiting for her to snap it up and hold the moment close to her heart. She knew what she wanted, and to prove her point, she'd bought a camera and had the machine sent over to the hotel. She meant to photograph all her adventures, every nook and cranny, every monument, every intriguing person.

Across the street and down two blocks, Devil Blackmoor had just taken the saddle off his horse. He brushed the stallion's back, all the while petting the animal's sleek coat and crooning into the horse's ear. Mesmerized, she watched his hands and the gentle way he stroked the horse.

She wished she had her camera.

Devil Blackmoor commanded her attention. He symbolized everything a father cautioned his daughter to be wary of. Despite the warning, Devil's strong jaw, his powerful shoulders and the confident way he held himself beckoned to every feminine nerve in Angela's body.

Angela clutched her hands to her chest, willing her gaze to shift to something or someone who wouldn't shatter her senses and set her blood boiling. Helpless to control her wayward heart, she kept looking back at Devil. She noticed everything about him, the way he moved, the way his denim jeans clung to his legs and the way they molded to his backside. Devil laughed at something the bouncer from the saloon said, and when he smiled, one edge of his mouth tilted crookedly. Angela's heart swooned and fluttered, and she thought she might never breathe again.

Beside the livery Mrs. Limpkin set several pies on the window-sill to cool. The smell of her apple pie dancing a jig on the same breeze that had lifted Angela's skirts earlier tantalized and teased Angela's stomach until it howled for a taste. Her mouth watered with anticipation, and a heady need to sink her teeth into all that life could offer her and more--much, much more--sent goose bumps straight to her toes.

"What ya doin' moonin' at Devil, Angela?" Fourteen-year-old Rusty Limpkin sidled up close to Angela and grinned. A mass of red freckles covered the boy's face. He smelled of the stables behind her and the horse manure he'd been shoveling all morning.

Trying not to inhale the pungent air beside her, Angela replied, "I'm not mooning at anyone." Angela turned on the boy, ready to defend her honor and unwilling to admit to the little scamp she was indeed staring at Devil Blackmoor. No, she was doing more than staring at the dangerous man: she was fantasizing about Devil and herself.

Rusty poked her shoulder. "For a kiss, I'll introduce you to Devil." He puckered his lips.

A shiver of disgust rippled down her spine. She searched for a reply. "And I'll tell your ma I saw you walking down Holladay Street."

"Aw, that's nothin' to be afeard of. Do that all the time. There's only whores down there. But that Devil Blackmoor--that's a whole different story. I heard tell Miss Iva over at the Gold Nugget told one of her customers that Devil had pleasured her in seven different ways."

Indignant, Angela ignored the stench emanating from the boy and inhaled deeply so she could put force behind her words. "Hush your mouth before I tell your ma. You've got no business listening to gossip like that." Angela felt the rise of heat to her cheeks, her mind reeling with the information Rusty had spouted without a blink of an eye. She'd seen firsthand how Devil had stroked his horse, and she'd wondered how she would feel if he stroked her so gently.

"It's not gossip. No sirree..." Rusty hitched his pants up. "I heard he's got hisself one of those harems and there's a hundred women or more inside. Heard tell when he's home, in Con-stan-ti-nople, he sees ten or more of them women each night. Besides, I'm not afeard of you. You're no bigger than a mite."

At a loss for words, Angela glared at the boy. "Go saddle my horse, Rusty." She shooed the boy away. But thoughts of harems rolled around in her head, and she wondered just what Devil did with those women each night.

"You gonna follow him out of town?" Rusty asked her as he brought Kangee out of the stable.

"It's none of your business what I do. I can ride anywhere I want. Now go on with you."

Rusty gave her a cockeyed glance and darted into the stable. Angela looked back to where Devil had been. He was gone. She wanted to find him. What she'd do if she encountered him went beyond her, but she felt sure she'd think of something.

Kissing him came to mind first; thoughts of touching his face with her fingers sent a hot shiver down her spine; imagining sliding her hands through his long black hair to find out if his gorgeous black locks were as soft and silky as they looked followed. With those ideas foremost in her head, she blushed from head to toe.

Totally disconcerted, and with a huff of indignation at her wayward mind, Angela mounted the stallion and headed out of town. Kangee, the name she'd given her horse, meant *raven* in the Sioux language. He was black as a raven's wing, and right now he pranced nervously, frightened by all the strange sights and sounds of the city.

He wanted to run but she held him back. He sidestepped once, twice and then a third time. They were almost to the edge of town, long, endless miles stretching out in front of her, with only a homestead here and there to remind her she'd just left civilization behind. They passed the last house.

"Easy, boy, we're almost there. Then you can run with the wind." Angela stroked Kangee's neck.

A horseless carriage sputtered and rumbled along beside her. Suddenly the machine backfired, sounding like a shotgun blast next to Kangee's ear. He reared, his forelegs pawing the air. The vehicle popped loudly and then roared to life, raising a cloud of dust in the process.

Along with the vehicle, Kangee shot forward, leaving Angela in a desperate battle to control her powerful mount. She let him have his head and they raced down the road then into the countryside beyond.

Wind sifted through her hair, her long braid uncoiling from its ribbon, wisps of hair dancing around her face. She let out a wild Sioux yell, reveling in the ride. From birth she'd been trained to ride like a man--to think like one, too. Her father and her brothers had taught her skills few white women knew. One-quarter Sioux, she'd always known that life for her would be challenging and sometimes hard.

One with her mount, Angela veered to the south on Kangee, taking a well-used trail through scrub brush and pine, a trail that led downward to a winding creek.

She let her hat fall back, her hair flying with the wind. With Kangee's hooves beating a powerful staccato on the earth, she felt alive and free.

They flew past Devil. She heard the loud, anxious whinny of his horse.

Thunder pounded behind her and she heard ' 'Son of a bitch" reverberating down the trail. Thrills shot down her spine.

She looked back as Devil Blackmoor bore down upon her. His horse gained ground, its tail streaming back. He was almost upon her. Captivated by the straight set of Devil's shoulders, the rigid set of his jaw and the steel in his dark eyes, she nudged Kangee to ride faster--then faster still. Rising to a challenge and needing to win were intricate parts of her character.

The hammering of the stallion's hooves grew louder and ever closer. She imagined the hot breath of his horse on her arm, felt Devil's leg brush across her own, knew a moment of fear.

"Hold on!" he cried out to her. "Don't be afraid."

Her pride wounded, she veered to the right. He had anticipated the move, seemed to know what she would do next. In the following instant, she found his hands encircling her waist; then he swooped her from the back of her mount onto his. In a matter of seconds his horse slowed and came to a complete stop.

She had wanted to know how it would feel to be held by him, but not this way. Giddy with unknown sensations deep in her belly, torn with indecision and battered pride, she reacted to him with her temper instead of common sense.

"Devil take you. Get your grimy paws off me." Then to her mortification, she landed a solid punch to his jaw. His head jerked back. For a long, tense moment she stared at him, stunned at her own brashness, yet unable to control her seething emotions. She wanted him to kiss her, yearned to feel his lips against hers and to feel the power and warmth of his embrace. Instead she'd hit him.

"Ungrateful little ..." was all he could get out before once more he seemed to notice her fist held high in the air and directed straight at him for the second time. He caught her hand before the impact.

"Let me--"

"Go?" he finished for her, a crooked smile on his face even while his eyes shone dark and penetratingly hot. "When you promise not to swing that wicked left hook again. I don't relish a battering even if a beautiful woman is on the other end of the fist."

Unable to do anything but stare at Devil, she stared. The diamond stud in his ear caught the light and sparkled. She wanted to touch the earring.

Beautiful woman? Her heart stopped.

The horse held its ground, the reins trailing on the grass. She could feel Devil's powerful thighs beneath her, saw close up the expanse of his chest, and the determined male superiority in the set of his shoulders.

Except for the diamond, he wore nothing but black.

The sun was behind him, bright and forceful, casting a strange light around his face. A glint of humor curled his lips, and the sudden urge to touch him--to touch all of him--swept through her. At the same instant a heated blush rose to her cheeks, then back down to settle in the pit of her stomach and lower still.

His hair was rakishly long and he'd tied it back with a leather thong. She wanted to run her fingers through his hair, but he held her hands behind her back, her breasts now pushing against his chest, almost as if he had planned the scene. Settled across his lap, she felt the power of his muscles, the danger of the man.

He had unseated her from her horse, had played Sir Galahad to her damsel in distress--but he was no white knight. She meant to tell him what she thought of his actions before she allowed him a kiss--and she did mean to allow him a kiss, two if he asked nicely. She hesitated, shocked by her wish. She had to decide if she really wanted to find out what kissing a man felt like.

Gathering what little was left of her willpower, and on the edge of frustration, she once more reacted before thinking.

"Let me go, you spawn of Satan," she said, stunned at her own audacity and by the fact it was the last thing she wanted to say. She wanted to make this man kiss her, not hate her. She pursed her lips in silent study of the man, an inquisition into his thoughts.

A game was being played--her mind against his.

Her breasts shifted against his chest. She moved her bottom to fit more snugly against him, testing her power over him. She liked the feel of his thighs beneath her, his chest meeting hers and his arms around her.

An innocent in some ways, but wise to the world in others, Angela longed to try her skills at seduction. She'd never been this close to a man, and she meant to enjoy every minute.

His jaw clenched tight, his words spoken in a tense monotone, he said, "What a sassy little spitfire." Then he seemed to relax. "All spark, nothing more," he murmured, his breath ruffling her hair. "Can you deliver on the promise in your eyes? A kiss, perhaps, for the man who just saved your life?"

She swallowed hard. A kiss--it was what she had silently asked for-- his lips on hers. But she wanted him to know she didn't give her favors to just anyone.

"Take your hands off me," she said in her most commanding voice.

The challenge didn't sway him. He laughed and pulled her closer, the intimate brush of his wild black hair across her shoulders setting her mind into a whirlwind of imagination. Her breasts felt swollen, her body's response to his shocking. She wanted him to touch her, ached for him in ways she'd never before imagined. Her hands rested on his upper arms, and with every movement he made, the large muscles of his biceps tensed around her fingers, tightening then relaxing in a most tantalizing fashion. She realized suddenly that she could not wrap her fingers even halfway around his arms.

Again she heard his deep, throaty laugh, a rumbling chuckle, and when she looked into his eyes, they sparkled with emotion. Desire erupted to assume control of her common sense. In his arms she couldn't think of anything but the way he felt against her and the need that seemed to overpower all rationality.

"Never, sweet angel," he whispered. "I like my hands on you. And you like them there, too. I want to kiss you. Grant me leave for one kiss and I promise you'll beg for more."

Lord, he made her melt. Could he really do that to her? Make her beg for more? She had the heady feeling that everything he said was true. She battled a moment of apprehension.' 'Arrogant ..." she said softly.

He winked. One mesmerizing brown eye twinkled merrily at her. "True," he said, just as he lowered his mouth to hers.

A brief thought--she shouldn't let him do this without a resounding *no*---hit her hard then vanished without a trace. This man was the very devil himself, but, oh, how she wanted him. Butterfly kisses caressed her mouth, his tongue moistened her lips. Her reputation would be shredded beyond repair, but she was discovering how a devil kissed and she had no regrets.

Not one.

He was right. She did want to beg and plead for more. He commanded with his lips and tongue. Her fingers clenched spasmodically around his huge arms. To the devil with her reputation.

His hands circled her waist, smoothed higher. Angela tried to say his name, but his thumbs brushed the underside of her breasts, once ... twice, and words crumbled like dry parchment in her throat.

She melted closer to him.

She moaned softly.

His fingers stroked her, moved slowly down her back, and she responded to his sensual domination. His aristocratic command of the situation intrigued her. He took control of her mind and her body.

A tidal wave of energy and an overpowering lust surged between them, ripping through her until she longed to satisfy every carnal desire he might have for her. She wanted to please him in every way.

She didn't know how.

Never in her life had she experienced a maelstrom of emotions such as she felt now. His tongue traced the seam of her lips, imploring her to open. She did. With lips, teeth, tongue, he consumed and ravished.

It seemed she could deny him nothing.

Her heart exploded against her chest. Devil pressed her back, seducing her lips and the inside of her mouth. Without thinking of the consequences, she slid her hands up his arms, wrapped herself around him and kissed him back, pressing herself against him instinctively in a primitive, exciting dance passed down through all time.

Her fingers smoothed along the back of his neck; she longed to possess him. He possessed her. Once again his hands moved down the length of her back, pressing her close, and ripples of pure bliss pulsed within her.

He took everything she offered.

She purred softly in the back of her throat. Her fingers combed through his hair. She felt him pulse against her where they touched intimately.

Each new contact brought her sensations she'd never felt before. His erotic sensual flare, his knowledge of just the touch that would make her his, sent her closer to heaven than she'd ever dreamed possible. His masculine groan, his hardening body, shocked her to the tips of her toes. He cradled her in his arms, her imagination playing havoc with what little she knew about male anatomy.

He bedeviled her, caused her to forget all but the hard angles and planes beneath her exploring hands, his lips, the strength and power--the danger--of his flesh against hers. Tenderly, he kissed her jawline, stopping at her ear to nibble and taste and make her yearn for more.

"Hold on to me, angel."

Angel...

Feeling wanton, she did cling to him. In one smooth motion, and with her still in his arms, he slid off his horse.

His fingers toyed with the buttons running along the front of her bodice. Cool air touched her skin, then warm fingers. One by one he flicked open all the buttons.

Embarrassment had no place here. Reverence, yearning--those were the emotions she saw in his eyes when he parted her blouse. A few more seconds and he would see her, touch her. She needed his touch.

He smelled of fresh sunshine and danger. His every movement spoke of breathtaking adventure, knowledge of new places and exotic people, everything Angela wanted to experience firsthand, not read about.

He settled her on the prairie grass in the wide-open space. She couldn't think, didn't care if anyone happened along. On top of her, he covered her with the length of his body. His weight upon her was enticing--it felt so good she knew it was right. She belonged here--in his arms--

beneath him.

"You're so damn sweet," he murmured just before his lips closed over hers once more. "Pure sugar."

Sanity rushed through her in a maelstrom of guilt and humiliation, her own wanton behavior hitting her hard between the eyes. She jerked from him. This was no game. She was about to lose her virginity, right here, in the wide open for anyone to see, to a man she knew only by reputation.

A man who advertised as a gun for hire.

Her father would kill him. And it would not be an easy death.

"Stop ..." The word didn't sound convincing even to her. He hesitated, watching her with calculated purpose and a knowing grin. Her fingers resting on his shoulders trembled violently. "Don't," she managed, her voice quavering with determination and regret. All it would take on his part was one more kiss and she'd be lost to the promise of carnal knowledge. Cold air and a terrible feeling of loss swept across her as he separated himself from her.

He leaned back on one elbow in casual repose. "Stop? Only a minute ago you were moaning and purring in sensual delight. Your body played mine; you strummed me with your long, delicate fingers. You liked my touch."

Dazed by the truth of his words, she somehow managed to respond. "You attacked me...." she whispered, barely getting the lie out. She gathered the bodice of her dress together, fumbling with the buttons in her haste. She did so badly at the task that he brushed her hands away and fastened her dress for her.

Her fingers were still trembling when she lifted her heavy mass of hair and began to braid it. Once again he stopped her. Taking her hair in his hands, he arranged the strands for her. They made eye contact. She wanted to see inside his mind, and she wanted to know what she'd stopped him from finishing.

Adventure had been at her fingertips, a breath away, and she'd rejected what he'd offered.

"I rescued you. If looks could tell the story, you loved every minute. Your lips are swollen from my kisses, and your eyes are flushed with passion."

The truth of his words sent a streak of wildfire through her. She ran her tongue across her mouth, testing his words. "I had no need of rescue."

One aristocratic eyebrow rose. "It didn't appear that way. You were racing through the trail, out of control, yelling your head off. If not yourself, you could have hurt your horse."

She flashed him a disdainful look and stood, brushing the dust and grass from her formerly canary yellow skirt. "You should have looked closer. I was not in danger, and I don't need saving. I can take care of myself better than most men."

From behind her, she could hear Devil Blackmoor chuckling. Striding to her horse she tried to ignore him, forced herself to keep going and not look back. Looking back could be the worst thing she'd ever done.

But she did look back.

He still sat in a negligent pose, a blade of grass between his white teeth, and a lopsided grin slanting across his arrogantly kissable mouth.

Just before she nudged her horse forward she heard him say, "I will find out who you are, Angel. I promise. And then you will need rescue from yourself."

~ * ~

As she rode from the scene, the day assumed a sudden chill, storm clouds brewing on the horizon and in Angela's heart. She veered Kangee to the right, heading into the forest and to higher, safer ground. Her mind and her body cried out to her.

Fool, fool, fool, her words said to the beat of her stallion's hooves. *You made an idiot of yourself, Angela Chamberlain. What would your dear mother say to you if she knew what you'd done? And your father?*

Alarm shot through her straight to her belly. She choked back a sob of fear---fear not for her but for Devil. If Sam Chamberlain knew what she'd just done with Devil, he'd ...

Sam Chamberlain's reputation was known throughout Colorado and the Dakotas. Where his enemies were concerned, he was ruthless. If Devil Blackmoor harmed Sam's daughter in any way, Devil would become a hated foe.

She closed her eyes, willing the picture of Devil staked out on the ground and at her father's mercy to vanish. Poor Devil--he didn't deserve Sam Chamberlain's wrath or Mother's. Hadn't she melted in Devil's arms, begging for more of his kisses? She'd liked his mouth on hers, the tender then possessive touch of his tongue deep inside her mouth.

A strangled noise rose from deep in her throat.

Angela leaped off Kangee before he stopped. A little brook stitched a path through the dense trees, and Angela strode back and forth beside the gurgling water, thinking--thinking and remembering.

Try as she might, she couldn't still her heart, and she couldn't keep her mind from Devil Blackmoor. Aristocratic, arrogant and all male, he intrigued and infuriated her.

He made her melt. And he was so very dangerous.

"I saw you and Devil."

"What?" Angela whirled around, practically falling full tilt into Rusty Limpkin's chest.

"Saw you kiss him and--"

"Why, you little scamp." Angela reached for the knife she always kept around her waist, a weapon she used with expertise. It wasn't there.

"Lookin' for something? Dressed up fancy like you are, you must have forgotten your weapon."

Angela stepped forward, Rusty backward. "You're wrong if you think I'm going to let you blackmail me. And I know that's what you're up to. You didn't see anything because there was nothing to see. You hear me?"

He nodded, his Adam's apple bobbing up and down.

She would have wound her fist into his shirtfront, but Rusty was too quick for her. He darted sideways and out of the path of her fury. Keeping his distance, he backed toward his horse, which he'd tethered farther down the hill.

"Go on now. If you stick around here I'll make you sorry."

Distance from Angela seemed to give Rusty his courage back. He grinned widely. "I'm going to be watching you, Angela."

She pulled at her braid and the unruly strands of hair that had knotted at the base of her skull. "You stay away from me," she warned, knowing Rusty would do just as he pleased.

Rusty Limpkin was a certifiable nuisance. Ever since she had arrived in Denver, he'd been hanging around her. She couldn't turn around without him showing up beside her. Rusty Limpkin was a perverted Peeping Tom and full of mischief. Well, she'd know by the time she rode back to town whether or not he'd really seen her with Devil. If Rusty had any juicy tidbits to feed the other boys, he would do so and within hours the whole town would know.

Rusty's word didn't mean a whole lot; he'd been caught in more than one lie, and several grown men had threatened to slice and dice him if he ever lied again. But if her father heard anything, rumor or not, there would be questions to answer.

Her fists clenched at her sides, her nails biting into the palms of her hands, Angela glared at Rusty as long as she could see him. When he disappeared from view, she shook her fist at him. "Darn you, Rusty Limpkin. If you do anything that hurts my father or my mother, I'm going to boil you in oil."

With that said, Angela stripped off her stockings and slipped her toes into the frigid alpine water. Her breath caught but she didn't stop at her toes; she submerged both feet and waded until her teeth ached.

Nothing dispelled the confusion in her brain, not the comfortable forest sounds or the soft breeze caressing her hot cheeks. In a few minutes of divine pleasure, Devil had burrowed his way inside her heart and she could not shake him out. She didn't want to exorcise him. She was eighteen. She could do what she wanted. But she needed her parents respect. Defying them was not something she meant to do, not unless they refused to back down from their stand on the finishing school. She'd wither and die there. Angela knew her father would understand if he'd only stop to think. He'd left the East and a prominent position for the freedom in the West. He knew exactly how she felt.

If only he'd remember.

She found a soft spot of moss to sit on and, tucking her knees beneath her chin, she watched the stream go by. Just like her life, the water followed the path set before it.

She meant to control her destiny.

Finishing school back east was her father's dream, not hers. She wanted adventure and travel and a man who would cherish her for herself, not for the way he wanted her to be. Perhaps not in that order, but she yearned with all her heart for all three.

Devil touched her as no other man had.

Sheet lightning suddenly lit up the sky.

The mountain storm hit hard and fast. The deluge began after the awful rolling of thunder and then more lightning. Angela took cover beneath a canopy of solid granite to wait out the storm.

Chapter Two

Devil Blackmoor watched her ride away. He struggled for the indifference he usually felt with women, apathy inbred through decades. The woman he had just encountered stirred unwanted feelings deep in his heart.

She was a study in contrasts, sultry tawny skin coupled with shining hair the color of golden desert sand and the bluest eyes he'd ever seen, eyes that seemed to probe his darkest secrets and search for the man beneath the facade he'd carefully constructed.

Leaning back against the soft bed of grass, he cursed himself in three different languages. He'd lost control and that was unthinkable. He'd almost made love to her here in the wide open, where anyone could have come along and watched. Where his friend, cousin and self-proclaimed bodyguard would show up in a few seconds. Misha was always close by, too close at times. The thought made him groan.

Her silken hair running through his fingers, the satin feel of her flesh against his fingertips, the light in her eyes, darkening to the deepest blue of the ocean were images that remained vivid in his mind. More than he'd ever believed possible he wanted her, desired her with an intensity that surprised him.

When he made love to her, and he knew he would, he wanted everything perfect. Soft pillows, the scent of jasmine hanging in the air, muted light--he would make sure she had all of that and more. He wanted her to dance for him, in the way of his father's people, with Turkish music and the soft, billowing garments of the harem women. Without closing his eyes, he could see her in the transparent clothes, enticing him with the subtle sway of her breasts, the provocative flare of her hips and her smile. Hers was a smile he couldn't resist, one that made him lose all perspective. When she looked at him the way she had only moments before, he wanted to possess her so thoroughly she'd never glance at another man.

It was not in his nature to be possessive or jealous, but with this lady he felt both emotions. They were strong and insistent, encompassing every part of him.

She was courageous--she had fought him despite his great size. He admired courage, yet he'd never encountered bravery in a woman. She had been honest in her response to him, and he respected honesty and integrity. Her kisses were innocent yet wildly passionate.

He might not ever see her again.

His maternal grandmother had sent word over a year ago that he must return home. She'd handpicked a wellborn bride for him. All that remained was his approval of the lady in question. He'd received the letter but two days past. He didn't want to leave America, but duty to his people and his land prevailed.

He was a second son, and the duty should not rest in his hands. With his stepbrother's death, his life had changed. He could no longer do as he pleased. He didn't need a wife, yet once again the dictates of society mandated he wed and bear a legitimate heir.

In his mother's homeland he was a prince. In his father's he held great riches. In America he felt free.

He had come to America seeking adventure and had fallen in love with the wild, untamed land--wild and untamed, just like the wanton angel he'd encountered seconds ago.

A friend had called him Devil because he looked so fierce, and Blackmoor because he seldom wore anything but black. The Americanized name had become as much a part of him as the land itself. Advertising as a hired gun had put excitement in his life, yet he'd stayed on the right side of the law. Now his reputation preceded him.

He felt that Lawrence Stevens, his latest employer and powerful U.S. Senator, had taken advantage of him. Devil believed Stevens had lied to him about Emma and Dakota Barringer when he hired him to find the pair and bring them to Denver. He meant to find out the truth before he handed Emma over to Stevens, meant to discover who committed the crime, who really murdered Emma's mother. He wanted to know why Stevens was willing to put up a small fortune to have Emma in his hands and at his mercy.

And then he meant to find his angel.

What would it take to convince the angel to follow him to Europe, where he would assume his duties, or to Constantinople, where his father lived and where he'd grown up? He'd spent the first fifteen years of his life under the influence of the Ottoman Empire. His father had abducted his mother, enslaved her--until his mother had managed to capture his father's heart. Then she had received a promise from Father at her deathbed that their son, if he choose to live in Russia, would go by the Popov name to continue her family's dynasty. If he still lived in the East, Devil would not have to ask to have this angel. She would be his for the taking.

In America he would have to ask.

All he could offer was the promise of adventure and for most ladies that was not enough to lure them away from their home and their family, entice them across the Atlantic to foreign places they might have only read about. Allah, but if she craved adventure, he could give her that and much more. He would give to his wanton angel her heart's desire.

Determined to find her, he headed back to town. The sooner he finished with the job he'd accepted the sooner he could search for this woman who'd touched something deep inside and take her home with him.

But would she go?

As if on cue, Misha appeared on the horizon, his approach cautious and slow.

"Your timing is perfect." Devil lay back, his hands tucked behind his head, eyes closed.

"But of course, Alexi," Misha Petrovich said, using Devil's given name. He gave a chuckle then doffed his hat. "How was your wild ride?"

"Enlightening," Devil said, still wondering what enticement he could give the angel of his dreams to convince her to travel with him.

"And did you win the fair lady?"

"Not yet, but I will."

"I'm sure that is the truth. Tell me, Alexi, have you ever been denied anything in your entire life?"

"Ah, Misha, in truth, I cannot think of a single time."

My Angel

~ * ~

"Hello, Papa."

Hours later, a bedraggled Angela Chamberlain closed the door to her father's office. Sam had rented a suite of rooms at the hotel for their short stay in Denver before resuming their travels and had turned one of the rooms into a private sanctuary where he could work. They would spend some time here then her father would take her to the train she would ride to boarding school.

She brushed the dripping strands of hair from her eyes and tried to smooth the wrinkles from her skirts. Sam sat at his desk, sifting through an array of papers.

He grunted. To Angela, his preoccupation with the notes in front of him was a good sign he might not notice her state of dishabille.

Without looking up or glancing her way, her father said, "Sit down."

The message came through loud and clear: *I'll* / / *deal with you as soon as I finish what I'm doing.* Waiting was torture, and her father knew just how impatient Angela was. He knew she wanted life to happen to her now, not later.

She meant to find a way out of the questions that were sure to start when her father got around to them. "Papa?"

"What?"

He didn't look up. She didn't like the tone of his voice.

"I'm cold and wet. Could we talk later?"

Silence hung in the room. She heard the steady tread of footsteps outside the door, and smelled the leftover of the roast beef her father had had for an earlier meal. The shuffling of papers sent a little shiver of apprehension up then down her spine. The unstoppable ticking of the grandfather clock paralyzed her.

Everyone else controlled her life. Time ruled each precious second, and it was slipping past her right now. She would not let that happen. At eighteen she meant to live rife to the fullest.

"I'm finished." He looked at her, really looked at her. "What happened to you?" Sam pushed back from the desk, his arms crossed stiffly over his chest. He held the position then relaxed everything but his critical gaze.

"A mountain storm." She hesitated to go on. The intense look in her father's eye flashed like nothing she'd seen before.

"Not the first storm you've weathered by yourself. But this one got the best of you."

"It hit fast and hard."

"I thought that between Dakota and Trey you knew where to find shelter."

To the Sioux, Dakota was known as Wildcat-Who-Stalks-The-Night, and Trey as White Eagle. Trey was her half brother, and Dakota acted like kin. While she was growing up they had taught her the ways of the Sioux people. Right now Dakota had disappeared into the Rockies with his wife, Emma, and it seemed that half the bounty hunters and Pinkertons in the west were looking for them, including Emma's brother, Jacob St. John. However, Jacob seemed more interested in clearing Emma's name than finding the pair. He'd even stepped out of retirement from the Pinkertons to help Emma.

"I did find a dry place."

He eyed her, a crooked slant to his lips, his silence unnerving.

"After the storm drenched me to the bone," she added.

The rumbling chuckle that followed surprised her. "And did you leave the dress shop buttoned so haphazardly?" he asked, and for a moment she saw a twinkle in his eye. She didn't know what he spoke of; then a horrid thought assailed her.

Devil. Angela looked at her bodice. What else could she do? She didn't know if she gasped or shrieked at the sight of her buttons, so hastily done by Devil. And undone. Not in that order.

From the tips of her toes she felt the heat climb to the roots of her hair, felt the blush steal across her cheeks and settle on her nose.

"I didn't know," she said, her hands fluttering along the row of pale yellow buttons, unsure of what to do about the predicament.

Her father let out a snort of disgust. "If I wasn't convinced before you needed finishing school, I certainly am now. You're a mess, Angela. A sweet, endearing mess, but no lady would parade around dressed as you are. I love you. Otherwise I wouldn't care, and I'd let you run around the mountains your entire life wearing nothing save your buckskins and a shotgun propped on your shoulder. I want more for you, and so does your mother. Always remember that."

She closed her eyes in a heartfelt prayer to the spirits above that her father had dismissed her appearance as nothing more than her untamed wildness.

"Yes, Papa," she said, her eyes lowered in an unusual show of compliance. She respected him and loved him dearly, even though she didn't agree with him.

Sam Chamberlain did want more for his daughter, and he was as immovable as the mountains themselves. Nothing short of a catastrophic event would change his mind.

"Papa, have you heard from Jacob? He's been gone too long. He should have found something out by now. I'm worried."

"Emma has Dakota to look after her," Sam said.

"I know, but Mama has been so worried. What are we going to do? They can't hide forever."

"Trust Jacob. He's the best Pinkerton around, and he'll discover the truth."

"I saw Emma's picture on a wanted poster."

Sam leaned forward and eyed Angela critically. "And I heard you followed Devil Blackmoor out of town." Sam's tone changed from firm command to hard control. "Any truth to the rumor?"

At his question, her heart stopped, froze mid-beat, and all thoughts of Emma and Dakota flew from her mind. She'd entertained thoughts of riding after Devil. Did that make her guilty? "No, Papa," she said. "I didn't follow him."

"Then you didn't meet him on a little-used trail?" Sam's finger tapped the mahogany desktop. He had loving hands, comforting hands--hands that could kill if provoked.

"Well..." She hesitated, her fingers wound together and clasped tightly in front of her. Only her father could make her cower in fright. Terror oozed through her bones.

"Angela?" His voice nearly roared in the unnatural silence surrounding them.

She couldn't lie. "I... we had an encounter."

"I don't like the way that sounds. An encounter?"

"Yes, Papa. He thought I needed rescuing." She didn't. Dakota and Trey had shown her how to ride and shoot a bow and arrow at the same time. She rode better than most men.

Sam sat back in his chair, his arms folded negligently across his chest and his expression grim. "You?" One eyebrow rose in mock disdain. "You're the most unlikely candidate for rescuing I've ever known."

"I know that. He didn't." She nodded, feeling a slim thread of hope grow in her heart. She could defend herself, could trap and could follow a trail. She knew how to survive in the high country, hunting her own game and foraging for food.' 'There is a measure of truth in the story. One of those horseless carriages spooked Kangee and he took off. Since we were on the outskirts of town, I let him run. The next thing I knew, Devil scooped me off my horse and rescued me."

Sam sat forward, his forearms resting on the desk. "And then what?"

She jerked, surprised that he might have guessed about the kiss. Angela sucked in her lower lip, remembering how Devil's mouth had crushed down on hers, recalling the spine-tingling sensations that had rolled through her, languidly at first then with the speed of stampeding horses. "Nothing, really." She wasn't going to tell her father the man kissed her. He'd go after Devil with only one thought in mind: torture. If she told Sam how willing she'd been, there'd be a shotgun wedding by noon tomorrow. She didn't want that either.

"You're not going to tell me."

Angela shook her head; then changing her mind, she nodded. "I hit him."

Sam leaned back again, his eyes lingering on his daughter. Once again Angela waited for someone else to decide her fate. "And then what?"

"He let me go."

Sam drummed his fingers on his desk, a thoughtful expression written clearly in the lines of his face. "Really..." His gaze raked over her. "You're not telling me everything."

"Papa," she began only to find herself interrupted.

"We can talk again later." With a wave of his hand and a low chuckle, he said,' 'Go on now. Clean yourself up properly."

Chapter Three

Two weeks later, long after Angela had given up hope of convincing her father not to send her East, Devil Blackmoor reappeared in Denver. Standing at the window of the hotel room she and her father shared, Angela watched Devil escort a woman through town then turn down the infamous Holladay Street into the red-light district.

"Emma?" she wondered out loud.

Angela stretched forward, pushing her nose out the half-open window and leaning precariously over the edge of the sill. She had prayed every day that no one would find Emma and Dakota. But now it seemed her prayers had gone unanswered.

"Emma .

Trey was Angela's half-brother and Dakota was Trey's blood brother. When Dakota's parents died on their way west, Dakota was adopted by a Sioux war chief. Trey and Dakota had grown up together with their Sioux families, had fought at the Battle of Little Big Horn against General Custer and the Seventh Cavalry. While Trey was part Indian by birth, Dakota wasn't. Dakota's skin was stark white but his soul was pure Sioux warrior, and he didn't have a drop of Indian blood in him.

Angela had been with Jacob when the telegram had arrived. The Pinkertons had wanted Jacob to find his sister and bring her in. Jacob had been torn between rushing to his sister's rescue or joining the Pinkertons to find the real murderer. And Jacob knew if Dakota disappeared into the Rockies, no one would find him until he was ready. So Jacob had set about to find the real criminal.

Now Devil Blackmoor had brought in Dakota's woman for money. Emma's face had been on wanted posters all over Denver and the state of

Colorado. Angela pulled herself inside the room, determined to do something to help Emma.

Nervously, Angela tapped her fingers against the window-pane. Her forehead rested against the cold glass, and she inhaled a ragged breath.

"Think." *Think.*

In a blind panic and knowing Devil and Emma would disappear from sight any second, Angela whirled from her perch at the window. She raced through the room, grappling with the doorknob in her haste to reach the street before they turned a corner. Her skirts tangled around her feet and legs, she stumbled awkwardly through the long hallway and down the stairs to the lobby of the hotel.

"Oof." The impact jarred her all the way to her toes. "I'm sorry... I..." Angela bent to retrieve the packages that had flown from the man's arms when she ran into him.

"You should be," the man told her, his tone indignant.

"I'm so sorry." Her voice was soft--strained. "Here." She handed him the last package and dashed out the door. "I'm sorry." But she almost smashed into a lady.

"Where I come from young women are polite." The man's harsh words followed her. "They watch where they are going."

She ran, her skirts held high.

The buildings blurred into one.

In the middle of the street she stopped, searching for some sign of Devil and Emma. A few seconds later she headed into the red-light district. More than anything Angela wanted to help Emma prove her innocence. More than anything she wanted to see Dakota happy.

Her sweaty hands clutched the fabric of her skirt. Angela turned slowly, searching out every dark nook, every door left open. She saw no one she recognized. Not Devil. Not Emma. In the few seconds it had taken her to race from the hotel, they had disappeared.

"Where did you go, Devil Blackmoor, and what did you do with Emma Barringer. If you've hurt her in anyway, I'll skin you alive."

Angela had been trained by the most skilled warriors in the Dakotas. She should be able to find two people. She had to--for Dakota and Jacob. They shared a common bond of love and friendship.

What affected one, affected them both. Loyalty to each other ran strong and deep.

Now Devil had brought in Dakota's woman. Devil was a gun for hire. In the weeks that had passed, Angela had found out all she could about Devil Blackmoor. Nothing she'd heard except his profession could be accepted as fact. What she'd heard had to be rumor, the tales too fantastic to believe. Yet...

He was a Russian prince. *My foot.*

He was the son of a Turkish sultan and owned an exotic harem of over one hundred women at his beck and call. Even less believable.

She'd heard that Lawrence Stevens, Emma's stepfather, was paying Devil twenty thousand dollars to bring Emma back to Denver. Emma was part of her family now, and in Angela's eyes, family was everything.

That allegiance made Devil Blackmoor her enemy.

Dakota wouldn't let Emma go without a fight. She was suddenly very worried about Dakota.

"Angela!"

Her heart skipped a beat. She'd recognize that voice anywhere. "No," she said. "Not now."

Her father's fingers wound around her arm, effectively stopping her blind rush into the nearest saloon.

"What are you up to?" he asked.

"Nothing, Papa."

That earned her a sour look, but she didn't dare tell her father she'd been about to step through the swinging doors in front of her into the Gold Nugget Saloon.

"Emma..." The impact of what had just occurred hit hard.

"Angela?" Sam asked, seemingly confused.

Angela turned to him. "Papa!" She sounded frantic. She was.

"What are you doing here?" Sam stood beside her, waiting for an answer to his earlier question.

"I saw Emma with Devil Blackmoor."

Sam swore under his breath. "Dakota and Trey were supposed to protect Emma."

"It's true then," Angela said softly, her heart hammering her fear against her ribs. Devil Blackmoor was dangerous. She knew firsthand just how dangerous he was.

"Perhaps. I'll look around. I mean to find out where he's taken Emma." Sam turned Angela in the direction of the hotel and nudged her forward.

"I'm going with you." She was determined.

"No." Sam was more tenacious.

"But--"

"No." With that said Sam once again nudged her toward the hotel and watched her walk down the street, away from the red-light district. When she looked back, he watched her still.

~ * ~

"You have a hell of a lot of nerve coming here."

The voices in the other room woke Angela. She brushed the hair from her eyes, blinking the sleep away. Even though she'd tried to wait up for her father, she'd fallen asleep without seeing him and finding out what happened to Emma or where Dakota was.

Now she heard the clink of glasses, the slosh of liquid.

The quilt covering her slipped silently to the floor. Angela swung her legs off the bed then made her way to the door. She leaned against the wall. Her fingers trembling, she opened the door a crack.

She saw her father hand Devil a drink.

Devil nodded his expression cold. "I promised Emma I'd check out her story. I have, and I'm disturbed by what I found out."

Absorbed in the conversation, Angela wiped her sweaty palms on her nightdress. She inched closer, the floorboards creaking under her weight.

"But you turned her over to the bastard anyway." Dakota stepped in front of Devil. His jaw was clenched, his fists tight.

Angela sucked in her breath. *He didn't.* Angela" s words were spoken only to herself, but silence suddenly filled the room. And she knew deep down in her heart Devil had betrayed them all.

Devil tensed.

"I'd given my word to Lawrence Stevens. He is her stepfather, and I did believe he had her best interests at heart. The lady is wanted for murder.

Stevens promised me he'd protect her. Besides, Emma left me no alternative when she refused to explain her part in this matter. I gave her ample opportunity. She could have told me what happened, why her face adorned wanted posters all over the state. Instead she chose to remain silent. Emma didn't trust me until I was in the process of handing her over to the man himself. By then her words of innocence were uttered too late."

He did. Angela slipped to the cold, hard floor, her back pressing against a table leg. A shudder began deep inside and worked its way out until she could barely control her limbs. A bittersweet ache lodged in the back of her heart.

He did.

"Now I'm asking you: if I was wrong, tell me and I'll help in any way possible. Who killed Emma's mother? And why was there a wanted poster on Emma Barringer?"

"Stevens killed Emma's mother," Sam said.

"He poisoned her and blamed it on Emma, hoping to install Emma in one of his whorehouses." Dakota paced back and forth in front of the door, his muscles flexed with tension and primed for a fight.

"I will help right this wrong," Devil said, his voice strong and determined.

Angela couldn't see Dakota but she heard him stop, felt the tensions escalate. "Ask the devil to help? I'm not a fool."

Devil sat still, showing no emotion when Dakota turned on him. No one seemed eager to further the explanation.

"Lawrence's man shot Jacob. He's going to be all right in a couple of days," Devil said.

No! Angela felt the floor drop out from under her. *Jacob has been shot?*

"I think he discovered something." Devil showed no emotion, his stoic features still hard and unreadable. "I would keep an eye on Emma and watch the house. What better man to give aid than one who is trusted by the opposition?" he asked. "If you keep me informed of the truth, I can make sure no real harm comes to Emma."

Suddenly Angela meant to find a way to help Emma. Emma could hang. Jacob had been shot. The Pinkertons were after Emma, as was every bounty hunter this side of the Mississippi. Dakota and Emma needed all the allies they could find.

"Lawrence is keeping her drugged," Devil said.

"Son of a bitch!" Dakota's fist hit the wall beside Angela.

She flinched, her startled gasp echoing around the room she was in.

Once more Dakota paced. His long, sleek strides back and forth got him nowhere.

Wild and untamed, Dakota had always been one to act first and think later. Angela knew he wanted to barge into the bordello and drag Emma out. He couldn't. If he did, the two of them would be hunted fugitives once more. Or dead. Emma was wanted by the law, dead or alive. No, the time had come to find proof against Stevens and Madame leBon.

If the sheriff discovered Emma before they had any facts that would prove her innocence, Emma could very well hang. Dakota's hands were tied until they had something to hold over Lawrence Stevens's head.

Devil's fingers rested on the butt of his gun. They drew Angela's gaze. *Oh, Lord,* She heated from the toes up. It was all she could do to concentrate on the conversation instead of remembering the touch of his hands upon her, the way they made her body come alive.

His mouth against hers, his lips--the liquid heat he evoked.

His caress had been strong and sure and so very tender. With his touch came pure bliss and heavenly satisfaction.

"An auction is being planned for Friday night." Devil spoke again, his voice low. The sound wrapped around her heart and stole her breath. "Emma is the main attraction. Lawrence is advertising heavily and holding peep shows three times a day."

"I'll kill him!" Dakota slammed his fist against the palm of his hand.

Despite the outburst Devil continued. "Men gather to watch her bathe. Tomorrow he plans on letting those who will bid in earnest take a closer look, examine the merchandise."

"I'll kill Stevens with my bare hands." The words emanating from Dakota came as a low growl. Dakota yanked Devil to his feet.

Devil's gaze turned murderous. "Let go," he said. "If I didn't have so much respect for you, Dakota, you'd be a dead man right now. I suggest you don't push your luck. I'm here to right a wrong. I suggest you be at the bordello tomorrow."

At the bordello? Oh, Emma. Fear for Emma shook Angela to the core.

"Stevens knows who I am," Dakota said.

"Find a way."

Dakota let his hands fall to his sides. Devil relaxed. Angela breathed more easily now. Dakota's jaw wasn't quite so tense, nor were his hands still flexed. There wouldn't be a fight here in the parlor.

Emma needed someone trustworthy inside the bordello.

Once again Angela sat back, leaning against the nightstand, her eyes closed. Her father would be adamant, his *no* final. She would have to take this into her own hands. Dakota loved Emma; that much was obvious. But Dakota needed to know Emma would be watched over or he'd ruin the carefully laid plans they'd been constructing all evening. Angela prayed Devil's presence at the whorehouse would be enough to hold Dakota back.

If Dakota went flying into the bordello with bullets ricocheting, it was a sure bet he'd land himself in jail and Emma with a noose around her neck. When someone Dakota loved was threatened, restraint was not something he could handle. That fact would make the situation even more dangerous for anyone inside.

She could handle a gun and a knife better than most men. No one inside the brothel would recognize her. As a housekeeper or maid, her own safety was not in question.

Faced with the obvious, Angela no longer had a choice. She'd have to disobey her father. It was the only way to protect Emma. Somehow she would get off the train Sam meant to put her on tomorrow morning, and then she would think of a way to get inside the bordello.

~ * ~

Standing on the platform at the train station, one valise in hand, Angela realized this was her last chance to tell her father about her plans. She couldn't.

Angela had gone over everything in her mind. There was no other way to keep Emma safe.

She was afraid, but not for herself. She feared for Emma.

"I love you, Papa." Angela didn't like herself very well at the moment, but she squared her shoulders, stiffening her spine and her determination in the process. Her knife, newly sharpened, lay in its sheath. Strapped tightly to her leg, the weapon was easy to reach, and she had a derringer in her valise.

"I love you, too."

Sam Chamberlain kissed Angela's forehead and stepped back, his hands resting on her shoulders, his eyes memorizing every inch of her. Guilt was a powerful force to reckon with, and right now it had a stranglehold on her heart.

She nodded. "I know," she said.

"Write to me, and I want you to send a telegram as soon as you reach Boston."

"Yes, sir." Long good-byes were not her father's style, and right now she thanked her lucky stars for that fact. Her remorse was so powerful that if he spent much more time here, she'd give in and tell him what she meant to do.

The train let out a loud whistle, steam rolled from the engine and the wheels began a slow shudder. She stood on the steps, watching her father walk away as the train lumbered through the center of town. The car she rode in was about to pass by the Wells Fargo station and the livery.

She had seconds to act. Turning away, she stepped to the other side, her valise in hand, and jumped from the train. The impact jarred her, stealing her breath and stopping her heart. Dazed, she lay on the ground for a few minutes. Low, gray clouds covered the sky, a slight mist dampening the ground where she lay. Where there should have been two buildings, there were four.

Angela closed her eyes. When she finally opened them and tried to sit up, nausea forced her back. She thought for a moment that she would be well and truly sick. A few minutes later she tried to rise again, this time more slowly. The ground moved beneath her and the sky spun crazily, but she held still and the motion slowly stopped.

This was not what she'd anticipated, but she'd had to wait longer than she'd intended. And now that she was off the train, safe and sound, she didn't want to think about the fear she'd felt moments before she'd jumped or the second thoughts that had rushed through her head.

She stayed behind the livery for over an hour before she ventured out. She had dressed plainly, hoping no one would notice her movements through town. Her dove gray dress buttoned to her throat, and her hair pulled back in a snug bun at the nape of her neck gave her a somber look. Cautiously, she stepped onto the sidewalk in plain view. Her knees wobbled. No one saw.

Now she had to devise a plan to get inside the bordello. Bravado and bluster had always worked for her before. Perhaps it would again. She inhaled once for courage then started forward.

The sound of Devil's voice reached her. Pressing back against the building, Angela held her breath and waited for him to move on. She remembered Devil's pronouncement that he meant to find her again. Not today. Not until she was ready.

With her heart pounding erratically, she waited until Devil disappeared. Then she set her mind to finding a way to the beautiful mansion outside of town that had become a whorehouse only a few months before.

The coach she hired dropped her off at the front door of the bordello, and Angela watched the vehicle sway down the long driveway. She schooled her nerves and inhaled one long, deep breath. The cold metal of the knocker seeped into her fingers, bringing with it a sense a glimpse of grim reality.

Just as she was about to knock, the door swung open and a huge man stared down at her. His eyes swept the length of her prim gray dress with the white lace collar. He grunted and began to close the door.

Angela stepped forward, her booted foot catching the door before it shut in her face. Her voice shook. "I'm here for the maid's position."

"There's no maid's position," he said, his voice thick, deep and gravelly, his stance immovable.

"Beggin' your pardon, sir"--she curtsied politely--"but I've got the ad for the job right here. I've come all the way from Rapid City. See?"

"There was no ad for a maid," he said.

Emma held out the yellowed newspaper, her fingers trembling so the paper shook. "You're wrong. It says"--she cleared her throat in a ladylike fashion--" 'An experienced woman needed for the upstairs rooms in the mansion just east of town.' That's me, experienced."

"You've got the wrong address," he said.

"Zeke?" a sweet voice called from somewhere inside the darkness. "Zeke, darling, who is it? Anyone interesting?"

"An upstairs maid, Miss leBon."

"Well, just don't stand there; let her in," came the breathy reply. "I've been trying for two days now to find someone who could take care of our guest."

"See, I told you there was a job."

Shaking his head, Zeke moved aside as Angela, with her chin held high, swept past him. He pointed down a long, dark corridor to a spot of light. "Go on," he said. "Velvet will be waiting, seein' as she's expectin' someone."

Pausing a moment to let her eyes adjust to the right and the strange, erotic sights in front of her, Angela let out a little gasp of surprise. Two of the banister posts were carved into private male parts, and the walls were covered with plate-glass mirrors.

Trying not to let her mouth gape open, Angela moved on wooden legs toward Madame leBon's office, a surge of fear pounding through her heart.

The parlor was deathly quiet, and the clock's chiming sounded like a death knell. A cloud of hazy smoke hung in the corridor, and even the incense floating from the madam's office didn't alleviate the musty odors clinging in the .air.

"Hello." Angela stepped forward, her hand extended in greeting. "I came for the job. The one upstairs. I'm very qualified." Angela flashed the biggest smile she could manage and hoped it was enough.

The madam didn't move, nor did her expression change. She was, Angela thought, the most beautiful woman she'd ever seen. Angela let her hand fall to her side; then, not knowing what to do she wound both hands tightly together in front of her.

Madame leBon's fingers were tucked under a perfectly shaped chin, an amused smile gracing her lips. Her shiny blond hair arranged in a coronet circled her face halo-like. The dress she wore was buttoned tightly to her chin, yet the bodice accentuated the lush, full- curves of her breasts.

What struck Angela as singularly expressive were the lady's eyes.

They were huge, round and a little slanted, and they were exquisitely blue. The madam's eyes sparkled like the high mountain lakes when the sun glistened on the rippling water.

Madame leBon scrutinized her for a few long seconds. Then, sitting upright, her hands resting on the desk, she said, "You'll do, but not for a maid. I've need of another girl to work the floor. Have you ever done that before?" Her eyes searched.

Angela nodded, her breath quickening. "Yes, ma'am."

One dark blond brow rose in skepticism. "Where? You're awfully young." The madam stood then proceeded around the desk, never taking her eyes from Angela's bosom. Angela refused to squirm under Madame leBon's perusal.

The madam's question was to the point, and Angela didn't know what to say. Feigning ignorance with a bit of bravado seemed the best path.

"Aunt Mathilda's boardinghouse," she said. "I worked the main floor. Aunt Mathilda insisted on doing the bedrooms. But Auntie promised that when I turned nineteen, I could help out upstairs, too."

A slow smile formed on Madame leBon's lips. "Really? And which would you like to work?"

Angela didn't hesitate in her reply. "Oh, the bedrooms, of course. I'd really enjoy that. Auntie says it's absolutely delightful."

Now the madam's eyes twinkled with merry laughter. "And have you any experience? I don't want an untried girl ruining the reputation of my establishment." The madam held a lock of Angela's hair in her fingers. "We'll have to do something different with this wild mess," she murmured a bit distractedly.

"No, ma' am. Auntie wouldn't' let me near the upstairs rooms. Said I wasn't old enough."

Madame leBon shrugged, "You've said that. Your age isn't what matters here." The madam tapped her perfect chin with a perfectly manicured fingernail and stared at her even harder. Angela felt sure Madame leBon saw right through the fabric of her clothing. "You're a tiny little thing." She paused for several heart-stopping seconds. "Undo your bodice and let me have a look. I'm not going to hire anyone I haven't seen. Men like big breasts, and I'm not hiring a girl who won't fill their hands and their needs."

Angela's heart stopped and her mouth went dry. This wasn't what she'd expected. For a fleeting moment, she almost turned and fled, but thoughts of Emma, helpless and alone somewhere upstairs, overshadowed her fear.

Emma.

Angela looked apprehensively over her shoulder. Zeke had gone. Only the two of them remained in the room. Her fingers trembled as she lifted the first button, but she reminded herself that she'd committed herself and that what she did now might be the difference between life and death-- hers and Emma's.

She could not falter.

"Hurry up. I don't have all day." The madam tapped her slippered foot on the Persian carpet. "No experience?" The question was rife with meaning.

Angela pulled her arms from the sleeves, the bodice hanging now around her hips.

"The chemise, too, everything."

Cool air touched her skin. The madam stood and now stepped closer, circling her.

"Put your arms behind your head."

"Why?"

"Don't ask foolish questions. As I said a minute ago, if you don't have big breasts, the gents just don't go for you. But I think yours will do nicely. More than a handful," she murmured, "and the coloring is exquisite."

Madame leBon sat on the edge of her desk, one leg swinging idly. Angela quickly pulled her chemise up and her bodice back on then buttoned it tight.

"We'll have to give you some instruction on the proper manner and decorum. I don't want my guests disappointed in you."

"Then I get the job?" She tried to sound eager, but with each passing second she wasn't sure about the wisdom of this. "When do I start?"

"I'll put you in Lottie's care at night and for the next few days. I want you to wait on Emma, make sure she gets everything she needs. Emma is in the room next to yours. She isn't feeling well and I have to have her ready for the auction Friday night. She's the main attraction. Even if Emma doesn't want to eat, make sure she drinks the water--all of it. After that is seen to, all you need to do is watch what Lottie does and learn everything you can. Ask her anything you want. I'm sure she'll be more than happy to answer."

"Oh, thank you." Angela curtsied, her knees almost buckling-

"In two days there will be an auction. I'll need you ready and able to work. There will be a lot of things to do upstairs, and I'll expect you to do the very best job you can. Lawrence Stevens will want you first. He tries out all the new girls just to make sure they are ready."

Angela's stomach turned over at that thought. /'// *kill him before I let him touch me.* "I won't disappoint you, Madame leBon. I promise."

"Please call me Velvet. And I'm sure you won't disappoint me. Zeke will show you to your room, and Lottie will come by later with more appropriate clothes."

Angela rubbed her sweaty palms down her dress. "Thank you." She tried for enthusiasm but realized her thank-you sounded more like a plea for help.

Chapter Four

Devil Blackmoor stepped into the dress shop, the fourth place of business he'd visited this Friday morning. A well-groomed, white-haired lady shot him a pleasant made-for-business smile.

"What can I do for you?"

Devil cleared his throat, feeling scrutinized from the tips of his toes to the top of his hat. "I'm looking for a young lady with an angel's smile, about this high." He held his hand at chest level. "Eyes that could tame Satan himself. A waist no bigger than the circumference of my hands." He gestured and grinned at his own words.

The lady gave an inelegant snort of disapproval before turning away. "Your mistress?"

"No." Devil continued his description. "A waist no bigger than my hands." He showed her again. But he was thinking of the way she felt cradled next to his chest, the way her wild, innocent passion had caused a tempest to rage in his soul.

His body tensed, hardening instantly.

"Never seen the young woman." The modiste swept from her seat behind the desk, moving to a table set with patterns and magazines of the latest fashions. Her stiff back turned to him, she sorted and stacked the material there.

"Yellow makes her look as fresh as a spring day." *And ripe for picking.*

He thought he saw the lady hesitate a moment, her shoulders and arms tensing as if she knew something she wasn't about to share with the likes of him.

"The lady you speak of hasn't been in my shop." Her voice sounded as prim and proper as a Boston tea party.

Liar, "So you say." He tipped his hat in a gentlemanly show of manners while he inwardly seethed.

"I most certainly do," came the terse reply, the woman's features drawing together into a sour pucker. "A gun for hire has no business questioning my integrity. Now unless you have further business here, I suggest you leave immediately."

Devil tipped his hat. His frustration simmering into anger, he let the door bang shut. The air smelled fresher on the other side of the door anyway.

Walking down the street, he listened to the jingle of his spurs as they hit the ground and the wind's soft moan as it swept around the buildings. He passed by Market Street and Holladay Street, part of the red-light district, without giving the buildings a second glance.

Mrs. Limpkin's berry pie sure smelled good. He could see five pies sitting out on the windowsill of her boardinghouse.

Rusty poked his head out from the door to the livery, a mischievous grin planted squarely on his round face. The boy slipped between the double doors and started toward him with a gangly gait.

"Sir." The feminine voice behind him sounded airy and breathless.

Before he could turn and acknowledge the woman, he felt small fingers close around his wrist in an invitation.

"Sir?" she asked, still breathless and slightly agitated, her chest heaving, despite the short run.

Devil smiled and tipped his hat. One of the girls who worked at the dress shop stood in front of him, her face flushed with the exertion of chasing after him. She inhaled deeply--to catch her breath, he presumed. Her hand was placed just above her heaving bosom.

"Sir..." she repeated.

His fingers rested on the butt of his gun, his stance wide as he stared at her, waiting to hear her out.

"I overheard your conversation with Madame Giselle."

Madame Giselle was as French as he was. Devil waited.

"I... I know it's none of my business, but the lady you described has been to the shop. A man old enough to be her father bought her a yellow dress a couple of weeks ago, and he ordered an entire wardrobe, including..." She paused, still trying to catch her breath.

"Including?" Devil didn't care for the direction of this conversation. He saw delicate under things, and filmy confections that tantalized and beckoned, things he meant to buy for her--as soon as he could find her.

"Unmentionables and beautiful nightclothes," the girl said.

Devil's fists closed around his gun as bile rose in his throat. The implications of what the girl told him hit him hard in the gut.

"The man wasn't satisfied with the merchandise and insisted that some of the garments be redone." After looking Devil straight in the eye, she added hastily, "He still isn't satisfied and he returned several garments. He won't pay the bill until the clothes suit him.

"Madame Giselle says he left her high and dry without a cent. She says the dresses are perfect the way they are, and the changes he's insisted on are impossible. That's why she was so cross with you just now. She wants her money."

"Tell your boss that if I find the lady in question, and if the lady is willing, I'll settle the bills."

"Oh, thank you, sir." The girl swung around, her skirts billowing, and headed back to the shop.

"Bad news, Devil?"

The slight sneer in Rusty's voice didn't sit well with Devil at the moment. He wasn't in the mood to deal with the little scamp, nor did he care to listen to the boy's lies. His anger and frustration burned deep even while he thanked Allah he'd found at least one clue to the angel's whereabouts.

"No, now that I think on it, the information is very good." Devil's stride lengthened. "What do you want, Rusty? More advice?"

"Mother wanted me to ask if you wanted a piece of pie."

"No." He paused thoughtfully. "Get Jabbar ready. I'm going for a ride."

"Think you'll meet up with the little blond hellion again?" Rusty taunted.

Devil schooled his features.' 'What do you know about her?"

Rusty shrugged his thin shoulders. "Not much." He glanced sideways at Devil then at the tall man striding toward them.

"Misha," Devil said.

Misha tipped his hat.

Devil waited for an answer, his arms crossed over his chest, a stern expression on his face. "Out with it, Rusty. All of it."

Rusty had the look of the cat who caught the canary and wasn't about to spit it up. "She kept her big stallion here."

Devil waited, and his hand came down on the back of Rusty's neck, exerting pressure. The boy squirmed then settled.

"The man she came to Denver with rode out of here a few hours ago. Headed into the hills." Rusty looked too smug.

"What do you know about him?"

"I think the man gave the big stallion to her and then decided she wasn't worth the money he spent on her. I think she's run off. Haven't seen her in two days."

"Have Jabbar ready in an hour," Devil said and watched patiently while Rusty scurried into the livery, rubbing his neck where Devil's fingers had exerted pressure.

"I'll make sure the boy gets into no more mischief," Misha said.

Devil nodded. "Watch him carefully."

On impulse Devil started for Holladay Street. Questions about Angel came to mind, questions he wasn't sure he wanted the answers to.

Rusty clearly baited him. Why?

The man the boy spoke of had a place in Angel's life. What exactly his Angel was to the man, he had to find out. Mistress? Lover? Wife? The thought of Angel being anyone's wife made his heart stop.

But the thought of his Angel ending up on the wickedest thoroughfare in the West made him sick to his stomach. He didn't know where to start looking for her, but at the moment Holladay Street seemed like the best idea he could come up with. As he walked he passed shabby cribs, elegant parlor houses, and fancy brothels. She could be in any one of them.

Revulsion swept through him. His angel was no whore. He would have sensed her experience, would have recognized the practiced moves, the knowing kisses. Yet a desperate urge to find her gripped him with talon-like fingers. He stared at the filthy cribs, praying he wouldn't discover her in one of them.

Devil pulled his pocket watch from his vest pocket. Time seemed to slip by, the hour of the auction drawing closer. All hell was about to break loose while he walked aimlessly up and down a street filled with whores.

He ran restless fingers through his hair. After the auction he'd locate her. Right now he didn't have the time. He had made promises and he had to keep them. He prayed his Angel was not a prostitute, and he prayed he would find her soon. He didn't like the thought of her left alone and vulnerable.

Devil headed back to the livery, his mood tense and irritable, calling himself a fool in several languages. His Angel was too sweet to become one of those hardened ladies of the evening. She had responded to his kisses as if she'd never been kissed before.

He had jumped to conclusions.

His heart relieved, he whistled a tune from the old country as he walked down the sidewalk.

~ * ~

Devil mounted Jabbar and cantered the big horse through the streets of Denver until he reached the edge of town. Misha rode with him. They turned their horses into the hills and let the stallions have full rein. A hot spring sun shone down on them. Sweat-slipped down Devil's neck.

One hour later Devil rode between two granite cliffs and then down into a hollow sheltered on four sides by stately evergreen trees. A cool breeze dried his sweat-soaked shirt. Misha stayed behind, preferring not to show himself to the other men.

In front of Devil, Dakota, Sam and Trey were mounted, and a fourth man leaned against a boulder. The fourth man's head was wound with a stark white bandage.

"Jacob?" Devil asked.

The man nodded. "Devil Blackmoor."

"You've found proof?"

Once again Jacob nodded. "A senator, a colleague of Stevens', came forward." Jacob's smile was grim. "Told us enough to put Stevens away for life."

Devil understood the subtlety behind Jacob's words. "I take it the man wasn't excited about telling the truth."

"He needed a bit of pressure."

"Our witness as well as Stevens has been dishonest for years," Sam said. He pushed back his hat.

"Emma didn't kill her mother," Dakota's voice was quiet, his dark eyes pensive. "I'm getting her out of the house now." Dakota turned to leave.

"Wait!" Sam's command held Dakota back.

"For what?" Dakota's voice, pencil thin and threatening, stopped Devil cold.

"For the sheriff to arrest him. We don't want him to fly now."

"Not when we're so close to putting the two of them away for life." Jacob touched the bandage on his head, pausing as if distracted. When he looked back to Devil, he offered an answer to Devil's question. "Lawrence Stevens killed her, and the madam helped," Jacob said. "He poisoned our mother slowly, day by day, until she didn't have the strength or the will to live.

"Emma would be free right now except for the fact that Stevens has her in the bordello. He's killed once, and as long as he has nothing to lose, we're afraid for Emma's life. Until we can get her out of there safely, he can't know what's going on."

Dakota dismounted, and the tension in the set of his jaw and the lines of anguish in his face disturbed Devil. This was a tricky situation. A hotheaded husband would accomplish nothing.

As if guessing Devil's concern, Sam spoke up. "The auction goes forward as planned."

"Dakota has already placed a silent bid. In disguise he's been to see her," Jacob said. "If the bid isn't enough, we're prepared to go as high as necessary. If he pays enough for her, he can walk out of the bordello with Emma on his arm then we can storm the place."

"Did Emma recognize Dakota?" Devil dismounted.

"She knew him."

"Perhaps that has its own merits. She'll understand we'll be there for her."

"Perhaps."

"And pigs fly." Dakota's heated reply made Devil jerk around. "She thought I betrayed her."

Once again Jacob touched the bandage, choosing to ignore Dakota's outburst. "Tonight at the auction Sam will be at the bordello, as well as Trey. She'll be protected. The sheriff will have his men there, and the Pinkertons will infiltrate the house. Nothing will go wrong."

Another hour passed while they went over the plans. Devil was to stay inside the bordello and watch Emma. If anything happened upstairs, Devil would step in to help. He would make sure the auction proceeded as planned, and that the proof against Stevens and leBon would be damming. Emma would have to be at the auction no matter what.

Devil watched the men ride away. He prayed nothing bad would happen, but he didn't trust Lawrence Stevens. Devil guided Jabbar back to town, his thoughts on the night's work.

"Misha?"

The big man rode from his hiding place, a look of apprehension in his eyes. "Yes." His voice was hard.

"I want you to go to Cheyenne."

"Now?"

Devil looked to the mountains. "Yes," he said. "I want my private car prepared for the journey east."

"I don't think this is wise."

"Perhaps not. But it's what I want. If Allah is smiling down on me, I'll have company. Don't spare any expense. And Misha, I know you will come up with a thousand and one reasons to stay. Don't. You won't change my mind."

Misha's shoulders stiffened, and his fists were clenched tight at his sides. "All right," he said. "I'll leave as soon as I get back to the hotel."

~ * ~

Angela carried the tray along the outskirts of the opulent ballroom. Scantily clad ladies danced and whirled on the parquet floor in the arms of the gentlemen here for the auction. Greed, women, and the ready availability of opium seduced the wealthy men of Denver to this spot.

She had learned a lot the last few days--too much, she'd thought at times. The ladies would drink expensive champagne, flirting all the while with gentlemen who had wives at home waiting for them. Then they'd eventually lead the eager men up the stairs covered with Oriental carpeting and into one of the fancy bedrooms. There were twenty bedrooms on the second floor, and most nights every one was in use by midnight.

Lottie had been kind to her, had told her what to expect from her first gentleman. Lottie's father had sold her and her younger sister to a bordello. Lottie had been thirteen years old, her sister twelve. At thirteen, her sister died in the whorehouse, birthing a stillborn child. From there Lottie had tried to make it on her own, only to find that without a man, she couldn't earn enough money to eat or rent a room in a respectable boardinghouse. No longer seeing the women who worked in the bordello in terms of good and evil, Angela felt her heart go out to them and the events in their lives that had brought some of them to this point.

Now as she walked up the stairs, she felt a steady gaze upon her. For a moment a sense of unease ruffled through her, but that vanished, to be replaced by a strange quivering sensation. Only Devil had ever made her feel that way.

Her nerves stretched taut, she whirled around and searched the room for him, but saw no one. He was here. He had to be--and she'd find him and twist his heart out if he thought to buy the services of one of these ladies. She reminded herself she was here for a reason, she had to stay near Emma and make sure nothing happened to her.

Yet with each step, her breathing quickened, her heart pounded. It wasn't the climb that had her panting and her knees wobbling. Devil watched her.

She smoothed then tugged at her dress, so different from the sweet yellow froth of material and the petticoats she'd worn the day they met. Now her breasts pushed invitingly from the low-cut bodice of exquisite red silk. The high cut of the hem showed a length of her leg she wanted only Devil to see.

Once she'd hoped to tempt a devil. Now she felt underdressed and wanton.

He would think she worked here. Angela sucked in her breath and pushed that thought to the back of her mind. She had a job to do.

Empowered by the knowledge he watched her, would protect her if necessary, she strode up the long flight of stairs to Emma's room. She wanted to see to Emma then Devil, but not in that order.

Devil had some hard and fast explanations to give her. Despite what he'd done to Emma, Angela would forgive him if he said the right words. Lord, but she didn't know what to think of Devil Blackmoor.

"Angel..." Devil whispered, stepping quickly from the shadowed alcove he'd been standing in and taking the pitcher from her hands. "May I help?" he asked his grin almost as broad as his shoulders.

She moved back, her smile of greeting wavering. "You," she said, suddenly shy and very breathless, her heart in her throat. She hadn't really expected him to pop out of nowhere.

"Alexi." His voice was resonating and warm. "I wish for you to call me Alexi," he said, his lips twitching at something humorous she didn't understand. " 'You' seems too impersonal for what I have in mind." His voice seduced, calmed and soothed all at the same time.

Cocking her head in thought, she remembered the only name she'd known him by, Devil Blackmoor. She liked the name Alexi, and she liked the way he watched her, almost admiringly.

His gaze on her lips, he stepped forward, so close she felt the warmth of him, and the power of him. Her entire body flushed and heated with anticipation, and the memory of his hands upon her made her tremble.

She wanted him closer to her, needed to be alone with him for at least a few cherished seconds before seeing to Emma. Angela squared her shoulders, her breasts rising to overflow the bodice, the pink color of her nipples almost showing.

Shyly, she placed a hand there to hide herself then decided against it. If she were to win this man for herself, it wouldn't be by hiding. With a practiced, seductive grace Lottie had drilled into her for two days now, she put her hands behind her back and stepped into the alcove so her back was against the smooth wood paneling. The movement accentuated her breasts, thrusting them upward and almost out of the flimsy material holding them.

Wanton came to mind. A fleeting glimpse of her parents' disapproving faces slipped through the clouds in her head, only to vanish.

She wanted this man, and if she had to be reckless to get him, she would. Lottie had told her exactly how to go about capturing the heart of a man like Devil Blackmoor.

If he pulled the drapes, he could make love to her right here in the alcove and no one would be the wiser. She focused on the gold brocaded seat that was obviously put there with carnal delights in mind.

She moistened her lips and watched him, knowing she wanted him, somehow understanding he was meant for her and she for him.

He leaned, one hand on the wall, the other rising to touch her lips. His finger brushed against her in a butterfly touch, a fleeting caress that made her want to beg for more. Parts of her body swelled and tightened in response to him. She ached in dark, feminine places deep inside her.

Pure bliss was what she felt.

Being near him almost satisfied her needs, and she longed to discover more. He peered down at her breasts, then back at her lips. Where his eyes caressed her, she wanted him to touch her.

"I've been looking all over Denver for you, but I never thought to find you here," he said, his voice soft and filled with concern.

His finger feathered across her chin, down the column of her throat. Hot, unstoppable shivers spiraled through her, overwhelming her. Once more she moistened her lips. She wanted to pull him to her, to circle him with her arms and hold him close against her.

When his words registered, she sucked in her breath. "You mean in a whorehouse?" she asked, puzzled and at the same time angered by his assumptions and suddenly on the defensive. In an indefinable way she'd come to respect Lottie, and some of the other girls, too. "Do you have something against women who have to work to survive? To eat?" she asked.

Alexi looked surprised by her vehement question. "No," he whispered huskily. "I have nothing against this--any of this. In truth I prefer a woman who is not afraid to use her body for pleasure. And at the moment I prefer you above everyone else. Come to me, Angel."

Thrilled by his ardent declaration, Angela wasn't afraid to use her body for pleasure as long as it was Devil doing the pleasuring. Oh, yes, she wanted to tell him over and over again, she needed to feel those wonderful sensations he had summoned from her body weeks ago.

"You have no use for virgins then..." Her breath fanned his lips. All the while she wondered what he thought of her.

She didn't want him to wait. Tension ripped her insides to shreds. He trailed his finger just above the bodice of her gown. She loved the contrast between the dark bronze of his skin set against the whiteness of her own. She thought he might dip his finger into the valley between her breasts. She needed him to touch her, to soothe the vibrant need rising within her.

If he asked, she would go anywhere with him, allow him anything he wanted. If he would only ask.

He was less than an inch away. She strained against him, silently urging him closer, but it seemed to Angela he wanted to prolong the inevitable. He wanted to control their lovemaking.

She wanted fulfillment.

"I do not want anything to do with virgins." He paused in reflection. "Although I will be duty-bound to marry one."

Frustration pierced her heart then fear. "You wouldn't marry someone who wasn't innocent?" she asked, unsure of herself and what she should tell him.

"Your words, sweetheart, not mine. I would never belittle a beautiful woman who gave herself to me in passion, but I would not wed her."

Confusion ran rampant in her mind. "Even if you loved her beyond anything imaginable?"

"Love is for fools and fairy tales."

She moistened her lips and swallowed, her eyes languidly following the path of his fingers as he inched closer to her breasts. His statements regarding virgins and wives vanished from her mind, replaced by the searing heat of his hands as they explored and tempted her from the path of virtue. When this man touched her, she could not think.

"But then..." She wanted to know more.

"Curiosity? I admire that in a woman; it shows a deep-seated intelligence. I would find a place in my heart for her as my mistress, and I would lavish her with her heart's desire."

His words and their meaning swept through her. The mistress of his heart, yes, she thought. She would be the mistress of his heart, his soul mate.

"I would hope, my angel, I would be her heart's desire, too. Would

I?"

She melted against him, her knees weak with pleasure, her spirits soaring higher than the clouds. Yet she recovered enough to realize she needed a small measure of sanity to deal with him. She must regain a few seconds of control or else he would surely have her behaving just as he wished.

"You're arrogant," she breathed softly.

"In the Popov men, arrogance is inbred. A most annoying habit if I do say so myself. If you like, I can try not to show that very infuriating side of my personality, but I will make no promises. There are some traits a man cannot hide no matter how hard he tries."

She could not think, could barely breathe. He pulled away from her and stared at her. Almost reverently he lowered her bodice, her breast now free of restraint and brushing against his callused fingertips. Second thoughts swept through her. Unsure of her feelings for Devil yet still driven by the heat of his touch, she thought to cover herself. He held her hands.

His dark brown eyes were wide with desire, his muscles flexing beneath her fingers. In the shadows of the dimly lit room, he looked dark and powerful, a warlord from ancient days, large and incomparable.

"Do you want me?" he asked.

She nodded her head, her fingers closing around his arms.

"You haven't chosen a partner for tonight?" he asked softly, his voice husky with desire. "Tell me your name, sweet, sweet angel."

She swallowed once before she said, "Angela."

"Angela what?" he asked, a smile on his lips, his eyes twinkling with approval.

"Just Angela..." She didn't want to ruin this moment. To tell him her last name might change their lives forever. She could well imagine what he'd do if he discovered her surname. He was seducing a Chamberlain. Only a man with a death wish would carry on so. And she did want to be seduced by Devil.

Her father would never find out, she decided.

"Do you have a partner for this evening?" he asked again. "If you do, I want you to tell him that you've chosen another. I don't want you with any other man. Where is your room?" he asked, low and hushed.

Sudden clarity hit her, and with it a realization of what she was about to do. Indecision overwhelmed her. "I can't," she said, alarmed by the prospect of giving herself to this man, yet wanting to surrender completely.

Her fingers were clenched tightly around his arms, and she was determined to hold him off until she was ready. The heat of embarrassment rose from the tips of her toes to the roots of her hair. Even while she wallowed in denial, she knew he could persuade her to share his bed. That was, after all, what she wanted. Wasn't it?

She was unsure of herself, wanting him desperately one minute, afraid to make the commitment the next. She didn't know why she'd said no.

"You have time before the festivities..." he murmured, the sentence rife with meaning. "For me. Give yourself over to my hands, Angel. Kiss me."

"No, please," Angela breathed, but the *no* was so soft, she didn't believe it herself. Her *please* was more a plea than a refusal. And he thought she was a practiced whore, well versed in the subtle game of love. Lottie had told her that lovemaking withheld for a short time could sometimes be more gratifying, but that wasn't her intent. Now that the time was here she was deathly afraid.

Alexi, his smile having vanished with the words *I can't*, reached for her. She didn't move, only watched his arms come out to touch her. His hands gently closed on her shoulders, and she shuddered helplessly in a quiet alcove surrounded by raucous celebration. Their breathing seemed to be part of the music and the laughter, her heart pounding with the tempo.

With intoxicating deliberation he drew her near. The scent of danger mingled with the fragrance of unleashed power permeating Alexi's clothes as the distance between them closed, her body unresisting beneath his hands, her face unconsciously lifting for his kiss.

"Yes," he said, and touched her lips. "Say yes and I'll be a man well satisfied."

The softness of his voice robbed her of conscious thought. When she was with him, she couldn't think. When he touched her, she melted.

It was a chaste, butterfly-light kiss for only one scant moment then Angela stroked his shoulders, her caresses becoming increasingly bold. His hands slid down to her hips, and he pulled her fiercely close. Unrepentantly, she ignored her better judgment, intent on tasting the hot boldness of his mouth, welcoming the thorough invasion of his tongue between her parted lips.

Angela lost herself in his strength and power, moving against his body in a sensual dance until every part of her melted into his hard-muscled frame. Only short seconds later, in an agitated state, his mouth lifted from hers abruptly, as though his patience had a measurable limit that had just expired.

"Where?" he asked, his voice curt and urgent, his mouth drifting languidly across her collarbone. "Where can we go?"

Startled by the potency of his touch, she cried out softly.

Her cry joined another. "Angela... where have you gotten to? I've been waiting forever. Angela!"

Devil stopped suddenly, as if she'd struck him. Roughly, he pulled the bodice of her gown up so the material covered her as modestly as possible. "Later," he said, promise in his voice. "We'll finish this later."

She watched him blend into the shadows of the alcove just as Velvet walked by. Angela felt as if she'd been used very well, and by the look in Velvet's eye, the madam didn't miss the hard evidence in front of her.

"Well, I'm glad to see you haven't wasted any time. Fifty percent goes in the fund. Make sure you record what he paid you." Velvet's voice was stern, and Angela prayed the madam couldn't see through her schooled emotions into her heart.

"Put the water in Emma's room then go to Lawrence. I believe he'd like to uncover as many of your charms as your hidden lover has just seen. He'll use you well and pay you handsomely. It's an initiation of sorts--or you could look at it as a test. Either way, do your best to satisfy him." Velvet stood back, giving Angela room to pass by and perhaps watching to see if she'd go to Lawrence afterward. She wasn't about to. The thought of Lawrence's hands upon her sickened her. Her hand touched the knife strapped to her thigh. She would use it if Stevens tried to force her.

~ * ~

Devil watched Angela move down the hall to Emma's room, helpless to stop her and wondering if she'd show up in Lawrence's suite ready and willing for sexual games.

Now that he'd laid claim to her, she'd better not. He didn't share what he considered his. And after this afternoon, Angela was indeed his. True, he'd had to look twice to recognize his angel. Kohl-rimmed eyes and painted lips had kept him wondering for more than a few minutes. It had taken him almost an hour to reconcile the wild, untamed hellion flying recklessly on her horse along the prairie with the prostitute in Madame leBon's house of ill repute.

He instantly liked all he saw. Her breasts pushed provocatively from a low-cut bodice of exquisite red silk. He remembered exactly how they looked and felt. They were lush, rounded globes, just the right size to fit his hands. Perfect rose-colored nipples tipped them. And he remembered the way her lips tasted. He'd also decided that after this night, no other man was going to view her beautiful feminine charms.

The high cut of the gown nonetheless left him straining to see more of her shapely legs and slim, narrow ankles. Her hips flared enticingly to a hand-span waist--

Velvet interrupted his carnal thoughts.

"You are such a devil," she purred, her delicate fingers resting on his shoulder. "You find my newest girl and practically ravish her in front of everyone who passes by." She was stroking Devil's arm, "You know Lawrence gets them first."

Angela had stopped halfway to Emma's room. "Angela, go on, see to Emma. Make sure she's ready." There was a long pause. Then, "Go on..."

Velvet's strident voice irritated Alexi. He wanted the auction to be over. He had other plans for his sweet Angela. He meant to make her his mistress and, if he could convince her, take her with him tonight when he left for the old country.

Devil looked past Velvet to Angela. She looked furious, a spitting hellcat came to mind. Ah, yes, with Angela in his bed his nights would be filled with passion and excitement.

Through the fabric of his pants, the madam touched his arousal. He jerked back, his fists clenched, ready to retaliate. He'd never before been so primed and on edge or furious with a woman. Velvet laughed, a deep, throaty sound that grated on Devil's nerves.

"She didn't give you what you needed. If you come with me, we can finish what she started." Velvet's hands moved swiftly and expertly on the buttons of his pants.

"No," he said, his fingers closing around her wrist in a dangerous threat, his voice cold and hollow.

She hissed but let go. Her chin tilted upward in a silent threat of her own, her bright red lips drawn back in a sneer. "So it's to be that way?" She moved closer to him. "I hear you're a man of *many* pleasures."

He put her aside, and, refastening his pants, he stepped from the alcove. "You heard wrong."

Suddenly disgusted with Velvet and with his own base desires, Devil strode down the stairs and into the parlor. At least twenty ladies plied their wares, laughing, drinking and smoking. He moved down the hallway and out the front door until he encountered fresh, clean air.

Leaning against a pillar, he let his mind wander back to Angela. He saw a lifetime of hot pursuit and exciting surrender with her.

He wanted Angela's long, coltish legs wrapped around him every night. With her by his side, her smile captivating all the seconds of his day, he could almost feel he'd achieved nirvana. Her bold honesty enticed him. Her innocent passion beckoned him. Instinctively, he knew she was the woman for him, his mate for the rest of his life.

The thought of taking a wife for the sole purpose of begetting an heir filled him with loathing, but he could see no solution to his dilemma. His grandmother would never accept Angela as his wife--as the mother of the heir.

He could not marry a whore.

Who would know?

Allah, the most desirable woman he'd ever known was a prostitute. That was fitting revenge, he supposed, for all the women he'd made love to in his lifetime. The one woman who made him feel things deep inside as no other, he couldn't marry because she wasn't a virgin.

The fact changed little. He still wanted her in his bed and his life. With an arrogance he freely admitted, he planned to have her beneath him in his bed as soon as he could provide the proper environment. When he made love to her, it would be on a soft bed, and the room would be filled with candlelight. He wouldn't let the depraved Lawrence Stevens or the greedy Madame leBon stand in his way. As soon as he'd done his part in rescuing Emma, he would find Angela, kidnap her if necessary, and hightail it out of the country.

Of course, the realization that she would give herself to him without protest or the time-consuming seduction needed with a virgin lightened his mood. Hot passion and seductive nights with a spirited hellion in his arms was a lot to look forward to.

He struck a match on the pillar and lit a smoke. Embers floated lazily down from the cigarette. He watched and waited, coiled tightly and primed for anything. A cool breeze came down from the mountains, hinting at a possible late snow.

A head start on the weather would be nice, he mused. His gear was packed and ready; he needed only to add a few extra essentials for Angela. Midnight. He breathed deeply with thought. When the clock struck twelve or possibly sooner, he and Angela would be on their way east. In a few days they'd catch the train in Cheyenne then on to New York, where his ship waited for him.

She'd had such a strange reaction to his comments about women and their bodies. She'd bristled like a little tigress defending her cubs. And he'd told her the truth. He did prefer a woman who was not afraid to use her body for pleasure. Remembering the cold, aristocratic women his grandmother had introduced him to when he lived in Russia with her sent rivers of ice down his spine. To bed one of those ladies would be like bedding a statue. He would not--could not--endure that without the thought of his Angel to return to.

During his life with his father, he'd seen and made love to many exotic women. His father, the grand vizier, had a harem full of beautiful women. None, he thought, were as mysterious as Angela. His father had abducted his mother, brought her to his palace as a slave, but he'd quickly learned of her nobility. And just as quickly he'd fallen in love with her, naming her his first wife.

His father had no trouble forgetting his mother's earlier marriage to a Russian aristocrat, claiming the marriage no longer existed. Yet when her former husband and firstborn son had died, it had given Alexi control of untold wealth and an inheritance in Russia that could be denied by no one.

Velvet had interrupted what would have turned out to be a fast, unsatisfying first encounter with his Angel. Even though he'd been irritated with the madam, he was inwardly pleased she had come upon them. Now Velvet knew how he felt about Angela, and the madam would think twice before abusing her.

Control had been inherent in every move he made throughout his life, and somehow the little slip of a lady of the evening called Angela dissolved that control with a smile. He had the uncanny feeling Angela wrested control from him with every breath she took.

He'd have to be wary.

The soft, unnatural swaying of shadows at the edge of the forest beyond caught his attention. He searched the perimeter but saw nothing unusual.

Every instinct cried out to him.

Devil pushed himself off the pillar and moved toward the trees and the vision he thought he'd seen. Lawrence Stevens rushed from the back of the house, unaware anyone watched.

And Devil pursued the pursuer. Someone or something had put a crunch on Lawrence's plans, and Devil could only guess the cause.

Emma...

The faint shadows, the indistinct fluttering of light and dark at the edge of the woods, had been Emma Barringer. She had done the impossible. She had escaped.

He had to find her before Lawrence Stevens did.

Chapter Five

The second Angela stepped foot in Emma's room she knew something had gone wrong. She looked from the rumpled bed to the nightdress pooled on the floor near the armoire.

The curtains had been drawn, something that had never been allowed. Emma's water glass and pitcher were tipped, and opium-laced liquid seeped across the floorboards and into the rug.

Silence prevailed throughout the expanse of the room. Shivers of fear raced up Angela's arms, primal and implicit. She rubbed them as if the gesture could dispel the cold.

It couldn't. Nothing could.

"Emma? Oh, dear God, where are you, Emma?"

Angela stood near the center of the room now, searching for answers. She could see signs of struggle: an overturned chair, a picture on the wall slightly askew. For Emma to have left the room by herself, she would have had to overcome a great obstacle: her drugged state. Emma was in no condition to brave the wilderness outside the bordello, and she certainly couldn't walk down the road. Velvet leBon had bought the most secluded mansion in the wilderness outside Denver.

Angela had thought to dilute the drugs Velvet had given Emma. Instinctively, Angela had known Dakota meant to rescue his wife or buy her at the auction. There was no other recourse. If Jacob had proof, they could bring in the Pinkertons and the sheriff. They could catch Lawrence Stevens and Velvet leBon.

Even in Angela's wildest imagination, she could not have foreseen an escape. Despite the threat of punishment from her father, she would have warned Sam or Dakota if she'd thought Emma was strong enough to leave on her own. She could have told Devil. Both men sat downstairs in the parlor waiting for the auction, completely unaware of the events unfolding upstairs.

An auction at which Emma would not appear.

With Emma gone, she had no reason to stay. She was at risk here, not just from Lawrence Stevens, should he find out who she was, but from her father, too. She was more afraid of her father. Guilt had a way of eating a hole in one's heart, and this deception had left Angela feeling more guilt than she'd known in a lifetime.

After a few courage-rending deep breaths, Angela fled Emma's room, walking swiftly down the hall, determined not to draw attention to herself. She reached her own room and, after closing the door, leaned against the wood, letting go a little sigh of relief.

She had only minutes until Emma would be discovered; then chaos would take over. She didn't want to be anywhere near the premises when the pandemonium began. Before anyone discovered Emma missing, Angela had to get away.

Angela began packing, a heavy sigh coming from her. Why couldn't her father listen and try to understand? Hearing her side of the story didn't seem unreasonable. Her father wanted to see her polished. She wasn't a piece of silver, and she had no need for fancy Eastern society. She stuffed the dress she'd worn to the bordello into her valise.

No matter what Sam Chamberlain had in mind for her, he could not erase her Sioux blood. Her mother, White Flower, was half Sioux. Angela had inherited her blond hair and blue eyes from her grandmother, who had been captured by a Sioux chieftain. Many summers she'd lived with her tribe, been part of their customs, admired their courage and honesty. She admired Emma, too. She paused a moment.

"I'm proud of you, Emma Barringer," she said, "but you've put a hitch in the plans."

Angela dug through her remaining clothes. She continued her search until she found her buckskins and moccasins. Dressing quickly, she turned to the mirror to braid her hair.

"Good Lord," she murmured. The sight of herself made her grimace with distaste. There wasn't enough water in the state of Colorado to wash the paint off her face. She pursed her lips, then puckered her mouth into a funny expression.

Her search for the soap took too many minutes. The scrubbing took longer. She washed until her cheeks were pink and raw. The kohl around her eyes smudged and burned. When she was finished, the paint was not all gone, but she liked the wide-eyed look a small amount of makeup gave her.

"Too bad you can't see me now, Devil." She flashed the mirror a mischievous grin before turning away. She slipped her knife into its sheath and tucked in her shirt. If Devil wanted her, he'd have to find her. She'd give him one week, she decided. Then she'd start looking for him.

"Angela! Open the door." Her father's voice from outside the door sent a ripple of fear down her spine, followed by a calming moment of resignation.

"Angela!"

Her name was uttered with such force, her heart missed a beat and she broke out hi a clammy sweat. She wasn't ready to face her father. Sam's frantic, angry pounding on her door was sure to break it down. "I'm coming." Her voice quavered and her nerves jumped. Knowing she had no other recourse, she slowly opened the door.

"Papa." She stiffened her shoulders and braced herself for her father's anger.

"What are you doing here? Never mind. I already know, but you'll answer my questions when this over. Do you understand?"

"Yes, Papa." She'd never seen him so angry. "But only because I need to explain my actions. I want you to understand."

"You're leaving," he said, taking her by the arm and leading her out the door. "You're going to the stables right now and you're going to find what looks like the fastest horse and you're getting out of here."

"Yes, Papa," she said.

"Stay in your room until I get back to the hotel. You've a lot to answer for, young lady. As of this morning, I thought you were safe and on your way to Boston."

"I know," she agreed. "But, Father, I'm not a child. I can take care of myself and make my own decisions," she said, her voice strong and sure.

He stared at her, a white-hot anger emanating from him. Her heart pounded erratically against her chest. She'd never before disobeyed him this blatantly. His fury with her was understandable, yet her own determination to make her own way stood at the forefront of her mind. She wanted his respect, needed his blessing, but if neither was forthcoming, she'd deal with the consequences.

"Angela?" His voice was filled with heated rage. "What are you up to?" His hands on her shoulders shook, his eyes alight with anger and fear she suddenly understood went beyond all reason. And she knew he held himself in check, that it was all he could do to keep from shaking her until her teeth rattled.

Despite her new resolve, she trembled beneath his scrutiny. "Nothing, Papa. I wanted to help. If Emma's not here, there is no reason for me to stay."

"Damn right!" he said, still watching her with unleashed anger. Angela had never seen that look before, had never pushed him over the edge this way.

The pounding of footsteps on the back stairs and the hushed whispers accompanying them forced Sam to push Angela back into her room and close the door. They waited until the sounds vanished and a door clicked shut farther down the hall. Then Sam cracked the door and peered out.

"It's clear. You go on now. Go down the back way and I'll be in the parlor. I want to find out what has happened to Emma." He handed her the packed valise. "I'll be at the hotel in an hour."

Angela nodded to her father then stepped gingerly down the carpeted hall, trying not to make a sound, and when she was sure her father had left by way of the front stairs, she slipped into the alcove.

Maids hurried back and forth. Two men brought pails of water to Emma's room. She could hear the frantic voice of Madame leBon, raised to a furor.

"Where is the chit? Where's Angela?"

Lawrence spoke a few words before leaving, and Zeke appeared. Then, through a space between the curtains, she saw Emma pass by, cradled in Devil's arms. Emma's eyes were wide with fear, her skin a sickly white.

Emma was back. Somehow Stevens had found her.

And Devil had played his part. He'd returned Emma for auction. It had been the plan from the beginning, the only way to gather enough evidence to convict Stevens and leBon, and in the process send them to jail for life.

Yet anger swept through Angela. She'd wanted so desperately for Emma to succeed in her escape and Devil had stopped her. He had only been doing his part in this, she reminded herself.

And I have to do my part.

Angela had made a promise to herself, and she could no more leave at this moment than she could stop breathing. The hour for the auction quickly approached. Two of the girls to be placed on the block, appearing eager for the games to start, strutted down the stairs and past the little alcove where she stood watching.

Sounds came from Emma's room.

The hall was empty. Angela rushed back to her room, tossing the valise she carried onto the bed. Then, rummaging through the petticoats and silk dresses, she found the red satin dress she'd worn earlier.

Dropping her valise by her door, a few minutes later she appeared at the threshold of Emma's room, only seconds after Velvet had called for the girl. Emma was in the bath behind a bathing screen and Zeke had just come from Velvet's room, a pitcher of water--no doubt laced with opium--in his hands.

"See that she's dressed and ready. Emma will have her turn on the auction block in about an hour, and I want her to look willing. Do what you have to," she said to Angela.

"Yes, ma'am." Angela nodded, a smile on her face and deep sorrow in her heart. She ached for Emma and all she'd accomplished only to fail in the end.

Emma rose from the bath. A pale yellow wrapper was placed around her shoulders. The dress she was to wear hung nearby and Angela swallowed hard, imagining what Emma would look like in the sheer gown and imagining how Dakota would feel when he saw her wearing the gauzy confection in front of all who came to watch.

Dakota would be driven to murder. Lawrence Stevens would burn in hell. The strength of both Trey and her father would be needed to hold

Dakota back.

~ * ~

Inhaling a deep, ragged breath, Angela stepped behind the bathing screen.

"Everything will be all right." Angela spoke in soothing tones to Emma.

Emma tried to speak. She moistened her lips but only a choked sound could be heard.

"I know you're afraid, but Dakota's downstairs," Angela said. "He won't let anything happen to you. Trust him."

Angela thought she saw Emma's eyes widen with a spark of hope. But she couldn't be sure.

An hour later and with a heavy heart, Angela watched Emma leave the room, a silent prayer in Angela's mind. Emma's future was now in Dakota's hands.

She had done all she could.

In a state of shock Angela stared into the now-empty hallway. Bawdy shouts rose from the ballroom below, and Angela could only guess the noise was due to the auction and the anticipation of Emma's arrival.

Velvet would have made sure the men were aroused to a fever pitch. Emma's dress alone would have caused the excitement to escalate.

Midnight approached, and Angela's father no doubt thought she was safely out of the bordello. Angela strode to her room, only to find the bed occupied. Her valise still sat by the door, where she'd dropped it an hour ago. Hastily grabbing her belongings, she shut the door and slipped away.

She darted into the alcove, determined to get rid of the skimpy dress and put on her buckskins--even more determined to be tucked into her bed when Sam arrived at the hotel. Unable to help herself, her fragile emotions stretched thin, she laughed. It was nervous laughter, and for a few minutes she collapsed on the couch, her head in her hands and her shoulders trembling with the release of the anxiety she'd felt for the last hour. Torn between her desire to know and love Devil Blackmoor and her loyalty to her family, she had never felt so confused and scared.

If she left now, she might never see Alexi again, might never again feel the gentleness of his touch or taste the sweetness of his kisses. Oh, how she prayed she would see Devil one more time. But she had to leave, now. And, she vowed, she would keep this one promise to her father.

A few minutes later she'd quickly slipped out of the dress and into her breeches and shirt. She was pulling on one of her moccasins when she heard Alexi.

"Angela."

Her prayers had been answered. Once again she laughed, the sound high and thin, her fingers shaking as she tried to put on her other moccasin. Words lodged in her throat and she couldn't answer him. She had to see him one more time.

"Angela, where are you?"

Angela heard the creak of a door nearby and then...

"Excuse me," Alexi said. She heard the amusement in his voice. Then he called out in whispered tones to her. "Angela, if you don't come out this minute before I embarrass myself again, I'll see the same happens to you. I mean it. I will embarrass you until you blush scarlet."

Covering her mouth with her hands, she tried to stifle the nervous laughter she couldn't stop. Then, remembering she meant to leave the house, she bent down to retrieve the other moccasin from the floor. The curtain separated for a second while she struggled with her valise and her balance. Her bare foot slipped through the opening then back.

"Devil...come here," she said, but her breath was ragged and her voice was slightly husky. She wanted to talk to him, to explain. She regained some of her composure and most of her wits. "Nothing and no one can embarrass me until I turn scarlet. Not even a devil." A restless energy swept through her.

"Is that a challenge?" His tone held warning.

She could tell from the sound of his voice he stood outside the curtain. "Of course." Angela knew it was. He was hot and speeding in her blood. He sent her nerves sailing wantonly and her heartbeat into a rapid staccato. "Next to riding hard and fast, I like a challenge best," she said breathily. Her imagination played havoc with her body. Devil had sought her out. He looked for her.

She wished time would allow her to tease and flirt with him. But she'd promised her father. She had to leave now. Shouts came from below her; loud whistling and wild catcalls followed. Angela cringed, knowing Emma's appearance to be the cause.

"As much as I'd like to play games with you, angel, this isn't the time or the place. I'm getting you out of here while there is still a chance. You're coming with me. All hell's about to break loose downstairs, and I don't want you caught in the middle. Emma will be safe; the Pinkertons, the sheriff and his deputies, they're all out there."

Her heart warmed. She liked the feel of his concern. They were in complete agreement, a quick exodus paramount.

Alexi flung back the curtain. The look of anticipation and then surprise on his face startled her. She gasped, clutching her moccasin to her chest.

"Why you little..."

"Tease?" Without thinking, she spoke the word that was foremost in her thoughts. She wanted to tease and flirt with him. Then, unsure of herself, she smiled at him. Even in this dreadful situation, she enjoyed the easy banter between them. With Devil nearby, she found it easy to forget everything but him and the way he made her feel.

"Devil," he murmured as his avid, strained features focused on her and his horrified gaze ran the length of her--down then up again.

With a slight lowering of her lashes, she countered softly, "Angel."

Standing in front of her, dressed from head to toe in black, he appeared shockingly mysterious, enigmatically hard and definitely the man they called Devil Blackmoor. He looked as if he were ready to tackle the portals of hell. His pants molded his powerful thighs and hips so every male part of him showed clearly, leaving her imagination racing. Broad shoulders strained the fabric of his shirt, which he'd left unbuttoned far enough to entice. She wanted to touch what she saw. She swallowed hard.

He stared avidly at her. "Just what are you wearing?"

She couldn't mistake the anger in his voice. Angela didn't know what to say. *Buckskins* came to mind, but her throat felt paralyzed.

"You're not going anywhere dressed like that."

He grabbed her wrist, pulling her from the alcove so quickly she stumbled into him. Her breasts were suddenly thrust against his chest. When she felt the hard, unyielding muscles of his upper body, the sensations evoked memories best not remembered at the moment.

With his hands he explored her. His long fingers traveled the length of her spine and back to settle on her waist. She allowed the heady exploration, reveling in the magical feelings born of his caress.

"Son of a bitch!" His voice exploded around her, ricocheting off the walls.

She flinched then smiled, a nervous reaction. She knew what he thought, because his roving gaze had stopped as did his hands just below her breasts. He stared at her hardening nipples, clear little imprints against the buckskins. In her haste she'd not had time to put on undergarments. Had she stopped to put on her underclothes, he would have found her naked.

Angela wanted to hide her anxiety behind bluster. With Devil Blackmoor that would never work. She meant to brazen this out and ignore his rising fury. She ran a fingertip along his collarbone then looked down, her lashes fluttering against her cheeks.

She'd never really looked at his arousal before. Now she did. Even through the fabric of his pants she saw him hard and pulsing.

"Don't swear so, Devil. It might give the wrong impression." Her words were throaty, and they weren't at all what she wanted to say. With Alexi standing so close to her, how could she think?

"Damnation. I'll swear if I want to."

"Of course you will," she said, making eye contact once more, all the while tracing his collarbone with the tip of one trembling finger and wishing she had time for him. He had short black hair on his chest, and it was soft to the touch. She scraped her nails across his flesh and he almost smiled. She marveled at the control she held over him, suddenly felt empowered and bold.

He stopped her roving fingers with his own, his eyes focusing on her hand then back on her clothing.

"What do you think you are wearing?" he asked again, this time more commanding.

Angela had never heard that particular tone or so much force put behind words spoken to her. Even the second time around, his question seemed unnecessary. Any fool could tell what she wore.

"Well?" he asked again, impatience unraveling his smile and turning his expression cold and dangerous.

She, stepped back, distancing herself from him, hoping the separation would cool her burning nerves and bring calm, rational thought to her jangled mind. Nothing seemed to help. Even with the distance her breasts heaved. She smiled, hoping for time to think. She placed one hand on her hip and turned away.

"My clothes," she said, wondering at his sanity. "I'm wearing my clothes. You've seen buckskins before."

One brow quirked upward, questioning her answer. "True enough," he agreed. "But not on a lady. What else have you got in that bag of yours? I want you to put a dress on--now."

She shook her head no. Angela meant to begin as she would finish. He would not dictate to her what she would wear or what she would do unless the situation was life-threatening and she agreed with him.

"I'm not changing my clothes. We don't have time. You said so yourself." She paused for breath, shrugging. Her sensitized nipples rubbed against the leather, and she almost groaned from the contact. "Besides, it's none of your business what I have in the bag." She picked up the discarded moccasin, and in one quick movement slipped the soft leather over her bare toes. Angela stepped from the alcove with a toss of her long braid.

She strode toward the back stairs, brushing past him as she went.

"God almighty."

Despite the noise coming from below, she heard his whispered words and flinched at the tone. He would have seen the knife when she walked by. Alexi had a lot to learn about her, one being that she never went anywhere without the knife Dakota had bought her when she had turned ten years old.

He faltered even as he tried to speak. A strangled, "Angel," was all he said.

With that one helpless look, he bolted into her heart like a streak of lightning. His fascination with her was purely sexual, she reminded herself, but she meant to change that fascination to love as soon as possible. Lottie had given her at least one hundred intriguing suggestions. She would take care of his every need.

"Are you coming?" she asked, putting as much sass and flirt into her voice as she could manage.

She wanted a strong man, one she could not bend to her will, but one who would listen to her.

"I'd be crazy not to." His voice was a low rumble deep in his chest.

He caught up to her halfway down the stairs and touching her arm, he turned her.

Angela stared up at Alexi with clear, unblinking eyes, ready, she knew, for whatever he wanted. Right now she wanted him to kiss her, nothing more. Later she wanted him to take her in his arms and teach her about love and fierce, hot passion, the kind that would last forever.

Angela inhaled an uneven breath, her gaze never wavering from his. "What, Alexi? What do you want?"

"I want you, darling girl. I want all of you."

She watched Alexi close his eyes. Her own eyes were wide open, and guilt assailed her. The thought that she hadn't told her father what she was about to do was like acid eating at her soul. He would worry about her, but if she gave him any indication what she was doing, he'd move heaven and earth to stop her. She wouldn't allow anyone to stand in the way of what she wanted.

She knew she didn't want to live without Alexi.

"I know," Her breathy whisper surprised her. "I want you too."

"You're so damn sweet. One would think ... no," he said.

"Alexi?"

"I'll pleasure you until you cry out my name, until you sleep the peace of a woman well sated."

She wanted to know what he meant--and so much more. "Promise?" she asked. Nervously she moistened her lips. It seemed to Angela that whenever he was near, tension closed in around her, suffocating her.

After long seconds of staring, he lowered his mouth to hers, brushing lightly--almost tentatively--across her lips. But her tongue came out to meet his mouth, to challenge, to take control. She'd had enough of the gentle teasing and mild caresses he'd given her so far.

He sensed the change in her and battled her for dominance. Almost as if he had to make sure she knew who set down the rules and made the decisions, he wound his fingers in her hair, tilted her head back, and commanded and directed the kiss. His lips closing over her, his tongue delving deeply inside her mouth, he continued relentlessly until she moaned softly, melting into his arms. He'd mastered her more easily than she'd thought possible. She was liquid heat in his arms, an inferno about to explode.

He pulled back, grinning, caressing her cheeks with his thumbs. "That was your first lesson, angel. A very important one, one that you must remember for all time. I am the man here, and I'm the one in command. You will follow my orders, and in turn, I will protect you with my life."

For a moment confusion swept through Angela, but then she flashed him a sassy smile. *And I will protect you with my life,* she added silently.

"Do you understand, darling?" His voice was soft and deep and very throaty. He kissed her eyes closed then her lips again, this time a soft, feathery kiss, a promise of more--or perhaps the tender kiss was meant to seal a bargain, she wasn't sure.

"Oh, yes," she said softly then her spirit flashed daringly. She gave her head what she hoped was an arrogant toss before breaking loose from his embrace. Looking over her shoulder, she laughed, and with a bold wink she said, "But Devil, didn't you know? Unless I see fit, I don't obey anyone."

For a brief span of time he looked as if she'd just hit him with a sledgehammer in his gut. Yet after he recovered, he smiled. The smile was one of retribution.

"You will bend to me. And you will cherish the very idea of obedience to me."

"When I choose to do so," she told him with a flippant air.

Once again he faltered. "We'll talk later," he said in a growl. "When we have more time."

"That suits me," she said, and jumped down the last three steps, landing on the balls of her feet.

What have I gotten myself into? she wondered, but all the while she couldn't stop grinning. Good Lord, but he was an arrogant man, and for a moment she wondered if she could ever change his aristocratic need to give orders.

Angela didn't wait for Alexi to follow; she knew he would. Outside, a soft mist filled the darkened night. There was no moonglow to give light to the earth. The blackness of the evening encompassed everything.

Bawdy shouts reverberated from the inside of the bordello, making Angela eager to leave. Through the window she could see men sitting in elegant chairs, scantily clad ladies draped over their arms, watching the show.

Emma would be all right. Her father and Dakota were in there. In the shadows, his gaze fastened on the window, she saw Jacob and what must have been other Pinkertons. They were all dressed in suits. The sheriff was there too. She supposed the rescue party was about to begin.

She was so absorbed in the scene beyond the windows, she wouldn't have known when Alexi reached her side except for the fact that he placed his arm around her and guided her toward the horses. Jabbar immediately recognized his master and nickered softly in greeting. A brown mare stood next to the great Jabbar, and a packhorse was behind them.

"We're going overland?" she asked, her mind reeling with the implications. He meant to take her with him. She would be alone with this man. Completely alone. From the first time she had set eyes upon him, being with him had been what she longed for.

He nodded. "Until we reach Cheyenne. Then we'll take the train."

"Four days..." Her voice drifted and he slanted her a strange look.

"Can you manage?" he asked.

She laughed. *Manage?* "Yes."

Before he could ask another question, she was on the mare and, giving her a swift little nudge, she was on her way. Alexi muttered something she didn't understand; then she heard the sound of his stallion's hooves and those of the packhorse.

Their relationship might very well be a battle of wills. Yet she wanted to win only half the time--or when she was right.

In a few minutes Alexi rode beside her. Content to ride in silence, she let the sounds of the night ease her conscience and her fears. Alexi would be a good husband to her. He was a kind man, if not indulgent. She would teach him indulgence. After all, her mother had taught Sam Chamberlain, and that must have been very hard indeed.

Just before dawn they passed a ranch house. A man and his son were outside working the cattle.

"Alexi." She tempered her voice. "Can we stop a minute? I want to send a note to one of the ladies at the house. I don't want anyone to worry about me."

He nodded, pulling his hat down slightly.

Angela slipped easily from the horse; then, opening her valise, she found paper and pen. She sat down on the grass and began to write a letter to her father, begging him not to follow her and pleading with him to be happy because she'd found the love of her life, her mate.

"The lad here is going to deliver the message for you," Alexi said. "I've paid him," he added.

"Thank you," she said. Indulgence might come naturally to Alexi, after all. She smiled brightly at him.

"We have another few hours' ride ahead of us, if you're not too tired."

She wasn't. "I'm just warming up." Her cheeks felt flushed, and Alexi had just helped lift a burden from her heart. "I could ride for hours."

"You don't have to. We'll stop, take a short break then move on." His observation of her was not subtle. He looked boldly at her, a promise in his expression.

The rise in her temperature was remarkable. She didn't like to think he could do that with just a look, but he could.

An hour later the sky opened up in shimmering display of fireworks. There was little they could do but take refuge beneath overhanging rocks.

Alexi helped her dismount, his eyes lingering on her mouth, his hands at her waist. He cleared his throat and, dropping his hands as if she burned him, he turned away.

"I'll start a fire," she said, patting her mare's neck.

The sideways look he shot her gave way to laughter. "You sure you know how?" he asked, a chuckle in his voice.

"You'd be surprised what I can do," she purred.

"Temptress. If the weather and the accommodations weren't so miserable, I'd find out right here what you can do." He touched her nose with the tip of his finger then followed the brotherly gesture with a kiss. "Right now."

Pushing away her maidenly fear and her wet hair, she winked. "I'd like that."

"As I said before, temptress, when we make love I'm going to have a soft bed and feather pillows all around me. I' ve waited for this a long time. I can hold off for a few more days."

Just then a wild bolt of lightning hit a nearby tree, and thunder boomed across the sky. Fire scorched the trunk, and sparks flew. Surprised, she flinched, and the horses went wild, rearing up and crying out their fear.

"Easy, girl." Angela recovered quickly. Her horse was terrified, Jabbar crazy.

Alexi stroked and spoke to the stallion, his words foreign and mysterious. He spoke in a soft whisper, as if he tended a cherished lover. Angela found herself drawn to him, mesmerized by the steady cadence of his voice and his actions. She wanted him to ease her maidenly fears in the same way. The depth of her emotions was so intense and compelling, she turned away from the sight.

"You afraid of thunderstorms?" he asked, his powerful chest suddenly pressed against her back, his arms around her, holding her close.

She didn't know when he'd left Jabbar's side, only that his heat radiated through her damp clothing. His warm breath whispered across her neck.

"No." *I'm afraid of my feelings for you.*

"You could have fooled me." He pulled her wet hair from the back of her neck and expertly wound it into a knotted coif on top of her head; then he secured it with a scarf he unwrapped from around his neck. "There."

Lightly he massaged the back of her neck, tension slowly draining from her. She felt lethargic, and her knees were weak with wanting. She let her head fall forward, enjoying the play of his wondrous fingers upon her.

He flicked the buttons of her shirt, and the fabric fell open, her breasts free. Expertly he slid her arms free of the sleeves. When he finished, he hung the shirt near the fire to dry.

He didn't touch her, barely looked at her. She felt as if he did. Her breasts swelled and ached, the crests tightening to taut buds. Crossing her arms over her chest was natural. He stopped her.

"Now your breeches," he said.

"But..." She slipped free of the moccasins, unsure of herself and the feelings of vulnerability her nakedness evoked.

"Do you trust me?"

Angela did trust him--with her life and her happiness. She nodded then slipped out of her pants while he rummaged in her valise.

"Here."

He walked to her, holding out a black riding skirt and a white blouse. Quickly she slipped them on, unaware that while her back was turned he had disrobed and hung his clothes near the fire to dry.

When she turned around again, she stared openly. "You're beautiful."

He quirked one dark brow, chuckling deeply. "Beautiful?"

To Angela he was the embodiment of an ancient warlord come to life. She could well imagine him wielding his cutlass against his enemies. Surrounded, he would fight valiantly, until he vanquished his foe.

"Yes." She felt her smile all the way across her face.

"Come here." He held out his arms to her and she walked slowly to him, knowing he would hold her throughout the tempest.

Rain turned to hail, pounding the earth. Wild winds tormented the tree limbs, sending dirt and debris into the raging air.

The moment was wild and passion-filled.

He swept her into his arms and walked with her to the driest part of their shelter. "You are beautiful," he whispered, his breath touching her cheek. He smelled of tempest and fire, of wild, wild winds and unyielding strength.

He left her there for the time it took him to dress. When he came back, he pulled her into his arms. "Feel better?" he asked.

"Yes." She snuggled next to him, absorbing the warmth he offered, content to let the man of her dreams hold her. More knowledge about passion and love would follow, not today, perhaps not tomorrow, but she knew that soon he would make love to her and she would give all of herself to him. Then she would teach him to love her in return.

"Where are we going?" she asked, while she idly ran her hands across the muscles of his chest.

The moment that Alexi had dreaded had come. Not for one second had he doubted her willingness to become his mistress. But this question had tormented him.

He held her hand in his, their fingers intertwined. The tempest howled around them. "Europe," he said softly. "Would you like that? To see the world with me? We can go to England, then France and perhaps on to Constantinople."

Raw thunder filled the air.

Angela moved away from him. Instantly he felt the separation, the coldness that would surely come between them. She brought his hand to her lips and kissed each finger, a gentle smile on her face.

Lightning ripped the sky in half.

"Yes." The single word was a breathy whisper surrounded by the raging storm.

In her eyes he saw that she would go anywhere with him. His free hand rose to lift her chin higher, to demand confirmation of what he saw.

She answered. "I've always wanted to see the world."

His fears eased. She brought his hand back to his lap, her fingers resting on his arousal. He held his shudder of masculine desire in check. *The little hellion.*

"Constantinople," he said. "My father lives there."

Her eyes were wide, her fingers moving gently upon him, stimulating him to a simmering current of unleashed passion. He felt battered and bruised, with only one solution to the wonderful sexual ache she did little to assuage with her shy yet wanton attentions. He didn't know how she maintained the act--practiced courtesan one minute, innocent virgin the next.

"Little hellion," he whispered, his tongue tracing the delicate pink shell of her ear. She purred for him.

His heart stopped.

"I thought I was your angel."

"Not when you toy with me and play games at my expense."

She looked at him with questioning eyes.

"You know exactly what you're about."

Her tempting pink tongue moistened her lips, her lashes lowered and she moved closer to him. Through her white shirt he could see the rosy tips of her breasts, could almost taste their sweetness.

"Of course I do," she admitted. "I mean to seduce you."

"And you're doing a fine job of it."

Angela ran her finger down the deep vee of his shirt. He'd tucked the length into his pants but had not buttoned it. Her fingers touched the top of his pants. He throbbed beneath the fabric, longing for her and her pleasure-drenched warmth.

Allah, why had he decided to wait for feather pillows? This little wanton did not need wooing. She needed hot and unbridled carnal delights. She could teach the women in his father's harem a few tricks of her own.

She ran her fingernail back to his throat, his muscles tensing in ardent anticipation of a sensual act that wasn't yet to be.

"Then I'll have to make sure you receive your just deserts."

He nipped her ear lightly. Without hesitation he leaned down, his mouth closing over her nipple, and through the white linen he suckled and teased. He ravished her breast with his teeth then turned to the other one.

He delighted in the sounds she made and the raw, primitive thrusting of her hips against his own. Covering her with his body, he let her softness ease him. There were ways to make her purr with sexual anticipation. He would do all that then he would watch her climax. He wanted to see her eyes at the moment her muscles spasmed and he brought her to the ultimate physical release.

"Little mistress mine, you'll melt in my hands."

Her fingers slipped beneath his shirt and teased his male nipples; her nails scraped across his flesh to the line of his pants again and again.

Her nails moved back and forth.

Her shirt ripped, buttons flying from their fastenings and scattering on the ground.

"Alexi."

His name on her lips rilled him. "Easy," he whispered. "I'm going to make you soar on the wings of the storm. Just hold on for the ride, sweet angel."

In seconds she lay naked beneath him. Her breasts were perfect, her waist narrow and her hips widely feminine. The soft expanse of curls at the apex of her thighs begged for his touch.

When his fingers dipped into her soft recesses, she jerked, her eyes widening.

"Alexi!"

She sounded panicked.

"Hush," he said, and kissed her lips, easing his tongue inside her mouth. His finger followed suit more intimately in her warm sheath.

Allah, but she was hot and tight.

He found the small bud of her wildest desire, deep in her feminine folds, and caressed her, her hips moving in rhythm with him. One with her at this moment, he understood her most urgent needs and granted her every wish.

She cried out in little mews and purrs. Even though she tried to speak, only one coherent word passed her lips. "Alexi..." she said again and again. The sound satisfied him.

And then not even his name passed her lips. She writhed against his hand, making sounds of gratification and crying out her passion and the pleasure of her release. Seconds passed and her body rhythm slowed, adapting to the tender ministrations he offered.

"You'll ride me, my sweet concubine. Soon, but not tonight, I will be deep inside you and I'll feel you pulse against me. Soon," he said. *Very soon.*

She turned her face into his shoulder when he wanted to look at her passion-filled eyes.

"Shy?" he asked, stunned by the thought and the inconsistency it presented. "Modesty has no place between lovers," he said as he ran his fingers down the length of her spine. In the aftermath, he held her close.

He felt suddenly angry. The pretense and the acting did not sit well with him, and he wondered what game she played.

Chapter Six

Four days later Angela and Devil rode out of Cheyenne on the train headed east. The accommodations were not what Alexi had told her they would be. Instead of his private car with all the luxuries money could buy, they rode with the other passengers on hard seats. They had no place to sleep, and Alexi's frustration and anger at the situation ate at her. His promise of a bed and pillows was unfulfilled.

Emma's rescue and the arrest of Stevens and Velvet leBon had made the front page of the paper in Cheyenne. Stevens's crimes had gone undetected for so long, the revelations at the trial were like the stirring up of a hornets' nest. Stevens had used his position as a senator to launder money and set up a white-slave trade that reached into South America. The list of his crimes went on and on.

Angel yawned and punched her valise into a more satisfying lump. The impatient gesture didn't work. Wide-eyed, she watched the endless miles of the Kansas prairie roll by. Occasionally she saw animals and here and there a farm. Mostly she saw miles and miles of billowing grasslands.

In the early afternoon there had been another wild storm, rain and hail pelting the ground. The storm had cooled the air somewhat, making the ride more bearable. Now sunset approached, one star shining low on the horizon.

She wondered how it would feel to once again be free as the wind, to feel as one with the earth. She wanted to ride Kangee across these wide-open prairies.

On the bench in front of her a smudged-cheeked urchin peered over the backrest, his brown eyes wide and sorrowful. With a smile, Angela reached out and gave his worn gray hat a little tug. He blinked once then lowered his face until Angela could see only his eyes. She loved children fiercely, and wanted at least two of each sex.

Alexi's children ...

"Peppermint stick?" she asked, trying to wheedle a smile out of the little boy and find her way into his good graces.

The youngster's eyes grew wider and darker. He looked interested and a little bolder. Yet he didn't answer. His little pink tongue darted out to moisten his lips in anticipation. All afternoon she'd watched him and tried to entice him with the sweet. Finally he nodded.

Angela pulled the confection from her pocket and held it in front of him in silent invitation. She gave the red-and-white-striped stick a gentle wave, making sure it passed directly in front of the boy's nose. His face screwed up tightly.

The little boy's fingers twitched.

"Say yes and it's yours," she said, wondering how the little boy felt, embarking on such an adventure. Probably the same way she did, excited and frightened all at the same time. She wanted to be wherever they were going, but she didn't want the trip to end.

Alexi had promised to show her London and Paris. They would sail the Mediterranean and pass by Constantinople, then into the Black Sea.

The little boy's mouth moved, either in his eagerness for the stick of candy or with his effort to say the one word she wanted to hear. Four grubby fingers with four equally dirty, ragged fingernails showed themselves on the back of the chair. She could see his mouth now and his soot-stained neck. He looked as if he'd been rolling around in ashes.

He was mischief and little boy all tied into one adorable bundle.

Angela smiled encouragement and held the treat closer. He reached out for it, tentatively at first, his frayed jacket sleeve coming only halfway down his forearm, his fingers almost closing around the sweet.

Just before his fingers grasped the peppermint stick, Alexi appeared, striding with his head held high down the aisle of the train. He tipped his hat and the ladies all nodded at the handsome gentleman. All the while he acted as if he owned the car they rode in. He sat down next to her then turned his attention to the little boy.

"You'd best be wary of this lady. She could steal your heart just as she has stolen mine." His eyes were warm and alight with mischief while he watched Angela. His hand rested possessively across her back.

The boy's eyes closed and his shoulders shook. He ducked down beneath the seat.

"Shame on you," Angela said, brushing Alexi's hand aside. "You frightened him. It took me hours to coax him that far, and you ruined my progress in less time than it takes to snap one's fingers."

"Temptress..." he countered, the word warm and teasing, his eyes twinkling in silent mirth. "My little *houri*, all ready to ply your charms on unsuspecting males. I will have to be stem with you."

"I am not a temptress or a tease. I meant to give him the candy. What's an *houri?*'"

"You will give him his reward only after you exacted your price. And an *houri* is someone who would give me my heart's desire. Will you, my angel? My brave, incorrigible angel."

She ignored the barb and his pointed questions, so she could bend over the seat and find the little boy who had disappeared almost the very instant Alexi sat down beside her.

"Need any help?" His hand rested possessively just below the small of her back. She moved her hips, trying halfheartedly to dislodge his hand, while she successfully gave the boy the candy. Alexi moved his hand lower, squeezing gently.

"No." She gasped, sitting back indignantly after giving Alexi a warning scowl. His hand sneaked around her waist, then higher, until she felt the warmth of his fingers below the rounded curve of her breasts. He caressed the underside slowly. She jerked with the sensation.

"Alexi!" She panicked.

"I want to taste you right here," he whispered, his ringer touching her nipple through the fabric of her shirt. "You'll taste better than strawberries and cream."

The warmth of his words and his touch engulfed her, simmered deep inside. She wanted him to deliver on his promise. "Devil," she whispered, then poked his chest with her forefinger. "I shall scream."

He shrugged his shoulders indifferently. "Ah, but you love my attentions." Beneath her jacket, his thumb passed over her nipple, once, twice. "And, my darling, you wouldn't want me arrested, because then you'd have to do without me."

She did love his attentions--and everything else about him--and that was the crux of the matter. They'd arrived in Cheyenne only to find that his personal rail car had been demolished two weeks earlier by an engine that had raced out of control. The promises of sensual bliss he'd made to her as they rode during the day and slept chastely in each other's arms on the ground during the night could not be fulfilled.

Ever since the bad news, he'd been alternately in a foul mood then a teasing one.

One minute he couldn't keep his hands away from her, the next she'd find herself alone and Alexi off pacing somewhere.

"I love your attentions only when you're nice." She breathed deeply, willing sanity to return.

"I'm always nice." He moved closer, his body shielding her from any eyes that might be directed their way. He tossed his greatcoat around her shoulders, hiding her from any lingering eyes. "Let's go for a walk. I know just the place."

She looked into his eyes, and the heat and the desire she saw there swamped her. Moistening her lips, all she could do was nod. He pulled her to her feet and let her pass in front of him. His hands resting on her shoulder, he guided her to the end of the car and outside, where the wind whistled and the iron wheels roared as sparks flew heavenward. They were alone, isolated from the rows of sleeping passengers. Only the endless miles of empty prairie surrounded them.

In less than a second she was in his arms, his cloak around them shielding them from any prying eyes. His mouth crushed down on hers, his tongue prodding, searching for entrance. She allowed it, desired him more than life itself. All the while, his free hand languidly slid up her dress and across her bare thigh. His callused fingers were abrasive against her inner leg. The caresses was practiced and intimate. The contact promised so much.

"Alexi." She squirmed and tried to dislodge his hand. She had not dreamed that he would be so daring. He wouldn't be denied.

"Hush. There is no one here except the two of us."

"But Alexi..."

Nor, it seemed, would he allow her to run from him. "I want to pleasure you."

"Alexi…" She couldn't think. "This isn't a good idea," she finally got out.

As he taunted and teased her--and as the evening darkened--his caresses became bolder. He would have his way; she knew that. She'd given up trying to control him or command dominance. Yet she often spoke her mind. .He would scowl then he would soothe his anger at her outspokenness with passion.

"Ah, sweet concubine," he drawled softly next to her ear. "Allow a starving man a few comforts of home and let me see to your pleasure." His hand moved upon her stomach, making her shudder and want him more than anything she could imagine.

"Please... Alexi, there are people just inside that door. They could come out here just as we have done." Her heart pounded and she could barely breathe. "Everyone can see us."

"No one will step through that door. I will not allow it. It is dark and you are completely hidden from anyone's view, even mine." His eyes smoldered with sensual promise. "Close your eyes and pretend my mouth is here, where my hands are. I'll do that to you soon. I'll kiss you right here." His hand moved inches, delved intimately. "And here." His lips touched her ear; his breath, hot and erotic, feathered across her neck. Adept fingers flicked open buttons on her shirt then the ribbons of her camisole. Sensually, flesh against flesh, he stroked the valley between her breasts, teased and taunted in ever smaller circles without touching the hard, budding crests.

The moon shone in all its splendor through a scattering of clouds, and the stars twinkled brightly. The world was asleep.

"I can't think... Alexi!" She breathed his name, the words short and staccato. She couldn't tell him she wanted him to stop. She couldn't lie to him.

One of his hands teased the crest of one breast, the other caressed feminine secrets beneath her skirt. She could not deny him.

"Open your eyes," he said. "Touch me. Feel my passion for you." He set her hand against his arousal.

For a few long seconds she could not respond. Her head fell limp against his shoulder. Her eyes were closed and she instantly obeyed.

"Now think of my mouth here"--and he touched her--"and here. You're hot and crying for me." With masculine command and arrogance, he stroked her and made her writhe against him, her attempts to control her response to him feeble.

"You want me." Two fingers slid deeply inside her. "I'm one with you now. Not like I will be, I promise you that. Tell me how much you want me."

Her words were said softly and into his chest. "Alexi--you can't..." But she didn't sound at all sincere, and she felt the rumble of his laughter against her cheek.

"Tell me you want me," he repeated, his fingers sliding ever deeper. "Tell me, angel."

"I want you."

She didn't want him to ever stop loving her. Her fingers closed around his arms, nails biting into his flesh, her breaths coming in tiny little pants. Her face buried against him, she tried hard not to let her impassioned sounds echo in the roar of the night.

"Alexi!" Every muscle in her body pulsed and tensed and shuddered. She clung to Alexi, her lover and friend. He held her tight while she climaxed in his arms, the thunder of the train exploding in her head, the sparks of light and heat shattering her reverie.

She rested against him, her mind and nerves spent. To save her immortal soul, she could not move.

His strong hands soothed and comforted her now that he'd brought her to heaven. Still, all Angela could do was cling to him, hiding her face in the shadows he'd made for her. Pretending he hadn't just touched her intimately on a train where anyone might know what they did left her embarrassed but with no regrets.

Where this man was concerned she would never have reservations or regrets. She had desired him from the moment she had set eyes upon him, had known he was meant for her and her alone.

"I would give you more," he said, still stroking her back, "but someone might notice." He laughed softly, his voice intimate and suggestive.

She lifted her burning cheeks high enough to look through the dirty, smudged window into the train. No one paid them any heed. No one knew or guessed what they had just done. Life went on as it had a few minutes earlier. The train rumbled down the tracks, and the people inside slept uncomfortably on the hard seats.

She began to relax, her tension easing as sleep began to close in around her. Sheltered in his arms, she saw his hardness beneath the fabric of his trousers. She wanted to see her dark, mysterious warlord naked again. She wanted to see his arousal and touch and stroke him as he did her. She wanted to feel him deep inside her.

"We'll go inside now." He swept her into his arms and carried her back to their bench. Settling her on his lap, he let her rest her head against his chest.

"I love you," she said so softly that he barely heard her, but he did and he smiled, a possessive male smile.

He held her tightly and he pretended they slept comfortably, side by side, in his personal car. His angel was like no woman he'd ever met. Strong and sure of herself, she gave him her loyalty, and he admired her bravery and her innate goodness. Now, besides pillows and a soft bed, he had other plans for Angela and their first union. He intended to make everything perfect for her.

Patience had always been his strong suit, and although he knew Angela was ready and eager for him, he would make her wait. Anticipation would make the loving sweeter and even more enduring.

They were headed to New York, and what better place was there to treat Angela to all the luxury he could afford? In Cheyenne he'd wired ahead to the Waldorf Hotel and reserved a suite of rooms for their short stay. By his calculations they could waste two days in the luxurious rooms. He would take her to a play or an opera. He'd wine and dine her in the best restaurants. He meant to spend hours making love to her, showing her all the ways he knew of to give and receive pleasure.

~ * ~

Sam Chamberlain wiped the back of his hand across his sweaty brow then pushed hard on the door in front of him. His shirt stuck to his clammy skin, and a line of perspiration beaded on his upper lip. Unseasonably warm weather beat down on the sidewalks and streets of the city. A dry, hot wind whirled between the buildings even while thunderclouds gathered on the horizon.

Stepping from the telegraph office, he strode with his hands clenched at his sides through the streets of Kansas City, a man determined to defend his daughter's honor. After he caught Devil Blackmoor, he had every intention of staking him out on the hot desert sand, and asking questions later. He had visions of stripping Devil's flesh from his body slowly, one narrow piece at a time.

Taking a shortcut to the train station, he turned, moving quickly through an alley that ran between a quiet row of houses. All he could hear were his own footsteps and the whistling wind. The uncanny silence warned him of danger, but not soon enough.

He felt the blade of a knife against his throat, a powerful arm across his chest. Survival instincts kicked in and he tensed, waiting for the right moment to fight back.

"What do you want with the prince?" the man holding the knife at his throat asked while the arm around Sam's neck tightened.

Sam drew in a shallow breath, thinking hard. He tried to keep his voice calm and his wits about him. It wasn't easy. "I don't know who you're talking about. I don't know any princes. Let me go and you can explain yourself."

"It is you who needs to explain. Why are you following the prince?" The man's voice was harsher now and obviously impatient.

This man holding him hostage was danger personified. Sam felt the hardness of him, the breadth of him, and knew his attacker could deliver whatever he promised. Death, it seemed. "I've never met a prince."

"Liar." The word came out in a raspy whisper. "I've no use for liars. You will tell me the truth or you will not live to regret it."

Sam felt a drop of blood slide down his throat, then another. The burly arm around his chest tightened until he could gasp only a tiny drop of air. He found himself slowly drawn into the shadows of the alley he'd carelessly walked down. His life flashed before him.

"You've got the wrong man." He choked out one painful word at a time. Sam tried to reason with the giant. "I'm willing to cooperate."

"I think not. I heard you asking questions in the saloon a few minutes ago; then I followed you. Tell me what you want with him and I'll let you go."

"Now who's lying?" Sam asked. "You're not about to let me go."

"You have one second. Talk."

"All right." Sam agreed rather than waste time, still unsure who this prince was--but he did know who he'd been asking questions about.

The man's arm tightened around Sam's chest. He found it harder to breathe, and speech wasn't any easier. He had the most uncomfortable thought that the man wanted to know about Devil Blackmoor. The man couldn't be a prince. Or could he?

"The man I'm looking for kidnapped my daughter. I have every intention of finding him and bringing him back for trial." Sam didn't dare tell this man that he meant to stake Devil out and let the buzzards see to his end.

"Now who's lying?"

When the man's arm tightened once more, Sam grunted.

"The prince wouldn't do that. He has no need to abduct a man's daughter. Women follow him like bees to honey. Some are after his money and title. Others want his body. He is, some would say, an insatiable man, but he would never kidnap a woman. Your lie is laughable." The man behind Sam loosened his hold. "He is traveling with a woman, his newest mistress. I'd advise you to look to the woman you call daughter for answers, not to the prince."

"My daughter is a virgin, and I don't like what you're implying." Sam's jaw tightened and he spit the furious words at the man.

The man laughed and let go of Sam, his knife still ready. "I imply nothing. I state only the truth. According to the messages I've received from the prince, the woman is planning on making the trip home to Russia with him. There is nothing you can do to stop the prince from doing whatever he pleases."

"And I suppose you make sure he gets whatever he pleases." Sam barely controlled his fury. Facing his adversary, Sam knew he'd encounter death if that was what this man intended. At least two hundred fifty pounds of pure muscle stared him down.

"That is part of my job," the man agreed. "I also protect the prince with my life."

"Then you're going to have to make sure I stay alive. If the prince"--and Sam let the word *prince* hang on the air in a derogatory manner--"wants to keep my daughter happy, that is, you'd best see that I'm still breathing when I meet this paragon."

The man smiled broadly. "I've no intention of killing you." On his pants leg, he wiped Sam's blood off his knife and held out his hand. "It is the American custom for friends to shake hands in greeting. My name is Misha. I am cousin to the prince, and his protector and confidant."

One eyebrow quirked, "Friends? That is debatable. You and I are at cross purposes," Sam said, his tone rife with sarcasm now that the knife wasn't slicing his neck open. He extended his own hand. "Sam Chamberlain."

"Well, Sam Chamberlain, we have much in common. I want to keep the prince happy and you want to protect your daughter. I believe that at the moment your daughter is keeping my prince very happy indeed."

As if Misha noticed the immediate scowl those words brought forth, he tempered his next words.

"Alexi will not hurt her. It is not his way. He will make love to her, protect and cherish her as long as she is a willing partner, and then he will let her go, making sure she will want for nothing the rest of her life. You have naught to fear from Alexi."

"He will marry her," Sam gritted out between clenched teeth. He was determined to set Misha straight. "He will marry her or he will die refusing me. I care not which happens. She will never willingly be his mistress."

"He cannot wed her. He is duty-bound to bring an heir into the world, and he could never marry a commoner. His grandmother already has his mate picked out for him."

"There is nothing common about my daughter. His grandmother can unpick his mate." Sam's voice resonated deep in his chest, his fury growing with each arrogant statement out of Misha's mouth.

Misha looked down at Sam. There was a condescending air about the giant, yet there was sorrow in his eyes. "I understand how you must feel, but it is already too late. Come," he said. "We've a train to New York to catch. I'd advise you to go home, but I doubt you'd listen to me. Shall we speak more of this while we ride? Perhaps I can make you realize what is at stake here."

"Perhaps I can enlighten you." Sam's voice took on a decided chill. "He will marry Angela."

With that Misha laughed again. It was a slow, warm chuckle coming from deep in his chest. Despite the fury and the anger Sam held in check until he caught up with Devil, he liked this man, Misha.

"With a father as determined as you are, perhaps he will, although I see little hope for a marriage between the two of them." Misha looked sad, his indrawn breath almost a hiss. "A great love perhaps, but never marriage."

~ * ~

"Misha writes us that Alexi is traveling with a woman, a commoner. Can you imagine that?" Feodora asked, her tone filled with spite and malice.

"What Alexi does is none of your business," Natasha, Alexi's grandmother, countered.

"It will be." Feodora pouted, her lips pursed and her eyebrows drawn into an ugly scowl. "When he becomes my husband."

White lilies adorned the table, and a soft spring breeze spread the curtains wide. Outside, the sky was a brilliant blue, and a few white clouds peppered the horizon.

Natasha Popov bent her head and played the keys of the grand piano fiercely, evoking all the dizzying sensation she held within. Her fingers wildly roamed the keyboard, back and forth, the melody intense and violent. She'd been playing the piano for hours now, her fury at her grandson and his newest paramour almost spent.

"That will never happen." Natasha looked up from the piano long enough to say the few words that needed to be said. "You should pack your bags and be gone from here."

"You'd like that, wouldn't you?" Feodora' tone was condescending. "Now I'm not good enough for your grandson. Is that it?"

Natasha's anger at Feodora would never vanish, and she sought a way to drive the young woman from the Popov home. "Very much," Natasha said. "Any woman who whores is not fit to be the wife of Alexi. He would never condone it."

No, she could never forgive the lady reclining on the couch, eating sweets. Feodora was a beautiful woman, and her family was well respected. But she was no gift from God, as her name implied. Feodora was a cold, calculating bitch with the morals of a practiced courtesan.

Natasha regretted with all her heart ever telling Feodora's father that Alexi might marry the chit. But she had. And now she must find some way to undo the damage she'd inadvertently created.

She needed to bend all her energy into seeing that the marriage would not take place. Short of an execution she could not think of one ploy.

Two mornings ago, Natasha had gone into the stables and found Feodora naked and in the arms of Ivan, the riding master. Three weeks ago she'd heard rumors of a longtime relationship between Feodora and some count living somewhere along the Danube. Feodora would not make a biddable wife for Alexi, and Natasha could not bear the thought of Feodora being mother to Alexi's children.

"He dare not bring her here," Feodora continued. "He'll rue the day he flaunts a mistress under my nose."

"You are not wed yet, nor are the two of you betrothed in his eyes," Natasha said, trying to calm her voice. "You are putting the cart before the horse, as they say, making demands on his actions and his life. Alexi is not a man to be ruled by a woman."

Natasha suddenly stopped playing, her fingers resting lightly on the piano keys. Critically, she studied the woman she'd once thought the perfect mate for her grandson. Old ladies should not try to play matchmaker; they inevitably fail, she told herself. Alexi was capable of finding a mate. Her intentions had been good. Selfishly, she'd meant only to hurry the process along.

"Have you changed your mind, then, about the marriage?" Feodora rose from the couch and minced toward the piano. "I would wager you have not. You need the fortune I would bring with me to renovate this crumbling heap you call an estate."

Feodora leaned over the keyboards, her plush, ripe breasts pushing against the low cut of her bodice. Natasha wondered what she'd ever seen in the spoiled young woman standing before her.

"I need nothing you have. The choice is my grandson's to make," Natasha said.' 'Be careful what you say. This crumbling estate is the home I love."

"And you will tell him all that you've heard about me. The rumors are all lies." Feodora's lips pursed slightly, a practiced gesture, one she used to bring a man to heel.

"No." Natasha smiled serenely, knowing Alexi would see through Feodora's seductive ploys. "He will not need me to tell him anything. I would never presume to spread gossip. The truth of your character will be seen by him soon enough. A whore cannot hide behind her money or an innocent game. He has enough experience with women and whores. He'll know the truth without help from me."

Feodora bristled, her anger turning her gloriously beautiful face into a hideous creation. "Witch!" she exploded.

Natasha relaxed and her fingers drifted into a slow waltz, the music calming her and offering her respite from the error of her own actions. *I will never play matchmaker again,* she vowed silently.

Feodora left the room. Natasha was sure the lady would go to one of her lovers for soothing, perhaps to Ivan, whose loyalty to Alexi was strong. It was all right with her. Perhaps by the time Alexi returned, Feodora would be huge with child, a bastard child.

She had personally thanked Ivan for seducing Feodora. He'd grinned and told her it was his pleasure. Karim, Alexi's father, had sent him with the express purpose of protecting Alexi and discovering the truth about Feodora. Natasha understood why Ivan had seduced Feodora. He'd seen beneath her character to her darker side, and he'd made sure the prince would never marry her by spoiling her himself. But then Ivan had confirmed the rumors to her personally.

As suspected, Feodora had been no innocent maiden when she'd bedded Ivan in the hayloft. Feo knew well what she was about.

Natasha said a silent prayer that Alexi was out of the country and could not be accused of fathering a child on Feodora. Yes, perhaps this would all work out for the best.

Feeling more lighthearted by the minute, she began to play a favorite of hers, "Oh, Dem Golden Slippers," then changing the tune quickly to "Little Brown Jug."

Chapter Seven

Feodora let the back door slam shut behind her, rage building inside her. She would have it all, Alexi and his money. She'd taunted the old lady about the condition of her estate, but the truth of the matter was, she had nothing: no money, no estate, no name and no future. Her father had been desperate to be rid of her. No nobleman would have her for a wife simply because they'd all had her as a lover.

"Bah! Men!" They were good for only one thing.

She liked the stable master better than any of the aristocratic dandies she'd bedded. He was a real man. If she'd had money, she would have never agreed to her father's schemes. Well, she still intended to have it all: the title of princess and the famous lover who'd learned how to give pleasure in a Turkish harem. If she could accomplish the feat, she meant to have both Ivan and Alexi.

"Ivan," she called out, her voice a sultry purr. When he didn't answer, she bristled. "Where the hell are you?"

A tall, broad-shouldered man appeared from the back of the stables. His hair was blue-black, his eyes a dark, smoldering brown. At the moment his shirt, unbuttoned, hung loosely from his shoulders, his muscles rippling, sweat sliding down his chest. She wanted to touch him so badly she ached.

His smile widened when he saw her. He was handsome, and he knew how to give a lady her pleasure. She was damp with need just looking at the man, her nipples taut, hard buds beneath her blouse.

He stepped closer and touched her cheek. "Little darling." He smelled of straw, horse manure and sweat, but Feodora didn't care. She ran her hands up his chest, pushing the fabric aside. Her fingers slipped beneath the material, her nails raking over his flat male nipples. With her sharp little teeth, she nipped and teased his flesh.

"Eager, aren't we?" he asked, a slow grin spreading across his face, one callused hand running up and down her back. "But you see, my darling, I've got work to do, and I don't have time for a dalliance in the hay. Perhaps you should come back another time."

"This won't take long," she said, her finger shoving the shirt from his shoulders. Stroking his back and his buttocks, she squeezed and rubbed and thought, *How could I have waited so long for this man, my lover?*

He tugged at her loose-fitting bodice until he'd uncovered her breasts and her arms were pinned to her sides by the constraining fabric. "How very clever of you, Feo. No underclothes?" His mouth closed eagerly over one breast, his hand over the other. The suction came hard and insistent. She arched back and groaned, satisfaction throbbing within.

"Ivan..." She sighed his name in a throaty whisper. "Do it to me. Please, Ivan. Take me here. Right now."

"Shameless hussy." His tone was endearing.

"You love it."

His hands were beneath her skirts, molding to her buttocks, caressing her from behind, squeezing, loving her as no other man had.

"Little Feodora, you must learn patience. A good tumble in the hay takes time." He laughed. His teeth clamped down on her nipple, his tongue teasing her, his fingers taunting her carnal appetites, bringing her so close and then backing off until she was a raging, seething bundle of sexual tension and need.

"Ivan!"

"I like my name on your lips," he told her, his voice calm. "I want to hear you scream it with pleasure."

She writhed in his hands, thrusting her belly against his arousal, feeling the length and heat of him through the fabric of their clothes, and he laughed again.

"Wrap your legs around me and I'll show you what you've been missing."

Intoxicated with carnal need, she instantly obeyed. He walked with her until her back was against the stable wall. A stallion reared his head back and kicked his stall door. Ivan reared his own head back, the air charged with sexual energy.

"Easy, fella, I'll find a mate for you as soon as I'm finished with my little mare." In answer the stallion bucked, kicking with his hind legs against the wall once more.

Ivan pulled at her bodice, the fabric falling away in shreds. Her breasts swayed free, and he licked and kissed her until she cried out again. "Ivan!"

"That's it; show me how much you want me."

She unlaced his pants and he sprang free. In one swift move he sheathed himself deep inside her, touching her womb. But he didn't move. She climaxed around him. "Ivan..."

When she stopped, he began to move inside, starting over from the beginning, tonguing her breasts, nipping and licking the crests again and again.

Feodora moaned his name once more, and in a matter of seconds she was moving and thrusting herself against him. All she could think about was Alexi and how much she hated him. More than anything she wanted Alexi to see her in another man's arms--in Ivan's arms. She wanted to punish Alexi for daring to bring a mistress to what was soon to be her home.

She came then with a shuddering cry.

Negligently, he withdrew from her and fastened his pants, leaving her disheveled and on the ground in the stables.

"Come back tonight," he said, his voice holding no trace of emotion. And he walked away from her. All she could see of him was his broad, powerful back and swaggering hips. Still she stared after him, hating him and his arrogance almost as much as she hated Alexi.

Cursing her need for Ivan, Feodora pulled her tattered bodice together, plucked a few pieces of straw from her wild hair, and fled to the house, hoping that no one would see her. Her luck failed her.

At the upstairs window, Natasha watched and smiled a knowing smile.

Feodora shuddered, a feeling of doom sweeping through her.

~ * ~

"What will be your first pleasure, sweet flower?" Alexi whispered, his lips almost touching Angela's as their private car came to a stop beneath the newly built Waldorf Hotel. "Food, a bath or me? Personally, I'm starving, and it's not for food. I wanted you yesterday, the day before and the day before that. I've been a patient man. Now the waiting is over."

Alexi's hand was on her arm as he guided her down the steps of the train and into the lavish hotel. He'd anticipated this night for what seemed to him a lifetime. Having his adorable Angela in his arms and in his bed beneath him could not come soon enough.

Angela smiled broadly at him, giving him a saucy wink in the process. "A bath, food then you," she told him.

Yet beneath all the bravado, he felt her shyness and wondered at it. It was a game not to his liking. She had no need to play the coy maiden with him. He'd already told her how he felt, told her that her other affairs meant nothing to him. They were in her past, not her future. They stepped into the elevator.

"Hellion," he said tenderly, knowing he'd put up with any games she wanted to play with him. "I might not give you a choice. If you don't stop tempting me, toying with my fragile masculine emotions, I will ravish you right here in the lift for all who happen by to see."

"You wouldn't dare," she said softly, with wide-eyed innocence.

But she should know he'd dare anything. Heat rose to color her cheeks. He hoped she was remembering other times when he did dare everything.

"Is that a challenge?" He backed her against the wall, his hands braced on either side of her head, leaving no room for escape. His hips pressed against her, and he hoped she could feel his growing hardness.

She wanted to be as brazen as Alexi.

"Yes..." She exhaled the word, daring him.

The lift made a grinding noise and began to move. She swallowed hard, her hands coming to rest on his shoulders. Her heart in her throat and her pride in shambles, she wanted desperately to tell him the truth, to tell him she was a virgin, had never slept with a man or felt a man deep within her. Yet she couldn't summon the courage.

Suddenly his expression turned tender, his eyes clouding with emotion. "Are you afraid?" he asked in a whisper. "Is that why you tremble beneath my touch and at my words?" His thumb lightly caressed her thrumming pulse. "You have nothing to fear from me. I would never hurt you."

"Yes," she said, burying her face and her humiliation in the folds of his shirt. "I don't want to be afraid. You've given me no reason to fear you." She sounded like a petulant child, and she hated herself for her innocence and all the self-doubts that went with it. It was not knowing that left her breathless, her heart pounding.

He was a man of the world, a man who'd had more than one lover. He would expect a great deal from her, skills she didn't possess. Yet he thought she was well versed in the sins of the flesh. Alexi did not want a virgin in his bed. He'd made that abundantly clear.

His arms came around her, cherishing her, and in the process he seemed to understand her anxiety and apprehension. "Lean on me, angel." She did. "Nothing bad will happen to you in my arms. I will protect you with my life. I will pleasure you in ways you've never dreamed of before, and I will see to your happiness. Inside and out, you're the most beautiful woman I've ever met."

The lift settled on the top floor, the gates opening for them with a grinding squeal. He swept her into his arms and carried her to their room.

"I told you I meant to ravish you." He kissed her nose, then her eyelids. "But I didn't want you take me seriously. I want to make love to you slowly, very slowly, and have that love returned."

"Please, Alexi. A bath first and then..." She allowed the sentence to end. "Give me some time and then I promise you..." Once again she let the sentence hang unfinished. She didn't know what to promise.

Now that the moment was at hand she was terrified. During the trip his sexual play had been unexpected at times and very tender at other moments, but she'd always known it would end at precisely the same place. Tonight he would show her everything about love. In his eyes, she was an experienced lady of the evening. He'd openly admitted that he preferred women who enjoyed the pleasure of their bodies and women who knew how to please a man.

He would expect her to know what she was about.

He let her slide down the length of him and, holding her at arm's length, he watched her with questioning, curious eyes. "What is this? A bashful lady? I thought you wanted me as much as I do you."

She nodded and her lips began to tremble. She held her bottom lip still with her upper teeth and swallowed painfully. "I do want you, Alexi. I want you so much it frightens me."

His smile broadened, his eyes twinkling. "I'll have to do something about all this shyness," he said, and feathered a leisurely kiss across her lips. His fingers wove through the strands of her hair, slowly tipping her head back. He deepened the kiss, his tongue sweeping in and out, a parody of what he meant to do later, Angela thought distractedly, when they were in bed.

He pulled away and watched her, his eyes bright with longing and promise.

A bold knock at the door startled her.

Alexi left her side to open it. Bellhops swept through the room. Some brought food and wine; others carried bouquets of flowers and candles. The men waited patiently after arranging the items in the room. Alexi handed them coins.

Angela inhaled several long, deep breaths.

"Now," Alexi said, "dinner will arrive shortly. I took the liberty of ordering last night, when I confirmed the reservations. The bath is this way." He ushered her into a small room with numerous facilities. "Hot and cold running water." He turned gold-handled devices, and steaming water ran into a huge porcelain tub.

She'd never seen anything so elegant or so inviting. She let the water run over her hand. "It's delightful."

His grin was broad. "So are you."

"Alexi..."

"I also ordered lotions and soap for you. I hope you like them." He waved the perfumed bottle in front of her nose. "Jasmine, my personal favorite." He kissed her gently and then he was gone.

For a few long seconds she stared at the closed door, unsure of her tremulous feelings and so very hesitant. What she was about to do would change her life forever, and it seemed too permanent. She could not regain what she was about to lose--her innocence.

They would leave the country soon. The thought loomed heavy on her mind. She'd wanted adventure, had prayed for it, but now that it was so close, she had second thoughts.

She might never see her father and mother again, or her friends. She'd miss them. But not half as much as she'd miss Alexi if she let him go without her. She'd regret that for the rest of her life.

"I love Alexi," she whispered, her hands clasped together in prayer. "I will go with him wherever he wants. It is a small price to pay for love. There is nothing to be afraid of."

She sat down on the rim of the tub and watched the water cascade into the white porcelain fixture. A heavy sigh followed, and then, gathering her courage, she stood, ready to face the new world she was about to encounter. She loved the endearing names he called her--little *houri*, his concubine--and she wondered at them, had never heard them before. In the last letter she sent to her father she had told him about the endearments to convince him of Alexi's love for her.

Angela disrobed quickly then sank into the hot, fragrant water, blessing Alexi and his thoughtfulness. On a table nearby someone had set a decanter of wine and a crystal goblet. She poured herself a glass and sipped hesitantly, the heady warmth of the wine filling her and relaxing her.

She finished the glass then poured another.

Luxuriating in the feel of the water and the cleanliness she had not enjoyed for weeks, she stayed in the bath until her fingers crinkled and her skin felt waterlogged. The water turned chilly, but instead of adding more, she climbed out. .

Behind the dressing screen Alexi had left a filmy peach nightdress and a wrapper. After dressing in the sheer confection, she blushed when she looked at herself in a mirror. Her damp hair hung loose around her shoulders. Where she'd not completely dried herself, the material clung to her breasts and nipples, her body clearly delineated for Alexi to see.

Brazen came to mind, and on the wings of that thought came another. She didn't doubt for one moment he might have planned this, her seduction. But he didn't know the truth about her.

He should know. She wanted him to know.

Alexi did want her in his bed, and to some extent in his life. But would he still have those same feelings for her after they made love and he discovered for himself just how inexperienced she was? Would he feel the same when he understood that she had not told him the truth?

Sitting in front of the vanity, lost in thought, she combed her damp hair and wrapped the length into a coil around her head. She pinched her cheeks to make them glow.

She looked carefully at the image she presented. Alexi liked her hair down. She quickly pulled the pins free and let it tumble in wanton curls around her shoulders.

"Angela?"

The door creaked open, and Alexi stood there bold and absolutely gorgeous. His black hair was disheveled, his shirt unbuttoned and pulled from his pants. His chest was powerful, his hands large and tender. "I believe it's my turn to bathe. Go on; you can dry your hair in front of the fire. I'll be out in a few minutes."

She didn't know what to say. Her heart lodged in her throat and her pulse danced a jig. "Did I take too long?"

"Yes," he said, his gaze upon her, his eyes roaming the length of her. "Far too long." He smiled, his eyes shining with masculine approval and something else--desire.

On trembling legs she rose and walked toward the door. He didn't move, just kept watching her.

"Alexi?" she asked. She touched his shoulder, her fingers trembling.

"A forfeit before you pass," he said, his voice mysteriously gruff. One of his fingers lifted her face, his mouth moving closer to her lips. She watched, mesmerized by his eyes, frozen with anticipation.

"What is it you want?" she asked.

"A kiss to tide me over until you offer me more, until you show me all you have to give. Until I can see your eyes when I fill you." His lips met hers, his tongue tracing the seam, demanding entrance. She responded, her tongue meeting his, playing and enticing him to give more. He did. He pulled her into his arms, his fingers sweeping through her hair; he deepened the kiss then suddenly there was space between them. He stared into her eyes touching her cheek with the back of his hand, a tender smile on his face.

"Allah, give me strength."

"I'll wait in the other room," she said, watching him, wondering why he needed strength.

His muscles tautly rigid, he set her aside, a dark, foreboding shadow in his expression. "Temptress," he whispered. "Sweet temptress." He stepped back and let her pass. She turned then, watching him shut the door behind her, and wishing she had the nerve to go to him while he bathed.

She did not. She was not the wanton angel he thought she was.

She inhaled deeply, despair in her heart, fear burrowing into the deepest part of her. "What will happen when you find out I'm a virgin? Will you set me aside?" she asked softly. "Will you call me a liar and abandon me here in New York, where I know no one? You wanted someone experienced, a lover and a wife who could give you hours of pleasure. I cannot do what you expect. I can only follow your lead."

~ * ~

In the bathing room, Alexi hummed a bawdy tune he'd learned in his mother country. Allah, but his angel was a beauty. She was sensitive and caring, and if he had his way, he'd never let her out of his bed. His mind spun with all the delightful interludes they would have soon.

Too bad she wasn't a virgin, he thought. The idea of her as his wife felt good, but then he thought again. As a mistress she would be at his beck and call. He would find a beautiful home for her near his own estate, and he'd make sure she had everything she wanted --except a horse and carriage, he amended. He would never give her the means to leave him. Angela was his --his alone --and she would be his forever. The thought of losing her left a hollow pit in his heart, one he knew could never be filled.

He ducked under the water, coming up sputtering and still singing. Soap ran into his eyes but he didn't care: He finished washing, dried himself off and dressed himself in black pants and a silk smoking jacket.

When he stepped into the room, the table was set with silver and delicate bone china. Two slim candles flickered and the lights had been dimmed. It was romantic, just the look he'd sought. And outside the balcony doors a full moon stood clearly in the sky. It would be a sultry night of love and romance, a night of new beginnings.

Pleased now that he'd waited for comfortable surroundings, he watched his angel for several peaceful minutes.

Angela sat by the fire, her long hair catching the light from the flickering fire, shadows dancing across the lush curves of her body. Allah, but she was beautiful, a divine treat sent from heaven meant just for him.

"Angela," he said his voice a throaty whisper in the dimly lit room. She turned, her smile catching him solidly in the gut and throwing him off balance. "A bath--now food. Then you can fill a starving man's heart."

She held out her hand to him, her fingers trembling. He didn't understand her fear. He wanted to change that fear to desire. A woman practiced in the art of loving should not be afraid.

"Devil..." she said.

"Angel..." he answered her. "Why so afraid?" Suddenly the only reason he could come up with for her fear surfaced. "Have you been misused? I'll kill the bastard."

Her cold, shaking fingers rested in his. When she looked at him, her eyes were wide and filled with moisture. A lone tear slipped from a vividly blue eye and ran down her cheek. He brushed it away.

"No," she said. "No, I haven't."

He breathed a sigh of relief, vacillating now in his emotions. "If not abuse, then why the fear? Have I done something? Anything to put the fear of God in you?"

"No." Her smile and voice were hesitant.

He meant to reassure and seduce. Slowly he brought her hands to his lips. Before kissing her, he turned her hand over and touched her palm lightly with his lips, his fingers tracing circles on the underside of her wrist. He led her to the table and made sure she was seated before going to his own chair.

He poured her more wine and watched her eyes sparkle with long-pent-up desire. Good, she wanted him as much as he wanted her. She toyed with the food on her plate, and he knew eating first had been a foolish plan.

"Relax," he said, the word soft and meant to soothe. "It's not like this is your first time," he said, and knew immediately he'd wounded her pride.

Alexi watched her slowly stiffen, her back, her arms, even her fingers around the stem of her glass, and he watched her smile fade into a staggering sadness. *Why?*

She played with the napkin on her lap, her lashes lowered. He decided the gesture was part of the game she'd played from the very beginning. Tonight he could tolerate games, but after that he wanted nothing but honesty between them.

"Alexi." She paused, her small pink tongue moistening her lips.

Little tease, he thought, but he liked her flirtatious manner and the audacious things she sometimes did. She needed adventure and excitement in her life. He meant to give that to her and more.

"What?" He leaned toward her, wanting to smell the jasmine--and the lady, wanting to learn everything about this woman he claimed as his own.

"The truth is always the best course?" she asked, her fingertips digging into the crystal.

His smile lifted at one corner. "Most of the time," he said. "You want to tell me something you've been hiding these many weeks?"

"Yes." Her voice was pencil thin, stretched to its limit.

Alarm rang in his ears. The worst scenarios he could imagine flashed through his mind at an alarming speed. He knew she'd changed her mind, and she meant to tell him she wouldn't go with him. Traveling across the ocean to lands unknown had been too much to expect. She might give him this night, but she would not give him the rest of her life. He searched frantically for the words that would convince her otherwise, but came up empty. Like dust in the wind, his dreams vanished.

She rose then and moved slowly toward the fire.

He watched her back and the provocative sway of her hips, his nerves suddenly drawn taut.

Through the material of her gown, he could see the shadow of her legs, the indentation that was her waist. He wanted her, yet he knew something was holding her back, keeping her from giving all of herself to him. Before he made love to her, he had to know what that something was.

After long minutes, when all he could hear was the hiss and pop of the fire, she finally said, "I'm not what you think l am. I'm not--"

Relief swept through him. "None of us are completely what another person believes them to be. It doesn't matter to me. I want you just the way you are. You are beautiful, Angela--from the inside out." He stopped, realizing he didn't know her last name, something he should have insisted on knowing, yet she'd seemed so unwilling to give it.

"That's the trouble," she said without turning around. But he could see the noticeable slump of her shoulders, the dejected curve of her spine. She seemed saddened, filled with remorse, and he couldn't fathom what his lovely angel could find so hard to tell him.

"I don't see a problem," he said. He moved behind her, his hands resting now upon her shoulders. He pulled her toward him, wanting to feel the length of her against him. "I feel like a bridegroom on his wedding night. I didn't expect that. I've waited so long to have you, the anticipation has had my nerves dangling on the edge of a cliff. Is that what's bothering you? Are you feeling as if this is your wedding night?"

"I do feel like a bride." She turned into his arms. "You make me feel cherished and loved."

"That is the way you should feel. Come now; let's not put this off any longer. The feather bed and the pillows await us."

She held back. "Alexi... I'm a virgin," she blurted out.

"Angel?" His heart stopped. He inhaled sharply. "Angel?"

"I've never done this before, never made love with any man. That's why"--her lashes lowered for a moment before she looked at him, courage in her eyes--"that's why I'm afraid. I'm terrified I won't please you."

His hands fell away from her. Shock waves swept through him. *A virgin.* Dreams formed in his head and began to seriously take root. Where he'd tossed the thought aside, thinking her a lady of the evening, now he could consider her worthy of his name. His grandmother might object at first, but in the end his arguments would prevail.

"The whorehouse?" he asked.

"I was there for Emma," she said. "No one knew. Not even my--" She stopped herself.

He suddenly didn't like himself very well, or the direction of his thoughts. He'd slept with countless women, and that didn't make him less of a person. He hadn't thought less of her when he believed she'd sold herself to a man or two.

Why would he consider her different now when he knew he was to be her first? Simply put, he could never have taken Angela as his wife, because he was a prince. His family expected him to marry a woman of his own station in life. A commoner would not do. A commoner could only serve him as a mistress.

Years of inbred prejudices surfaced. Anger at himself grew and he fought to push the fury aside. For so many weeks he'd thought of little else but this night, a night of love he meant to share with the most desirable woman he'd ever met. Now anger at his motives threatened to ruin all he'd waited so long for.

Wanting to forget the direction of his thoughts, he pulled her to him, could feel the deep seated fears of a maiden's heart and the trembling of her limbs. His heart soared. "I will do my best not to hurt you." He kissed the top of her head, reveling in her sweet innocence. Against him he felt her breathing ease as she relaxed.

"I know." Her hands upon his chest, she pushed herself away from him long enough to look into his eyes. She looked at him with complete trust. "You of all people, I know, would never willingly hurt me."

"Are you sure you want this? By giving yourself to me, you bestow a great honor upon me. It is something I can never return," he told her with great sincerity.

"I am sure," she said, her voice virtuous.

"I am blessed." With that said he swept her into his arms and carried her into the bedchamber, where he reverently placed her upon his bed. His bed was the only bed she would ever know, he vowed. He turned from her and shrugged out of his dressing gown.

Alexi lay down beside her, doing nothing more than stroking her with his gaze. "You are beautiful," he said.

She touched his cheek, and he shuddered at the potent heat searing him. Angela could do this to him, humble him with just a look and a shy caress.

His fingertips whispered against the long white column of her throat, stopping at her pulse. He delighted in the swift, sure beat of her heart, and the shallow, rapid breaths that revealed her need for him.

Only him--no other man.

"I will make this the most wondrous night of your life," he said, and lowered his head to caress her with his lips. He fluttered kisses wherever his hands had been, down her neck and across the tops of her breasts, her response to his touch wild and primitive.

Innocent in the extreme.

She touched his shoulders and pulled him closer until he felt her breasts touch his chest. Her fingertips were a light caress against his nakedness, her softness against his hard planes and angles a boon he would never refuse. "I don't know what to do," she said. "Teach me."

"Relax, sweet angel, enjoy. We will have many nights together..."

He touched his lips to hers and she arched against him. "Easy," he said softly, "just a little longer." His whisper was gentle across her cheeks. He untied her wrapper and opened the material so he could see through the sheer fabric of the gown she wore. Soft pink nipples beckoned him, and like a hungry man waiting to feast, he dipped his head and through the material tasted what he'd waited so long for.

"Alexi."

His name upon her lips encouraged his attentions.

She purred and curved into his mouth, begging for more. He delighted that she was filled with passion and need.

With Angela as his wife, he could be content forever. On the whisper of that thought came another: with this woman as his wife he would have no need of a mistress or a harem of inviting exotic ladies. This lady of his could and would fulfill all his dreams forever.

Angela was feminine mystery and demure strength. Despite her common roots she would make him a strong wife and bear him healthy children. He would need her support in the times to come. Taking over a dynasty ruled by greedy, avaricious men and changing the rules the people on his estate had lived with for centuries would not be easy.

He pulled on the delicate ribbons of the gown she wore and they came free, baring Angela completely to his tortured gaze. She ran her fingers through his hair and pulled his mouth to hers.

"Alexi." She sighed his name again, her breath sweet, her lips pliant and soft beneath his own. "I want to please you."

"Angela," he replied, "my angel. You please me more than life itself."

Her hands ran the length of his back. Potent shudders racked his body.

"I want to see you," she said, her voice purring the words. While she spoke her hands wandered to his hips and the fastenings of his pants.

He left the bed to remove his clothes. She watched him, wide-eyed and fascinated. She moistened her lips, a gesture that almost brought him to his knees. He stepped toward her again, his eyes absorbing her form, the perfectly rounded globes of her breasts, the tiny waist flaring provocatively to feminine hips.

"Sit up," he said. She complied, and in one deft move he swept the gown over her head and let it fall to the floor.

He loved her slowly, sipping and tasting each delicate, sensual part of her. Then his fingers closed around her breast, his thumb against her nipple, and she cried out.

Alexi smiled down upon her, pleased with the response, and continued the slow seduction, praying he would not hurt her. She writhed with his increasingly bold caresses and intimate kisses. A whiplash of fire darted through him, burning him all the places that touched her.

Somewhere he lost control. When he kissed Angela, her mouth flooded his body with warmth; her touch upon the naked flesh of his back seared through him straight to his sex, and then even deeper within, to reach his soul.

She was his mate for life. He would have no other.

She gasped for air, digging her nails into his back as his lips left hers to suckle her nipple where his thumb had so recently teased.

"Please," she said. "Alexi, please do something."

He smiled, a self-satisfied feeling sweeping through him at her words and the trembling need in her voice. His hand moved slowly along her side, curving around her hip, between the two of them then between her legs. The pressure of his fingers moved intimately between them, down through the soft curls that hid her femininity, stroking her so thoroughly and sensually that she would not feel the pain of his entrance.

She pressed her palms against his chest, touched his nipples. Volcanic heat swept through him. She twisted and writhed beneath the onslaught of his loving; he gave and gave some more. With each new stroke of her hands upon him, he burned for her and prayed to Allah that she'd always respond with such wild, untamed passion.

Trying not to alarm her, he moved between her thighs, pushing her legs apart. He felt the soft dampness there and rested his sex against her welcoming sheath. He eased into her with patience and care. Farther into her tightness he went, until he found himself sheathed to her womb.

Allah!

Chapter Eight

She had lied to him, the truth apparent now that he knew her intimately. She was no more a virgin than he was.

His body shook, his anger rising to a fever pitch as he realized there was no barrier to be broken, no resistance within her, and he understood she'd played him for a fool. Fury swept through him, a rage so deep and heartrending, one so hot and intense, that he'd surely burn and perish.

In one wild, passion-filled moment, all his dreams crumbled to dust.

He would never forgive her, but he would use her as she had used him.

An eye for an eye.

"Alexi," she called out in a paper-thin voice.

He'd once longed for his name upon her lips. No more.

Beneath him she writhed and her hips lifted to bring him deeper and more fully inside. His little wanton angel knew what to do. He meant to stop this travesty before it went any further, but she wrapped her legs around his back and he was undone, brought to his knees by a jezebel. A massive shudder swept through him, and he gave himself over to the sexual delights he knew she offered. To hell with her feelings and her so called tender sensibilities.

To hell with his dreams.

She never cried out or suffered pain because there was no reason. He would not hurt her because she was not a maiden.

Angela would never be his wife. A shudder racked his body. A tight knot of pain burrowed deep into his heart.

~ * ~

His arms braced on either side of her, Alexi paused. She felt him looking down at her, just as she felt his sudden unexplainable anger, saw the cold, hard lines of his face, the ice in his expression. She wished fervently she had the power to see into his mind. His expression was suddenly so hard and cold, she felt rivers of fear rushing through her.

For too many long seconds he held still, watching her, his sex deep inside her, filling her.

He began to withdraw.

Only to plunge into her again, this time with little regard for her feelings, yet she found herself drawn higher and higher until she cried out in pleasure and stars seemed to shimmer in her mind. She bit fiercely into her lower lip then felt his mouth upon hers, his tongue sweeping along her lips, imploring her to open to him, demanding all she had to give and more.

He tensed then a thrust brought him so deeply within her she shuddered with the intensity of it. The heat of his climax filled her with liquid fire. And almost as instantly, he eased his weight off her, pulled the covers on top of her and, rising from her bedside, strode from the room. On his way out, he picked up his pants and stepped into them.

"Don't move from that bed," he commanded. "I'll be back later."

"Alexi?" she whispered, the sheet held to her swollen breasts, shame and humiliation swamping her.

Angela stared after him, confused and heartbroken. Defying his command, she rose from the bed and, shrugging into her wrapper, followed Alexi into the parlor. Several minutes passed while she watched Alexi in the other room, pacing, a dark, cold glare in his eyes. He didn't look up or acknowledge her presence.

Needing to understand what had changed between them, she stepped out of the shadows. "What did I do wrong? I would make things right if I could," she told him softly before taking another step into the room, afraid to confront the demon in Alexi but too terrified not to.

"You need an answer to that question?" His words and tone were harsh, and he sounded every bit as taken aback by what just happened as she felt.

"I know I don't know much about lovemaking, but--"

"My God, woman!" he thundered so loudly she thought the entire hotel must be able to hear. "After what just happened in there, and the irrevocable proof I met head-on, you have the audacity to tell me that?"

Angela stepped back into the shadows of the room, confused about Alexi's feelings for the first time since she'd met him.

"I don't understand." She tried desperately to still the quavering of her voice and the trembling of her body. She could not.

What proof?

Alexi gave her an icy stare. She stepped back again, retreating into the darkness of the room and her soul.

"Liar." His voice was soft, but the one word had the impact of a locomotive crashing into her heart. She was sure it stopped beating. And she was sure she did not know what he spoke of.

"I am not a liar," she told him, her voice so low she was not sure he heard.

He poured himself a glass of brandy and downed the alcohol in one gulp. One arm rested against the fireplace. The flames licked upward and embers popped. He did not move. Suddenly, with no warning, Alexi threw the crystal into the fire. What liquid remained hissed and exploded with the heat. The delicate glass shattered into a thousand glimmering shards.

"I'm going out," Alexi gritted out between clenched teeth. "Be here when I get back. I want you in my bed, nowhere else. Do you understand?"

She didn't move.

"Do you understand?" Harshly, he repeated his commands as if she were a wayward child, incapable of comprehending what he wanted.

"Where else would I be?" she asked, confusion pooling in her stomach, fear in her heart. "What have I done?"

He came to her then. His hands wrapped around her arms. She could not help but meet his gaze and recognize the simmering rage he held tightly in check. It seemed it would not take much for him to explode.

"I am not a fool, Angela. You've lied to me, and I find that a sin I cannot forgive. Pack your clothes. We'll leave on the morrow with the tide. I see no reason to spend any more time in New York, courting you like the besotted fool I've been. I never make a mistake twice."

With those hollow words rattling around in Angela's mind, she watched Alexi dress in evening attire and leave the room. On an ominous note the door closed, the latch clicking.

Confused and utterly alone, Angela walked in a daze through the rooms of their suite. Unable to cry, she watched the fire slowly die, just as her heart was dying.

Pack your clothes. Be here when I get back.

Like hell! she thought, furious with the man and his bold audacity. His great arrogance no longer appealed to her. His impervious commands she would no longer obey.

Angela plopped down on the ornate gold couch, her head in her hands, tears now sliding down her cheeks, all energy drained from her. She would not cry, she vowed, but she could not help herself.

Like hell.

She clutched a pillow to her chest and fingered the tassel, determination rising to overcome her despair. Night sounds swept in through an open window, a horse and carriage, the rumbling of the underground train. Nothing filled the emptiness inside her.

"Alexi," she whispered, bereft, "what have I done to change everything so? What sin do you believe I've committed?"

She closed her eyes, and when she opened them again, the embers of the fire had died to almost nothing. The clock on the mantel chimed twice. She rose and looked in their room. It was still empty, the bed cold. The sheets were rumpled from their lovemaking, something so incomplete and lacking it left a hole in her heart she didn't think could ever be filled. The promise had been so sweet, the deed empty.

Courage she'd always possessed until these last few heartrending minutes surfaced. She knew what she had to do. She had to leave, and she had to vanish before Alexi returned. Because he would never let her go.

Despite the hate he felt for her and the rage that simmered so blatantly on the surface, he would keep her with him until she hated, too. She could never let that happen.

Determined to see this through, she shook off the weakness and the uncharacteristic vulnerability that had held her to Alexi. Then she packed her clothes, just as he'd demanded.

Her one valise in hand, Angela, with her head held high, strode out of the suite and out of Alexi's life forever. Small electric lights lit the hallway and the stairs leading to the first floor. The foyer was awash with a golden glow. The bellboy gave her a cursory look before going back to work.

Tears stung the back of her throat as she silently made her way out of the hotel, but she valiantly fought them back, keeping her head high. Outside, beneath a crescent moon hovering in the sky, she made her way down the lighted street and away from Alexi and the hurtful rejection she didn't understand.

~ * ~

Alexi hailed a carriage and gave directions to one of the most prestigious bordellos New York City had to offer. Slowly he walked up the long brick walkway. Huge lion-headed knocker in hand, he pounded against the door.

"Good evening, Devil. Nice to see you, sir. It's been a while."

"Good to see you also, Stubbs. Is Venus still here?" Alexi asked as he handed Stubbs his jacket and loosened his tie. If anyone could ease the pain, Venus could. She knew tricks even the experienced harem women he'd dallied with as an untried youth would swoon at.

"She sure is, Devil. You want me to fetch her down?"

"Not if she's in her room. Does she have a gentleman with her?" Alexi let his gaze wander up the expensive Oriental carpet to the top of the stairs. Venus had always been one of his favorites. He could talk to her, and he wanted to talk tonight, as well as satisfy his other, baser needs.

He needed to forget the deep, merciless pain.

"She's by herself right now. Her last gentleman caller left a half hour ago. Figured she'd be down in a few minutes, looking for more clients."

Alexi's gut turned over at the mention of another man in Venus's bed. He didn't want a whore; he wanted Angela. "Angela, why couldn't you have been my angel?" he whispered, desperate for answers. "Why didn't your past matter to me until I thought I'd be the first one in your bed?"

His gait dragging, Alexi climbed the steps to Venus's room. The sparkling chandeliers didn't brighten his heart, nor did any of the scantily clad ladies lounging on the banister and reclining in chairs below.

He'd seen it all. Done just about everything.

Alexi knew which room was hers. He'd been there several times before and enjoyed himself immensely. This time felt different. He raised his hand to knock but the door swung open of its own accord.

One lamp lit the room. Venus sat at her dressing table, naked except for her silk stockings and garish red garters. When he stepped in, she turned, her full breasts swaying like pendulums. He'd always loved her breasts. Until now.

Until he'd seen and tasted Angela's breasts, felt the satin of her flesh, stroked the ivory column of her long neck.

Venus smiled at him and posed seductively, her breasts pushed forward, the rouged nipples blatant in their demand. Her legs were spread wide, beckoning any man who might walk through her door, her arms resting back against the chair to best present herself to him.

He didn't want her. He needed Angela and her wide-eyed innocence, her angelic smile, breasts that would fill his hands, a body that fit him like a personally ordered glove.

"Devil." She rose and slipped on an orange satin wrapper, a color that clashed with her red hair. "It's been a long time, to long. You've come to see me? " She stretched out her arms for him.

He closed the distance, but a quick hug and a kiss on the cheek were all he could bring himself to give her. Her smile faded.

With wisdom he'd never credited to her, she searched his soul and perhaps his heart, too.

"Why, Devil Blackmoor, you're *in* love." One hand rested on her hip. "Who is the lucky lady? And what on earth are you doing here?" She pulled out a gold brocade chair for Alexi to sit on, then curled herself up catlike on a couch. "Come, tell Venus all about her. It's plain to see you're no good for anything else." She touched one long, painted nail to her lips. "I will be wantin' my usual fee, mind you."

"Of course," Alexi said, relieved she saw his feelings so easily. "I wouldn't have it any other way."

"Now tell me. What's she like, this woman you're in love with?" Venus uncurled herself long enough to pour both of them a snifter of brandy before settling back against the couch.

Alexi allowed himself a minute of reflection and a slight smile. "I'm not in love with her," he began. *Fool, she stole your heart the first day you saw her riding on her horse, her hair flying wildly behind her.*

"Bah." Venus waved her hand in the air to dismiss the notion. "Best you start telling yourself the truth, Devil Black-moor, or she's going to have you wrapped around her little finger." Venus paused, leaning forward so her face was only inches from his, her breasts spilling from the silken robe.

"She's a wild one," Alexi said softly.

He squirmed inwardly at Venus's bold scrutiny of him. In a mysterious way Venus touched him with her gaze, boldly perusing his private thoughts. "She already does have you wrapped around her ringer. I never would have believed this if I didn't see it with my own eyes."

"She lied to me," he said. "I can't forgive her. I won't."

"In this world every woman is forced to lie at one time or another to protect herself. I didn't take you for a fool. If you don't love her, you care for her. Forgiveness is easy. Best you find a way to understand her side of the story or you'll be tied in knots forever."

Alexi poured himself another glass, sipping the brandy slowly, going over her words. "Why?" He didn't understand why Angela had lied to him.

"Because men like you behave like asses," she told him dryly. "That's why. You want one thing from a woman and expect another. When you don't get what you need, you behave like little boys."

"You couldn't mince words a little and save my tender sensibilities?" he asked.

"Do you have tender sensibilities? After what you've just revealed, I'm hard-pressed to see them. Forgive her, Devil. Can it really be so hard?" She winked, a matronly grin, completely out of character, exposing her own feelings. "Now, tell me what falsehood this woman of your heart has told you."

"She said she was a virgin."

"Now why on earth would she say that if it wasn't true? Was she? We both know you aren't."

Alexi had never wondered why. And that bothered him. Why? He asked himself again. He could come up with no answer except that she truly was a virgin, which wasn't true.

"No, she wasn't innocent, and I don't know why she'd lie about it," he finally said.

"Well, when you figure it out you'll probably understand more about yourself and your lady than you ever wanted to know. Especially when it's almost impossible for a lady to prove she's never slept with another man unless her maiden shield is intact. If she wasn't a virgin, she would have known that little fact." Venus stopped rambling, her lips forming a broad smile in immediate recognition of the problem.

"You know why she lied."

Venus shook her head. "Think about it, Devil. That's all I'm going to say. Think. If you really love this woman, think long and hard and don't let her virtue mean so much. In the long run it doesn't, you know. It's what a woman has in her heart and soul that counts."

Alexi leaned back in the chair, drink in hand, going over Venus's words. Angela had heart; that much was true. Once he'd admired her courage and integrity. The rest of what Venus implied, he didn't understand.

For a few long hours they sat in quiet solitude, drinking fine, expensive brandy and once in a while speaking of old times. Alexi dozed off once. Venus woke him, prodding him to go on home to his lady. She, after all, had a living to earn, Alexi recalled.

Once again Alexi gave her a chaste kiss; then, slinging his jacket over his shoulder, he sauntered out of Venus's room and the expensive bordello.

Stepping out into the cool night and thinking over what he and Venus had talked about, he realized that Angela was meant to be his mistress, nothing more, and given time, he could forgive her the lie that had passed so easily from her lips. Dreams of a loving wife were not for him. He would go home and do his duty, keeping Angela by his side. Forgiving her for shattering his dreams was hard but not impossible.

He would find a way.

"A virgin." The thought and the inconsistencies still rankled. He'd wanted her to be an untried maiden from the moment he'd first set eyes upon her. She'd sent his emotions on a tempestuous ride through hell. No other woman had possessed his heart and soul so thoroughly, and now that he looked back, he was thankful for the truth and the freedom.

He could possess her, own her, but she would never have his heart again.

He rounded the corner in time to see the object of his thoughts striding manlike down the street, valise in hand. The rage that once again consumed him nearly brought him to his knees. He'd given her orders. How dared she think to disobey him?

How dared she leave him?

He strode after her, his heart pounding and his hands trembling with restrained fury. When he caught her, he meant to make her understand she did not want to run from him. He would follow her to the ends of the earth to convince her.

As she turned another corner, he panicked. Two men stalked her. Alexi began to run, his feet pounding the pavement, his heart in his throat. He cursed himself a hundred times over for not setting Misha to guard the door of his room and his wayward mistress. He knew Misha was in town. Misha had sent word of his arrival while Angela had been bathing. At this very moment, Misha should be on board his ship, waiting to depart for their homeland.

He swore again. He should have guessed Angela would try something foolish.

The way he'd acted in bed that night had not been well done. He would make it up to her as soon as he caught her and explained a few things. There would be no recriminations and no regrets.

Suddenly Angela's war cry rose in the stillness of the early morning, sending shivers down his spine.

"My God, woman," he cursed, picking up his pace. He remembered the knife she'd carried and prayed she didn't dare use the weapon.

Alexi rounded the corner and came to an abrupt halt, fear for Angela his immediate concern

"Easy now, little lady. We don't mean you no harm." The man's voice was sleek and calculated.

Two sleazy-looking men had Angela backed against the wall. Her knife was drawn and glistening in the small amount of light that filtered through to the alley.

The men were pimps, yet they were dressed in black evening clothes, their smiles false. Angela wouldn't know what they were.

"We've got a nice, warm room for you to stay in. Won't cost you a cent." The smoothness of the man's voice sent another river of fear down Alexi's spine.

He would kill the man.

"I'll just bet you do." With one fluid motion, Alexi grabbed the larger man by the back of his shirt and tossed him aside. "This lady is mine. No one touches what is mine."

"Who says so? Looks like she's runnin' away to me," the other man said. His eyes roved over Angela, resting on her breasts. "Yup, who says she's yours?"

"I do," Alexi gritted out through tightly clenched teeth.

"Alexi..." Angela's whisper sounded like a death knell in his ear. "I'm all right." Angela slowly eased closer to Alexi.

"Put the blade away, darlin'. You don't need it now," Alexi said. "I won't let anything happen to you."

She didn't sheathe the knife. With her knees bent and every muscle flexed, she waited for one of the men to strike.

"Do as I say," Alexi said, his voice hard and commanding.

Alexi watched Angela's body shudder and heave, but she didn't sheathe the knife. At least she had the sense to be afraid. If he'd been a few minutes later, she'd be turning tricks in New York's red-light district in the morning.

He turned his attention back to the men. One had a small derringer trained on him; the other had drawn a knife of his own. Then he heard Angela's voice, bold and more daring than he'd ever imagined.

"Lay one finger on Devil Blackmoor and you'll wish you were dead. I've learned ways to make a man pray for death."

The pimp laughed outright. "We're not afraid of a wee thing like you."

"You should be," Alexi said, not knowing whether to shake some sense into her or take pride in her courage. She was a feisty, daring little thing, stubborn to a fault.

"I've had my fill of this," the man holding the derringer said. He moved slightly.

His trigger finger twitched.

Everything seemed to happen in slow motion. The gun exploded. Angela anticipated him and dove in front of Alexi, knocking them both to the ground.

"Son of a bitch," the gunman hollered.

From his position slightly beneath Angela, Alexi had hardly enough time to raise his arm and fend off the blow directed at him by the second man. The knife slipped through his shirt and the flesh of his arm. He heard Angela groan.

Ignoring his wound, Alexi rose to his feet. He readied himself for the next attack. It came from both sides. With practiced speed, he ducked and kicked out. The first man caught one of Alexi's feet in the chin and was thrown back against the wall. The impact caught him so hard the assailant slowly sank to the ground. The other man turned and ran.

Barely winded by the quick exchange, Alexi watched the man run just long enough to reassure himself he was not going for reinforcements.

He knelt beside Angela, who had not moved. He saw the crease of the bullet against her forehead, and the blood. Her face was pale, her hair in disarray around her shoulders. He touched his finger to the pulse at her throat. It was strong and steady, and he breathed a silent prayer. The bullet had only grazed her, the impact stunning her. Alexi prayed she would waken, but not, he thought wryly, until he had her on the *Mystic,* safe and sound and bound for Europe.

Once out of the harbor there would be little she could do to protest a journey she had once been eager for. Quickly he tore a strip of cloth off his shirt and bandaged her head. Then he saw to his own wound, binding his arm tightly. Blood soaked the cloth. He tore more strips until finally the bleeding stopped. Then, sweeping Angela into his arms, he moved down the sidewalk toward the hotel.

Bold as brass he walked into the lobby, explained to the man at the desk what had happened and ordered a carriage to take them to the docks and another to bring their bags.

Once in the carriage, Alexi held Angela on his lap. With her gently cradled in his arms, he remembered the first time he had held her like this. His heart swelled with tenderness and the need to protect her.

"Allah, but what would I do without you? I could have lost you tonight." As if the impact of all that had transpired suddenly hit home, Alexi shuddered. A cold sweat had him shaking uncontrollably. She had taken a bullet meant for him. She had thrown herself in front of him to protect him. No woman had ever cared so much for him she would risk her own life.

"Little fool," he whispered. "Allah protect this woman." Alexi buried his face in her hair, moisture rising to his eyes. He heard the beating of her heart and the steady, deep breaths of sleep. Her pulse was strong, and he felt sure she would awaken in a few hours with a grating headache, but otherwise fine.

During the ride to the docks rain started to fall, a fine drizzle at first then turning into a torrent. Lightning lit up the eastern sky and, with Angela still in his arms, Alexi had to run up the gangplank to his room. Even then they were both soaked through to the skin. She looked so fragile and helpless, but Alexi knew better.

He laid her down on the bed and undressed her completely. The sight of her stirred the most primitive urges within him. He wanted her again. But this time he wanted her to know real pleasure.

He cursed himself for a fool. She wasn't conscious, and here he stood lusting after her body, a body he knew she'd given to at least one other man.

Does the past matter so damn much?

The only answer he could come up with was no. The past was simply that--the past, and best forgotten.

The knock at the door brought him back to the present and the deep, all-consuming ache in his groin, an ache that had left him only once since his first encounter with the devil incarnate in front of him. He chuckled softly at the illusion. Yet he knew that in heart and deed she was an angel, his very own wanton angel. He covered her with a blanket.

"I didn't expect you so soon," the captain of the ship said. He stood in the doorway to Alexi's cabin, his hat in hand, in dress uniform.

"Nor did I think to be here until late tomorrow." Alexi let out a long, slow breath. "Can we leave on the tide?"

"We can set sail as soon as the storm passes."

"Good, then do so. And Misha?"

"He left the ship. Said he had one last thing to tend to before sailing.

Should we wait for him?" the captain asked.

"He can fend for himself. He knows exactly where I am. If he chooses to show, he will. If he doesn't, he must have a damned fine reason for leaving me high and dry to protect myself and my little charge."

"Leave you high and dry? Never! You know I'm as good as your shadow." The booming voice exploded from somewhere behind the captain. "I have my own stories to tell, but all in good time. Besides, I saw the fight. You had everything under control, and you would not have welcomed my interference."

Alexi grunted.

"You would have allowed her to run off and leave me?"

"Of course not." Misha laughed and slapped Alexi on the shoulder. "You were spoiling for a fight, and don't deny it. Don't you feel better all ready?"

Alexi felt relief instantly, and as if the presence of Misha here on the ship gave him leave to succumb to the wound that had been bleeding now for several hours, Alexi slumped to the ground.

Despite the fog surrounding him, Alexi heard Misha swearing at the captain then Misha picked him up from the floor as if he were a rag doll and laid him next to Angela on the bed in his cabin.

He shivered then began to sweat. Heat swept through Alexi. Even in his sleep, he knew a fever raged within his body. Nightmares flowed, one into the other. He was in the desert with his father, the oasis miles away, and yet he saw the line of trees clearly, smelled the water, felt the cool liquid lining his parched throat. Ivan appeared out of nowhere, bringing wine and food, laughing outrageously. They were both young and hot-blooded.

He heard bells, and the enchantment the women his father procured for him would bring. There were two tents set up for their use. One, of course, was for his father, the other one for him. If any of the women suited him, he would be allowed to buy them for his own personal use, and begin his own harem.

Alexi had never done that--bought women to keep as slaves. He was content to pick from the newest women brought to the harem. His father allowed him to do that. Once he'd used the women, they would be touched by no one else, not even his father.

But that was years ago.

None of the women had ever stirred him as Angela did. Angela, his fiery angel of retribution. Even now while his mind wandered back to the desert sands, he felt her cool soothing touch upon his fevered skin.

Angela... She'd been small and tight when he entered her. She had not been used by many. But she'd lied to him. Still, he'd find a way to forgive and get on with their life together.

The memory sparked a hollow chord of discontent and he allowed his mind to wander back to the tent and the dancing women. Scarves fluttered, and the women swayed enticingly to the music of the desert.

The music haunted his soul.

Adara...

Adara had been the first woman to show him the ways of love and pleasure. Fire and tempest had been the result of that union, but there had been no other satisfaction. Alexi had learned then that women served little use besides momentary delight.

Until Angela had robbed him of his soul. Angela was a fever within him, stirring up a tempest of carnal pleasures and sexual yearnings he could not live without. She enticed then held back favors. She played games, but when he had been sheathed so deeply inside that he touched her womb, he had for a moment believed he touched her heart.

That moment had been short-lived. It had taken less than a second to realize that Angela's maiden shield had already been broken, and not by him--less than a second to understand what a fool he'd been.

He'd been on the verge of proposing marriage. He thanked Allah he'd not been so rash.

The coolness of a cloth washed over his chest. He opened his eyes, the light blinding, yet the vision in front of him was beautiful. Angela, his very own angel, administered to his needs. Her hair hung loose around her shoulders.

"About time you came back to the land of the living," she told him. Her voice was soft, and he could have sworn he'd died and gone to heaven.

"I didn't know I'd left."

Her expression changed to grim determination, her eyes hollow. "Since I know you'll live"--she rose from her place by his side--"I won't waste any more time here."

His hand was around her wrist before she could leave him. "You're not going anywhere, not until you tell me why you were leaving me."

"I don't owe you an explanation or anything else," she told him as they made eye contact. "You don't own me."

Her tone was cool, and he felt a stab of regret at the way he'd acted in the hotel, ruefully admitting he should not have left her in bed--alone.

"You owe me your life," he said, and immediately regretted the statement but could think of no way to take it back. He owed her more than he could ever repay. It was a bullet meant for him that grazed her head.

His point made, she blushed a deep crimson. "I could have handled them. You didn't give me a chance to defend myself. They were nothing."

That much was true, he admitted reluctantly. Even with a wounded arm, it had taken him little time to overcome them and send them packing.

"Angela." He wasn't about to give up. "Why were you leaving the hotel? I told you to pack your clothes and stay put. We had an agreement, you and I."

She tugged on her arm but he wouldn't allow her to escape until she answered. "I don't obey orders. I told you that a long time ago. And as far as I'm concerned what you did last night rendered our agreement null and void."

"What I did last night? You will obey…"

"I think not," she said casually, and, applying pressure to his thumb, she quickly made her escape.

Chapter Nine

"Misha."

She heard him yelling for the burly giant who had stayed by his side throughout his illness, dispensing orders as rapidly as Alexi himself.

"Misha! Get her now." His impatience knew no bounds.

Not wishing to meet up with Misha, and knowing Alexi would order his man to bring her back to him, she scampered out the door and down the long hallway, with every intention of losing herself on the huge ship.

Luck was not with her. Misha appeared on the stairway leading above decks, and as if guessing his master's thoughts, he pointed her in the other direction, a grim expression on his face.

"I do not relish the thought of chasing after you. Unlike Alexi, I have no reason to treat you gently."

Misha was taller than Alexi by at least five inches, and his shoulders were broader, his arms even more muscled. He had the same aristocratic way Alexi had of expecting all orders to be obeyed before they'd even been spoken. Misha's eyes were an iron gray when he was angry and almost a pewter color when something amused him. They were pewter now, and his lips twitched with a threatening smile.

"Alexi wants you, not me," she said a bit too quickly. Misha did laugh.

"I see through your ploy." His hands rested negligently on his trim hips. "Now what on earth did you do to get him in such a foul humor?"

"Nothing." She tried to push past him and was stopped instantly.

"Turn around and go back to him or I'll be forced to drag you to his room," Misha said, still chuckling softly.

"What Alexi wants, Alexi gets," she told Misha petulantly. "Drag me."

That stopped his laughter. Misha's eyebrows drew together into a frown. "That is true," Misha told her, his voice holding within it a wealth of amusement once again. He made no attempt to lay a hand on her, just stared at her, waiting patiently.

With a muffled oath, Angela walked back to Alexi's room. Almost as soon as she stepped inside she heard the latch turn. She was locked inside a room with only one bed--with Alexi. He would pay for this.

He grinned at her, his smile devilish.

Her heart turned over. Angela didn't move from her spot by the door. She couldn't. She wasn't ready to forgive Alexi.

"Come sit." Alexi patted the place on his bed she'd occupied earlier, his smile growing even broader.

She shook her head, intending never to willingly allow herself close to this man again. He would seduce her if she let herself get too near. One touch and she'd melt into his arms. He'd kidnapped her, stolen her away from her homeland, and called her a liar.

"You're afraid," he taunted. He smoothed the covers down and leaned against the headboard, his bare chest looming above the sheets.

She swallowed hard. "No. Wise beyond my years," she returned, not daring to move closer, yet wavering in her resolve. The man had an iron grip and a will so strong she doubted she'd ever win a battle waged against him.

He smiled then, and the sight of it went straight to her heart. Oh, how she turned to molten fire with one look from him. She willed herself to control the vacillating emotions inside her.

"Come and sit down. I won't touch you."

Once more she shook her head no. "I'm fine here," she squeaked, then swallowed hard, trying desperately to regain control of her voice. The man planned something, and she didn't intend to fall so easily into his schemes. He would explain his own actions to her, and he would tell her why he left her so suddenly the night before.

"Why did you call me a liar?" she asked, blurting out what was uppermost on her mind.

All signs of amusement left Alexi, his expression turning hard and cruel once more. It seemed she'd said something wrong again.

"You would have been better off not reminding me of that."

Forgetting her vow to stay as far from Alexi as she could, Angela stepped forward, her fists clutched at her sides. "I want to know," she said, her eyes beginning to fill with moisture, her heart swamped with pain. "I'm not a liar."

"I believed you," he began so softly she stepped closer. "I believed you when you told me you were a virgin." His tone was bitter now, and his words were edged with ice. "You lied to me, and I'm afraid I cannot forgive so easily."

"I am. I was," she amended, dropping to her knees beside his bed. "Why do you say such a thing?" she asked, completely baffled, her heart in her throat, tears stinging her eyes. "Alexi ..."

His laughter echoed around the room, raising goose bumps on Angela's arms. "I might forgive you the lie if you would only admit to it now. Tell me the truth, angel, or forever hold your tongue. You cannot think to carry on this charade. I'm no fool you can wrap around your little finger. I know a virgin when I have one."

His words bit deep. They were hurtful words, tainted with bitterness and regrets Angela didn't understand.

So very confused, Angela stared at him, silent tears of pain and betrayal sliding down her cheeks. "I cannot lie, Alexi. Please don't make me. As God is my witness, I'd never lain with a man until you."

"Son of a bitch, Angela, the proof was there, or not there, inside of you. Did you truly think I would not notice the lack of your maidenhead? I told you before, I'm no fool."

Every emotion inside Angela cried out in denial then she realized she'd felt no pain, nothing.

"But..." She felt the shock reverberate within. There had been no proof of her innocence. There was no way she knew of to convince him, save trust.

His finger to her lips silenced her. ' 'No more. We will speak of this no more. You will come with me to my homeland and be my mistress. I'll take care of you just as I told you earlier, and you'll want for nothing. I will cherish and protect you. I--"

"I will be a wife or nothing." She rose, her insides a quivering mass of hate and love for this insufferable man. "I was innocent until you touched me. I don't care what you think. I don't care if you found me lacking. I should have insisted you listen to me." She turned, her spine stiff, and marched to the door.

Her anger knew no bounds. The door was still bolted shut.

"Misha! Misha!" She pounded on the door until her fists hurt as badly as her heart, until she could not raise her hand. Angela sank to the floor, her skirts rippling around her. She leaned against the wall and closed her eyes, willing Alexi and the horrid truth of his words to the back of her mind. Convincing him was hopeless.

He wouldn't allow her to escape, even into the hollow recesses of her mind. His voice came to her gently and soothingly.

"Come here, little one. In time you will learn that being a mistress is much better than being a wife. I will give you a house of your own and servants, all the jewels you want. You can see me most every night, lie with me, bear my children."

"No." But her answer sounded weak. She had no force behind the word.

He held out his hand to her, and woodenly she came to him.

When she stood beside the bed once more, she inhaled deeply, praying for the courage to tell him what he needed to hear. "I will not be your mistress. I will not climb into bed with you ever again except as your wife. And if you ever touch me"--she took another deep, cleansing breath-- "if you ever touch me intimately, I-I will scalp you."

His laughter came from deep inside, rambling up to fill the room. "You can try, angel. You can try. Believe me when I tell you that you aren't the first to threaten me with that particular dire event. No one has succeeded yet." Once again he patted the bed. "Come now. Sit on the bed with me. We can speak of more pleasant things."

"I will do more than try," she said, her fists clenched tightly.

"Very well," he said. "I will allow this tantrum for a while. But you will see the way of things soon then you will come to me. Angela, I cannot marry you. A marriage with you was difficult yet possible when I thought you were coming to me a virgin. But now..." he shrugged. "There is no way I could convince my grandmother of your suitability."

"Suitability!"

Fury raged within her, and, ready to explode, Angela drew her hand back but caught herself. The twinkle of amusement was still in Alexi's eyes. "A passionate woman is all I've ever dreamed of. I will give you everything your heart desires," he said. "And more, much, much more."

"You look for a wife as you would a horse."

"Bloodlines are important."

"Ha! When the same bloodlines are mixed so thoroughly that people turn crazy, they mean less than nothing."

"Point taken. I still cannot marry someone like you. I will give you trips to Moscow and to the sun-drenched Crimea. After my heir is born, we can explore Italy and France together. Everything you want is yours."

"Everything but your name and respectability."

She thought she saw regret--or perhaps a moment of pain--in his expression before he shuttered his feelings to her. "As my mistress, you'll have respectability," he told her, his tone soft, soothing.

If he meant to ease her mind, he only made the situation more intolerable. "I meant what I said. Lay one hand on me in the way of a lover and I'll see that you regret the day you were born. When I'm through with you, if you can still walk, you'll be minus your scalp."

He sighed deeply.' 'I will agree to this hands-off arrangement for a short time and under one condition. You must be able to tell me no."

"All right," she agreed quickly, her voice trembling, knowing that if he set his mind to her seduction, he would have her in the palm of his hand. "I have to say no, and you have to stop. Agreed?"

He grinned shamelessly. "I do believe I've won the first battle. I promise you I'll win the war, and you'll find yourself in my arms and in my bed. While I admire your courage and your convictions, I do mean to make love to you."

Stubbornly, she sat down on a chair on the opposite side of the room as far from the bed as she could manage. Folding her hands in her lap, she looked at her fingers, twined them together then undid them. The silence between them seemed to stretch on forever.

She had nothing more to say to him, and she didn't dare look at him. The rustling of sheets across the room set strange sensations pummeling her insides. She clenched her fingers together then peeked at him through lowered lashes. He'd put his hands behind his head and relaxed. The sheets lay draped across his lap, concealing very little. His eyes were closed, but she knew he watched her. She knew, though, that the pose was merely pretense. Her dark warlord would not give in easily.

Wind whistled through the sails of the ship as it began to pick up speed. Crewmen bellowed orders, and bells clanged. From her position, she could see outside. New York swept by, the Statue of Liberty stood tall and proud then there was nothing but open sea and the breaking dawn of a new day.

The rhythm of the ocean and the sway of the ship began to lull her to sleep. She nodded, then jerked awake. A comfortable position eluded her.

"You can lie down beside me." The deep voice sounded soft and gentle.

She did want to lie down beside Alexi, but she wouldn't.

She ignored the offer and curled up in the chair. Once again she nodded off, her dreams haunting her, but she did sleep.

~ * ~

When she woke she was in Alexi's bed, naked, the sun shining through the open window and the smell of salt spray vibrant in the air.

"Alexi," she whispered, Alexi wasn't in the room. Angela stretched, every muscle in her body screaming out painfully. She rose and wrapped a sheet around her.

A pitcher of water and a bowl sat on a table. She washed then took care of her other needs in a closed-off room of the cabin.

"You have a lot of nerve, Devil Blackmoor," she said indignantly, one hand holding the sheet in place as she searched for her clothes. "You're insufferable, and I'll have you know that your little game won't work. Keep me naked, for all I care."

"Now that's what a man likes to hear."

How he'd opened the door without her knowing or hearing was beyond her. He stood just inside the doorway, his hands full of platters of steaming food, a lascivious grin on his face.

Her stomach rumbled.

"Hungry?" He laughed.

"You know I am." She picked up the ends of the sheet, walking awkwardly to the table where he set the food down and looked at him expectantly.

"No food until I get a kiss," he told her solemnly and straight-faced.

She felt a sledgehammer hit her gut again. "That's blackmail."

"No, it's payment for all the work that went into the breakfast." Platters still in hand, Alexi moved farther into the room.

"Then I should kiss the cook," she told him tartly.

"I am the cook." He laughed. He set the dishes on the table, silverware and china rattling noisily. She rose quickly, thinking to step by him.

"You're not going anywhere," he said and wrapped her in his arms, his mouth descending to hers. The kiss was hard and demanding. His lips pressing against hers evoked pent-up emotions and a deep-seated anger. Alexi ravaged her mouth and she responded hungrily, once again giving him power over her heart and body. But he didn't seem to want the power. He ended the kiss by nibbling on her bottom lip, then soothing the small hurt with his tongue.

The smile bestowed upon her then was all-male and powerful. He knew he could have swept her off her feet. He could have made love to her if he'd wanted to. His smile told her that he chose not to.

She stepped back, shamed by her reaction, admonishing herself for her own weakness.

"You didn't say no," he told her, his voice gentle, almost as if he understood the raw emotions ripping through her--and the indecision. Almost as if he knew she battled herself.

"I'm saying it now." Bravery in the face of such tenderness was hard to come by. She gathered it, shielding herself from her need to give him all the love she felt deep in her heart, reminding herself that he meant only to use her and shame her.

"Ah, but I do believe your denial comes after the fact. Deny me all you want, but it won't change what just happened here. I could have made love to you, and you would not have protested. Nor will it undo the kiss you just bestowed upon me. One you thoroughly enjoyed. Be honest with yourself. You want me as much as I want you."

"Wanting you was never an issue." She spoke with heartrending honesty. Still, he didn't understand. She was afraid he would never understand.

He studied her carefully, a puzzled expression on his dark features. "Angela," he began. "You're carrying this too far. A little rebellion I can tolerate, but..." He piled her plate high with eggs and ham. Fresh bread was set beside the plates, sliced and spread with butter.

She changed the subject. "When are you going to give me something to wear? When I sleep with you?" she asked, wishing she could see this his way, knowing she couldn't. No amount of coercion on his part would make her. She would never give in to his proposition.

"My fair lady, you do me wrong."

"Then where are my clothes?" she asked, trying desperately to keep the anger and the childish tantrum that threatened to explode from doing just that.

"In the laundry," he replied, forking a piece of egg and holding it out to her. He ran the food across her lips. Her stomach rumbled and he laughed. "Come on; eat," he said, and like a lamb being led to the slaughter, she allowed him to feed her.

He kept her mouth filled, which kept her stomach happy.

"I do like your compliance," he said, just as her lips closed over a succulent piece of ham.

Compliance?

She nearly choked on the food. Her hand went to her throat, and her meager covering slipped. She grappled with the sheet for a few minutes, knowing Alexi must have surely glimpsed parts of her she didn't want him to see.

"This is not compliance. What you see is hunger."

"Of course, whatever you say, angel." He rose.

Angela squirmed on her chair, not liking the look on his face at all. He walked slowly behind her chair. His hands suddenly rested on her bare shoulders. She squeaked.

"Hush, I'm only going to massage away the kinks you got last night when you foolishly tried to sleep in that horrible chair. You really should take better care of yourself. When there is a perfectly comfortable bed available, you should use it. You have nothing to fear from me. I always hold true to my promises." His hands worked magic on her muscles. She didn't want to relax. Relaxation could prove too dangerous.

He kissed her neck where he'd pulled her hair away, then brushed his lips lightly down the column of her throat.

She sprang from the chair. "No!" Angela had turned and faced him, her anger and fear roiling inside, sweeping through her. If nothing else, she was determined. "No," she said again, a little less forcibly, but the panic was still in her voice.

He smiled a jaunty smile and walked from the room.

The lock grated closed.

~ * ~

For a few glaring minutes, Sam Chamberlain let the fury rumble deep in his chest, let it grow until the anger and frustration he felt erupted in a wild Sioux war cry.

In unison the men loading a merchant ship nearby turned to stare at him. At his sides his fists clenched and unclenched. He thought of the knife he'd strapped to his leg, hidden by the pants he wore, and what he'd like to do with it--bury it deep inside Devil's heart. High-handed aristocrat or not, Devil Black-moor would pay for what he'd done to his daughter.

Drizzle spilled relentlessly from the heavens above, and a cold wind stung his cheeks. He longed for a fight, for release from the pain he felt. He had meant to protect his daughter from her own foolishness and had failed. The *Mystic's* sails slowly dipped below the horizon as Sam paced the docks in New York harbor, cursing Devil Blackmoor and Misha and whatever gods had allowed this to happen.

Blackmoor would pay a hundredfold if he'd touched his daughter intimately, if Angela had been hurt in any way. There would be no place on earth Blackmoor could hide.

The next ship to England wasn't due out until the evening tide. Frustration pooled in Sam's gut. Anger surged in mercuric flows in his bloodstream. At least he would be only a few hours behind that son of a bitch. Staking the bastard out in the desert would have to wait. When he caught Devil, he meant to feed him to the sharks--forget the desert ants and foul-smelling buzzards.

"Fool," he berated himself. "Idiot." He glared at the heavens above. When Angela had stepped on that train heading for the finishing school, willing and eager, he should have known something was wrong. He should have known she was up to something. Her running away with Devil Blackmoor had come as a complete surprise.

He should have never placed his trust in Misha. Misha had led him a merry dance, one that took him over most of New York City and into the early hours of the morning.

Misha would pay, too.

After Misha left him, he'd finally located Devil's room in the Waldorf, only to find out that Devil had departed along with his paramour--as the bellboy had delicately put it--early that same morning.

"Angela." His breath vanished in the gray afternoon, the single word swallowed by the cold drizzle. "How on earth could you have let that man deceive you so? Didn't I teach you to be a better judge of character?"

The blame was his own; he knew that for a fact. He'd allowed Angela to chase after wild dreams, never imagining that she'd run from him. Yet Angela had always been surrounded by people she could trust, had never known the shadier side of human nature.

Blackmoor was a devil.

All along he'd known Angela craved adventure, but he'd never guessed she would run after it and abandon all the rules of propriety he'd taught her.

He should have seen the warning signs.

It was not like him to misread his daughter so completely.

He had never believed she was old enough to think herself in love.

"Son of a bitch!"

He could curse himself a thousand times in several languages, yet all the swearing in the world would not bring Angela home or keep her out of Blackmoor's bed. She'd already slept with the devil, of that he was sure.

The room in the hotel had been ripe for romance, a candlelit table, a soft, glowing fire--and the bed had been well and truly rumpled, as if they'd frolicked there for hours.

From his coat pocket he pulled a crumpled piece of paper. The note Misha left him was water-logged, the ink running in rivulets down the parchment. The words, etched hi his mind, infuriated him even more two hours later than they had when he'd first read them.

Nice meeting you, Angela's father, I'm sure we'll meet again, but not for a few months. Alexi's clipper ship the Mystic *is faster than any other ship in New York harbor.*

And Europe is a huge continent. I'd wish you good luck in your endeavor, but I wouldn't mean it. It might take you years to find us in his homeland. My heart would go out to you if I weren't such a loyal subject to the prince.

Sincerely,

Misha--your friend in another circumstance.

"Damn you, Misha. You knew how I felt about Angela. How could you?"

Another low growl emanated from the pit of Sam's stomach. Despair and a deep foreboding settled in the core of his heart. If it wasn't already too late, it would be by the time he reached Angela. His precious daughter had been or would be used thoroughly by an aristocratic snob who thought it was his right to abuse women and their hearts.

He would have to be there for Angela, be there to pick up the pieces of her broken heart. Beyond any doubt, Sam knew his daughter loved a devil.

Devil was in for his day of reckoning.

Chapter Ten

Alexi welcomed the tempest that sent salt spray licking the deck and wind pummeling the sails. Gale-force winds challenged his ship and the captain. The *Mystic* slumped into a deep trough and then rode the next swell. Waves rushed across the deck, sweeping everything that wasn't tied down into the ocean's murky depths.

Two long weeks had passed since the ship had sailed out of New York harbor, and he'd gained no ground with the recalcitrant lady below in his cabin. Angela refused to understand or even listen to his vows of good faith and the privileges of becoming his beloved and protected paramour. She refused to listen to the reasons he gave her as to why she could never become his wife.

He meant to protect and cherish her. He meant to lavish her with gifts.

Wasn't that enough?

She turned a cold shoulder to him each time he walked into his chambers. Lately he'd taken to sleeping on deck, just to ease the ache inside that looking at her caused him. He knew she hurt, too.

Allah, but a hard, furious fight would do him a world of good. He wondered if Misha would oblige him.

"Hit the deck." Misha's loud call jolted him out of his brooding.

The crack of a mast far overhead, which meant rigging hurtling downward, filled him with fear for his men and, strangely enough, renewed energy. Even with the sails trimmed to fight the furious winds, the masts had taken a beating. Another crack echoed loudly, and one mast toppled forward. The men looked for shelter from the bombardment.

Waves washed over the deck, and the ship tilted precariously. The captain eased back on the rudder, barking orders, and the ship righted. By all that was holy, he should go downstairs and see how Angela fared. He dared not. He could withstand the icy tempest more easily than he could fight the frigid glares she cursed him with. She was the most stubborn woman he'd ever run across.

Suddenly he caught a brief glance of billowing skirts, a familiar and well-turned ankle; then recognition slaughtered his self-control. Without thought he started forward, unable, for a few lengthy minutes, to utter a sound or a warning. She had no idea what she was up against.

"Angela, no ..."

Her face shadowed and pale, she appeared on deck, clinging to the railing. What did she think she was about? Surely she would be washed overboard if she didn't go below, and soon. A huge wave washed across the deck. He watched, his heart lodging in his throat as the water swept her feet out from under her.

He'd never known such fear. "Angela," he cried out.

Racing toward her, hanging on to whatever was secured, he felt as though his feet had lead weights tied to them. The rope knotted around his waist to keep him tied to the ship caught on debris. He yanked it loose. *Little fool.* He would not lose her now.

"Angela, hang on!"

He watched her grope for a handhold, her fingers closing around anything that swept by. She fought valiantly, yet each surge of water pushed her closer to the side of the ship and an icy grave.

"Damn you. You little fool!"

He gave voice to his thoughts; then he swept her from the deck and in one swift movement hauled her against his chest, his hands roaming everywhere, making sure she was all right. He set her aside, studying her beautiful, pale face. Her hair streamed in dripping silken threads down her back and along her cheeks. He brushed them back.

"Why?" He wanted to shake sense into her, and perhaps a little respect for Mother Nature. He meant to hold on to her forever and keep her from harm. If she would only allow him to protect her. "Why did you leave the safety of the cabin?"

Another wave swept by, but he pulled her below deck, closing the door behind them. He felt the shuddering of her body and heard her teeth chattering. Against him her body felt like ice.

"Answer me." His fear knew no bounds and rapidly changed to fury. Allah, but he would never forget the sight of her lying on the deck, ocean water swirling around her. He would never forget his fear.

She tried to answer. Her lips moved.

He could not live without her. He swept her into his arms and carried her to his cabin.

"Can I help?" Misha had followed. He stood at the top of the steps, staring at the two of them, gentle understanding in his expression.

"See that hot water is sent down and apprise me of the crew."

Misha nodded. Once again Alexi was alone with Angela and torn between the urge to blister her with a lecture she'd never heard the likes of before or make love to her. "You must learn to obey," he said, brushing her hair from her eyes, holding her face between both hands. "I told you to stay below."

He never wanted to go through anything like that again. She would obey him. In the name of safety, he would see that she did. She had far too much courage for her size.

When they entered the cabin, it was bathed in a gloomy darkness, the only light coming from the lightning flashing across the black sky outside. He strode to the lantern then searched his desk for a match. After several frustrating minutes he found what he looked for, and once again the cabin was aglow in light.

He turned to her, his heart going out to her, his fear now under control. She stood in the middle of the room, water sliding down her hair and her face to pool on the floor. She was soaked through to the skin, but now her chin was tilted upward in a show of defiance.

"What were you doing out there? I told you to stay in the cabin," he repeated himself, his fears leaving him beside himself and slightly incoherent.

He had already guessed the answer to his question. She'd come outside to find him. The darkness and the horrible wail of the storm must have terrified her.

"I..." He watched her swallow, saw her fight the trembling of her shoulders with a stiffness he was unaccustomed to seeing in her. "I went to find you." Still her teeth chattered.

"You were afraid," he said, knowing the truth. He held out his arms to her, offering comfort, nothing more.

She nodded, and he knew she wanted him to hold her but was afraid of their bargain. "It's all right, angel. I would never take advantage of your fear. I promise."

With a strangled half sob she bolted into his arms. Beneath his slicker, he enfolded her in his embrace. Her cold, wet clothes penetrated every pore of his body.

"I didn't know." She sobbed into his chest. "I've never seen anything like that."

"You must be chilled to the bone."

"I've never been on a ship before, in the middle of a hurricane."

"You feel like ice. And, darling, this is merely a summer storm, nothing more. Even now the winds are easing."

Her only answer was a muffled sound and a shiver that swept her entire body then his. She clung tighter, as if she never meant to let go of him. Another time he would have felt a deep male satisfaction; now he was only concerned for her health.

A knock on the door tore his mind from his brooding.

"Water, sir."

"Bring it in." He tried to pull her arms free from around his waist but could not budge her.

Misha followed the cook into the room and pulled the tub out. He assembled the privacy screen and directed the crew carrying kettles of hot water. Steam rose invitingly. Alexi wondered if she'd allow him in the tub with her.

"Anything else?" Misha asked.

Alexi shook his head, his gaze still lingering on the woman shivering in front of him.

His body hardened instantly, and this state of need was not unusual. He'd been constantly aroused since rescuing her that long-ago day.

"You've got to get warm," he told her, gently trying to maneuver her to the tub.

Alexi felt her nod of agreement against his chest and thanked Allah for her renewed courage. It would be only a matter of minutes before she became the spitting little tigress he so admired. Ah, but how to tame a tigress? He'd certainly failed so far.

"Come on," he said, and led her around the privacy screens to the bath. "Do you need any help?" he asked, and his voice, he knew, was filled with hope.

She smiled then. The beauty of it hit him in the heart. She'd recovered. Perhaps it would have been nice to have her compliant a bit longer. No, he decided. He would not take advantage of her. When she came to his bed, he would have the vibrant, headstrong woman he'd come to admire.

"Promise to stay on your side," she said in a much-recovered and saucy tone.

He grinned shamelessly and shook his head no. "Now that your teeth aren't chartering and your shoulders aren't trembling with fear, all bets are off. I'll do all I can to get you in my bed and in my arms. Nothing has changed, Angela. I still want you."

She squared her shoulders, her arms crossed defiantly in front of her, her chin lifted stubbornly. "Then I won't put on dry clothes, nor will I get in the bath."

The ship rolled slightly with the waves, and the water in the tub sloshed over the edge. She groped for something to hang on to and found Alexi.

"If you wait much longer, you won't have water for a bath," he said, his grin widening. "Then you will have to climb into bed with me to get warm."

She looked at the tub, then the bed, as if weighing her chances; then she slipped behind the screen. He watched her disrobe, her silhouette beckoning to him, her feminine curves lush and ripe. Her long, slender leg stepping over the rim was almost his undoing.

Water splashed over the rim as she slipped into the bath.

He could bear no more. On one heel he turned and left the room. He had a ship to see to and men who might have been hurt by the fallen mast and rigging. What had once been meant to be a pleasure trip had undoubtedly become the longest ocean voyage of his life.

~ * ~

Angela let out the breath she'd been holding when she heard the door to the cabin close shut. She slipped lower into the hot water, willing her shivering to stop. There was, she told herself repeatedly, nothing to fear. Already the winds slowed and the violent shuddering of the ship had almost stopped. Soon they'd have calm waters.

Despite all she told herself, she could not stop the violent response of her body to her stupidity, could not force her teeth to stop chattering. Going outside in the storm had been the most foolish thing she'd ever done. Angela Chamberlain was not by nature a foolish woman. But when the lights had gone out, she'd been petrified, and all she'd been able to think of was Alexi.

For a few fragile moments, she let her head fall back on the tub, and allowed the soothing balm of the water to comfort her. Alexi's arms around her had felt much better than the water. When she'd expected him to pull her sodden clothes from her, he'd acted the gentleman and allowed her privacy.

He'd wanted her. When he held her close, she'd felt the evidence of his arousal against her belly. If anything, the heat of him against her--and knowing what he felt like deep inside her--had warmed her more thoroughly than the bathwater. He could have seduced her then, but he chose not to.

Why? she wondered. Was it the deep-seated honor and the code of loyalty he lived by? He'd made a promise to her, and now he meant to keep it.

Jasmine, his favorite perfume, floated with the steam to swirl around her. The door opened and closed. Alexi had returned. He padded barefoot around the room, hanging up her wet clothes then his own. Through the screen, she could see the outline of his body, watched as he disrobed and donned dry pants and a shirt.

"Angela?"

Alexi stepped around the screen, a huge bath sheet in hand. She moved lower into the tub, her hands covering her breasts. He looked concerned for her.

"You warm enough now?" he asked. He bent over and tested the bathwater. "The worst of the storm has passed by. You should snuggle down in the bed and warm yourself."

"Alexi?" She swallowed hard, unwilling to let go of her values, but wanting him so very much. If he touched her now, she'd come undone.

"No, you misunderstand; as much as I'd like to, I will not join you. I've too much to do topside." He chucked her under the chin and laughed softly. "You want me. I can tell."

She nodded, a tear suddenly slipping down her cheek. "But I won't give in to you. I deserve better than to be a man's plaything. I deserve to be your wife, and I'll settle for nothing less."

For a moment he stiffened, his breath held tight. Then his expression softened, his eyes growing warm with caring. "You would never be my plaything," he said softly, the backs of his knuckles brushing her cheek.

"In my eyes--"

"Hush. I would cherish you. When you come to realize how precious you are to me, life will be more satisfactory for both of us."

"You would do the same if I were your wife." She turned from him, unable to continue the discussion. It was a useless pastime. He had made up his mind and wouldn't budge. She felt him withdraw from her. His fingers clenched tight against the rim of the tub.

She sighed softly, her lashes closing as if she could shut the pain away. "I wish you could understand my point of view--my needs."

"Allah, but you are a stubborn woman. I could ask the same of you."

She felt an immediate need to defend herself.' 'You are twice as stubborn, arrogant, presumptuous... The list could go on, and still we would not be able to reach an agreement in this. I will not be your mistress--ever. The moment we reach land I will purchase passage home."

The pulse beneath his jaw jumped rapidly. "With what? You don't have enough money and I will not give you any for that purpose."

"If I'm a whore, I could always sell my favors."

With a fierceness she'd never seen before, he lifted her from the water. He held her at eye level, her breasts pushed against his chest, her feet dangling in midair.

"Never!" Sweeping her into his arms he strode to the bed. They fell upon it.

He held her there with his eyes and his body. Petrified, she could not move, could barely breathe. "You will not sell your favors to anyone," he told her coldly. He did not touch her. He hovered over her, his expression fierce, his eyes determined. "Do you hear me?"

"To anyone but you?" she countered. "Isn't that what you expect me to do? Sell my body to you? In return you will lavish me with gifts." She was shaking, so unnerved by the man she saw above her. She had pushed him too far. She knew it the moment the words were out of her mouth.

"A wife sells herself for respectability and a name. You, I would love and adore with every part of my heart and soul forever." She tried to turn her face away. The pain she saw in his eyes was more than she could bear.

"You have the roles reversed," she told him, trying to maintain some level of rationality when she wanted to yell and scream at him.

"No," he said, and rose from the bed. "I don't." He walked the length of the room and back again, not pausing even a moment to look at her. His hands raked through his damp hair until it stood on end.

Angela buried herself beneath the covers of the bed and watched in silent dismay. Finally he stopped in front of the window, his hands clasped behind his back, and watched the rolling ocean, the calming weather.

Silence dragged on for what seemed an eternity. She could not stop herself from looking at him, could not stop wishing he'd believe her.

The door opened, light from the hallway spilling into the cabin.

"Alexi?" Misha's voice called out. "There are men who need you. The captain has fixed our location and would like to know where you want to put into port for repairs."

"Coming," Alexi said. Before he left, he walked to her and, kneeling by the bed, ran his fingers along her jaw. "A very determined jaw you have." He closed his eyes thoughtfully. "Sleep, little one. You need to rest. Please do not fear me. I would never hurt you." His voice was gentle and full of grave concern. "Soon you will understand that I want only the best for you--for the two of us."

Angela knew his words for the lie they were. He had already hurt her deeply. Nothing he could ever do, save marry her, could heal the pain he'd inflicted upon her. Worst of all, he didn't understand, might never understand.

~ * ~

The clock chimed midnight before Feodora collected enough courage to leave her bedroom and make her way down the narrow servants' staircase to the outside. With each step the wooden planks creaked and groaned their protest.

She held her breath, thrilled with the excitement. Before this night ended, she'd have Ivan in the palm of her hand. She'd have him begging for her favors.

Her heart sped out of control with anticipation of Ivan's big, strong arms around her and the delightful things she knew he'd do to her. He was the best lover she'd ever had. Her insides quivered like jelly with the thought of seeing him naked. She'd never seen him completely bare, but tonight she meant to see all of him. She giggled.

Deep inside her most feminine parts she ached and dampened with desire for him. He'd put every other man she'd known, intimately or not, to shame. Thoughts of him driving into her, licking and nipping her breasts and her secret feminine folds drove her wild with desire.

Sweet Jesus, but she could hardly stand the wicked anticipation. It had taken all the control she had to wait for Natasha to finally go to bed. Then watching the hands on the clock for the entire hour she gave herself just to make sure no one would see her leave had her hot and panting with need. She was ready for him right now.

She risked a great deal. Of course, that was part of the thrill.

She touched a finger to her lips and let her tongue moisten the tip, thinking of Ivan and the little drop of moisture that would inevitably spill from his shaft just before he drove inside and satisfied her. She ran the palms of her hands across her breasts, keeping her flesh sensitive and alive with the heady passion she felt for him.

Outside the house a sliver of moon sat low on the horizon, giving little light. She didn't need light, the path to Ivan's bed ingrained in her memory.

Looking both ways and seeing no one, she lifted her skirt and dashed across the back lawn to the darkened stables. Ivan would have doused the lights, but he'd be up waiting for her. She pictured him in his bed, naked, his hands behind his head, a knowing grin on his gorgeous face.

Another giggle slipped from her at the surprise she had planned for him. Her bare nipples swelled and budded against the silk shirt she wore. She wanted to touch herself again but decided to wait for the master's caress. At the thought of Ivan stroking her, her stomach muscles and those farther down clenched tightly. Her body felt swollen and damp with need.

She slipped through the stable to the back room where Ivan slept and ate. The room smelled of hot coffee and wild male animal. The door stood open, the bed vacant. She gasped, frightened for a moment by the hand that closed over her mouth.

"Be still. It's only me," Ivan told her, his warm breath whispering softly across her heated skin.

She'd know his voice and the feel of his powerful chest anywhere. He smelled like unleashed power and hot desire, and she loved his wild virility. She leaned into him, pressing her back against his chest, letting his forearm rub against her breasts. His thumb caressed her lips, and one finger ran down the column of her neck.

She shivered, her womanly impulses quivering with anticipation of the erotic delights awaiting. Her tongue flicked out to touch the palm of his hand, and she delighted in the masculine rumble deep inside his chest.

With his free hand, he flicked open the buttons on her blouse, her breasts spilling free. He turned his attention to the fastenings on her skirt. After a few seconds, the fabric pooled on the ground. She stood before him naked, completely exposed and vulnerable.

He would never be able to resist her siren's call.

"Are you still intent on marrying Alexi?" Ivan asked, his breath hot and sultry against her cheek, his tongue gently exploring her ear, tracing the shell she'd exposed by pulling her hair back. He nipped her ear.

She groaned, pressing herself closer to him, reveling hi the unleashed power of the man.

"Are you?" he asked again after several minutes of silence. He tongued kisses down her throat, across her shoulder. With both hands he lifted her breasts, pushing them together, caressing them with the callused pads of his fingers.

"Yes..." she whimpered.

He pushed her away, his lip curling hi haughty disdain. "Even if you carry my child?"

She felt the chill sweep between them. "You can't offer me what he can."

"I haven't proposed anything, nor will I. When you carry my child, you won't lie with anyone except me unless I say different."

It was an arrogant command--one he couldn't enforce. Anger as well as passion replaced the chill until she burned with unleashed fury.

"Bastard," she said silkily, shifting her hips so her breasts swayed, inviting his touch once more. She knew she was beautiful and irresistible. All her lovers had told her so. "No one, not even my father, tells me what to do. Especially not a lowly stable hand," she taunted, one hand on a hip, a pose she meant to entice him with.

"Bitch," he told her. "I will tell you what to do, and you'll do what I say, even if I have to tie you to my bed to enforce my demands."

He gave her a swat and pointed to the bed. She walked to the only chair in the room and sat down. She draped one leg casually over the arm of the chair.

She beckoned him with one finger, posturing. Ivan leaned against the door frame, watching her, his eyes roving with an appreciative gleam. Already he was under her spell.

"I told you to go to the bed, wench." His voice softened. "But if you mean to disobey..." The threat hung in the air, his smile wicked as his gaze traveled the length of her.

She shuddered at the implication. "Have you forgotten so soon? I do what I please. There isn't a man on earth who can command me, least of all you," she repeated, then moistened her lips, her top white teeth tucking her bottom lip beneath in a seductive gesture.

Ivan didn't move, yet his muscles coiled and he looked primed and ready to attack. She loved and hated him all at the same time. She knew she'd gone too far, taunting him the way she had. But he needed to understand that he was a hired hand and she was about to become the mistress of the estate. His job--his livelihood--depended on her approval.

One dark eyebrow quirked upward. "Is that so?" He still didn't move. His arms were crossed in front of his chest, his voice low. The smile she'd seen on his face earlier no longer curled his full lower lip.

"Yes." She tilted her chin upward, but her reply sounded weak. He would heel to her before this night was over, she vowed. The princess and her stable master, yes, she liked the sound of that.

Feodora put her hands under her breasts and pushed them up and out. Momentarily his gaze dropped to her breasts then back up. She ran her hands down her naked body, posing for him.

"Come to me," she purred.

"You must be cold," he told her. "When you're ready to climb into my bed, I'll pleasure you. Otherwise I'll take you when and if the whim hits."

Ivan turned his back to her and walked out the door into the stable.

"Ivan!" Her cry was hoarse, and she hated him at that moment more than she'd ever hated anyone. He'd just rejected her offer. How dared he. She wanted to strike out at him, wanted to leave and show him he couldn't get away with this uppity manner.

She heard the whisper of his footfalls, the soft sounds he made to the horses to calm them. If she closed her eyes, she could imagine his touch upon her. He'd smell like the stable when he returned--if he returned.

She shivered and looked to the bed, knowing what she wanted, yet unwilling to give him the upper hand. Her teeth gritted together hard; she was determined she would not back down in her quest to tame the stable hand. A cold draft suddenly spilled through the crudely made walls of his room. Once more she stared at his bed and the plush warm quilt that lay atop it, stared longingly. Goose bumps rose on her arms and legs, and her nipples became taut little buds.

Suddenly she felt vulnerable and at a great disadvantage. He'd done that on purpose. "Damn you, Ivan," she shrieked, and didn't care how witchy she sounded.

She rubbed her arms and her legs. Still determined to win this battle, she didn't move. Instead she looked for her clothes.

They were gone, vanished into the blackness of the stables. "Bastard," she grated out, knowing full well Ivan was responsible for their disappearance. He must have kicked them out of the way when he strode from the room, defying her. Petty revenge, she told herself. They would surely be just around the corner, just outside.

Feodora scrambled on hands and knees, searching through the straw and dirt of the stable for her clothes. He'd done something with them. In the suffocating darkness she found nothing.

"Well, what a tantalizing sight for my senses," Ivan said.

His laughter infuriated her.

At the same time he spoke, she felt his hands on her naked bottom, squeezing her gently, caressing her intimately. A whimper escaped her before she could push the sound back. She tried to stand, but one hand on the small of her back held her in place.

"You aren't going anywhere," he told her. "I suddenly feel like having you."

"Ivan, I can't find my clothes."

"For what I've planned, you don't need them."

He gently caressed the tips of her breasts. "Ivan..."

He was behind her. "That's what I like to hear. My name on your lips. Say it again, sweetheart, and perhaps I'll show a bit of mercy."

She stiffened, realizing how quickly she'd lost the upper hand. One long finger, then two, delved inside her, his thumb teasing her, seeking her pleasure. For a moment he withdrew from her and she almost cried out to him. Then behind her she felt the coarse wool of his trousers upon her back, the worn material of his shirt, and now she felt his arousal, hard and probing.

He thrust inside her, his hands hugging her breasts, his lips brushing light kisses down her spine. "You are mine until I tell you differently. Don't ever refuse an order." His whispered words warmed her neck; his kisses nipped across her shoulders. "You can't ever win."

"Ivan... please."

He prolonged the ultimate satisfaction, taunting her, playing with her. "By the time Alexi arrives home, you'll be huge with my child," he told her. Grabbing hold of her hips he thrust again and again, deeper each time until she could hold nothing back from him.

She cried out in pleasure.

He emptied himself deep inside her and held himself there. Minutes later he withdrew, and, sweeping her into his arms, he walked with her to his bed.

"You will get under the covers and you will stay there," he told her, his meaning clear.

She nodded and obeyed, unable to do anything else. Feodora wanted him again, and it shamed her that she could not control the man. He was only a lowly stable hand, nothing more, but he gave orders as if he'd had years of training, as if he'd been born to command.

She fell asleep in his bed without the warmth of him next to her. She awoke alone in his bed, the sun shining through the dirty, streaked window. Her clothes lay neatly folded on the chair. She dressed quickly and, sweeping her hair into a knot on top of her head, she dashed across the lawn to the narrow, dark stairway and headed for her room.

~ * ~

From a downstairs window Natasha and Ivan watched Feodora.

"You really think this will work?" Natasha's whole body trembled with fear for her grandson and worry for her friend who was ill. "I will not sit by and watch Alexi fall prey to that witch."

Ivan nodded thoughtfully. "This plan of ours will work. Don't worry about the trip you've planned. You have to go. You've waited far too long as it is. That friend of yours needs you at his side."

"I can't help but worry."

"Don't. There is nothing Feodora can do here. Misha and Alexi will be home in a few days time."

"But--"

Ivan held up his hands to stop Natasha. "No arguing. Feodora can do no harm. And in the meantime I will enjoy the satisfaction of sweet revenge."

Feodora had a lot to answer for where his family was concerned. Her father had waged war on his people, and had all but annihilated them. She sailed artlessly through life, never thinking of anyone but herself. She was a spoiled, greedy little brat.

Yes, Ivan had plans for her, and if Feodora refused to cooperate, she would find herself abducted and settled into a harem--from which she would never escape.

Chapter Eleven

The sun had just cast its first golden spires of light upon the ocean when Alexi stepped onto deck. Over a week ago he'd spent the better part of his days standing by while his men wenched and drank in the taverns along London's waterfront. Unable to keep his mind from thoughts of Angela's soft golden hair and her lithe young body, he'd returned to his cabin a few minutes after midnight.

When he'd looked in on Angela, she had been asleep in his bed, her hair in careless disarray across his pillows. Dressed in a soft white nightdress buttoned all the way to her neck, she had unknowingly invited him, beckoned for his touch. He'd given in to his baser urges, and without further thought had walked to her. He'd held a few silken strands in his fingers, touched her cheek and let his imagination play havoc with his heart.

And during that same week, while the ship was in for repairs, he'd tormented himself and everyone around him. His anger at the smallest things had sent most of his men scurrying if he merely looked their way. Even Misha had wisely kept his distance.

Nothing had helped. He could not seduce her. She still said no, and he still slept on deck, away from Angela.

Several days ago they left London. Two hours ago they'd rounded the corner of Spain, heading into the Mediterranean Sea.

She was such a stubborn little spitfire. How on earth could he convince her that he wanted only the best for her? He inhaled a ragged breath then let it out slowly.

Today was a beautiful day. High, feathery clouds floated whimsically in the sky. They sailed in the Mediterranean, a deep sapphire blue--the color of Angela's eyes--the same color as the precious gems in her ears.

Dolphins swam alongside the clipper ship, playing in the wake then darting in front of the bow. The smell of sea spray lay heavy in the air. Calm water lay ahead of them as far as the eye could see. It would be smooth sailing for all aboard except Angela and himself.

He would have to change his strategy where Angela was concerned. Obviously she didn't realize or understand what a great honor he bestowed upon her by asking her to be his mistress, to share her life with him. He must convince her.

"She is still asleep, Alexi." Misha materialized by his side. Alexi wasn't surprised. He'd asked his friend to look after Angela in his absence and report back.

"Why does she resist?" Alexi turned on his friend. "Am I not charming?" His anger and confusion warred with the needs of his family and his desire to give Angela everything she wished for, including him. His arrogance overwhelmed him at times. But he knew she wanted him.

She could deny him forever, but all he had to do was look into her eyes to see the desire that flared within her when he drew near. Her cheeks would flush a becoming pink shade, and her bottom lip would tremble until she tucked it beneath her top teeth to still it.

"You do not know why she is so stubborn that she still refuses your loving even though her eyes say something different?" Misha asked, a smile curling his lip, a deep chuckle rumbling across the deck. "It is not for me to tell you, my friend. You must take the time to work out your problems. Talk to her. Besides, I fear you've gone too far this time, Alexi. Ask Angela for the truth. Find out who she is--who she really is. Not the fairy tale she has made up."

"Therein lies the trouble. She hasn't made anything up. I don't believe for a minute she is capable of such a great deception. A small lie here, or there maybe something to soothe a troubled lover."

"Then find out what she hasn't told you."

"You make her sound mysterious. She is a commoner, a simple woman." Alexi stared out to sea.

"Is she?"

"You're as easy to see through as glass. What do you know about Angela that I don't? What hasn't she told me?"

"You need to ask her. If she still refuses to tell you, and if the situation warrants it, I will explain to you what I learned on the trip east. But this is something between you and Angela. It will do the two of you no good if I interfere."

Alexi braced himself against the railing of the ship, staring out at the water. They would be docked soon, the overland trip beginning. He would have to watch her carefully. There wasn't a moment that passed that he didn't fear her promise to leave. Given the opportunity, she would find the first ship back to the States.

"She is so angry with me, she wouldn't tell me. Even if I got down on one knee and begged." He ran his hands through his hair, raking it off his forehead and from his eyes. "She's as stubborn as a Colorado mule."

Alexi massaged his pounding temples. The ship dipped sharply, spray drenching his face. The cold water did little to invigorate his dampened spirits. Alexi strode the length of the ship and back.

Back and forth.

Misha watched, a knowing grin on his face, a smile that only served to infuriate Alexi further.

As Misha suggested, he needed to go below and confront Angela--find out exactly what she wasn't telling him.

~ * ~

Angela felt the weight on the bed before she realized Alexi had entered the room. She'd been awake most of the night, wishing for a way to escape the ship and Alexi's hold over her. She would not--could not--give in to his plans for her. Morning light brightened the room but did little to assuage her wounded emotions.

Misha had been vigilant in his watch; then Alexi had returned. The door had remained locked, but she'd heard their footsteps outside the cabin and their quiet conversation. There had been no lapse in their guarding of her. No chance for her to escape on the London docks.

Alexi pulled back the covers she'd drawn to her nose, a deep chuckle following. Despite her resolve, his tender smile made her heart turn over.

"I know what you're about, my sweet concubine. You cannot hide

146

from me."

He brushed a gentle kiss across her lips. She opened her eyes. "I know," she said on a sigh. "I don't want to hide from you. I want to change your mind."

"The day is beautiful, the ocean incredibly blue, and I don't want you down here. You're far too pale." His fingers caressed her cheek. "The sunshine will give color to your skin and breathe life into your body."

"I'd like to go outside," she said, startling herself. Until this moment, she'd wanted to escape the gossip and the stares. Everyone must know she slept in Alexi's bed. They would believe the worst. Shame swept through her, anger close on its heels.

"Good, then get dressed. I'll wait for you in the hall. Don't take too long; the dolphins might get tired of their games, and I'd hate for you to miss them." His smile filled her heart with memories.

"Dolphins?" She sat up, the sheets held tightly to her breasts. "Are there really dolphins out there?"

"Dolphins..." He winked. "Hurry up."

He rose from the bed. Emptiness and a profound loneliness welled deep inside Angela. A deep chasm of mistrust stood between them. The loss was acute, magnified with each passing second.

In a few long strides he stood by the door, his body framed in sunlight. Dressed in formfitting breeches and a white shirt, he gave off an aristocratic air. He might really be a prince, she thought. A prince, a devil, a tender lover--she wanted the man, needed him, but he was unwilling to sacrifice for her, or believe in her. She was good enough for any man--even a prince.

Should he have to sacrifice?

Reminded of what she gave up to be with Alexi and the self-respect she'd lose if she gave in to his wishes, Angela felt heated tears gather in the back of her throat. Loneliness and a deep-seated fear knifed her heart. Stubbornness welled inside her, a determination so strong she almost relented just to ease the pain.

For some time now, Angela had wondered if a little bit of Alexi wasn't better than nothing at all. Her father would be so ashamed of her thoughts, but she wasn't. She loved Alexi with all her heart, and all she wanted was a life with him, a chance for happiness.

He believed a mistress was held in higher regard than a wife. Once she'd vowed that she would settle for nothing less than what her mother and father had known, a love everlasting.

But now...

Did two people have to be married to love forever?

Angela didn't have any idea what she could expect from this life he planned for her. Perhaps it would be better for her to settle for a place in the background rather than a place at his side. Second best...

She'd never played second fiddle to anyone.

"Hurry up, lazybones," he said, a rakish smile on his handsome face.

Angela's heart broke in two. She knew what she had to do. The door closed behind Alexi and shut him off from her.

She pushed her hair from her face--her desperate thoughts from her mind--and did exactly what Alexi commanded. She hurried.

A few minutes later, she decided aloud, "I'm ready."

Angela stepped from the room, dressed in lemon yellow and prepared to face life rather than hide from it.

She understood how much she needed his love. When she left him, she'd hold his memory close to her heart. The few moments they'd had together she'd cherish forever. Memories would have to be enough to last a lifetime.

"You look lovely." Alexi offered his arm and she accepted, her fingers closing over his strength, absorbing his energy and courage. She knew and loved the power of this man, and she loved his gentleness, too.

He commanded men, expecting absolute obedience, yet he accepted her wishes and had not forced her or tried to seduce her. She knew he'd wanted her. So many times Alexi had looked at her with such longing and desire she knew he missed her desperately.

Yet he'd held back. He'd kept his word to her.

They walked in companionable silence, Angela soaking up the fresh air and warm sunshine. Alexi had told her the truth about this day. It was one to remember.

Beside her, he cleared his throat. He touched her gently on the shoulder and she turned to him, her eyes lifted to meet his own. His diamond earring sparkled in the sunlight. "Misha says you're not telling me something I should know. Is that true?" he asked.

They stopped at the bow of the ship. At his words her fingers gripped the railing, biting into the smooth wood. She leaned forward, letting the wind ruffle through her hair and her clothing. More than anything she wanted to tell him what he wanted to know.

Two dolphins played tag in the wake of the ship. She smiled, pointing to them then laughing at their antics.

"Angela." His hand rested on her shoulder, turning her gently. "Don't run from me."

Once more she wanted to hide, needed to run as far away as possible. She closed her eyes to the bleakness she felt, tried to push it all to the back of her mind and enjoy the day. She found she couldn't.

Fear stopped her. Fear for Alexi's life kept her from telling him her name.

"I'd like to go back downstairs."

Alexi shook his head and eyed her critically. "Hiding again? I never thought of you as a coward. If you don't tell me what I need to know, Misha will."

Misha will. Those two words hung on the air.

When she looked at him, his eyes warmed with tenderness. Perhaps she had nothing to fear.

Misha would tell all. But what could Misha know?

Her already frayed nerves unraveled. "I don't understand what you're talking about." Confusion gripped her. "There is nothing that can be said that will solve what's wrong between us."

"Who are you?" he questioned.

She shook her head, denying him what he asked for. Panic, raw and dangerous, danced through her. She could never tell him she was Sam Chamberlain's daughter. The shame would swallow her whole.

His voice turned hard, unforgiving. "Just Angela. That's what you told me in the bordello. Just Angela, as if your name had no meaning or value. Who are you, Angela? What do you hide from me?"

The words left unsaid between them burned like acid in her soul. "When we were at the bordello, I couldn't tell you what you wanted to know.

I'd given my word. It was a vow I had to keep."

With the back of his hand, he caressed her cheek, lifted her chin, a promise in his eyes.

"And now?" His voice turned smooth and as warm as the best Kentucky whiskey.

"Knowing my name will serve no purpose save to humiliate me. I don't understand why Misha is so persistent."

"He thinks I should keep one eye trained behind me. Misha fears for my life."

"Only if my father followed me, and I told him not to."

Her heart jumped to her throat, and she knew her mistake instantly. Her father would make sure his little girl was safe and protected. He would track her to hell and back.

On her shoulder, Alexi's hand tightened. "Your father? If I were the father of a beautiful girl and she disappeared, I'd follow her trail and I'd never stop seeking until I found her. I'd kill the man who tarnished her reputation, who abused her in any way. Is that the way of it?" he queried, his expression solemn. "Except I didn't tarnish your reputation, did I?" His voice was bitter. "You came to me. You were willing and loving."

"In this case you wouldn't have to, I told him I was with you and that I loved you." She laughed softly but her heart cried. "In my letter I wrote that I was happy and you meant to marry me. Wasn't that terribly presumptuous of me?" she asked, her words a hollow, empty sound whipped away by the wind.

For a brief moment he looked chagrined. Then he smiled, a soft, tender smile. "Are you happy?" he asked her, his voice low and magical. Once again one of his long fingers rested under her chin, lifting it so their eyes met.

Tears pooled in hers, a half sob escaping her. She tried to turn from him. He stopped her.

"No, I'm not. I've never been so unhappy and so lonely in my life." She trembled beneath his touch and the force of his darkening gaze.

"It doesn't have to be that way." He bent close, brushed a kiss across her forehead--a friendly kiss, nothing more. "Agree to my proposal and I'll make you the happiest woman in the world." He seduced her with the warmth of his voice, with the tenderness she knew he felt for her. "It is an honest and heartfelt proposal."

Angela turned in his arms, her heart pierced through to its very center. Yet she leaned against him, used his warmth to comfort and soothe her bruised feelings, used his strength to restore her own determination not to yield to him. "The saddest woman in the world," she whispered, and was sure her words were lost in the wind blowing off the sea.

His arms were crossed just below her breasts. His shirt was of finest lawn and rolled up so his forearms were bared. He smelled of the sea and the summer wind. She turned her face sideways and rested her cheek against him, enjoying his warmth, knowing if she'd give in to his demand, she could feel this way all the time. But if she gave in, she'd never be happy.

"Will you become mine, Angela? I need you. Just say the word and I promise you'll never regret the decision. You'll never regret coming to my bed."

Need, not love.

She wanted both. God, how she loved him and needed him all at the same time. She adored everything about him; his strength, his tenderness, his patience, his stubbornness.

He was her mate. She deserved more than the title of mistress. She deserved his name. Alexi offered her nothing else, nor would he ever.

"What if I agree? What then?" she asked, knowing that by taking this step she was throwing away a lifetime of teachings for a few years of pleasure.

A lengthy pause followed. "I'll cherish you forever."

Cherish, not love. In the scheme of the universe, did that minor difference matter?

Yes. She could never live half a life, and half a life would be all he'd give her.

He turned her in his arms once again, his fingers sifting through her hair until her head tilted upward. Their lips met in a bittersweet kiss--a kiss that sealed a promise between them, a promise she couldn't keep.

"Alexi?"

His knuckles rested on her cheek. "You won't regret this decision."

She turned into his warmth, kissed his fingers. / *already do.* She fought the burning tears that welled deep inside and clung to her throat.

She didn't know how to tell him that he'd misunderstood. She still had no intention of coming to his bed.

~ * ~

Why did victory feel bittesweet and so hollow? Alexi asked himself more than once. He'd seen the unshed tears in her eyes, watched her stubborn courage melt away as the days passed, slowly changing into weeks. She wanted him and had been willing to hold out for his name until she realized she would never have it.

From the start all he had wanted was to make her happy. He'd failed miserably. He felt an uncontrollable need to reassure her and make promises he couldn't keep.

He' d suffered, been through hell and back, while she'd played games with him, toyed with his emotions. None of what she did or said had made sense to him.

She'd suffered, too, or had this all been an elaborate hoax, a match, two against two? Had she played with him in hopes of gaining more?

It had all been needless. She'd had at least one other man in her bed, had pretended to be something she wasn't. When he'd discovered the blatant lie, she should have given in gracefully and admitted everything to him.

Still, she trifled with his affections, his honor, his very heart and soul. She thought nothing of loyalty and duty.

He watched her, never taking his gaze from her. To his eyes, her beauty outshone the sun and the stars. Once he'd believed in her and her innate honesty.

Somehow he still did.

Angela sat in the sunshine near the bow of the ship. The wind blew her hair from the pins she'd secured it with, and her face was tilted heavenward. Her pose was angelic, tempting in its purity, beguiling in its innocence.

She'd never looked lovelier than she did right now.

The messages she sent him were always mixed. The picture of innocence. Allah, but he wished...

"You asked her?" Misha suddenly appeared beside him, his arms crossed over his chest, a half smile on his face.

Alexi nodded. "Yes," he said, his thoughts centered on Angela. He didn't understand, but her sudden compliance disappointed him. She was, he knew, seeking all that he could give her: money, jewelry, clothes. He was willing to lavish upon her whatever she wanted, except his name. But that thought rankled. He had once thought she loved him, wanted nothing from him except the return of his feelings.

Misha leaned against one of the lifeboats, his stance nonchalant. "She told you the truth? She told you her last name?" Misha's voice was dry and a bit strained. "You realize that your life is in danger. Knowing the man and his reputation, he might stake you out on the desert sands and ask questions later. When we reach land, I will take all precautions necessary. We'll go overland quickly. You should arrive at your ancestral home in two days."

"Whatever you think best," Alexi said without emotion, not bothering to confess to Misha he still knew next to nothing about Angela.

Stake me out on the desert sands?

Of course he'd asked her, but she didn't tell him anything. She had a father--one who cared. She told him she'd written to him and told him not to worry, that she would marry the man she ran away with.

What father would believe that drivel? A father who didn't have the God-given sense to protect his own daughter.

Alexi could not marry a woman who lied about her innocence--one who continued to dally with his affections. Honor-bound to do his duty, he had no choice. Marriage for him meant that a lady equal to his station must be his bride.

He slammed his fist on the railing, furious with himself and the fact that he cared too much. Thinking of Angela would likely drive him mad. He'd thought to be the only man to possess her. Sharing had never come easily to him. Time and again he told himself it was the future that counted, not the past. The reminding didn't temper his possessive instincts.

"You should have listened to her," Misha said. "What did Angela tell you?"

"Not much. She has a father who will not venture out of his snug home to find her. A man who could not possibly care about her."

"Sweet Jesus," Misha said softly. "And you believed that bit of foolishness?"

Alexi shrugged, unable to admit the truth. "Why wouldn't I?"

"Because she's lying." Misha paused, struggling for a breath. "Just as she lied to you before. She's not what she seems, Alexi. Wake up before you find yourself staked out below a smoldering sun with vultures flying above you and your manly parts stuffed in your mouth." Misha's voice rose with each word.

"Crudity does not become you, Misha. When have you ever allowed your wild imagination to overshadow common sense? Only an irate father or another lover would seek revenge in such a brutal manner."

"Stupidity may well be the death of you. She has an irate father, one who believes he is chasing the devil himself."

Misha turned his back on Alexi, his fists clenched at his sides, his shoulders racked with tension.

Alexi laughed this time. "What father would go after a woman who was about to be married to a prince? You cannot expect me to believe there is really a man swearing vengeance against me. It is simply not possible. If someone is out there following the *Mystic,* it is to dance at the lady's wedding and smile at the fool who believed in her innocence. Perhaps he is after a share of my wealth."

Fury and frustration still tainted Misha's thoughts and words. "Are you sure she was not a maiden? Are you absolutely positive?"

"Allah, but your ignorance exceeds your arrogance. I know a maiden when I bed one. She was not."

"Very well then, it seems there is naught that I can tell you that you would acknowledge as truth. You will have to learn the hard way."

"She's agreed to be my mistress." His voice was filled with scorn and sarcasm.

Misha eyed him critically. "You don't want her now."

The statement surprised Alexi, but he nodded. "I find the thought appalling, her reasons abhorrent."

"You are a hard man to please. For weeks now you've been pacing the decks, a man full of lust, unable to appease it, not wanting another woman to

warm your bed, and now that she's agreed to your terms you don't want her."
Misha laughed. "The irony of it all. You are a sorry case, Prince Alexi. It is too
bad you cannot accept what you feel for her. Your life would be much
improved--and so would mine."

"What?" Alexi asked, still mulling over his admission. Now that he'd
won the chase and her compliance, he didn't want her. That was a lie, he
thought. He wanted her more this very second than he ever had.

"You're like a snarling bear to be around. Like your western name,
Devil, you've behaved atrociously. Unless you find a woman to ease your
baser instincts, it doesn't appear you will change anytime soon. Bed the chit
and get her out of your system. Make her your mistress, but be wary of the
price you might pay. Give her the jewels and fancy clothes you promised;
enjoy her so the rest of us can find some rest from your bellowing."

Misha left on those words of wisdom. Alexi watched him stride
arrogantly down the length of the ship to the steering gears. With a wave of
his hand, Misha dismissed the captain and took control of the clipper ship.

Alexi watched him, his trusted cousin. Misha braved the elements of
the sea like a man born to it. Misha--his devoted friend, a man who had
never lied to him.

Misha accompanied him on this trip of his own free will, seeking
adventure and an escape from the duties that would soon rule his life. Misha
was a count in his own right, yet he served Alexi faithfully.

"Bed the chit," Alexi muttered. "Get her out of my system." Perhaps
he would do just that.

~*~

Sam Chamberlain stood on the London docks, watching the *Mystic*
and Angela sail out of view. In his pockets were three unopened letters from
Angela. His fear for her sanity paramount now, he was almost afraid to read
the letters. He'd heard the gossip on the docks. Angela slept in Alexi's cabin.
By now his daughter was the devil's mistress. A man like Devil Blackmoor
took whatever he pleased.

Devil Blackmoor was in for an awakening. Devil Blackmoor would
rue the day he bedded Angela Chamberlain.

Sam fingered the letters. Giving in to his fears, he found a shaded spot and sat down. For a few long seconds he closed his eyes, letting the breeze soothe his nerves.

Three telegrams. They burned his hand.

Dearest Papa and Mama,

We--Alexi and I--have boarded the train in Cheyenne. His private car was demolished in an accident, so we had to buy passage. Did you know he is a prince? We're on our way to Russia. He fills me with happiness.

I'm sorry.... I seem to be rambling. We were slowed by several storms, but now we are on the train headed to New York City. Alexi says his ship, the Mystic, *will be waiting there for us. He told me we would see London and maybe Paris on our way to his homeland. He's promised me adventure.*

Nothing more, Sam thought, his anger simmering out of control. His jaw clenched, his fingers trembling with rage.

His father is a grand vizier in Turkey somewhere. If there is time, we 'll stop and see his father. I'm so excited.

"Hell!"

I've always wanted adventure, and that finishing school you planned for me would have been the death of me. I cannot envision myself eating with a dozen forks and deciding which wine to serve with fish.

I'm so happy. Alexi says I will be his first concubine.

"Son of a bitch!"

Isn't that romantic? I do love him so. Please, Papa. I know you're worrying about me. Don't. I would do this all over if I had the chance. My only regret is that I lied to you. I'm sorry, Papa, but as I said before, if I had it to do over again, I would do the same thing.

Alexi has promised to give me my heart's desire. He loves me, and I think that when we reach Russia, we'll be married.

Give Mother and Trey my love, and think good thoughts for me. Don't for get

Jacob; he was always such a wonderful friend.

I've been selfish, thinking only of myself. How is Emma? Did everything turn out all right?

I Love you, Papa and Mama.

Angela.

"She can't be that naive."

Sam crumpled the paper into a hard ball and tossed it into the Thames. Tears slid down his cheeks, and his shoulders slumped. He thought his heart had broken in two.

"Concubine."

Dear God, he'd kill the bastard. If he had to storm the seraglio or the devil's palace to get her out, he would do that--and whatever else was necessary.

Alexi kept a harem.

Concubine.

He paced the docks, unable to read the other letters, afraid of what Angela had gotten herself into. She was so naive in many ways, still a child at heart, even though her body was that of a grown woman. She trusted with her heart and soul.

The sun was low on the horizon. Night would fall soon, and he had nowhere to stay, except for the ship he'd booked passage on. The captain had told him he could sleep there if he wished, even though they weren't leaving for several days.

The merchant ship was bound for Turkey, and the captain had agreed to let him off in Constantinople. From there he'd have to find a way across the Black Sea. Once again he would be days behind Angela. By the time he reached her, she could be huge with child.

He didn't care, though. He'd love any child of Angela's. What worried him most was Angela's heart, and how badly it would break when she discovered Blackmoor's true character.

Giving in to his need for rest and privacy, Sam sought shelter in the cabin he'd secured aboard the *Martha Rose*. With a whiskey bottle on the table beside his bed and a filled glass in his hand, Sam opened the second missive.

My Angel

Dearest Mama and Papa,

The trip across country is tiring but exciting. I've seen so many new, wonderful things. Denver is a big city, but it is nothing compared to Philadelphia and some of the other places Alexi has shown me.

He wired ahead and he says he has a surprise for me when we reach New York City. Nothing has changed. We still haven't spoken of marriage, but I fall more in love with him every day, and I know he wants me.

Of course he wanted her. What man wouldn't?

The way he looks at me makes me feel so strange deep inside. Is that the way you're supposed to feel when you really love someone? Is that how you feel when you are in love?

Sam breathed a deep sigh of relief. "Yes, little one," he whispered. "It is how you feel when you're in love. I don't doubt you love that bastard. But if he's hurt you in any way, I'm going to kill him," Sam threw back his head and downed the glass of whiskey in one swallow, relishing the burn in the back of his throat.

He calls me his sweet concubine now. I still don't know what that is, but the way he says it makes me feel cherished from the top of my head to the tips of my toes.

"If you only knew, darling. I'm praying for you. When you find out what he really wants, don't give in to him. Whatever you do, sweetheart, don't bless him with your virtue. Hold on to it. I pray every day you see Devil Blackmoor for what he is: a cad and a reprobate."

Sam hurled another shot of whiskey down his throat. Unable to read further, he rolled a cigarette then stepped outside.

The night was clear and bathed in stars. Big Ben chimed the hour. The *Martha Rose* lay at anchor, waiting for her cargo to be loaded. Sam supposed he should be pleased that the captain had given him passage.

He flicked glowing hot embers into the air, watching as they floated lazily down to the river. His thoughts went out to Angela. He'd die for her.

He wondered if Devil would do the same.

Inadvertently, he slipped his hand into his coat pocket. The third telegram still lay there, its tale untold. Icy fear gripped his heart. A deep foreboding swept through him. This letter needed reading, yet he'd prolonged the inevitable.

It would begin the same, but it wouldn't end on the same positive note as the others. Somehow he felt some of Angela's fear.

I love him so...

He had to force himself to read it. Sam reached into his pocket and opened it. Darkness shadowed the ink on the paper, and he couldn't easily see the words, but he could almost feel them.

"Chamberlain," he berated himself. "It's all in your head. You have no reason to be thinking the way you are. Angela loves the man. That won't change."

But Sam sensed it had.

Slowly he walked back to the cabin, facing the ordeal in front of him.

Dearest Papa and Mama,

I'm so confused and unhappy. I left this letter at the hotel. The clerk at the desk promised to send it. Alexi thinks I've lied to him. He walked out of the hotel and he hasn't come back in the longest time. I don't know what I did wrong but I've never seen him so angry.

I've decided to leave him. I won't stay with a man who thinks the worst of me. If you could meet me somewhere. Kansas City, maybe. Then I wouldn't have to go so far by myself.

I'm afraid, Papa.

Sam set the letter on the table. He'd never felt so helpless in his entire life. His little girl was out there somewhere with a man who couldn't see the treasure he held in the palm of his hand. Blackmoor must have made love to her, and when he didn't get what he expected he must have pushed her aside.

What Sam didn't understand was why the man didn't let her go. Why Angela had to run from him. Well, she didn't get to Kansas City. And if his fears held any merit, she might be on her way to a Turkish harem.

"Son of a bitch!" He rose, toppling the table and the chairs. "Son of a bitch!" A chair crashed against one wall and shattered into a hundred pieces.

Sam didn't want to read on, but he knew he had to finish.

You have every right to be angry with me. I've been foolish and selfish. I've put my own wants and desires ahead of what is reasonable. I didn't think beyond my own wishes.

If you still want me to attend the finishing school, I will. I'll walk around with a book on my head all day, and learn which fork I'm supposed to eat oysters with and which wine to serve with the chicken.

Papa, I hate him. I hate him every bit as much as I said I loved him before. He's a despicable man. Papa, I love you. Take me home, please. Angela.

He would take her home if it was the last thing he did.

Chapter Twelve

The intelligent, logical thing to do would be to make love to Angela until she was out of his system, just as Misha had told him he should. But Alexi couldn't do that. He chose not to take her to his bed, not until she could learn to trust his affections, learn to believe in him. Not only would that clear the air- between them, it would cleanse him of the guilt he'd been harboring ever since he kidnapped her from New York City and set her on the *Mystic*.

He could no longer deny that he'd abducted her, forced her against her will to travel with him across the ocean. All that after he'd seduced her then ignored her.

No wonder she acted confused one minute, furious the next. He'd hurt her. She had every right to those emotions.

He paused outside the door to his cabin. Without knocking, frustrated beyond endurance, he pushed open the door. She sat by the window, looking out, a pensive expression on her delicate features. She was dressed in a light blue gown, an off-the-shoulder affair that made her look almost ethereal. The bodice was cut daringly low, provocatively revealing the tops of her ivory breasts. She wore no petticoats, no corset--not even shoes. He reflected that in his homeland they'd both be quite indecent--he was barefoot, wearing breeches, and his shirt hung unbuttoned from his shoulders, revealing his chest. A bead of sweat ran down his back. Yes, his grandmother would find him hard to swallow if she were to see him now. And Angela appeared far too fetching in her natural beauty, as delicate and angelic as the mythical sirens who lured sailors to their deaths with the magic of their voices.

When he cleared his throat, she turned to face him, her eyes shadowed, her smile gone. She looked vulnerable and lonely.

Angela held her hands in her lap. Her hair was pulled back, severely so, and tied into a tight bun at the base of her neck. Before the evening finished, she'd be in his arms, her hair wild and natural down her back.

Then her appearance would not be that of an angel, but of a wanton.

Alexi stepped into the room, letting the door slam behind him. He strode inside and stopped at the table.

"Did you mean what you said?" he asked with an indifference he didn't feel as he studied her carefully, taking note of her fidgeting hands and the paleness of her cheeks.

Angela watched him, then after a moment shook her head. She trembled slightly, her lower lip held still by her upper teeth.

"I committed to nothing." Her voice was shallow and thready. She'd never appeared more beautiful and vulnerable than she did right now. Her sadness besieged him, tore at his heart as nothing else could. He'd meant to make her happy, had never meant for any of this to happen.

He approached her, rounding the table set for lovers. But one unsatisfied joining did not make them lovers. "That was not my understanding." Thoughts of taking her in his arms overwhelmed him, leaving him powerless to think. Soothing her mysterious fears seemed necessary, yet strangely out of place.

"Misha brought wine for us," she said, then waved her hand in a careless flutter. "And food."

She looked resigned and terribly skittish, her face devoid of all color. He meant to change that.

Alexi poured a glass of burgundy and handed it to her. "Drink," he said. "It will make you feel better."

"I don't want anything." Her voice was soft, her shoulders no longer squared against him. She looked as if all the fight and brash determination he loved so well had vanished from her, and he hated the way she'd given in to his demands. His frustration was at an agonizing point. He tried hard to remind himself she was alone and frightened, that he'd wrenched her from her homeland, taken her miles away from everything and everyone she knew.

"You need it," he told her, holding back the oath that hovered on his lips. "I'd like to see color in your cheeks again." *Laughter in your voice.* He paused, his arm resting on the back of a chair.

She looked tired, thinner than when the ship had set sail out of New York. She appeared to him as a childlike waif. The friendly companionship they'd shared earlier had vanished. Somehow he'd envisioned long walks on the deck with the moon shining down upon them, the warm Mediterranean wind caressing them, her eyes aglow with desire.

"Whatever you say." She accepted the glass and sipped hesitantly, her wary gaze never leaving him.

He filled his glass. It seemed to Alexi that the unnatural stiffness between them stifled all his coherent thoughts.

"Good, I'm glad you see things my way," he said. But he wasn't satisfied. Fire and passion, headstrong stubbornness and willful disobedience were his Angela. He didn't know the submissive woman sitting before him.

What happened to her sass and vinegar? What happened to the woman he wanted so badly he could scarcely breathe?

His fingers closed tightly around the stem of his glass, nearly breaking it in two. He didn't love her. He desired her, wanted her, needed her in his bed.

Compliantly, she nodded and finished her wine. She set the glass on the table, still staring at him. He poured her more.

But Devil, didn't you know? Unless I see fit I don't obey anyone. Her words haunted him. The woman in front of him was not the woman he'd been so taken with only a few weeks ago. Somehow he had stripped her of her pride, her honor and her dignity. He wanted to restore them.

"Your wish is my command," she said so quietly he had to lean forward to hear.

The words infuriated him, and he responded without thought. "Sarcasm doesn't become an angel." His polished reply rang in his ears, and he hated himself, despised his lack of control and compassion. She had a way of disarming him.

She flushed. "You don't understand."

Under the circumstances, her innocent pose was intolerable. "No, Angela, you don't understand," he said quietly, his frustration rising. "But it doesn't matter, not any longer."

"Because I've agreed to your every command?" she asked with a delicate softness that stole his breath.

He had been on the verge of letting her go. "Yes," he told her.

She stood, tiny, fragile, her blue eyes caught by the muted light slanting in through the window. He wondered if she had planned this from the beginning, his unmanning.

He wasn't quite sure what he meant to accomplish when he began to move toward her; her reluctance had been understood, and he had no desire to push her too far too soon. But he also reflected that it was far too easy to dwell on lies, and the only way to accept what life had in store was to admit the truth. Perhaps it was time, long past time for Angela to tell him what he needed to know.

Perhaps he should have insisted long ago. In retrospect, he'd been too easy on her, far too patient.

"Before we go any further"--he pulled up a chair and sat down beside her, pulling her onto his lap--"I want you to admit that you weren't a virgin, as you pretended to be that night in New York. I've accepted the fact, but you need to do the same."

"Lies?" she stared at him as if he'd lost his mind. She studied him, and all he could see in the depth of her blue eyes was quiet despair.

He ran a finger beneath her chin, forcing her to meet his gaze, meaning to entice from her the words she seemed so reluctant to say. "You know what lie I'm talking about." His voice was smooth, his heart unyielding.

Beneath his fingers he could feel the blood in her veins race, and he watched her breasts heave frantically. When he brought his gaze to meet hers, what he saw there nearly stopped him from his determined course.

"I haven't lied to you," she whispered, even as his fingers dipped lower, felt soft, yielding curves. To hell with compliance, he thought. He needed his little hellion back. Sometime during this trip, his spitfire had vanished into the murky depths of his memory.

"Why won't you admit that I was not your first lover?" Having to ask infuriated him. "Why?"

When his finger touched the rose crest of her breast, she inhaled softly, her voice trembling. "Please, can we just forget that night?"

"No, I can never forget. It stands between us," he said, and he touched the other silken globe, his fingers tracing lazy circles, seducing her.

"Tell me, Angela. You like this, don't you? You like to be touched. In fact, you like it so much you don't care who touches you. Any lover will do. Isn't that a fact?"

He hated himself for the words he unthinkingly spoke, but there was no way to call them back.

Visibly squaring her shoulders, she pushed him aside. Her body trembled as she grappled with the fastenings of her bodice, which he'd expertly undone in a few short minutes.

"No." Her voice shook. "Go away. You are not worthy of my love, Alexi. I wouldn't have you if you were the last man on this earth. I hate you. Do you hear me? I detest the very sight of you." She trembled from head to toe.

"I could change your mind." To his ears, he sounded too polished, too smooth. "I can pleasure you until you call out my name."

"You promised," she said, her back turned to him, her head high, every muscle in her body tensing.

"To hell with promises! I've been patient and caring, concerned only with your needs. No longer. I want you. Now."

His rage astounded him. Allah, but she was a courtesan, a little tease, and she still thought to deny him. He would allow it no more.

His voice sounded like low thunder. He swept her off her feet. In the next second he deposited her on the bed like a piece of fluff. That was what she was, a delicate piece of fluff, an adorable lady with the morals of an alley cat. He would teach her that he was the only tomcat she could have.

"No," she said.

The single word sounded breathless and airy:

She was still playing games; she squirmed beneath him, responded to the onslaught of his hungry kisses. Stroking his back, she gave in to him, and the reality of his blatant seduction of her left him empty and cold. Yet he didn't hesitate.

He took advantage of the moment, her clothing coming off slowly, her dress, her petticoats, her stockings and undergarments, everything, until she lay naked to his gaze. Her soft curves tortured his senses. She was his Aphrodite, a goddess of sensual delights.

"You promised," she said.

Moisture filled her eyes. The tears wrenched at his soul and effectively stopped him.

Allah, but she was beautiful.

Revulsion at his own actions swept through Alexi. He backed off, his feelings mercurial where Angela was concerned. The truth should not be that hard for her to tell.

"I did promise," he reluctantly admitted, and rose over her, unable to keep the depth of his frustration from showing. "One day you'll give in to your desires. I'll be here for you, but I'm not going to beg or plead. Don't wait too long."

Naked and vulnerable, Angela lifted her chin defiantly. I've never slept with any man but you."

One eyebrow rose. His anger resurfaced when he should have ignored her statement. For the life of him, he could not understand why her confession meant so much to him. "The lack of your maiden shield tells me something quite different, don't you think?"

Once again Angela ignored his comment. Her face a deathly white, she wrapped the sheet around her, tucking in the ends to hold it in place, and rose from the bed. Her manner arrogant, she walked to the table set for them by Misha. The atmosphere was too strained, too tense, the air nearly crackling with the passion emanating from the two of them.

He didn't dare risk her anger.

Her nonchalance in the midst of such anxiety was a soothing balm to his soul. Even if he lived to a ripe old age, he would never understand her. She was so unlike any other woman he'd ever met.

Then, in a prim, stilted voice, her words softly spoken, she asked, "Would you like some wine?" She grappled with the sheet and the wine, her elbows pinning the recalcitrant material to her sides.

Suddenly he was assailed with the urge to smile at the endearing picture she made. In one hand she held a carafe of his best burgundy, and in the other a crystal glass he'd always reserved for special occasions. This occasion was supposed to be special. His intentions had been honorable. He should have made her his cherished mistress by now. Instead they were still at odds, and he still waited for a confession he sensed she would never give him.

Misha had set the table for them, and he'd placed a candle in the middle. With the setting of the sun, shadows danced in the room. The waters were calm, the weather outside balmy. He'd wanted to enjoy this evening on the Mediterranean with Angela.

Single-handedly he had ruined the atmosphere with his callous, uncaring words. In his mind, he owed her an apology, and she owed him the truth. Neither would be forthcoming anytime soon.

He waited to reply while he studied her. Finally he said, "Yes," and pulled out a chair for her. "I'd like wine."

The time he had spent wooing her now seemed like a strange learning period. For Angela it must have been a time of adjustment, and he hadn't helped. If anything, he'd made matters worse. Except for the fact that he could never marry her, there was no reason for his violent reaction to her lack of virginity.

The glass was full to the brim, and she hesitated, a mysterious light in her eyes. "Then I'd be happy to give this to you."

The second before she tossed the wine at him, he read her intent, but it was too late to stop her. He felt the cool liquid touch his face before he could react. Then he chose not to do anything.

Alexi wasn't sure how to deal with her tantrum. He needed to let her rid herself of the anger she'd been dealing with for several days now. Perhaps this would make her more accommodating.

"Your aim was a bit off. Perhaps you'd like to try again?" His words sounded practiced, as if he'd had wine thrown in his face on more than one occasion.

Her cheeks flushed a hot scarlet. "Fine."

Before he realized she truly meant to take him up on his suggestion, she'd poured another glass, and once more she tossed red burgundy in his face. Still unsure of how to react, he licked the wine from his lips.

Deep inside he was laughing at himself and applauding her.

"Good." He poured himself a glass, anticipation and his imagination making him bold. He had visions of exactly where he meant to pour the wine and just how she would taste wearing the rich liquid.

Silently he walked around her, traced a finger along her shoulders, kissed the column of her neck, and let the wine in his glass run down the valley between her breasts and across them, soaking her sheet.

She inhaled sharply. "You did that on purpose," she whispered. "It's cold."

"I could warm it up."

This fight felt too dignified, the woman too unruffled--too prim. She had stiffened, and with ladylike finesse she was slowly pouring another glass. He tried not to think of the cost and tried to focus on the taste of her wine soaked flesh.

Both crests were clearly defined beneath the wet sheet. He had stepped on the hem when she had moved to pour herself a glass.

"If you don't want me licking the wine from your silken skin, I *suggest*"--he emphasized the word *suggest*--"you drink what's in your glass. You can't win," he said, his voice assuming a tender note.

"What if I don't want to drink it?" She was backing away from him, her eyes wide, but no longer with fear or sadness. There, clearly seen in her eyes, was the sassy lady he remembered.

"Do you want to toss it in my face again?" he purred, and stepped toward her, creating a game of retreat and advance between the two of them.

She nodded, her grip on the glass tightening, her hold on the sheet around her slipping.

"Toss it," he challenged.

Her hands quivered, and within the crystal the wine rippled violently.

"Toss it, Angela. Throw the wine in my face."

"I've changed my mind," she said, her voice rich velvet.

"I didn't hear you." He leaned closer to her. Her back was up against the wall.

A little bit louder: "I don't want to throw it in your face."

"Then what do you plan?" he asked. He kissed the tip of her nose and her forehead. He licked wine from her collarbone, nipping at her silken flesh and reveling in the taste of her soft skin covered in burgundy. She made no protest.

"Angela!" he barked, and in the next instant he exploded away from her, the front of his pants soaked with sweet red wine.

Her grin was heart-stoppingly beautiful, her voice soft. "Is it cold?"

Her lashes fluttered endearingly.

"Allah," he said, "but you know about the element of surprise. I do believe you won this battle. I surrender to your tender ministrations. Have mercy."

Angela laughed, her hands raised to her mouth, her eyes twinkling. It occurred to Alexi that it had been a very long time since he'd heard her laugh. His deep, throaty chuckle joined hers.

For a few long seconds she looked at him, endearingly shy and utterly beautiful.

"If you get to lick the wine from me, it is only fair that you give me the same privilege," she said.

Every muscle, from his head to his toes, tightened. He thought of her lips on his wine-soaked body. "There is nothing fair about this," he gritted out, and once again he swept her off her feet, the sheet slipping from her breasts to pool around her waist.

They fell upon the bed, his mouth closing hungrily over hers and her soft, loving sounds echoing in his throat. A tenderness so intense he could barely hold himself back swept through him.

Then he felt her arms curling around him. Felt her fingers teasing through his hair, drawing him closer. Her mouth parted timidly, yet met his fevered urgency.

The ship sped swiftly across the water.

"Sweet angel," he whispered. "Don't deny me again."

He continued to kiss her, his hand stroking down to her ankle, lifting and parting the sheet as he brought his fingers back to her waist. She clung to him, meeting the demands of his lips, seeking and then finding him. Her eyes were closed, her lashes damp, her urgency undeniable.

She hummed when he stroked her, sighed when she touched him, purred deep in her throat when he suckled her. He thought he'd died and gone to heaven.

He tugged at the buttons to his breeches, freeing himself. Yet as he shifted, he felt the slowing of the ship beneath them, and for a brief moment wondered why.

His desire raged, yet it was tempered. He meant to take the longest time, meant to satisfy her in every way. Yet when he would have moved with slow precision, she cried out his name, moving against him, responding wildly to his caress. He struggled mentally for control, knowing it was a lost cause.

He meant to learn her softness firsthand.

The ship stopped. Alexi paused, his hand quickly moving to cover Angela with a bed sheet.

He listened.

Pounding feet overhead was the only warning. A cannon shot exploding near the *Mystic* had Alexi springing from the bed and groping for the buttons of his pants.

Three shots in rapid-fire succession. The boat rocked, water spraying outside the window in glistening droplets.

"Stay here," he said. "Bolt the door." He had fastened his pants and was even now slipping his arms through his shirtsleeves. "Get dressed."

"Alexi?"

He kissed her hard then he was gone.

~ * ~

Stunned by all that had happened, Angela touched one finger to her lips. She had almost made love to him. If not for the ship firing on them, she would have. Suddenly she fully realized the impact of what was happening outside.

"Pirates? Barbary pirates?" *Surely not.* He had Turkish relatives.

Yet the sounds and the thought of pirates sparked a sense of primal fear deep inside Angela. Before she'd first heard the staccato rhythm of booted feet above her, she'd promised herself she'd stop Alexi before he made love to her. The day had been filled with tension and fear for herself, and she knew that without a doubt she would never have been able to stop him. She would never have said no.

Perhaps this had been a godsend. Not if it were indeed pirates attacking the ship.

The clipper ship answered back with cannon shot of its own. Angela sat up. Without knocking, Misha opened the door. There was an urgency about him.

"Lock it," he said and was gone.

Then she heard the grappling irons, the grinding of wood against wood, the men yelling and shouting.

Through the window, she looked out across the wide expanse of sea that stretched away from the *Mystic*. Another ship close by unfurled its sails and seemed to hover, waiting in the stillness.

It did not fly the skull and crossbones, but the flag of its country of origin. There was nothing about the flag to spark fear in her heart. Ships didn't fly a country's colors then attack another ship.

It was unheard-of. It was a declaration of war.

Those thoughts came unbidden to her mind, and raw fear spiraled through her--fear and denial. She pushed her face to the glass, trying to see as much as possible.

Angela's heart raced, thundering loud and clear in the sudden silence that seemed to encompass the ship. As quickly as the sounds had begun, they ended. The men on the *Mystic* must have surrendered. Probably the wisest course, she told herself.

Boots hammered across the ship above her and down the stairs toward the cabin. She clung to the sheet, held it against her nakedness, trembling. She should have dressed. She should have locked the door.

It was too late now. If they meant to harm her, she would fight. There was nothing else she could do.

How many of them were there? A whole shipful. Alexi wouldn't let them have her without a fight. That meant only one thing: he lay dead in a pool of blood on the deck of the *Mystic*.

Strangely, she'd heard no sound of swords. Not one gunshot had filled the air. Only the cannon blasts had pierced the lazy day. Lazy, until they'd been boarded by pirates.

She trembled, desperately clinging to the sheet, her back against the wall. Alexi had wanted her, had offered to give her all she desired, and she'd refused him time and again.

Now what would happen to her?

Angela jerked when the door opened, her shoulders trembling with fright at the sight of the man standing boldly in the door. The pirate had come for her, and she knew she'd end up in some Turkish harem.

She heard laughter and shouts, and she wondered at that.

Holding on to her dignity by a fragile, single thread, she rose to her feet. Once again she had a sheet wrapped around her. Suddenly, while she stood trembling with fear, Alexi burst through the men, pushing all but one out of the doorway.

"I told Misha to have you bolt the door." He looked furious.

He had every right to be. She'd told him she would obey him if his commands were reasonable.

The door slammed shut. He glanced at Angela, then at the man standing boldly in the cabin.

"Don't be frightened, Angela," Alexi said, his voice now calm and soothing.

She could barely breathe, could barely speak, and he was asking her not to be afraid. 'What does he want? Tell me what he wants."

Instantly Alexi stood beside her, wrapping her in a dressing gown, hovering in front of her so the man could not see her. He lifted a hand, indicating the seat by the window.

"Alexi," she whispered again, "tell me what he wants."

The man laughed, his gaze focused on her. "I want to meet the woman who has stolen my son's heart," he replied.

The man who stood in front of her was bold and audacious. He was dark and mysterious, his eyes twinkling with mirth.

Her heart pounded. "Your son?" The rumors were true. His father was a Turkish sultan.

He nodded.

"And he's about to find out that he shouldn't have barged in here," Alexi said, his anger obvious to Angela.

"Alexi?" she questioned. Her eyes met his.

Angela's gaze returned to the man who'd entered the cabin unbidden, arrogantly assuming he could do as he pleased.

"Father," Alexi implored, "you must leave. This is not well done of you. She is my woman."

His father wore a white shirt and formfitting black pants. He carried no weapons, posed no threat as he stood with his hands braced on his hips. His face was chiseled, strong. His eyes were cold and hard, and they penetrated like ice as he looked her over. His hair was the same shade as Alexi's, his shoulders not quite so broad nor his height quite so intimidating. His mustache and beard were slightly silvered. She should have known this man was Alexi's father.

Alexi was made in his image.

"You've seen too much already." Alexi growled low and deep. "You're my father, but that doesn't give you the right to--"

"Stare at your woman?" he asked, a chuckle following.

"You're more Eastern in your ways than even I imagined and prayed. You do not forsake your real people even while you embrace your new family. This is good." He spoke softly, but the sound carried through the room. Like Alexi, it was the voice of a man accustomed to being obeyed.

Chapter Thirteen

Moonglow shone softly against the backdrop of the warm Mediterranean night. With his father beside him, Alexi stood at the bow of the *Mystic,* Karim's ships cutting the sea protectively around them.

Alexi had expected something like this from his father, but Karim had gone too far when he barged into his cabin to confront Angela. Karim and his bodyguards had seen more of her than Alexi deemed appropriate.

"Why are you here, and why do you take such liberties?" Alexi's fingers bit into the sleek wood, his emotions tempered only by the knowledge that his father must have good reason for acting so brazenly and against a time-honored code.

"You're not glad to see me?" Karim asked, a strange smile slanting across his face.

"I'm honored you've gone to so much trouble, and yes, I'm glad to see you."

Karim stared out at the ocean before turning back to Alexi. "I've received a message from your grandmother." Karim let that statement hang in the air. "Actually, I've received quite a few in the years you've been away. But this is the first one that sparked my interest. I knew you would return home."

Karim stood near Alexi, his hands clasped behind his back, his gaze once more focused ahead.

"I'm sure you have received many. I didn't tell her where I was going or what I was about. She would have interfered in my life, and at the time I needed to be left alone."

Alexi turned, trying to relax--not succeeding by any means.

"So it was you who forwarded the letter," Alexi said.

"I knew the missive would bring you home." Karim chuckled and pointed toward the east, his eyes cast there reverently. "The old lady is a powerful force--one to be reckoned with--and stubborn to a fault. I don't believe Attila the Hun could have ignored her for long." Once again there was a long pause. "I admire her. She means well, though at times I am hard-pressed to agree with her. She has made a grave mistake this time, and wished for my intervention in the matter. I sent Ivan."

"Ivan?" One eyebrow rose in speculation. "Grandmother is not easy to ignore. All her life she has manipulated events so she would have her way. What is this mistake you speak of?" Curiosity drew him. His grandmother was also not known to admit to mistakes easily.

"It would not be so in my country. She would understand her place."

"The Ottoman Empire is dying, and the ways of the Western world are already creeping into the country. What is it you heard from my grandmother?"

"Natasha writes that she's picked out a wife for you. Her name is Feodora. Do you know her?"

Alexi nodded. "There isn't a nobleman in all of the East who doesn't know of Feodora," he said, his tone filled with sarcasm. "I guessed she had picked a bride for me. I did not know who until just now." His instincts warned him his father had more to reveal--much more--and he'd do so in his own sweet time.

"Do you know anything about her?"

"Very little that isn't founded in rumor. Her noble blood would make her a suitable wife for me or anyone else. Yet if what I've heard of her is true, I'd never know who fathered the children that grew in her belly. She's had countless affairs, lifts her skirts to any man who glances her way." He hesitated. "I believe I would like to find out for myself what the lady is like. Although I'd trust Ivan's opinion."

For different reasons, Feodora would be no more suitable as a wife than Angela. At least he cared for Angela.

And Angela would be true to him...

Alexi's heart skipped a beat, and he inhaled a ragged breath. *She would be true to me.*

"That is good to know." Karim's voice was solemn. "Ivan

volunteered to watch over her until you returned. He vowed that Feodora would be big with his child by the time you found the estate again. That way she can in no way force an unwanted marriage and a bastard on you."

Alexi smiled thoughtfully. "Such a task he's taken on. One look at Ivan, and Feodora would be lost. She could never resist a handsome man."

"That was the purpose. Natasha and Ivan and I have plotted to save you from her loose ways. You must find a wife suitable for your station and one who is faithful; then you can take as many mistresses as you want."

Alexi wanted only one woman in his bed.

Angela...

She still hadn't told him about her father or her name. Misha hadn't told him either. Events were truly out of hand.

~ * ~

Feodora was sicker than she'd been in all of her adult life. Bent over at her waist, she lost her breakfast for the third day in a row. Moving slowly, she made her way to the pitcher of water on her nightstand and rinsed her mouth. She spit it out, afraid to swallow, afraid to move lest the horrible retching begin all over again.

Since Ivan had come to Alexi's estate, everything had changed for the worse. He would smile at her, and against her better judgment she gave herself to him. She could not exorcise him from her mind. His body looked and felt like an aphrodisiac. He left her aching and needing. When she looked at him, she would begin to tremble, and she would inevitably break out in a cold sweat, her heart pumping fiercely, her breath coming in shallow, ragged pants.

She hated Ivan, and he detested her, but they fit together like a hand to a glove. He filled her like no other. She knew his intentions were to soil her already tarnished reputation to a state where no one would want her, where Alexi would not marry her. Unable to stop herself, she still came to him in the middle of the night, begging for his attentions.

She knew she was shameless.

If she didn't wed Alexi, her father would have her thrown from his house and disowned. She would be left with nothing.

It seemed Ivan had succeeded in his mission. He had completely despoiled her, where no one else had. She'd always managed to lose the babies she'd conceived.

Until now.

"Sweet Jesus." She moaned and gave in to her sickness once more, every muscle screaming in protest.

She felt Ivan's presence beside her, before she was able to acknowledge him. He knew her condition.

"Go away," she finally said, unwilling to see his victorious grin. "Leave me to die in peace."

Soothingly, he touched her back, massaging her, working the kinks from her aching muscles. "You are not dying. This is perfectly normal, as well you know."

"How?" she asked.

He laughed, the sound booming in the quiet of the warm morning sun. "You dare ask? Why, I thought you were well versed in the ways of men and women."

"You know what I mean." She turned and accepted the cool glass of water Ivan handed her, once again not daring to swallow.

One of Ivan's dark eyebrows rose in amusement as he stared at her, humor written in every nuance. "I do?" he questioned, his eyes twinkling a challenge she wanted to ignore. "I would not dare to attempt to figure out the workings of your mind."

She quelled the response on the tip of her tongue. It wouldn't do to anger this man when her entire life rested in his hands, now that he'd succeeded in his mission.

"Of course you do. The potion..."

"Ah, the potion." He lowered himself to his haunches, his powerful thighs bulging as they accepted his weight. His finger lifted her chin so she could not turn from his gaze. "I doctored it so my child would not be aborted. All life is precious, especially a child's. You will protect this life inside you."

She stared at him, her mind blank. "You hate me so very much," she said softly.

He grinned, his smile broad. "That is where you are wrong. There is no woman on the face of this earth I could hate. I love them all, and they all love me. And, Feodora, I will see to it that this child of mine is well taken care of."

"What will happen to me--and the babe?" she asked, her hand slowly lowering to touch her abdomen. "Will you marry me and give the child your name?"

He shook his head. "The child will have a name, and you will be taken care of, but marriage to me? No. I am not yet ready for such a blessed state."

Anger flared, and the need for retribution surfaced. "I will kill you."

One handsome eyebrow quirked in speculation. "The father of your child? I think not."

"Yes. You dare imply that you could take care of the babe in the manner of his station, You--a lowly stable master." She sneered, her hate escalating with each beat of her heart. He wouldn't dare.

"Stable masters make love to the ladies of estates quite often. It is something acceptable in most circles."

"I will tell Alexi you forced me."

Ivan shook his head at her. "You will not. You will not be here when he returns from America. I will make sure you are safe and protected in a place of my choice. And I will see to your marriage. For you, I will find a suitable mate, one who will keep you well satisfied all the days of your life."

She gritted her teeth against the hate welling in her breast. "You cannot abduct me, and you cannot make me wed a man I've never met."

"But I can. The men of my family have been doing that very thing successfully for hundreds of years. Where I am going to take you, you'll never be able to leave unless I give you my permission. The man you marry will keep you in chains if you defy him, yet if you are a sweet, biddable wife, he will treat you with the care and understanding a wife deserves."

Fear snaked through her, yet her body shivered with delight at his words. She would marry a powerful man, a wealthy one. Perhaps this would not be so very bad.

"Who is this person? Where will you take me?" Curiosity seemed to be getting the best of her.

"Not far from here. I am glad to see that you are becoming more accepting of your new future." He rose, towering above her, one hand placed firmly on a lean hip, the other on her shoulder.

Ivan was all man, pure, unleashed masculine power, all she'd ever wanted. He would not be easy to forget. Perhaps she could have Ivan and a husband, too. Wheels were already spinning in her brain.

Suddenly she knew the truth of his words. She'd played the game his way and lost, and now she decided she might enjoy what he planned for her. She would never give him the satisfaction of learning how easily she'd given in to his wishes, though.

"You can't possibly think to hold me." She felt a carnal shiver at her own words. Perhaps they would trigger a primitive memory in him, and he would make love to her again, one more time before he gave her up.

"Your future husband will hold on tight to you."

"I will find a way out," she countered.

"Across miles of desert sand? In your condition? You cannot even leave this estate on your own. You haven't the resources. I'm leaving to meet Alexi and Misha. Natasha has left to see to a sick friend. You will stay here and you will cause no mischief. When I return, I will see to your future."

Primal fear swept through her. Ivan meant every word he spoke. *Across miles of desert sand.*

This arrogant man towering over her was no stable master. She'd made the worst mistake of her life and didn't know what to do.

"Who are you?"

He laughed deep in his throat, the sound booming through the trees surrounding them. His hands were held high over his head, his face pointed upward.

"I am the man who will see you mastered."

~ * ~

"Ivan!"

Through what seemed like a seething mass of humanity, Alexi saw his wayward cousin.

"Alexander. There you are!"

Luckily, Ivan was tall enough to stand above the men and women gathered on the docks. Amid fishermen and merchants unloading their wares in the busy port, Alexi hadn't expected to see anyone he knew, least of all Ivan.

Ivan had always had an uncanny sense of where he was and what he was about. He waved in return to his cousin's call and pushed his way through the crowded wharf. A vendor cried out to him.

Alexi wondered again for the hundredth time if he hadn't been a fool to bring Angela here. He'd never had so many misgivings in his entire life. His country and its ideals would be difficult for Angela to adjust to, just as she was having so much trouble adjusting to the idea of becoming his mistress.

She would have to take grave care in this city. For almost two hours this morning while they were waiting for the tide to change, he'd tried to explain both of his countries and the way of life he took for granted. As he explained, he found that some of the customs were no longer acceptable to him.

After his father had left the ship and given the *Mystic* safe escort through the Black Sea to this port, he'd not had the heart to return to Angela until the morning tide. He wanted to know if he could make her happy before she became pregnant with his child. He needed to know if she'd stay with him of her own accord. For the two of them it could be no other way.

On the other hand, he could not bear to let her go. Thoughts of living without her forced him into a cold sweat. If she already carried a child of his, he would lock her in a room to keep her with him.

Pushing through the throngs of people, he realized how much he'd changed, how much America had changed him. This was not a life he could adapt to easily, even if he wanted to.

He made his way to Ivan at last, who embraced him quickly and drew him away, smiling wryly. "Are the rumors true? Do you bring a lady with you to be your mistress? Come on to the caravan and tell me all that has happened since you left. The minute Natasha heard you would arrive she sent me to find you and bring you home. Naturally, you could have made the proper arrangements for yourself, but I thought it prudent to greet you and let you know what has been going on in your absence. Have you heard anything?"

Alexi shook his head. He had heard only what his father had allowed him to hear. He knew little of what had transpired in the years he'd been gone, other than the fact of his mother's former husband's death, followed in two short weeks by the death of one of his half brothers. And of course he had heard the news concerning Fedora, the woman his grandmother had chosen for him. He welcomed another man's view of this situation.

"I have to send word to Misha where we'll be. He'll see that Angela reaches the caravan safely."

"Make sure you veil her properly. If she is blond and blue-eyed, she'll be fair game for any slaver's in the vicinity. You'd never find her."

Alexi hissed sharply, his emotions reeling. "I've been gone for too long, cousin. I had forgotten the customs and the hidden dangers of this country. I've forgotten too much."

"Misha would have remembered. He has always been the practical one."

"Always," Alexi agreed.

While Alexi absorbed the atmosphere in the flamboyant port city, and thought about how good it should feel to be home, Ivan gave instructions to a trusted messenger and sent him back to the *Mystic*.

Alexi inhaled deeply. The air was redolent with exotic spice and sweat from the men and women clustered together, and it was swept by the dry desert winds gusting off the sands surrounding the city.

"When do we leave?" Alexi asked, eager to get home and away from the dangers here. Despite his reasons for leaving and the nostalgia he carried for the States, he was anxious to return. Everything would be different now. He would have full control over the people working his land and the estate money.

They walked through the city, passing vendors hawking their wares. Alexi bought a sack of oranges to share with Angela this evening. He eyed the colorful material, the silken, sheer fabrics and thought wistfully of Angela dancing for him garbed in the clothes of his mother country. Music filtered through the vending stands, reviving his memory.

On the outskirts of the city, Ivan had indeed assembled a caravan of strength. There were twenty of his desert warriors, playing cards in the shade of a few trees, their horses grazing near the spring. Camels waited nearby, and there were plenty of animals to carry them and their possessions. In the Turkish custom Ivan had spared no expense or luxury.

Ivan and Alexi took shelter from the afternoon heat in one of the tents set up for his use. Inside, a plush Oriental carpet was spread out on the floor. Pillows lay in abundance; every comfort had been obtained, and nothing was left to chance. A young girl poured wine and brought refreshments for the men, then left.

Alexi relaxed on the pillows, sipping his wine. It felt good to be pampered. His thoughts turned to Angela, and he wondered when she'd arrive and if she'd still feel amenable to him.

First things first, he thought. "Tell me about Feodora," Although his father had already told him that Feodora was unsuitable, Alexi was interested in Ivan's point of view.

Ivan slanted him a crooked smile. "In a few months she will be huge with my child, Alexi. No, Feodora would not make you a good wife. I plan to take her to my tribe in the desert, far away from the estate and any mischief she might find. Najjar lost his wife and child to an epidemic last spring. He needs a woman's comfort."

Alexi made no comment while Ivan rambled on, but let his thoughts spin back to Angela--the way she felt in his arms, the way she tasted when he suckled her, the smell of jasmine that always surrounded her.

Ivan continued. "Feodora is a bit of a shrew, but Najjar will not care as long as she warms his bed passionately. That I'm sure she will do just fine. Feodora is a woman who needs to be often and thoroughly pleasured."

"Najjar? He is..."

Ivan made a lewd gesture with his hands. "If what the maidens say is true, Najjar is... well endowed," Ivan finally said with a grin on his face.

"He will keep her barefoot and pregnant," Alexi laughed softly. And then, "You feel nothing for her?"

Ivan paused a second. "Nothing special. Nothing that would bind her to me. Najjar needs a woman of her talents, and in turn he will keep her well loved. He has a huge sexual appetite as does Feodora. They are made for each other. By the end of another week she would have worn me down."

"She would not have been suited as a wife for me?"

"No, when I made love to her she'd already known many men. She was no virgin, and you must marry an innocent woman with noble bloodlines. Nothing less will be accepted by your grandmother or the serfs who reside on your estate. Have your mistress, but you must find a wife soon. So much depends on it."

"I suppose Natasha has someone else picked out for me."

Ivan laughed and shook his head. "She threw up her hands in aggravation. Decided she was a terrible matchmaker and didn't dare risk it again. You must travel north to Moscow and pick someone out yourself. Your grandmother will accompany you. She has made the plans already. If everything goes smoothly, she will return in a week so that both of you can leave together."

Going to Moscow to pick a bride... Alexi didn't much like that idea. Travel would take time from Angela, and he would have to leave her alone. Ivan and Misha would take care of her. She would be safe in their hands. Fears that Angela would leave him if given half a chance loomed heavy in his mind. He would have her promise not to leave.

Alexi stopped brooding suddenly. "How long until Angela arrives?"

Ivan, who was standing at the opening of the tent, grinned. "Coming across the sand with Najjar right now. You can meet Najjar. I will wait for your approval."

Alexi pulled the flap of the tent back. Najjar stood a head and a half taller than Alexi's petite hellion. Najjar saw Ivan, smiled, waved and turned to Angela, who was walking with her hands folded in front of her and her head bowed behind the big man. Misha walked behind Angela. Alexi wanted to laugh at the strange picture. Angela had never looked subservient. She still didn't.

Angela was dressed hi black veils that covered her from head to toe. He could not see any part of her. As they moved closer he could see the outline of her face behind the sheer black veil covering her.

The buzz of the camp seemed to fade, and he made his way quickly through the throng of people to reach her. He offered Misha and Ivan a quick nod then reached for Angela's hand, drawing her into the fold of his embrace.

It was only then he realized that despite the brave show she put on for everyone around her, she was...

Quite simply trembling.

He frowned, worried he'd expected too much of her. He quickly readjusted his stance, slipping an arm around her shoulders and offering silent reassurance. Ivan's men seemed to press around them, even as he led her back toward the tent. "I'm sorry, Angela. I should have realized travel through the city would have been treacherous for a woman. I shouldn't have relied on Misha and Najjar as guides," he whispered to Angela.' 'Had I thought on it I would not have left you alone."

She turned slightly in his arms, her face angelic with forgiveness. "Alexi, I'm fine. The guided tour was fascinating. There is so much going on. Misha explained everything to me. It is truly an adventure."

"You're sure?" Alexi wanted to touch her gently, wanted to erase the fear she wouldn't admit to.

He didn't want her to be worried about travel across a land that was known for its thieves and dangers that could pop up at a moment's notice. And in truth, he wasn't at all certain she could make the trip. So far she'd shown amazing strength of character, but this land was rough and far more dangerous than anything she was accustomed to. A small, fragile piece of femininity such as Angela might surely die in this unforgiving land.

"You don't need to worry about me."

He didn't know what to say. She had changed enormously in the last month. She had grown pale and lost weight, but today she had a touch of color in her cheeks. Her lips were a deep rose hue, and her vibrancy gave her an enchanting appeal.

She seemed truly pleased to be there.

"Ah, so this is the exotic beauty, Angela, whom I've heard so much about," Ivan said as they reached the tent. "Now that you've finally arrived, perhaps we should go inside and talk about the trip north. We've food and wine, enough for an army of men. I've arranged for every comfort and need to be satisfied. You will want for nothing," he whispered.

"Quite right," Alexi heard himself saying firmly. "Ivan, as an expert on the desert, please advise Angela she should take every precaution as we cross."

Ivan ever so slightly arched a brow; in his life, he'd noted that strong women would never bow completely to their husbands or masters, they would always have their say. A wise man learned to humor his woman, pretend to listen to everything she had to say--and then made sure the woman was safe, even if it meant extreme measures had to be taken. America had changed Alexi. He certainly was not at ease with this woman; it was a new revelation. But Ivan played along with Alexi.

"Alexi speaks true. The crossing is dangerous."

On their way inside the tent, Alexi was startled to hear his name called then Ivan's. He turned to see one of Ivan's men. The man strode through camp, his hands clenched at his sides, his robes billowing behind him. Ivan clasped the man around the shoulders, greeting him.

"What are you doing here? You should be with the people, watching over them in my place," Ivan said, a frown deepening his brow.

"Would that I could." The man spoke softly, as if someone might overhear what he said. "I was the only man uninjured after the army of rebels swept down upon us, breaking all the treaties between us. The women and children who are still alive are crying out in hunger. The men are injured and dying. I have no idea which tribe it was. Indeed, I am not sure it wasn't mercenaries, they were so ruthless."

"Allah..." Ivan whispered.

"We captured one man, but he died before we could wring any information from him."

To Alexi's surprise and fury, Angela decided to answer for everyone. "We must go to your people and help them. We have food enough to feed an army. Isn't that what you just said, Ivan?" Angela looked pointedly at Ivan, her lips curved sweetly.

Alexi could have throttled her then and there, despite his tender feelings for her and the light in her soft blue eyes. She should learn not to speak out. Her advice would never be heeded. If she didn't watch what she said, she could put them both in a precarious position.

"Ivan, forgive her," Alexi said simply, stepping in front of Angela, wrapping an arm around her waist and pulling her toward him and to a position slightly behind him--a position of servitude. "She does not understand our customs. I will make sure there are no more problems."

Chapter Fourteen

Pain simmered deep inside Angela even while she acknowledged the truth of what Alexi had said. "Forgive?" Her whispered question went unnoticed. She was at a loss among these men and the strange customs.

"Go inside," Alexi said, parting the tent flap.

To find adventure had been her dream. Now all she wanted was to find a way home, to breathe the clean mountain air once more. She knew Alexi would take a wife and give another woman his name. She didn't want to be here when that happened. Yet even today, her thoughts when she had dressed had spiraled in a mad fashion. She already hated the unknown woman who would become his wife. Even if she had been of a mind to accept the position of mistress, being his lover would never be enough for her. She needed so much more.

Because she did want Alexi to love her.

She wanted their children to carry his name.

All that had transpired between them the last few months failed to matter now, and all that did matter was that she loved him. She loved him for his basic honesty, for his loyalty, for his stubborn determination, for his sense of right and wrong. And she loved the sight of him, the feel of his hands upon her, the way he looked at her with such smoldering intensity and possessiveness.

She loved the passion that darkened his eyes when he held her close.

Their lives were too different. They would never be able to reach an understanding, an amenable solution to their problems. He would never be able to put a lifetime of teachings and beliefs behind him, and she would never be able to live the lie he was asking of her.

Was trust too difficult?

Perhaps to Alexi it was.

The problem they faced now had nothing to do with them. She ached to do all she could to help his people and those of his friends. What she'd offered had not been so strange that she needed anyone's forgiveness.

Alexi sat by her later that night, commenting to Ivan on the strategies they would employ, and on the identity of the men behind the attacks on Ivan's people. He acted courteous throughout the evening, but subdued. His deep brown eyes looked almost black despite the light of the fire reflected in them, and Angela was afraid something was simmering in him that would eventually send her world catapulting apart.

At times she had the most disturbing premonitions of searing pain and blinding fear.

She meant to go with Alexi.

It was very late when the two of them were finally alone, watching the fire outside their tent die down. The embers glowed softly, the breeze from the desert blew warm and dry.

"Alexi?"

"I love this land," he said. The reverence she heard in his voice touched her heart.

Beside herself with emotion, she felt awkward and shy. "I don't want to leave here without you," she said, her voice a whisper. If he left her side, something bad would happen. With the wisdom born of her Sioux heritage, she sensed the future.

And she was afraid.

"We don't know what to expect," he said, still staring into the night. He extended his hand in a silent invitation for her to accept him. She did, and he led her inside the tent.

The long black robes she wore hid her body from view--had been purposely designed to do so. Inside the voluminous material, she felt strangely protected. Still, she was startled when she felt his hands upon the tiny fastenings at her neck. Insecurity gripped her. Even as she needed him to love her, she couldn't help but wonder how she could compare with the woman who would soon become his wife.

The robe unfastened, she held the black material to her breasts, whispered a thank-you, and stood in front of him wide-eyed and thoroughly distraught. He didn't seem to notice. He had already spread out numerous blankets and arranged the pillows then he lay down, his hands folded behind his head. She let the robe she'd worn over her dress fall to the floor. He paid her little heed as she sat down in the opposite corner, taking her hair down and brushing it out.

She touched her sapphire earrings. To Angela they signified bold adventure, daring feats and a bit of rebellion. When she wore them, she would always remember Devil Blackmoor.

Angela took them off and placed them out of sight and out of mind. She closed her eyes and for one long moment tried desperately to forget that what she wanted most was unobtainable.

"I don't understand what is expected of me," she said softly, determined that he must understand her position in matter concerning her behavior. "We had months on board the ship. You spent hours teaching me the language of your mother's people. You could have explained Turkish customs more thoroughly."

His gaze shot to her, and she froze uncomfortably, wishing she hadn't spoken. She had felt more at ease when he ignored her. "I won't let you put your life in danger. We don't know who attacked Ivan's village. I don't believe for a second they were neighbors. The treaties have been held and respected for too many years for any one of the neighboring tribes to put that at risk. There is something else afoot here, and I mean to discover the meaning of this outrage. Once, a very long time ago, Feodora's father attacked Ivan's village."

Fear spiraling deep inside her, Angela wrapped her arms around herself, feeling the shivers racking her body bone-deep. He wasn't listening to her. Instead he spoke of a treachery that must have occurred years past to Ivan's people.

Something terrible would truly happen to her if he left her alone in this strange place--alone to fend for herself. "You know I can shoot and ride better than most men. If I traveled with you, my life would not be in danger. I might even be of help," she challenged him, hoping he would recant his decision. "And you would be there to protect me."

"Really?" he questioned, the pause before his next question significant. His gaze bore into her. "Who are you, Angela? What is the truth?"

She turned from him. "I can't tell you."

"You expect me to trust you, believe in you, yet you won't trust me with your name?"

She turned back, and touched his sleeve, imploring him with her eyes. Her lies had gone on too long. If she told him now who she was, he might feel honor-bound to marry her. She didn't want to trap him. She wanted his love.

"Take me with you." Sam was in the Rocky Mountains, believing she was married to Alexi. Not for a minute would he believe she was about to become Devil Blackmoor's mistress. In her naiveté she didn't realize she'd just about told her father all in her final letter. She could have told Alexi more about herself, but she had been afraid the knowledge might lead to more truth than she wanted him to uncover. She wished heartily she could tell him she was Angela Chamberlain and he'd best treat her with respect and honor.

"From the start you haven't wanted to believe me. You formed a first impression and stuck with it. If I told you I grew up in a log cabin, that my father taught me to shoot and ride, that my uncle bought me an ivory-handled knife and taught me to use it with the expertise of a Sioux warrior, would you believe me? Would you believe I have a half brother who is a Sioux warrior... ?" she let her words hang in the air, watched for his reaction. To judge him now would be hard, but she had to know.

He rose on his elbows, his hair disheveled. "No," he said. "I'd believe you were a good storyteller."

Pain swept through her. She turned her back to him, unwilling to let him see the sheen of moisture gathering in her eyes, unwilling to let him see the depth of her fears. It seemed he would believe only half-truths and lies about her. She would tell him nothing more until he was ready to listen. Quickly she brushed away the tears, stifling a half sob before it erupted.

"Of course I'm a good storyteller. I learned that craft at my mother's knee. She is half-Sioux. Have I told you that? No? But then had I told you, you wouldn't believe me." She didn't want to belabor a worn-out point. "Apparently we are not going to settle anything this night."

She heard his exasperated sigh emanating from the blankets, the rumpling of pillows and crinkling of sheets. He seemed restless and out of sorts. The devil take him--he should be.

"There is nothing to settle, Angela." His voice in the surrounding darkness did little to ease her fears. "We're not in disagreement. Your past makes little difference to me. It is our future and your safety I am concerned with."

"Alexi, you don't understand. I've not accepted your bargain. I've made a promise to go with you, but my reasons are my own until I choose to divulge them. My background is not worth talking about; even though at times you wish to know about me, most of the time you care not. All you need to know is who I am now and who I will become."

"My lover," he said, his voice warm with passion. He rose suddenly, walking over to her, and she saw that he had not changed clothes. He had chosen to sleep in his buckskins, just as he'd done every night on the trail. He stood with his feet slightly apart, towering over her, pinning her with his gaze alone. "I know you don't accept the title of mistress, and I know you want something else from me, something I can't give--not because I don't want to but because I can't. Angela, I will prove to you I can take care of you and I'll never neglect you. You will want for nothing, and in time you'll be glad I insisted on this relationship."

"I'm sure you believe that what you say is true." She watched the moon and the stars through the open tent flap. They gave small comfort.

"You are stubborn to a fault, but I've come to admire that trait. Together we will have strong children."

"If things go your way, they will be children without a name," she whispered softly, then prayed Alexi had not heard.

"And if things go your way?" he asked.

"There will be no nameless bastards."

She could sense him stiffen, feel the anger emanating from him. She felt his presence before he turned her toward him, touched and lifted her chin. "You are under my protection, Angela. You will have to see this my way."

"But Alexi--"

"Men support and cherish the women they care for, and in turn the women give their love and affection," he informed her for what must have been the hundredth time, his voice rising slightly.

She tried very hard to control her simmering emotions.

"I've given you all I'm capable of. You cannot have my heart and soul. I will not allow you to have them. You cannot keep me here, and as soon as I find a way, I will leave."

He moved so swiftly she cried out softly, expecting to be swept into his arms and tossed upon the heap of pillows across the room.

She didn't know what she wanted--except peace.

But he did nothing other than caress her cheek and whisper softly against her ear: "I swear, Angela, you'll be the death of me before too much longer. I am damned if I touch you and damned if I don't. Go to bed. I'll join you later."

She was suddenly tired, and felt very strongly just how vulnerable she had become. This wasn't America, and Sam Chamberlain didn't look after her any longer. She was unmarried and on her own in a strange country, with only Alexi's good graces to rely on. She didn't want to make him angry. She wanted to curl up next to him and sleep with his arms around her, feel the warmth of him against her, and know his strength was there to ward off whatever might threaten. She'd wanted him to make love to her, yet now that they were alone again, she prayed for the strength to say no.

One time with him just wasn't enough, and yet one time had to last for an eternity.

He turned down the lantern by the bedside and walked to the tent opening, his back to her, his fingers gripping the canvas. He gazed at the same moon and the same stars she did. A slight breeze ruffled the fabric he held.

She curled up to sleep, turning her back to him as well.

When she closed her eyes, thoughts of Alexi burned in her mind. All the anger and the misunderstandings surfaced, and, searching her head for a way to convince Alexi of the truth, she found no peace. It seemed to her she lay alone in the bed forever, the wind whispering through the tent flaps, and soft moonglow filtering through the openings.

He didn't come back to bed.

At last she fell asleep but her own ear-splitting scream woke her what seemed like minutes later. He was beside her then, the makeshift bed dipping with his weight. He held her in his arms, stroked her back and made soft, soothing noises.

All she could remember of the dream was searing heat on her back, fire...

And endless pain.

The dream had been so vivid even closing her eyes did not make it vanish. Remembering it horrified her even more. She couldn't move. In her dream her wrists had been tied high on a pole, and with every second the fire searing her back raged higher. She cried out for help, but Alexi wasn't there to save her.

"It's all right, angel," he murmured softly, and with a sigh lay down beside her and pulled her to him. He didn't speak to her or ask what was wrong, and she was so glad that he'd given up his stubborn vigil that she didn't venture to say anything, afraid the fragile peace between them would rip apart at the seams once more.

She thought he slept, but he told her after a moment, "You need never fear as long as you're with me. I will see that no harm comes to you, Angela. You are mine."

"But you're leaving me alone," she said.

"Misha will be with you." The silence chilled her bone-deep. "Angela," he said, the weariness in his tone apparent, "I want your promise you won't try to leave, to escape him."

She shook her head, backing away from him. "No."

"Promise me."

Still she refused. "I can't do that."

He pulled her close. "I fear for your life. The desert is as treacherous as the mountains are dangerous. You don't know what's out there. Please, angel. When I return, we can talk. If you really want to leave, I will help you. Just give me this one chance."

His soft pleas blended with the exotic desert sound and stole Angela's will. She wanted to talk with Devil, needed to make him understand. "All right then." She spoke with little hesitation, knowing she would give him one more chance to right the wrongs he'd done. "I promise."

She heard his sigh, felt him relax against her. She closed her eyes, wondering about the future and what it would now bring. The wind whispered and the moon cast a glow inside the tent.

She pretended she slept. He would leave her soon, and who would save her from the searing heat that awaited her?

Who would protect her in this foreign land? Only Alexi could keep her from harm.

She could win no arguments tonight. With him it was a matter of semantics, and with her it was a matter of the heart.

~ * ~

Misha had taken Alexi's parting words to heart. He'd protect Angela and make sure every comfort he could offer was hers. Short of tying her down, he'd also make sure she could not leave the wagon train. Misha had personally seen to her food, made sure she had sufficient warmth in the evenings. It could get very cold in the desert, he'd said.

Over dinners he'd told her stories about Alexi, about his childhood and the manner in which he'd been brought up--things she'd never thought about. Alexi spoke nine languages fluently. He'd spent his early years in Constantinople with his father--the grand vizier--and his mother. He told her Alexi had only decided recently he would honor his mother's wish and adopt the Popov name. He had decided only when he'd been called home to Russia. Misha had told her what little he knew about Turkish customs. And he continued the language lessons Alexi had begun when they first started on this adventure.

Not wasting time on the road, they arrived at Alexi's estate at night. Even with a full moon casting its glow on the earth below, without Alexi the huge mansion high in the mountains appeared lonely and forbidding. No one came out to greet them.

It seemed as if everyone had deserted the home. The grounds and all the servants, she thought, slept peacefully, unaware of their arrival.

A horse nickered softly in the stable, and a lone dog barked somewhere behind the house. The common, everyday sounds warmed her heart. At least the animals spoke the same language here as they did in the States.

One faint light cast its glow from an upstairs window. Mysterious shadows moved around the front steps. For a brief second a curtain was drawn back. Someone watched them. The curtain fluttered closed, the light was blown out and all was as it had been.

Chills suddenly swept through to her bones. Angela shivered, running her ice-cold hands up and down her arms. She had never known fear like this. It was all-consuming, yet irrational. A clock inside chimed the hour. Its sound was that of a death knell.

"What is it?" Misha asked, almost as if he'd felt the same cold draft, the same spine-tingling terror.

"I don't know," Angela said, trying to shrug the eerie sensation off. "I'm just tired."

The journey had been exhausting and filled with fear. Her innate courage and strength had seen her through. She missed Alexi, his smile, his gentle touch.

Angela knew she was pregnant with Alexi's child, and she found herself needing to rest more often. She'd endured bouts of nausea and uncharacteristic fatigue for miles without complaining. She hoped the sickness and the exhaustion had gone unnoticed by Misha, but she wasn't sure.

Angela thought she'd be anxious to retire when they reached the house. Instead she felt an unexplainable anxiety, a foreboding deep in the pit of her stomach, and she knew she would be unable to sleep.

She looked at Misha, a man she'd come to rely on over the days that had passed. At times Misha had pushed them hard, saying the trail was dangerous and he would take no chances with Alexi's beloved. But at other times he'd made her rest, seen to her every whim.

Now the sight of the estate sent shivers all the way to her toes. She was thankful Misha wasn't going to leave her at the doorstep of this house that looked so very foreign and cold. This was Alexi's home. He'd spent part of his life roaming the grounds, catching fish in the rivers that swept by and playing in the abundant fields. Yet she didn't feel his presence here.

If she were to know more about Alexi, she would have to learn more about his home.

The people in the villages they'd passed earlier depended on him and his family for their education and their livelihood. What would her life be like if she were part of all this?

She would never have a place here. As his mistress she'd always be on the outside looking in. She would be an ornament, nothing more. Her heart ached for the love she'd never experience.

It was quite cold and damp, but when Misha helped her down, she forgot the discomfort and the ominous feelings she'd experienced when she first looked at the mansion. Determined to make the best of this situation, she shook off all the bad thoughts she'd harbored.

She spun around then realized everyone was watching her, including Misha. He looked tired as well, and was trying not to be impatient with her. It seemed he wanted nothing more than to escort her to her bed before finding his own.

"I will take you to your room. I'm sure the long trip has exhausted you."

"Of course," she said.

The long brick walkway was slippery; he held her elbow carefully, escorting her up the stairway to the porch. When they reached the top, Misha opened the door for her. As she stepped into the cold, empty hallway, the house became even more forbidding.

She inhaled a deep breath, summoning her courage.

"It will all feel different in the morning," Misha said.' 'When the sun is shining," he added, "this place will not seem so big and intimidating."

His encouragement lightened her steps but not her heart. She missed Alexi and his bold, sunny smile. Suddenly she missed the Rockies and the snow-covered peaks. "When will Alexi be back?" she asked, already feeling as if a part of her heart were missing.

"A few days, maybe a few weeks. It's hard to say." Misha led her up a curving staircase that rose immediately from the entry. The downstairs rooms branched off from either side of it. "You'll find the room quite nice. You must be exhausted," he repeated.

"Yes..." She touched his arm. "Thank you for all you've done."

He grunted away the thank-you, looking embarrassed by her words. "It was nothing. It's late, and you'll want a grand tour in the morning," he said, expecting her to follow behind him. "Alexi told me to put you in here." He opened a door, letting her step inside before he walked to another door across the room and opened it. "This door leads to his chamber."

Slowly she turned around, taking in everything. Her room was beautiful, more beautiful than any room she'd seen, except the one in the hotel in New York. It had a large bed covered with a thick blue quilt and piled with dark blue pillows. The oak furniture was massive, the wallpaper in a delicate blue floral pattern, matching the quilt, and the molding about the ceiling had been designed to mirror the paper.

"It's very nice," she murmured. But her heart felt lodged in her throat. It was her room. And it was next to his. Her parents didn't sleep alone. Alexi had insisted they share the same room and the same bed when they were on board the *Mystic*, but he didn't know for sure that she'd be his mistress then. Already he'd set her apart.

195

"If there isn't anything else, I'll leave you to rest." Misha started from the room but paused at the door.

She turned quickly. "Where will you be if I need you?"

"Down the hall and to the right," he said, then saluted sharply and left her. "I'll talk to you in the morning. I will give you that tour, if you want one." He smiled gently at her.

She watched him leave, staring at his back as he walked down the hall and through the door to his room. She heard the door click shut. She was alone.

For a long time Angela wandered the room, picking up a figurine, pulling back the white lace curtains at the window. She still felt restless and ill at ease. Her room looked over the front of the estate. She could see the long, tree-lined driveway leading to the front door. Moisture filled her eyes, and she fought the hot sting of tears welling deep in her throat. She didn't want to feel homesick.

She didn't want to miss Alexi either.

Someone had already brought her single bag to the room. She dreaded the thought of putting on the same nightgown she'd worn and laundered until it was slightly gray and paper-thin. She slipped off her traveling clothes and pulled the worn nightgown over her head.

She left the light burning and lay on her bed, staring at the ceiling, wishing sleep would not prove quite so elusive, wishing Alexi lay here beside her as her husband. Her hand drifted down to where her womb lay beneath. Inside her body she sheltered and nurtured a new life, Alexi's blood, his heir if he married her, his bastard if he didn't. They had lain together only once. A miracle, she thought; this tiny life was a miracle sent from God.

She would keep the miracle from God safe.

Angela did sleep, yet it seemed she'd just closed her eyes when a woman's shrill voice startled her awake in the sun-bright room.

"What are you doing in this chamber?" The question was harsh and biting.

Angela sat up, blinking the sleep from her eyes. Bright morning light filtered in through the window, the lace curtain painting delicate shadows across the bed. A young, very pretty woman stood beside her bed. Her black hair was tied into a tight chignon at the base of her neck, little ringlets dancing whimsically around the lady's face. Fashionably clothed in a mauve day dress, the woman looked down her long, aristocratic nose at Angela.

Beneath her skirts, the woman's foot tapped a rapid beat, an impatient staccato. "I asked you a question," she said, her lips pursed into a shrewish expression, her eyes tiny slits of pale brown. "You'd be well advised to answer immediately," she said in her native language.

Angela caught the drift of the lady's words and tried her best to answer in Russian. "Misha told me to stay here." For some reason this woman didn't like her. "Is something wrong?" Angela was determined not to let the lady frighten her. She pushed her hair back from her face, tried to blink the sleep from her eyes and resist the bone-deep weariness that assailed her.

"What is Misha to you? Is Ivan back? Natasha will not be pleased you're in this room. She wouldn't even let me stay .here, and I'm Alexi's betrothed. I want you out of here." The young woman gave a stamp of her tiny foot to emphasize the point. "Get out. Out!" Once again her voice turned shrill and she shook one finger in front of Angela's nose.

Alexi's betrothed?

"No," Angela said, her voice calmer than her racing pulse. The knife Dakota had given her lay nearby, but not close enough to reach. She'd suspected she'd be in danger here. She'd been right. This woman posed a threat to her greater than anything Alexi could have imagined on the trail, a threat greater than anything she'd faced in her lifetime--and once she'd gone nose-to-nose with a grizzly for a few minutes, until her father rescued her by shooting the beast. Common sense, the uncanny instinct for survival Angela had, cried out for her to be wary.

The young lady turned florid, her fists clamping together at her sides. "You will do as I say." She trembled as she spoke, her voice filled with loathing. "You will do it now!"

Angela smiled and raised her chin a notch. "Who is in charge of the house with Alexi gone?" Angela asked, unclear about her role or her rights. She knew Alexi would not allow her to stay in this room after he took a wife, but for now...

For now he wanted her here. He'd given Misha explicit directions.

The lady's chest swelled with arrogant pride. "I am, seeing that I'm about to become Alexi's wife. I'm in charge of everything that goes on here."

"Pity," Angela said, her voice soft but not low enough to keep the lady from hearing.

"Get out of my room." The woman's voice trembled with rage.

"This isn't your room." Angela rose, no longer afraid of this woman who seemed all talk and bluster. This creature had no backbone. "Very well." Angela had never wanted to sleep in this room, but she didn't want to give in to this lady's demands, either.

She would have to. Because she would not be safely ensconced in Alexi's room as his new plaything when he returned.

A long silence followed while the two women studied each other.

"What room would you put me in?" Angela asked, not liking the smug expression the woman gave her. Angela picked up her valise and headed for the door.

"You will earn your keep here," the lady said. "And you will address me as Miss Feodora."

"I'd like to speak with Misha first." Angela felt serenely calm and, for the first time since leaving New York, in control of her life. She wanted to keep it that way.

"Misha was called away. Someone is threatening his family's estate. His father spoke of an emergency--life or death. He will not be back soon."

Misha is gone.

She no longer had a protector. A sliver of ice slipped down her spine. Then she shook the feeling of doom off. She didn't need anyone to protect her. She was Sam Chamberlain's daughter. She could take care of herself.

Angela's fingers closed over the handle of her valise. She stood straight and tall, waiting for Feodora to give her directions to another room. Instead Feodora sent her to the kitchen.

"The cook will tell you what to do," Feodora called out, "and perhaps if you do all your duties correctly, she'll give you a pallet near the fire so you can stay warm. Russian nights do get so very cold."

Not for one minute did Angela intend to do Feodora's bidding, no matter what the woman thought. No, she intended to pass through the kitchen and grab a bite to eat, nothing more. After that she'd find someplace where she could think and figure out what she should do next.

Chapter Fifteen

Alexi had sent Angela's caravan across the desert and into the hills, and while he watched the wagon she rode in disappear from view, the wind whistled an ominous sound. Fear twisted down his back, and chills swept through him.

"Misha, keep her safe." His whispered words haunted him and lodged deep in his heart. "Don't let anything happen to her."

Angela had given him her word. She would keep her promise. So why did he feel this gut-wrenching fear? A fear he could not shake.

He prayed nothing would happen to them. Bandits and outlaws roamed the mountains freely, but he'd left the caravan well guarded. Rebel groups had risen around the country, but Angela was no threat to them.

"Ready?" Ivan stood beside him.

He nodded.

Alexi, Ivan and half of Ivan's men rode out two hours after Angela's caravan left the busy port city for his estate. They rode nonstop through the night and into the next day, taking an hour of rest at one of the known watering holes on the way.

Twelve hours later they rode into what was left of the ravaged village. The men who had decimated it left little but the burned-out shell of a few homes. Smoke still rose from the ashes of the buildings; Ivan's own home had also been decimated.

Men, women and children were gathered at the edge of the ruins in makeshift tents, tending to the sick and wounded. Babies cried from hunger and fatigue.

Alexi dismounted, then picked up a crying child and cradled the babe in his arms. The child looked at him with beautiful dark brown eyes and a curious expression just before he let out a loud, pitiful wail.

"Hush now, sweet one," Alexi said, rocking the child. He smoothed the dark hair on the baby's head, picturing a child of his and Angela's in his arms. His breathing stilled, the picture so vivid and real the impact on his heart stunned him.

"Hush," he whispered again. The little one was nuzzling him, his puckered mouth against his chest, searching for something Alexi could never give. Once again he thought on Angela, could picture her feeding his son, her angelic face, her soft hair flowing around her shoulders. "Allah."

What torment.

"Let's find your mother, shall we?" he crooned softly and rocked the child.

"That shouldn't be too difficult." Ivan nodded in the direction of a young woman who rushed toward them, arms held out.

The babe wailed louder. It seemed he knew exactly what he wanted.

Unable to stop the child's tears, Alexi handed the baby back to his mother.

"There you go," he told the infant, then turned. "Ivan!" he said harshly.

"I'm here," Ivan said, his shoulders tense, his voice racked with pain.

Ivan was there, talking to Najjar, making plans.

Ivan and Alexi set up a communications tent and began preparations to defend the villagers if the need arose again.

They spoke with everyone.

None of the villagers had seen anything but the death that surrounded them. All they had heard was the battle cry, "Revenge! Death to the tyrant!" When the attackers finally left, the people had worked feverishly to stop the fires and rescue their friends and relatives still trapped inside the burning homes.

The attack had been planned and executed with great expertise. The army of men melted into the desert sands afterward and left few survivors in any shape to follow.

Alexi vowed retribution.

Ivan swore to the gods--the Christian one and Allah--that the demise of their enemies would be slow and torturous.

They had struck in the middle of night. It had been swift and merciless. *Revenge.*

Alexi mulled the puzzling words over for hours.

Death to the tyrant.

Ivan was no tyrant, but his family was known for their despotic behavior. Then there was Feodora to consider. Her father had attacked once before. Now he had even more reason for retribution.

What if they never discovered the truth?

~ * ~

Angela Chamberlain sipped the hot black coffee and munched on the scones she'd pilfered from the kitchen when the cook wasn't looking. In a storage room, she had dressed in her buckskins and moccasins. Then she'd stridden from the grounds with her back straight and her chin pointed forward, never looking back.

The clear blue pond she'd passed while she rode on the wagon the evening before sparkled now with the dancing sun rays reflected upon it. The water beckoned for her to swim. Later, she thought, perhaps when the day warmed. A slight breeze blew in from the north, and a few high clouds lazed the day away. Toward the horizon was a bank of darker clouds.

The intolerable situation she found herself in left her vulnerable and angry, furiously so. Feodora was a dreadful woman, and Angela knew the lady had the potential to make her life miserable. Until Alexi returned, she'd have to be careful.

The intractable woman would become Alexi's wife.

Betrothed, indeed. Feodora would make Alexi's life miserable.

An answer to her problems would occur to Angela if she waited long enough. Yet she had an eerie feeling she'd hesitated too long in making a decision, and any delay might prove to be her downfall. If Feodora had appeared in her life at any other place or time, Angela would have left without a glance over her shoulder. If she chose to stay, she would have had the means to fight Feodora.

She had given Alexi a promise.

She'd promised him she'd be here when he returned. Angela had been brought up to honor a promise, to treat them as sacred.

She sat beside the pond. Her mind adrift, she idly plucked a piece of grass, twirling it between her fingers as she concentrated, and thought hard on her alternatives.

She could stay here, but Feodora had single-handedly decided Angela would become a scullery maid. Not just a simple servant, but one of the lowest-ranking people on the estate.

Hard work didn't bother her. It was something she was used to. All her life she'd had chores to do, hard chores. But this was different. Feodora had maliciousness foremost in her thoughts. The estate had more than enough servants; she'd seen that when she'd walked through the house, into the kitchen then across the grounds.

Angela knew she could leave Alexi, make her own way, knew she would most likely succeed. The language, thanks to Misha's diligence and Alexi's tutoring, she now spoke tolerably well. She had her knife, her compass and enough knowledge in her head to survive in any wilderness for months, perhaps years, if she had to.

She didn't doubt her ability to follow a trail or to find a hidden path in the rugged Rocky Mountains, but then again, this was another country. The American embassy could be hundreds of miles away. At the moment she didn't know the direction of the closest city. In her bag she had two changes of clothing but no money.

She could survive without money.

The idea of asking Feodora--no, Miss Feodora--for a map of Russia made her giggle hysterically until she almost sobbed. Frustrated with the horrid situation she found herself into, she lay back on the soft green grass and watched the wind whisper through the oak leaves and the sunlight play on the water. Hindsight was seldom helpful. Angela she should have insisted Alexi take her with him, should have followed when Misha let down his guard. When Alexi had presented his argument, she'd backed down much too easily.

While she lay on the grass, the sun slowly moved across the sky. Hours seemed to pass, the afternoon drifting by, and still she'd reached no conclusions. She'd promised Alexi she'd be here waiting for him when he returned.

A promise had to be kept at all costs, she reminded herself.

Alexi had believed in her, trusted her. She could not disappoint him.

She rolled onto her stomach, her feet swinging in the air above and behind her, her forearms supporting her weight as she watched an ant work diligently. The tiny insect was trying to tug a part of her scone up the hill; to the wee creature it must have seemed a mountain. The ant did struggle but kept going. It could have stayed there and eaten the whole thing, saving itself hours of work.

She felt like the ant. Surely she had the weight of a mountain upon her back.

The sun felt warm against her face, the wind soft. A few months ago she had embraced adventure wholeheartedly, never examining her motives or her purpose. Now, faced with a woman who thought herself above the common people, she yearned for the peace of a Rocky Mountain stream.

She ached to see her home--the mountains and the wide-open prairies. Deep inside, though, she knew her home lay with Alexi. She couldn't abandon him no matter the obstacles placed in front of her. Surely, Alexi's grandmother would have helped her. But she was gone, too.

Misha, poor Misha--his family was threatened. She could hardly blame him for abandoning her.

"Grab her!"

Angela jerked to her feet, her knees bent, her arms relaxed, yet ready to fight. She'd know that voice anywhere. "Feodora?" Angela paused, relaxing too soon.

"Yuri." Feodora's voice was harsh and grating.

The man stepped forward. They circled one another, each wary of the other.

"Miss Feodora, to the likes of you," she said, stripping Angela with her eyes. "You dress like a man," she said, spittle forming around her mouth.

Who was this woman really? She didn't seem the type who would appeal to the gunslinger Devil Blackmoor--or the aristocratic Alexi Popov.

"I do as I please." Angela couldn't keep the sarcasm from creeping into her voice. She decided not to fight, and stuffed her hands into her pockets, surveying the woman with purpose, sizing her up as an opponent. Without Yuri, Feodora was hot air, nothing more.

Feodora flushed with rage, her prim features puckering until she looked pinched and old. She turned to Yuri.' 'Bind her and take her back to the estate." She inhaled raggedly, practically gagging in her attempt to draw air, she was so furious. "Toss her in the woodshed." Feodora's hands shook, and her too-thin lips quivered. "A few days without food should be enough to convince this peasant that the serfs do not lie around all day. There is work to be done."

Angela stepped back, once more taking on the stance of a predator ready to fight. "I'm not a serf or a peasant. I'm a free woman. All of these people are free. You cannot confine me or order me to work. You're living in the past. If I'm not wanted here, I will leave." Angela picked up her valise, walking away, her back stiff and her mind made up.

"Yuri!"

Angela made the mistake of turning back.

Feodora looked her over one more time. "You will learn to speak to your betters with proper respect."

Angela's gaze went to Yuri. "The only person here who is equal to me is this man you call Yuri. Should I apologize to him?"

"Shut her up!"

Before Angela could reach for a weapon, she found herself pushed forward at knifepoint, her hands tied in front of her. She heard Yuri's whisper, "Sorry, but I've no choice. It was either you or my wife."

Angela looked at Feodora askance, bewildered beyond anything she'd known before.

Feodora followed Angela, prodding her along with the blunt end of a walking stick. Angela knew that bruises would soon form on her back. Angela stumbled awkwardly down the narrow, winding trail that led to Alexi's home, trying to avoid the blows. *Adventure?* It seemed she'd gotten what she'd prayed for. *And so very much more.*

She tamped down her fear and studied the situation from every angle. It was not so terrible. Not for one moment did she doubt her ability to escape the cords that were haphazardly wound around her wrist, or the woodshed she was headed toward.

If she escaped the woodshed, she'd have no recourse but to leave the estate. She couldn't very well walk up to the main house and present herself for inspection. Feodora would be outraged and unforgiving. Without Misha she had only herself to depend on.

They reached the shed, a formidable structure, and well made. Angela cringed, thinking of the spiders and the bugs hiding in tiny corners, things crawling around the stacks of wood. She thought of the darkness and the sweltering heat when the sun hit it, too. The building was made for punishment, for torture.

"There's your home for the next two days," Feodora informed her, a smug expression on her face, one Angela wanted to wipe off with her fists.

Angela shot her nemesis a withering glare--one that, if Feodora had had any common sense, would have warned her of Angela's determination to have revenge.

"You will come to regret this," Angela said softly, but her tone held a warning. "Your time will come, Feodora, and it matters not who wins this battle. I will win the war. Alexi will-return one day, and he will be furious with you. Forgiveness does not come easily to the devil, and that is how Alexi will appear to you."

Feodora lost all color.

The man Feodora called Yuri gave her a hesitant nudge, and Angela stumbled inside. The door closed shut, and total darkness assailed her.

She turned around, searching for some manner of light. Her eyes began to slowly adjust, and she could make out slight forms, the barest hint of other structures inside. Her fingers closed around a long cord of leather. A whip. Tremors shot through her.

Unable to stop herself, she reached out for the leather strap, remembering her dream of agonizing fire across her back. Touching the leather should have ended her unfounded fears, but when her fingers wound around the whip, she felt the pain of countless souls. The room swayed beneath her feet.

"No!" she cried out, yet only a whisper escaped her.

A promise given must be kept.

The vow haunted her. She'd given Alexi her word. She'd made a promise she intended to keep.

Renewed determination swept through her. She clenched her teeth, fighting the pain and the nausea that threatened. With great concentration, she was able to move, to bring her knees to her chest and reach the knife she'd strapped to her thigh, her fingers closing over the handle. It slipped easily from its sheath.

A fierce joy filled her, a wild Sioux war cry trembling on her lips. The sharp knife cut through the leather. She rubbed her wrists and flexed her fingers, willing the blood to return to her fingers.

Through the long, endless night, Angela found herself repeating her father's words about sacred promises and her honor. While her body grew numb with cold, she fought off the need to escape.

To keep warm she paced the tiny shed.

Morning came. Bright light filtered through a few uneven cracks in the shed. The storm that had threatened the night before had never materialized. With the new day came the hope that Feodora would show mercy and let her out, or even bring food and water for nourishment.

Once more Angela paced the small confines of the shed.

Back and forth.

Her body cried out in pain and agonizing humiliation as she fought its needs.

Afternoon crept into evening.

Hunger gnawed at her.

She stretched her muscles then paced the width of the room again and again. Restless energy ripped through her at an alarming speed.

"Angela." Yuri stood near one boarded window. "Angela, over here," he whispered. "Are you all right? Can I get you anything?"

Her mouth was so dry she could barely speak, her tongue swollen and parched. The word *yes* came out in a hoarse sob. "Water..."

He handed her a cup.

"I feared for your safety," he told her. "One more day is all you need endure. I cannot help you. I wish I could. When Alexi returns, he will set this to rights."

If I live that long. "I will tell him how you've helped," she said.

"No, he will be angry that I did not go against Miss Feodora. I'm afraid for my wife and my children. She threatened to beat them--and put them here. My wife is with child, and my daughter is only two."

Beat them? Women and children?

His voice on the other side of the wall comforted her. Yet he was gone too soon. His words echoed in her mind. She had fallen into a nightmare of an adventure, entered a country that verged on barbarism. An eerie blackness crept into her heart, and she was afraid. Once more she thought of flight, but reminded herself of her vows.

A promise must be kept.

"But at what price, Papa?"

A promise must be kept, little one. It is sacred. She heard her father's voice clearly, as if he stood beside her. *But Angela, if that promise means your life, you must make a choice. A good person would forgive under those circumstances.*

Alexi will forgive.

Through a chink in one of the solid planks, she saw muted light from the moon. After Yuri left, she made up her mind. She could endure one more day of confinement, one more day without food or water. She would use that time to seek her identity. It would be her vision quest. She would pray to the ancient gods for guidance and strength. She would become one with the earth and look for a sign for her future.

For the first time since the encounter with Feodora, she felt at peace with herself. Once more she could hear her father's voice in her mind. Once again she heard the earth speaking to her.

She sat cross-legged on the dirt floor and closed her eyes. She chanted and prayed, drifting into a strange world where there was no more darkness, where light and beauty filled every space.

She saw a white eagle and knew it was Trey, her half brother, soaring above her, encouraging her. Then she saw a wildcat, knew him to be Dakota. Her friends were with her in this ordeal; whatever she chose to do they would guide her, and they would help her survive.

She had only to listen to the sounds of the earth, the sky and the water.

As time passed and her visions intertwined, one into another, she saw a doe walk from the woods, grazing. The beautiful animal lifted her head and listened. All was quiet until there was a great heaving and crashing through the woods. At the edge of the forest stood a wolf, a magnificent black wolf. He was breathing hard, yet he lifted his head, and his strength overshadowed everything else. Unafraid, the doe watched, in awe of the power and the magnificence of the mighty predator.

On the other side of the forest a white man emerged, a rifle in his hand. He aimed it at the doe. She took flight as shot after shot whizzed past her, and still she ran. Several bullets grazed her back. She bled. The doe was determined not to go down, survival foremost in the animal's thoughts. She ran until she reached cover and hid herself beneath wild berry bushes. The skin upon her back burned, was on fire from the wounds inflicted upon her.

Determined to live, she held still. She became one with the earth.

When the first shots were fired, the wolf let out a tremendous howl of outrage. He charged toward the huntsman, ignoring the bullets and the danger. They fought to the death. The huntsman lay on the ground, dying. The wolf stood over the man for a few minutes, then searched the meadow.

Again he sat and let out an eerie wail that spoke of fear and loneliness--a sound that spoke of betrayal. With the mournful wail, the doe's heart broke.

The door of the shed swung open, and light blinded Angela.

Her dreams had been put to an end. Angela knew the doe was supposed to be her, the wolf Alexi, and the huntsman Feodora. Feodora was a deadly enemy. Angela should take grave care.

Feodora stepped inside. For the first time in Angela's life, she understood hate and knew her life was in danger. If she chose to stay, she would have to watch everything she said and did. One misstep could well mean her life.

The doe had chosen to run, and Angela knew, deep in her heart, she would eventually be forced to run as well, to break her sacred promise to Alexi.

Feodora stood in the open door, the sun at her back. Her gaze went to the leather straps on Angela's side. "Take the knife, Yuri, and search her. Make sure she doesn't have any more hidden surprises then take her to the kitchen. She has a floor to scrub."

For a second Yuri's eyes flashed vindictively at Feodora then he shuttered his expression. He looked at Angela and nodded toward the house. Angela followed.

Inside the kitchen the smell of freshly baked bread headed straight to Angela's stomach. Her gut clenched, and her stomach growled its hunger. Five loaves of bread sat on the counter cooling--two days had passed since she'd eaten.

"When you finish with the floors, you can have a slice of bread." Feodora swept from the room, her skirts knocking over a pail of milk.

Chapter Sixteen

Waves of apprehension swept through Alexi. Shivers whipped down his spine even while the sun blistered the sand beneath his feet. Throughout the morning the strange, ominous sensations that plagued him would not leave. Even under the hot desert sun, chills of disquiet brought goose bumps to his arms and cold sweat trickling down his chest.

He looked to the north, visions of Angela clouding his mind and pulling on his heartstrings. Suddenly he wished she were by his side. An urgent need to talk to her, to see her and hear her laughter, pushed out all other thoughts.

He wanted to touch her face, her hands, to know that no harm had come to her, that she was protected. Instead he touched the diamond in his ear and felt a bone-deep cold he could not chase from his heart.

The days had moved by swiftly, but not productively. All the clues they sifted through took circuitous routes or became dead ends. Not one moment passed when he didn't think of Angela or the wide-open spaces that could be found in the West. When his mind shifted to her, the strange feeling that something was seriously wrong pulsed stronger and stronger.

"I fear for your lady." Ivan stood beside Alexi, a faint smile on his broad, handsome face. "You've been gone too long. If anything were to happen to Misha, Feodora would sink her deadly claws into Angela. She would take a pound of flesh--and perhaps more--from your mistress. She will be truly jealous of your lady, and Feo is filled with spite and hatred."

"Angela can take care of herself," Alexi murmured, praying she would be able to withstand whatever trials awaited her. "What is it you fear from Feodora?"

"Everything." Ivan shrugged. "Nothing. With Feo you wouldn't know until she had you bound and gagged. I would like to bring her back here as soon

209

as possible. Put her in Najjar's hands, where she can no longer make any trouble."

"Najjar's bed, you mean." Alexi laughed, but he didn't feel the laughter in his heart. Angela needed him. His premonitions--the chills and the horrid dreams he had every night--cried out to him.

"Since the marriage to you will never take place, her father has disowned her. She has nowhere to turn. That fact coupled with Angela's sudden appearance will make her deadly. I told Natasha not to worry, but now that I think on it, I pray Misha can hold his own against the woman."

"Feodora is pregnant with your child?"

Ivan nodded. "She is, and I've stopped her more than once from aborting the babe."

Alexi swallowed hard, his thoughts in turmoil.' 'Could Feodora's father have been responsible for this carnage?"

The question hung in the air, unanswered.

Go home, Alexi. Go home.

He prayed daily his dreams were unfounded.

"I will feel much better when I know she can cause no one trouble, except perhaps Najjar, who can handle Feodora. It is time, friend. What will it take? A week and a few days to get to your home? We will find out nothing more here. For the time being, I have given up on this."

"No more than five days," Alexi said, determined to break all records on his trek across the desert. "I, too, have had the feeling that things are not the way they should be. I will rest much easier when I see Angela with my own eyes."

"Our fates are written in the stars, but that does not mean we can leave everything to chance. You've made a wise decision. I will ride with you. Together we will move faster than the wind."

~ * ~

When Angela finished the endless list of chores that day, she was too exhausted to eat. She wrapped the piece of dry, stale bread the cook had given her in a cloth and climbed the steps to her attic chamber, each step an ordeal. Her inhaled breaths came in ragged pants and her heart beat double-time as each second passed into another. The stab's seemed to stretch upward forever, seemed to be the longest set she'd ever encountered.

Feo stood at the top, waiting for her, a malicious look etched on her pinched face. "What do you want now?" The words tumbled out before Angela could stop them.

"You will learn to speak to your betters with respect." Feodora broke the silence with a scathing tone.

There was nothing Angela wanted to do more than tell Feo what she thought of her. But she didn't have the energy to waste.

"Cat got your tongue? Speak to me," Feo taunted her.

"What do you want me to say?" Angela said, stopping a few feet from the woman and inches from the closed room she wanted to disappear into and not come out of until she'd slept for at least twelve hours.

"I want you to apologize." Feo tapped her foot on the solid rock, her shoulders shaking with the effort she made to conceal her wickedness.

When hell freezes over. "I'm sorry, Feo," Angela said through clenched teeth, choosing to be prudent instead of rash. *Is that good enough, or do you want me to grovel?*

"He won't ever be yours. You should know I won't give him up to the likes of an American peasant. Alexi is an aristocrat, born and bred. He can't marry anyone as baseborn as you." She seemed to puff up with hatred. Her expression and the way she looked Angela up and down said more than her words. Her eyes narrowed hatefully. She'd put herself in charge. No one on the estate would gainsay her.

As much as Angela hated to admit it, Feodora was right. Alexi would never be hers. She would never hold his heart--but neither would Feodora. If Alexi married the hateful woman, he would have to keep Feodora in his bed until she bred then he'd be done with the woman.

And if Angela stayed, Alexi would return to her, make love to her, sleep in her bed, but his heart would be somewhere else. Alexi didn't plan to give his heart to anyone.

Forced by her position on the staircase to look up at Feodora, Angela swallowed what was left of her pride. "Excuse me. I'm tired and hungry." Angela brushed past her, trying not to touch her as she negotiated the narrow door into her room.

Feodora stood just beyond the doorway, watching. Angela could feel her eyes upon her back, could feel the hatred.

"What did you do to him?"

Angela turned then and, with one hand on the door, watched the other woman for a long time before shutting the door in her face. The action was rash, but Angela had no regrets. She heard a loud hiss from behind the wood barrier, yet Feodora didn't rise to the challenge Angela had just passed her way. Despite Angela's resolve to appear meek, her pride seemed to be her worst enemy.

Angela Chamberlain did not know how to grovel.

"Alexi, where are you?" she whispered into the lonely night, his handsome, dark features vivid in her mind. She longed for him to hold her and to tell her he'd return soon.

Sitting down on the small bed in the corner of the drafty room, Angela pulled her knees up to her chest and rested her head on top of them. She rocked back and forth, memories sliding by in her mind, warming her heart.

"Alexi," she whispered into the hot, sultry air, "please hurry home."

It would not do to bemoan her fate. She would have to make the best of this situation. Alexi would return; she knew that. Rising from the old mattress, she washed her face in the water near the nightstand and munched on the stale bread.

The room was tucked into the eaves of the mansion, and one tiny window looked down on the garden. Despite the gloom upstairs and the pending darkness, Angela could see brilliant roses and beds of nasturtiums and pansies. There seemed to be color everywhere except in her room, which was all a dull gray. Unlike the chamber she'd slept in two nights before, the walls were not papered, with blue flowers and the bed was not grand and fluffy.

The only decoration here was a tiny spider weaving its delicate silver web from the windowpane to a spindly table.

The small bed was covered with a tattered gray quilt, and beneath that, one worn sheet was spread across a thin mattress. She shook the coverings, afraid of what she might find beneath or in the bed, but she was almost too tired to care. She'd rather sleep in the woods with the stars overhead than here. At least the insects and animals that might snuggle up to her in the woods seemed natural and clean.

She sat on the edge of the bed and slipped her shoes off; then, wriggling her bare toes, she leaned back against the headboard. Every muscle in her body ached from the backbreaking work. She stretched, searching her soul and her heart for the courage to endure anything Miss Feodora might throw her way. It was a challenge of sorts, Feodora against her. She would win; she was determined.

Angela Chamberlain would win. A Chamberlain did not back down or run from an adversary. And she could work as hard as anyone.

Lying on the bed, her hands tucked beneath her cheeks, she watched the moonlight brighten the dark sky and the twinkling stars begin their march toward a new day.

"Alexi, where are you?" She whispered the words into the stillness.

Angela drifted off to sleep, the slice of bread uneaten, what was left of the tepid water still in the pitcher near the window. In a world somewhere between sleep and awareness, she pushed the covers away, sweat drenching her nightclothes.

~ * ~

Pounding on the door a few hours later woke her. The room was still bathed in darkness, and a hoarse whisper came through the solid oak. "Miss Angela, you've got to get up."

"Why?" She moaned, aware that her body still felt flushed with heat and her head ached. "It's still dark outside."

"The servants all get up earlier than the rest of the household. You're an hour late already. Some of the staff have seen to a few of your chores, but they won't be able to keep up the pretense much longer. You've got to rise before Miss Feodora finds out you've been slacking off. She'll have you flogged, and that's a fact."

Flogged? "Flogged?" Angela sat up, rubbing the sleep from her eyes. "She doesn't have the right."

"True enough, but she's taken the right. With the Popovs all gone and no one to gainsay her, she's become a tyrant. No one is safe, particularly not you. She has taken an extreme dislike to you. You must be very careful not to make her mad."

With good reason, Angela supposed. Feodora thought she'd stolen her man. She stifled the yawn and the urge to tell the lady on the opposite side of the door she was going back to sleep and to forget the extra chores, that she'd take responsibility for her own actions. Instead she called out, "I'll be right down."

Through the closed door, Angela added, "By the way, what are my chores this morning?"

"The kitchen floor has to be scrubbed every day. Miss Feodora insisted that was your job. And the coal bin needs to be filled." The woman's voice on the other side of the door paused ominously. "It will take hours to fill it. She won't let you eat until the job is done. I've an apple here for you."

After fastening the buttons on her dress, Angela slipped on her worn shoes. She tied her hair back into a tight knot at the base of her neck. Dressed and ready to go, Angela opened the door. A young lady no older than fourteen or fifteen stood there. She put out her hand, offering the fruit. "Do you have bread?"

Angela nodded yes. "Some. It's left over from yesterday. What's your name?"

"Sveta. Yuri is my brother. He asked that I keep an eye on you, seeing that you're Alexi's favorite. Eat the apple here. You won't have time once you've started to work."

Favorite? So they all knew what she was to Alexi. If it kept her safe, who was she to protest? "All right." Angela bit into the apple. Eating and walking at the same time, she moved down the long servants' staircase to the kitchen below, Sveta beside her.

Caution and survival were foremost in her mind. Feodora's punishments were nothing more than a little hard work. She would see this through. And as for a flogging, Angela didn't plan on aggravating Miss Feodora enough to merit a punishment that severe.

~ * ~

Yet as the sun climbed higher in the sky and her hands bled from the handle of the coal bucket biting into them, Angela was no longer sure she would see this through. Sweat soaked her blouse, and the hard edges of the house in front of her blurred. There was no respite, no rest and no food until all her chores were finished. Feodora had singled her out, and it seemed the woman might indeed seek her death.

Angela was strong as a horse, but she did fear for the child in her womb. The time drew near when she would have to make a decision. Angela knew in her heart she would have to consider her unborn child beyond any promises she'd made or any feelings she harbored for Alexi.

One day ran into the next, an endless stream of chores mounting to a level Angela was hard-pressed to finish each night. Her buckskins, which had once fit like a second skin, now hung on her. Her cheeks were hollow and her eyes dark with fatigue and worry.

She would not be Feodora's victim.

At the end of each day she was weary beyond belief, and still she clung to the stubborn notion she would outlast the horrid woman who made her life a living hell. She prayed daily Alexi would be back soon, setting everything in its proper order and place.

She told herself that even if he meant to marry Feodora, he would not allow the woman to abuse her.

Alex had other plans for her.

She hadn't thought about those plans for days now, nor had she tormented herself with the anguish the position of paramour would cause her. As Angela lay back on her thin pallet that night, she renewed her determination to settle for nothing less than Alexi's name. Alexi's fondness for her, his gentle caresses and words of love, had turned her soft.

Any child of hers deserved the father's name. The babe also deserved to be born. At this rate, working as hard as she did each day, exhausting herself to the point where she could barely climb the steps to her room at night, she could harm the child. She would give Alexi one more day to make it home. If he didn't return by this time tomorrow night, she would leave, all promises set aside.

With that decided, she dropped off to sleep.

~ * ~

Throughout the long day that followed, every horse nickering, every door slamming, every sound made her heart stop beating. The coal bin needed filling again, so she lugged buckets of coal until once again her hands bled, the wounds cutting deep into the old ones that had not yet healed.

She collected small parcels of food to keep her alive during her long journey, deciding to head north instead of crossing the desert. That night, when she entered her room, she was pleased with her endeavors. She had several apples, a loaf of bread the cook had thrown out because it was too old, two potatoes and five precious matches.

She was ready. Nothing would stop her.

She waited until the house quieted and all were in bed. A crescent moon hung in a cloudless sky. Stars drenched the night with their twinkling light. Soft breezes wafted through the open window. The world seemed to pause in thought.

The silence was too heavy, too foreboding. Her heart lurched.

Without warning the door to her room slammed open. Feodora stood in the opening, her fingers drumming a warning on her hips, her pinched face and narrow-eyed gaze resting smugly on Angela. "Search the room. Quickly."

Angela rose, protesting. "You've no right to go through my things," she said, and stepped in front of the man who had entered behind Feodora.

"I've every right," she said with a snarl. "There are items missing from the kitchen. If you've stolen anything, you'll live to regret your disobedience."

She had not brought Yuri this time. Another man searched her bag, which sat in the open, ready to go. A few more minutes and Feodora would have found an empty room.

The man pulled the old, tattered quilt from the bag, along with the small sack of provisions. Then he discovered her knife, the one Dakota had given her. She'd retrieved the precious gift just before leaving her work that evening and returning to her room. Feodora seemed to take the most joy in discovering the knife.

"Little thief," she said with smirking glee, holding the knife to Angela's face. "Take her to the flogging post and tie her there. We'll deal with her in the morning. Let her think on her sins and wait for her punishment."

"The knife is mine. It was given to me a long time ago by a friend," she said, her voice soft, her tone menacing. Yet there was nothing she could do to dissuade the woman.

Before Angela could object again or fight, she was flung over the man's broad shoulders and hauled downstairs. Within another few seconds, her hands were secured above her head and tied to a post in the middle of the yard.

Nothing she'd ever dealt with had prepared her for this. Unless she could free herself, come morning she'd be flogged.

She did not call for Alexi in her prayers. Instead she chanted to herself, praying for the strength and courage needed to withstand the ordeal that awaited. She'd seen this in her vision quest. Fate could not be circumvented. Just as the doe had bled from her back, she would, too then she'd leave this place forever.

~ * ~

The heat and the searing pain from her back nearly crippled her, brought her to her knees. Yet she had not cried out, not once. The punishment was over now, the spectators vanishing just as suddenly as they had appeared. Yuri cut her down and carried her to the woodshed, where he placed her facedown on an old mattress. Blood trickled down her back and her sides.

He gingerly put ointment on the open wounds covering her back, touching her gently--almost afraid. She bit down hard on her lip, trying once more to keep from crying out. Still the torment went on and on.

Once she heard Yuri sigh. "This should not have happened," he whispered "There was nothing I could do to stop Miss Feodora. I sent for Alexi's grandmother. They should arrive in another day or two. Misha, he cannot return."

The unspoken meaning was not lost on Angela. She might not survive.

She would survive. Angela closed her eyes, concentrating on her homeland, seeing the snowcapped Rockies rise up against the prairie. She imagined cold snow on her back, and the burning seemed to cool slightly. In her mind she sat at her father's knee while he told her legends of the Sioux gods and how the earth was formed.

She listened to the wind in the trees and the birds calling their sweet songs. When she dreamed of frolicking in cool, clear waters, she discovered Yuri tending to her again, cooling her back with the ointments he brought.

Two days passed before she felt strong enough to sit, two more until she could walk without pain. Still, Alexi's grandmother had not arrived. She would leave in the night, follow the river upstream until she reached a village. She devoured all the food Yuri set in front of her, hoping to regain her strength more rapidly.

She thought on the child she nurtured beneath her heart, and she prayed.

Feodora hated her. If the woman tried to find her, Angela prayed the effort would be halfhearted. Feo wanted her dead or gone; either would probably suit. Yet she knew Feodora was vindictive and unstable, and she was capable of anything.

Angela wanted to leave a letter for Alexi. She needed to explain. There was no time.

The sky was shrouded in clouds, a summer storm brewing on the horizon, racing this way with tremendous speed. Thunder and lightning lit the sky--an omen, perhaps. Wakinyan, the god of thunder, answered her prayers, came to her now in her hour of need. Rain battered the earth, and a swift wind blasted through the trees.

Angela left the woodshed just as the storm hit. Her tracks would be washed clean, and the dogs, if Feodora set them upon her trail, would never find her scent. She made her way to the pond and gingerly walked through the water along the edge until she reached the shallow creek feeding into the still waters. Forging ahead, pushing herself beyond her endurance, she walked along the edge of the creek. All through the stormy night she trudged on, fought her encroaching loneliness and fatigue, knowing that unless Alexi chose to look for her, she would never see him again.

For a moment her hand rested on her stomach; their child grew there, a child he might never see, did not even know about. Anguish pierced her heart and lodged there. The pain was unbearable.

The rain slowed to a soft drizzle, then the first morning rays of sunlight pushed through the aftermath of the storm. She took off her buckskin jacket, wringing out the water and tossing it over her shoulder. Still, she pushed on. Stubborn determination kept her moving.

A small, sheltered glade offered protection. She changed her clothes, leaving her buckskins draped over the valise to dry, and mentally thanking Yuri for smuggling the bag and a small sack of food to her. She ate one of her apples, continuing to walk, following the creek. Her pace was slow but constant, meant to save her strength. She broke off a piece of bread then washed the dry crust down with a handful of clear water.

When she stopped to rest again, she laughed at herself. "You've grown soft, woman. You must have more endurance if you intend to get away from the witch at Alexi's estate. To save her pride, she will have to send someone for you, and they will travel on horses. They will not rest every two minutes. Get up. Get up." She prodded herself along.

She thanked Yuri again in her mind for bringing her the food, then ate another apple, tossing the core aside, then moving, always moving. She was painfully aware of the stitch in her side and the burning ache across her back, knowing the wounds had opened and she bled. Still she forced one foot in front of the other.

She stopped at midmorning, feeling woozy and a bit dizzy. Bending over at the waist, she let the blood wash through to her head. She straightened stiffly and walked on.

Once she thought she heard barking dogs and a man calling out to them. Even while she searched for a place to hide, the sounds vanished, moving off in a different direction.

She forced herself to rest and to forget what might have been between herself and Alexi. This, after all, was for the best. When she reached a town, she'd find someone to help her. She'd send a message to her father, and perhaps he'd meet her in London.

Evening came softly, and as darkness fell around her she was forced to look for food. She dined on sweet blackberries and found a few wild potatoes that didn't need cooking. Foraging for food had been one of the skills her half brother had drilled into her head. She could catch a fish with her hands, but she didn't dare light a fire, and she wasn't hungry enough to eat the flesh raw.

Her stomach rumbled in an attempt to tell her she was wrong. Indeed, she was hungry enough to eat raw meat, but the thought repulsed her. No, she didn't dare start a fire this close to the estate and the trackers who were surely behind her. She ate the last apple then wrapped the tattered blanket she had stolen from the woodshed around her. Finding sleep elusive, she watched the moon and the stars, trying to identify all that she could. She did find the north star, and knew she could navigate her way cross country.

She didn't want to lose Alexi. In truth, she didn't know if she'd ever really had him, but there had been times when she had felt as if all was well, as long as he held her, as long as he was near. If she thought back, she'd fallen head over heels for him before she even knew who he was--the first time she'd set eyes upon him, that day in Denver when she saw him stroking his horse and speaking softly to his sleek black stallion Jabbar. Even though they disagreed about their relationship, as the days passed, a gentle, trusting love had grown between them.

Now he was miles away from her, and she had been forced to run for her life, never to return to his home or his arms. Everything had gone full circle. At the hands of his future wife, she had learned a bittersweet lesson and learned it well. She could trust and rely on no one but herself to keep her safe.

~ * ~

She woke the next morning much later than she'd planned. She ate the berries left over from the night before and started on her way. With each passing day she wanted to believe she grew stronger. But she didn't. Her stomach cramped horribly, and before an hour had passed she had to stop and rest again. Fatigue seemed to sink its ugly claws into her lungs, seemed to squeeze the air from her even as she tried to inhale.

The stream was fresh and clean here. She drank quickly and deeply; then, filling her hands with the cool liquid, she splashed the healing water over her heated face and hands. Leaning her shoulder on a granite boulder, she rested with the sun pouring across her face, drenching her with its heat. Her back was on fire, yet the rest of her felt cold despite the sun, and shivers seemed to take over, sending shudders through her body.

She tried to stand, but the bees stirring up pollen in the wildflowers nearby were pleasant to listen to, as were the birds overhead and the squirrels chattering in the trees. A few minutes more of rest in this lazy, sun-drenched afternoon wouldn't matter. Feodora would not come for her. She was safe.

~ * ~

Sam encountered one dead end after another. He'd always been one step behind Devil Blackmoor. But now that he reached Europe, he couldn't hope to catch the *Mystic*. Every time he asked a question about Alexi Popov, as he had learned was Devil's full name, someone sent him in the wrong direction.

He began to think that he should do the opposite of what people told him.

The man should have an enemy or two.

But Alexi Popov had no enemies.

He reached the port town on the Black Sea, where Alexi and Misha had landed two weeks earlier. There were no caravans going across the desert, nor was there any hope of finding one in the next few weeks. If the rumors were true, this was Alexi's homeland. There would be no help forthcoming here.

Fear settled in the pit of Sam's stomach. He ached to see his daughter and to know she was well and truly cared for. The letters she had written had bothered him at first, but Sam knew his levelheaded daughter well. She would spirit the truth from the devil, and she would do what she knew was right.

Satan himself could not wrench Angela's self-respect from her--and neither could Devil Blackmoor.

On his third day in the busy port town, he watched two men ride at breakneck speed just outside the marketplace. Their haphazard pace left men shaking their fists at the pair and shouting vile curses. Yet nothing stopped them, not even the wagonload of produce the lead man upended on his mad dash.

Even though he didn't recognize the man dressed in white robes that billowed around his huge body, Sam Chamberlain would recognize the piece of horseflesh he rode anywhere.

"Jabber." He whistled through clenched teeth. "Finally, my prayers have been answered. I've found the devil himself."

The two men streaking past Sam did little to alleviate his fears. His pulse pounded rapidly, his heart near to jumping from his chest. As he mounted his own stallion, Sam said another silent prayer and followed the men from town and toward the purple-cloaked hills to the north.

At long last he had the break he needed. He prayed he followed Devil and Misha. If not, he could well be signing his own death warrant.

The men rode relentlessly through the long afternoon and into the night. Sam's fears doubled then tripled. As the moon rose and cast light upon the path, Sam let the distance between the men in front of him diminish.

By midmorning of the next day, they'd reached the foothills surrounding the desert. Rocks rose on either side of the narrow, winding road that snaked ever northward. Sam knew the men had set a trap for him and waited for him to pass. At whatever cost to himself, he relished meeting Devil Blackmoor. He had a few things to right with the man. He had waited long enough.

While he'd like to stake Devil Blackmoor out on the desert behind him, it would solve nothing, least of all restoring his daughter's virtue or ensuring her happiness. The shot whizzing past his head didn't take him by surprise, nor did the man who landed square on the middle of his back, knocking him off his horse.

He heard a string of vile curses. Then...

"Sam Chamberlain. Son of a bitch!"

Sam had counted on the element of surprise. Devil Blackmoor didn't know Sam pursued him or why; he could tell by the tone of Devil's voice and the momentary relaxing of Devil's grip around his neck.

That was all it took. The element of surprise was now his. Sam now had Devil by the neck, and he meant to keep the advantage. Sam was on top of Devil, his knife at Devil's throat. "You have a hell of a lot of explaining to do, Devil Blackmoor. You're going to tell me the truth now or you won't live to see another sunset." Sam rose, Devil held against his chest, his knife tucked neatly under Devil's chin. Sam wanted to draw blood. For Angela's sake, he held back.

"Perhaps if you'd give me a clue." Alexi sounded perturbed but not frightened.

Ivan stood on the rocks opposite the two men, his hands folded across his chest. "You two old friends? Or enemies? It's devilishly hard to tell."

"I thought we were friends," Alexi said, his tone menacing even though Sam had the upper hand for now.

Sam pressed the knife closer, still not drawing blood but wanting to. "We were acquaintances until he abducted my daughter. Now he's an enemy. I want revenge."

Alexi felt all the blood in his body rush to his feet. *Angela? Sam Chamberlain's daughter?* So that was what Misha had referred to.

Sam *Chamberlain's daughter.*

But wasn't she a whore? How ironic Sam would follow her halfway across the world.

"Angela's your kin?" Alexi choked on the question, knowing the answer and dreading it at the same time. Confirmation could mean only one thing: Angela was no prostitute. All his preconceived ideas once again shattered into a thousand pieces.

"You know she is," Sam grated out then furiously pushed Alexi aside.

"I didn't. Not until this moment. She never told me. I thought..." Even while Alexi saw Sam's need to kill, to seek vengeance for the wrong Alexi had done Sam's daughter, Alexi knew Sam wouldn't hurt him. Not until he saw his daughter. Not until Sam heard Angela's tale. It would not do to tell Sam Chamberlain what he'd thought his daughter was. *A whore.* No, it would not do at all. Alexi's stomach churned in dismay. He'd never wronged another man in his life.

Allah, but he'd done Angela a terrible wrong--and in the process her father, too.

"What did you think? That she would be easy? That you could use her any way you pleased? I've heard the stories about you, Alexi Popov, and your harem of women."

Ivan laughed. "Harem? My, my, but your reputation precedes you."

"Shut the hell up." Alexi glared at his friend. He had thought of Angela as easy, and yes, he had thought he could do whatever he pleased. "I've no harem." He turned to Sam. "I've no harem," he repeated. "Your daughter came with me willingly. She wanted adventure, and I had no idea who she was."

This was not all his fault. But he felt as if it were.

His stomach turned over once more. Indeed, he'd had no idea, but would knowledge of Angela's identity have stopped him? The answer eluded him. He'd wanted Angela from the first time he set eyes on her, and he'd decided at that moment he'd have her.

No, nothing would have stopped him from seducing her, from making love to her.

Not Sam Chamberlain or Chamberlain's reputation. Not anything.

He wanted her still, even knowing who she was. He needed to undo the wrongs he'd committed against her. He needed to change the fear he'd seen in her eyes when he left her that night in the hotel room. She'd thought she'd done something wrong, and he had done nothing to change that thought.

That lack still haunted him. He had lashed out at her because of her lack of innocence.

The two men were circling each other now, one ready to kill, the other needing to make amends. Alexi could think of only one way to repair the damage done, and that was to offer marriage. The same obstacle still lay in his path, though. Nothing had changed.

Ivan laughed again, clearly amused by the circling men. He clapped his hands, gaining their attention momentarily. "We don't have time for this nonsense," he said harshly. "Have you forgotten our need for haste?"

Alexi grunted. "Tell that to the father of the wronged woman"

Sam looked at Ivan then Alexi, feeling the subtle tension that passed between the two men. Once again, fear for Angela was paramount in his mind. "You feel it, too," Sam said softly.

"There is danger to her. I thought she'd be safe, but the feelings will not leave.."

Sam nodded, understanding they childishly wasted time here. "We will settle this later," Sam said, his voice a low, vehement growl.

Alexi nodded. "We will solve the dispute. Though I fear nothing can be settled."

Chapter Seventeen

As the three men rode down the winding lane leading to the mansion, tremors of fear swept through Alexi. Each shudder ripped through to the marrow of his bones.

All around them, hounds bayed and men yelled. In the distance he heard confusion and mass hysteria. His heart pounded, and he spurred Jabbar faster, until the horse was lathered and heaving.

Ivan and Sam kept pace beside him.

In a swirl of dust, they stopped. Alexi jerked on Jabbar's reins so harshly the stallion reared, his mighty forelegs pawing the air, Alexi's heart racing with dread.

Suddenly the grounds surrounding the mansion stilled, became absolutely silent.

It should have felt good to be home. But Alexi felt only fear and a profound sense of betrayal. He knew without asking Angela was gone, understood she'd broken her sacred promise to him.

His heart seemed to stop, then shudder. He didn't want to believe the thoughts lodging painfully in his heart.

A lace curtain in one of the upstairs rooms stirred and for a brief moment Alexi thought he saw Feodora's pinched face studying him. He'd seen Feodora years before as a little girl. Even then the lines of her face had been harshly squeezed together, making her appear to hate the world.

Where was his grandmother? Where was Angela? Both of the women should have been outside to greet them by now.

"Master?"

Alexi turned once again, jerking Jabbar's reins. "Yuri..."

The man looked strangely forlorn, his shoulders stooped as if the weight of the world rested upon them.

"It's been a long time. I trust everything is well." But Alexi knew nothing was right.

Yuri took Jabbar's reins as Alexi dismounted.

He cleared his throat before speaking. "Everything is terrible," Yuri began, his voice filled with fear, but as the words began to flow he seemed to gain courage. "Mrs. Popov is gone. She did not know when you would be home or that the girl would arrive without you. Misha has left, too. He did not realize Natasha was not here because he left in the middle of the night. I fear--"

"Angela?" Alexi barked her name. The stark anger in his voice surprised him, fear pounding through his veins. All the misgivings he'd had for over a week once again swept through him full force. His heart clenched and tightened into a hard, strangled knot. "Angela?" he repeated, softer this time. His hands were on Yuri's shoulders, shaking the man. "Where the hell is Angela?" Alexi's patience unraveled.

"Gone," Yuri said, his head lowered as well as his voice. "Ran off yesterday."

"No!" Sam's voice penetrated the cold, unforgiving fog wrapping around Alexi and squeezing his heart.

"She would not leave unless something or someone threatened her life." Sam turned the full force of his fury onto Alexi. "What did you do to her?"

"I've done nothing but cherish Angela." *And promise to protect her, keep her safe.* "She came with me of her own free will, just as I told you earlier." But his gut clenched. He remembered vividly how angry and furious she'd been after he had deposited her on his ship like a sack of potatoes. She had not boarded the *Mystic* of her own free will. He lied to Sam, but the truth would not help. Not right now.

"We will see." Sam nodded. "When she can speak for herself, she will tell me what happened."

"Where did she go?" Alexi assumed control, firing his questions at Yuri. "Why? When?"

"We don't know where she's gone." Yuri walked with Jabbar toward the stables, the other horses following. "I could tell you why, but I think you should ask Miss Feodora. She's the one responsible. Angela stood her ground as long as she could, but ..."

"The hounds." Ivan spoke up, his tone fierce, his hands clenched together. "Did Feodora send the hounds after Angela?"

Another wave of terror gripped Alexi. The hounds would tear her apart. Surely Feodora knew that.

"Yes, she did, but they couldn't find a trail. Hid her tracks real well, she did. Knew just what to do to keep the dogs from finding her," Yuri said, a note of pride in his voice that Alexi did not miss. "She lit out of here even though she wasn't strong enough. If she hadn't gone when she did, Miss Feodora would have had her back to work the next morning."

"What aren't you telling me?" Alexi asked, his gaze trained on Yuri. His voice was threatening. "Angela wasn't here to work. She was to be my--" Alexi caught himself before saying *mistress*. This was not the time for her father to know the truth about his intentions, even though Sam had guessed as much.

After hesitating a moment, Yuri blurted out the truth. "Miss Feodora locked Angela in the woodshed without food and water for two days. Then, when she took a few apples, Miss Feodora had her flogged--accused the sweet angel of stealing. As soon as the wee thing could walk, she lit out of here."

Alexi and Sam were halfway up the stairs before Yuri finished. The word *flogged* had them both running. Alexi burst into Feodora's room first, murder foremost in his mind. How dared Feodora take it on herself to assume control of the household in his grandmother's absence. His muscles straining, his fists clenching, he was sorely tempted to do the same to the aristocratic lady his mother had picked for him to wed. He wanted her flogged, humiliated in front of the peasants.

Flogging was too good for the likes of her.

Sam stood behind Alexi. Ivan followed at a more sedate speed.

"I should kill you," Alexi grated out after bursting into the room he'd seen her in earlier.

"Killing is too easy." Sam spoke from behind Alexi, his voice low and menacing. "She needs a lifetime of torture."

"She will have a lifetime of banishment." Ivan spoke from behind both Alexi and Sam. "And to Feodora it will be torture."

Feodora rose from the chair she sat in, her hands fluttering, her lashes lowered demurely.' 'Whatever do you mean? I know nothing."

Alexi stepped forward but was stopped by Sam's hand on his shoulder. "Where is Angela?" Sam asked before Alexi could collect his pound of flesh from Feodora.

Feodora smoothed the folds of her ivory satin skirt, the lines of her face softening. The bodice of her dress was trimmed with lace, slightly off the shoulder, calculated to show an expanse of soft white skin. She bent over to expose herself to Alexi.

He saw and bile rose in his throat.

"I don't have any idea what you mean," she said, looking up, her smile the picture of innocence, her pose demure, enticing to any man stupid enough to believe in this woman's virtue. Alexi could not be duped. "You know I don't concern myself with the servants," she said offhandedly.

"Angela was not a servant. She was supposed to be safe here," Alexi said. "Under my protection."

"My misunderstanding." She fluttered her lashes, looking pointedly at Ivan. "Perhaps you should have sent word what your intentions were."

"I've told him everything about you, Feodora. Everything," Ivan said, his voice as harsh and commanding as Alexi's. A shudder swept across her shoulders. "I've told him how you came to my bed in the middle of the night and sometimes in the middle of the day."

"He lied." Her voice shook, her skin ashen.

Alexi grinned. He reached out, wrapping one of her dangling curls around his finger. "In all the years I've known Ivan, he has never spoken an untruth. You are nothing but an expensive whore with an aristocratic title, Feodora. Nothing more." He let the curl go, dismissing her.

"Begging your pardon, sir." Yuri appeared in the doorway. "Misha showed Miss Angela to the room you requested for her. Hours later, Misha was summoned home and Miss Feodora had Angela removed." Yuri finished the story, leaving nothing out, Alexi growing more angry with the telling. "Miss Angela set off in the midst of a raging storm."

"Yuri." Alexi turned to his man. "Lock Miss Feodora in this room. Don't let her out for any reason. Until I find Angela, I want to know that

Feodora can do no more harm to anyone. Ivan, sit on her if you have to."

"With pleasure." Ivan laughed. "It would indeed be a pleasure to see if she still carries my child. Her skirts seem to hide the swelling of her womb. She did submit to me so sweetly. It is a pity I could not bring your bridegroom with me. Najjar would enjoy taming a shrew, and he is very eager to taste your fire." Ivan seemed to enjoy taunting her.

Little was said between Alexi and Sam as they walked down the long staircase to the first floor. Alexi started out the door. Sam stopped him.

"While your eagerness to find Angela makes me look upon you in a little different light, it is not wise to begin the search now." Sam's words were spoken with the strength and the wisdom of a man well versed in tracking.

"I will not wait. If the hounds lost her, it can mean only one thing: she used the pond and the creek feeding into it to make her departure. I know where she's headed." Several times Alexi ran his fingers through his hair. And several times he inhaled deeply, cursing the woman upstairs.

~ * ~

Less than thirty minutes later Alexi sat on a fresh horse, Sam at his side, and they headed north into the mountains. Even to an experienced tracker there were few signs. Alexi understood all too well why his peasants had run in circles, trying to find Angela.

"Angela did not want to be found. Catching up to Angela will not be easy for us either," Sam said, his voice swelling with both pride in and fear for his daughter.

He had taught her well--perhaps too well. Her life might be the price for her expertise.

Day drew into night, and still they moved on, both knowing Angela would not stop unless she had to. She had two days head start. Anything could happen in this wilderness and country she knew nothing about.

Sam found an apple core and then another, and prayed they were Angela's. Fear for her settled in the depth of his gut. She would not have left such a sign if she had her wits about her. She was hurting. The need for speed welled inside him.

Then Alexi found the spot where she'd lain to rest, saw blood on the granite she'd lain against and saw, too, the tracks of other men.

Two other men had found her and spirited her away. Their tracks led deep into the mountains.

~ * ~

Alexi set a steady pace, his heart heavy with worry. He'd never felt so frightened. Angela was everything to him. To live the rest of his years alone, without her, would make his life have no meaning. The thought startled him. He'd never believed a woman could mean so very much to him.

Sam mirrored Alexi's apprehension in the grim set of his mouth. Alexi could read the fear in the older man, could see the anguish in the set of his shoulders, the tilt of his chin. He saw love and pride for Angela in Sam's expression, and heard the same in the man's voice every time he spoke of her.

Angela was a wild thing, an adventure ready to happen. Alexi prayed she'd had her fill of excitement.

She would have learned discipline at her father's knee, a moral code that would run straight and true. When all this was finished, Alexi meant to ask Sam just what the hell Angela was doing at Velvet leBon's whorehouse the night Emma Barringer was to be auctioned. The man was a fool for letting her dress as a whore, for allowing a man like himself to believe the worst of a fragile, sweet woman. Alexi smiled inwardly. Angela would never admit it, but she *was* soft and fragile, delicate in the extreme. She could fight like a man, yet she did not have the strength to pit herself against him. He'd won the only battle they'd ever engaged in simply by overpowering her then subduing her.

"Hell," Alexi muttered.

"You're feeling the danger, too. When we get Angela back to your home, I intend to find out what made you think you could steal my daughter without asking permission."

Alexi moaned. He didn't have an answer. Arrogance? The fact that he'd never been denied anything before in his life? "When we get back, old man... when we get back, I'm going to demand a few answers of my own."

"Very well," Sam gritted out.

Night settled in, and the wind blowing down from the mountains chilled Alexi. Or perhaps it was fear that sent the cold straight to his heart. His mind played games with him, his imagination running rampant, his terror at Angela's abduction wrenching his heart into two separate pieces.

He had promised to keep her safe. She had promised to stay at the mansion. According to Yuri she had endured as much as she could. She'd run only because there was no other way.

Firelight bathed the hard angles and planes of Sam's features. He lit a cheroot. The embers glowed red-hot against the black cloak of night. They both had a multitude of unanswered questions.

"What did you say to my daughter?" Sam asked. His tone held no menace, just curiosity.

"I didn't seduce her, if that's what you're asking." Guilt swept through him. Until now he had not believed seduction had played a part in this.

Perhaps in her innocence she had not known how to stop him. He'd been very persuasive.

"She's a grown woman with a mind of her own. I'll give you that much," Sam said reflectively. He flicked his cigarette into the flames of the fire. "She's stubborn and hardheaded. She ran from me--right into your arms. I will claim my share of responsibility here."

"I. wanted her the first time I touched her."

Sam choked on the coffee he'd just swallowed. "Touched her, did you? In what way?"

Alexi rose. He tossed the remains of his coffee into the fire. "How I touched Angela is between Angela and myself."

Sam stood. They were eye-to-eye, the fire separating them. "The way I see the situation, now that I'm here everything between the two of you is my business. If you've had her in your bed or even in your arms, I mean to see the two of you married."

Alexi's voice was filled with grave concern. He ignored the threat. "We have to find her first." Alexi walked to the edge of the light. He stared into the darkness. This was not the American West, but the untamed land was just as dangerous. The men who roamed these hills were a ruthless bunch. They lived by their wits alone. They robbed travelers of their money and provisions. Many of them were wanted for their political actions against the czar.

There was great unrest in his country.

After living in the United States, he believed as the rebels did, but he prayed no one knew of his attachment to Angela. Her life could be forfeit if they did, if she fell into the wrong man's hands.

He suddenly understood the truth of his feelings. "I will marry her."

Sam studied him for the longest time, his nod of approval encouraging.' 'I believe you are man enough for my daughter."

Alexi laughed softly at the compliment Sam gave, and felt a rush of energy sweep through him. "Thank you," he said, returning to the fire. "This light is a beacon to any who wish to see it."

Sam nodded. "You've set a trap and we are the bait. You are foolish and brave. Perhaps you know more about those who have stolen her than I do."

"This is not America, so I should. But I don't. If they knew who followed, they would be here, demanding ransom. We've heard nothing except the howl of the wolves." He hunkered down, playing with the embers of the fire. "I am worried. Very worried."

~ * ~

Angela stared straight ahead, and all she saw were stiff, rugged mountains and an iron gray sky. The grueling pace the men who captured her set challenged her endurance. Twice she nodded off on the back of her mount, slumping into the arms of her captor behind her, who bore a striking resemblance to Alexi.

The man was not as dark or as brooding, but he had the same deep brown eyes--eyes that seemed to find a way to penetrate her soul. Twenty-four hours later they rode into a small village nestled in a valley. Small children played in the dusty spaces between the huts, dogs barking and nipping at their heels.

No more than two words had been said between her and her captors--or benefactors, she wasn't sure which they were.

Christine Young

"You will rest," the man who rode in front of her said, startling her. His voice was ragged and sounded frustrated. "You will rest and we will wait here for your man to find you and pay for your ransom."

She started to nod. Yes, Alexi would find her. But then she changed her mind. "No," she said with more energy than she knew she possessed.

"No?" the man queried. "Then I was right. You were running. What is it that frightens you so badly that you become brave enough to venture through these parts alone?"

She clamped down on her impulsive tongue. He would laugh if she told him how a woman with skinny arms frightened her. "I will take your advice," she said.

"Ah, a rarity," he said, laughing. "A smart woman." His hands rested on her waist. He lifted her easily from the horse. An old woman came from the hut they'd stopped in front of.

She was wrinkled with age, her hair silver-gray, pulled back into a tight knot at the base of her neck. She wore a brown dress that had obviously seen several seasons of wear. When she smiled at the big man, her face lit up and for a passing second she looked years younger. The welcome seemed genuine.

Angela wanted to hold her hand out in greeting, but her knees gave way. The big man who'd brought her here scooped her into his arms.

"I can walk," Angela protested.

"Should I let you down so you can melt into a puddle at my feet? You do not need to prove how stubborn you are." He paused a few seconds to look at the woman, perhaps to gain permission to enter the hut. She nodded and he went inside, turning sideways and bending at the waist as he went through the door.

The one room was small and scrubbed clean. She could smell soap and disinfectant. A peat fire burned in the fireplace, sending a warm glow throughout the otherwise dark room. A bed, a rocking chair and a table with two chairs were all the furniture the old woman had.

The man chose the bed to set her upon.

"Turn over," he told her sternly, all gentleness disappearing from his voice. "I want to look at your back."

She sat wide-eyed, not venturing to move, a heated protest forming

233

on her lips. All she could manage was to shake her head in denial.

The old woman made a *tsking* noise. "Go on with you, you big oaf. Have you no manners? Shoo," she said, brushing the large man aside.

Angela held her breath, not daring to imagine what the man would do if the old woman angered him.

He laughed, chucking the old lady under the chin good-naturedly. "Anything you say, Mama. Just take good care of her."

The woman went on. "I will take a look, and if I've need of your advice, I will ask." She stepped between the man and Angela before turning to say, "Get a cup of coffee."

The man's expression turned grave. "I think she might be pregnant," he said. "Best you check that out, too."

Angela had already turned over, her swift inhalation of breath muffled in the pillow. The woman lifted her shirt, a slight gasp escaping her at the sight of her back.

"God have mercy." The man was suddenly beside the bed, his voice devoid of emotion. "Who could have done this to her?"

"Do you really think anyone will pay for her safe return? It seems to me they were more than eager to get rid of her. A few more strokes and she might have died."

Angela could hear the man pacing behind her. "We will keep her here. If no one looks for her or claims her, I will marry her."

"No," Angela said, her voice raspy against the pillow her head rested upon. "No, I'm going home."

"Hush, we can talk later. You are in no condition to go anywhere-- least of all back to a place where they would beat you so. The aristos should take better care of their people."

Angela could not reply. A cool cloth was pressed against her back. The fire there seemed to stop for a minute. The woman gave her something to drink; then she continued to clean the dirt from her back, the pain dulling to an indelicate throb.

As if lost in a fog, Angela heard the man and the woman speak. She heard words such as *rebel* and *angel--war* and *punishment*--words that would have astounded her if she could have focused more clearly. Their conversation seemed to go on forever then she slept a deep, all-consuming sleep in which there were no dreams or pain, no confusing words.

She woke refreshed to the busy clatter of cooking, only a dull throb across her back. The woman hummed to herself as she worked. The man was not in the room.

Angela began to sit up, stopping when she realized she was naked beneath the covers. She lay back down, her face turned to the woman, who had noticed the movement.

"How are you feeling?"

The woman moved slowly today, not at all as she had before. With stooped shoulders, she carried a bowl of steaming, liquid to Angela. "Now sit up and eat."

Angela practically choked, a blush heating her cheeks. "I've nothing on."

The woman looked taken aback, as if she'd forgotten or wasn't sure what to do about the girl's condition. "You need to eat," she insisted. "It is just the two of us."

"Where are my clothes?" Angela didn't care how many people were in the room. The man who'd brought her here could come back at any time. She wanted the protection her clothes would give her.

As if reading her mind, the woman said "He's gone. He'll not return soon."

Angela breathed a long sigh of relief, and energy seemed to surge through her. "How long have I been here?" she asked.

The woman sat on the bed, the bowl of steaming liquid in one hand, a spoon in the other. "Eat."

A spoonful of broth at her mouth, Angela obeyed, feeling the warmth seep through her, slowly at first. "How long?" Angela asked again.

The woman shook her head, setting the food aside. "Long enough for someone to have come looking for you," she said.

"Alexi," Angela said without thinking.

She heard the old women's quick intake of air. "You know him?" Angela queried.

"His father I knew very well, for he is also Stephan's father. Stephan and Alexi are half brothers. Alexi, I knew, only when he was younger." Her voice was harsh and cold.' 'His mother's first husband was a murderer, as was his older half brother. I did not know until it was too late. Until my welcome at his home wore thin and I was forced to leave."

As Devil Blackmoor, Alexi had killed when necessary, but this woman knew nothing of that man. She couldn't. Alexi's father lived in another country. His mother's former husband and his older half brother were both dead.

"Perhaps this Alexi is not as evil." The old woman said. "I would not second-guess any of the Popov men. They all come from bad stock. But Alexi's father is not a Popov. So perhaps he does not possess the evil that was inbred in the Popov men."

"He does not," Angela said her hand on the old women's arm. "If he comes to look for me promise me you'll..."

Angela did not know what she wanted.

"Yes?" The woman's voice was harsh. "Why do you hesitate?"

"I love him." Angela knew the truth more clearly than ever before. She did love him. But he didn't love her in return. She wanted nothing less than what her parents had.

A true and deep love. A forever love. One that would last a lifetime and through eternity.

The knock on the door startled both of them.

"Stephan!"

Angela pulled the sheet tight around her as the big man entered, her pulse racing. The man slanted her a cursory look, then went to the kettle of soup simmering over the fire. His back to her, he stayed at the kettle long enough for her to slip more securely beneath the covers.

"They followed the trail I set for them. But it won't take long for either of them to see the trickery." He turned after he spoke. "How is the patient?"

Stephan was suddenly by the bed, his hand on her forehead. "She is not as hot. Perhaps she will live then?" He laughed while the back of his hand touched her cheek gently.

"How long did I sleep?" Angela asked once more.

"What? The old woman wouldn't tell you? You've been asleep for a solid day. Long enough for me to discover you were indeed missed."

"Alexi?" she asked.

"Yes," he said, their eyes meeting, and she saw the anger and latent hatred there. "And an older man."

Puzzled, Angela caught herself sitting up. "Do you know him?"

"No, but I think you do. If what I overheard was right, he is your father," Stephan told her, his face set.

"Impossible." She sat up, clutching the sheet to her breasts, her pulse pounding. She would have to go back to Alexi; a confrontation was inevitable. Her father would know everything, would know she had slept with Alexi.

Panic swept through her.

Stephan trailed his finger across her naked shoulder. She bit back hysteria, caused not by his touch but by the knowledge that her father was here, looking for her.

"I will protect you, little one. You will be safe with me." Stephan read her fear.

She'd heard those words before. And here she was, unprotected and definitely not safe.

"No!" She scooted back out of his reach. He dropped his hand, his smile gone.

"I will fight him for you, for your honor."

"No."

He rose from the bed and walked to the door. "Too bad. They will be here *in* a few hours. You might want to dress. The position you now occupy in my home will not appear quite so damning if you're up and about. And dressed..."

"Your home? I thought ..." She could tell she'd angered him.

"You thought wrong,."

"Where are my clothes?" Her voice trembled. The woman had disappeared, and she was left alone with Stephan.

"My mother is retrieving them for you. I had them washed. The bloodstains are gone."

"Thank you," Angela said, but she could not keep her lip from quivering or her insides from turning over.

"No thanks are needed. If you change your mind about your feelings for me, let me know."

Chapter Eighteen

"Get out!" Feodora screamed at Ivan.

"Never." His voice sounded suave, sophisticated, not at all like the stable master he was supposed to be, and his aristocratic polish was unnerving.

In a blinding rage, Feodora threw the largest vase of flowers she could set her hands upon directly at Ivan's head. Moving with the grace of a Siberian tiger, he ducked, walking steadily toward her, the flying object crashing against the wall behind him. Water from the upset pot drenched his shirt, running in tiny rivulets down his face.

"Get out," she screeched again, and sidestepped his advance. His muscles flexed with every movement, his advance toward her never wavering. He appeared, every inch of him, a powerful male animal on the prowl.

She was his prey.

"Hmmm." Ivan paused in the attack, running his hand through his already disheveled locks. "Furious Feodora--it does have a nice ring to it. I do enjoy a fast, furious tussle with a lady who has a wounded heart. The passion and the heat can melt the very core of a man. Of course, you are no lady, and that fact will make this even more enjoyable. Although, Feodora, I'm not quite sure you have a heart to wound. In any case, it is not for me to mend the wound or feed the blazing passion inside you. The task is for Najjar; he waits for his submissive bride and the child in her womb."

"He can wait until hell freezes over," she said in a patronizing tone, her lashes fluttering against her cheeks.

"My lady, what language. I'm sure Najjar will be willing to cure your impetuous behavior."

She edged around the bed, her gaze riveted on Ivan, anticipating his every move. "You can't force me," she whispered, breathless, her chest heaving, pulling in great lungfuls of air in anticipation.

At any time Ivan was impossible to read: the broad smile, the imperious set of his lips, the knowing sparkle in his eyes when he happened to glance her way, as if he would like to kiss her senseless.

No wonder she could never get the upper hand with him. Feodora supposed she ought to take him more seriously, but she'd never in her life done that--taken a man seriously. Perhaps that had been her mistake, her downfall. Despite Ivan's irresistible and rakish nature, she had just learned the hard way that he was a very dangerous man.

God, but she still wanted him, longed to feel the weight of him on top of her, his shaft deep inside her.

"Never, milady. I wouldn't dream of such a thing. If I wanted you, which I don't, you'd fall into my arms quite willingly." Ivan undid the buttons on his shirt, still watching her, waiting for what, she wasn't sure.

"Then what are you doing?" She licked her lips, one hand resting provocatively against her breast. He was wrong. She wouldn't fall into his arms if he asked. She'd leap.

"I'm not going to ravish you now that you're promised to another man, a friend of mine."

"I was promised to another before. And that fact never stopped you," she challenged.

He paused, absorbing the new angle she'd tossed his way, "That man knew nothing about you. There was no promise, only a hope on his grandmother's part for an heir. We both agreed the match was wrong."

Ivan shook the shirt out, droplets of water evaporating into the sun-drenched room. "You'd like to call out *rape* now, wouldn't you? Even though we both know how untrue the cry would be." Bare-chested, Ivan sat down on a chair by the window, his long legs propped on a footstool, and poured two cups of tea. He munched on an almond cake, then offered one to Feodora.

"They're quite good. Eat up. Najjar likes his women plump, with a little something to hold on to and caress in the middle of the night."

"What do you want from me?" She stepped cautiously to Ivan's side, accepting the cake and the tea, her hands trembling with desire for him.

"Only your cooperation. I want Najjar to be happy with you, and in return I'll see that Alexi does not deal harshly with you when he returns." Ivan bit off another piece of cake, licking the icing upon his lips then added, "Although you deserve a good flogging." He leaned back, one leg now resting across the other, a man totally in control.

Fury replaced lust. "In return I find myself dragged off to the most barren land on this earth. To live in a tent." She knelt by his side, her hand wandering the length of his leg, resting almost intimately against him. It would do her no good to resort to arguments when seduction always worked to her advantage.

One eyebrow quirked upward. "In return"--Ivan leaned forward, taking her hand in his, his arms braced against the armrests of the chair-- "you live to breathe another day." Slowly Ivan raised her trembling fingers to his lips and kissed the back of her hand. "Life, even in the desert, is much more gratifying than death."

"Surely you jest." Feo did pray that he toyed with her emotions, baiting her, perhaps. She did not want to be banished to the desert, nor did she want to die.

The words were no more cruel than Feodora's actions against Angela had been. Where Feodora was going, life was often harsh, and no one would withhold punishment if it was deserved. Najjar would never hold back his hand if she caused grief to any member of the tribe. Feodora needed to be taught a lesson--and quickly, or she would not live a year in Najjar's world.

"Hardly." Ivan sipped his tea, once more leaning back in the chair. For a moment longer, he held her hand in his, enjoying the softness. "I could give you to Angela's father--or worse, I could encourage Alexi to give you to Angela herself. I'm sure she could devise a fitting punishment." He purposely let the words hang on the air. "I've heard tales of torture that might turn even your stomach."

She paled, her skin changing to ashen. The shallow breaths she inhaled no longer came from the need to entice and seduce; her pulse beneath his fingers beat rapidly in fear. He'd scared her. That had been his purpose.

"Now as to the babe. I suggest you either confirm the pregnancy or let me." His gaze drifted to her womb.

Her eyes widened. "Ivan?" If he lifted her skirts, he might make love to her.

"The truth, Feo, just the truth." His eyes were cold and hard. In that instant she saw the truth: he hated her. Everything between them had been a calculated lie.

She flashed him a defiant look. "Yes, I'm still with child. Does that please you?" she asked, snatching her hand from his, her glare hot enough to melt stone.

"Immensely." Satisfaction did indeed feel good. He'd achieved everything he'd set out to do.

~ * ~

Alexi pushed his hat back with his forearm, a fine sheen of sweat beading his forehead. The tracks in front of him were only a day old, but it was obvious the horse making them no longer bore two riders. They'd been duped. He admired the skill of the man who'd tricked them even while he cursed him under his breath. The need to see Angela safe was a seething tempest within him.

"What now?" Sam asked, his brow furrowed in concentration.

"We go back. She's at the village."

"You know who has her."

Sam's calm assessment infuriated Alexi. It was frustrating to know how close they'd been to her, that they could have stolen her away without a fight if they'd only been smart enough to read the signs sooner.

"I do now," Alexi said, a grim smile tugging at the corners of his mouth and dread weighing down his heart. "I haven't seen him for long time. I suppose the two of us are overdue for a meeting. I would have preferred an encounter because of something different from an argument over a woman, however."

Alexi felt the intensity of Sam's gaze on the back of his neck. The man was curious. *Let him wonder.* If Sam Chamberlain were not Angela's father, there would have been more than a few heated words between them by now. More than likely their anger would have erupted in bloodshed.

Stephan was a bastard son of Alexi's father, Karim. Only Allah knew how many bastards the man had sired, sowing his seed over most of Europe. But Stephan he had known very well. Stephan's mother had been a favorite of Karim and she'd spent a great deal of time at their mansion, Stephan at her side. Natasha had loved Stephan with all her heart, had treated him as a beloved grandchild.

As little boys they had spent fun time together. There was a fondness in his heart for Stephan. Not enough to let him have his woman, though.

Alexi had asked Stephan to come to America with him, encouraged him. Stephan had adamantly refused. The young man had had a purpose even then. Stephan was a born leader, a rebel, a man whom others looked up to--and Stephan was in the middle of the revolution sweeping across Russia and Europe.

Agreeing with Stephan and his ideals had always been easy for Alexi, but the hothead was going to get himself killed if he continued on the path he'd chosen. Alexi wanted to yank Stephan off his high horse. He wanted to take him to America, where one didn't have to fight for his freedom, something every man deserved.

That was all Stephan really wanted: his freedom. Stephan didn't want war, didn't want to fight.

The country was coming to that, though. Fighting would erupt soon, and everyone would lose. His friends would die.

"Are we going to ride in shooting, or are more peaceful means acceptable?" Sam asked, his hand on the butt of his gun, obviously ready for whatever Alexi decided.

"We will negotiate her release. Stephan wants money to further his cause." Alexi rose from his position and balanced on the balls of his feet. "He'll give her over for the right amount of coin."

"You're sure?"

Alexi nodded. "Positive."

~ * ~

The downpour started when Alexi and Sam were a mile from the village. Sheets of rain slanted against a broodingly dark sky. Alexi pulled his hooded poncho from his saddlebag, as did Sam, both slipping the capes over their heads for protection.

Riding between the huts on a mud-soggy trail, Alexi knew these people had never seen two men look so desperate or so mean. Children peered from cracked doorways then shrieked with fear, darting inside when they caught sight of the two men.

The children watched two of the American West's meanest desperadoes ride through their village. With his dark, brooding eyes and two days' growth of beard, Alexi knew he looked to be the very devil incarnate.

Alexi led the way to Stephan's home, stopping Jabbar in front of the doorway. Negligently, he leaned on the saddle horn. He didn't know what he expected when Stephan stepped from the hut, his rifle clasped beneath one arm, a furious scowl on his usually smiling countenance. Stephan appeared to have every intention of using the weapon if necessary.

"What do you want, brother?" Stephan spoke with a slight sneer. "It's been such a long time since you've come calling. I could say it was a pleasure, but..."

Alexi knew the tone Stephan used was meant for all aristocrats, not just him. "My woman," Alexi said, determined to set fear into Stephan's heart. "Pray to your God you haven't touched her." Alexi' s voice was low and powerful. He watched Stephan move under the power of his words.

"Pray to Allah," Stephan ground out, appearing unruffled by Alexi's cold threat.

"We've both grown up over the years," Alexi said, his emotions tightly controlled. "But you're still not man enough to hold your own against me. Where is Angela? Inside, I presume? Safe?"

Stephan widened his stance, squaring off against Alexi, his purpose unmistakable. "You may be bigger, but you never learned to care for a woman. She's under my protection now. I will keep her safe."

That jibe hit home. He, Alexi Popov, had promised Angela exactly that: to protect and keep her safe. Now Stephan was doing just that. They were indeed an unlikely pair.

"She's mine." Alexi growled low in his throat.

"Then prove it. Fight me for her."

At the challenge, tension coiled deep inside Alexi, all rational thought fleeing him. Alexi was off Jabbar in a flash, the two brothers circling. Alexi was huge and well muscled, Stephan long, lean and wiry. One man resembled a sleek gazelle, the other an enraged grizzly.

"Hold it right there!" Sam's voice rose above the fever pitch of the storm and the afternoon, penetrating the anger and the tension simmering inside each man. "Hold," he said again, this time in a fierce whisper.

Lightning-charged air threatened to jump between the brothers.

"Until Angela is legally wed, she's my daughter. Both of you stop this nonsense. I want to see her."

Both furious men suddenly looked chastised, the importance of Angela and her welfare suddenly resuming its proper place in their heads.

Alexi dropped his hands to his sides.

Stephan nodded. "She's in there."

Sam stepped through the door, brushing by both men as if they were nonexistent. He paused a few seconds, letting his eyes adjust to the dim light. Angela was on the bed, turned onto her side, her hands tucked beneath her cheek, her hair spread across the pillow and down her back. She looked like his little girl--his angel when she slept, his spitfire when she was awake. He adored her and wanted the best for her.

Well, she'd done it again. Her impetuous desire for adventure had brought her halfway around the world and earned her a wretched flogging at the hands of a madwoman. And if what he'd understood was true, she wasn't married, but she'd agreed to be this arrogant Russian's paramour. He should put her in a corner for a week for this.

He sighed, kneeling down beside her, tenderly smoothing back the hair from her face just as he'd done so many times. He meant to test Alexi--or Devil Blackmoor--whatever the hell he called himself. "You are going home with me. If he loves you he will follow. If he loves you, nothing will keep him from you. If not...

"If not, you are indeed better off without him." He growled softly in the back of his throat.

Moisture filled his eyes and stung the deeper recesses of his heart. "If not," Sam repeated, "he doesn't deserve you. And as for the other young puppy, I can tell by watching him he cares for you, but nothing more. He has a deep-seated desire to best his idol. I should have let them fight. Maybe one of them would have beat some sense into the other." Sam inhaled deeply, remembering his own arrogance. "One can't expect miracles in this godforsaken land--or anywhere else.

"Rest, little one. The journey home is long."

Angela stirred, her hand brushing against his. When had she grown into such a beautiful woman? Sam wondered. He'd been so determined to do what he thought best for his little girl that he'd never listened to her, never acknowledged her wishes as anything but childhood fantasies. She'd craved adventure.

He wanted her to go to finishing school. For the life of him, he could not come up with one good reason now.

If he had listened...

If he had heard what she'd tried to tell him time and again, all this might have never happened.

"Papa?" Angela asked, blinking slowly.

"I'm here. I've come to take you home," he said.

Even in her drowsy state, he watched her stiffen. "No, Papa. I have to see Alexi first. I promised, and now that you're here..." She touched his face.

She hadn't expected to see him, he thought.

"Now that you're here, I won't be in danger."

"Now that I'm here, you'll obey me..."

Her eyes flashed. "No."

He knew he was controlling her life again, not listening to her, but when had she grown so willful? "Angela?"

She had always been willful, he realized.

"Papa, don't you see? I'm not a little girl any longer. I'm a grown woman. And Papa, I ..." She paused, red staining her cheeks, and Sam knew what she was about to reveal.

"You don't have to tell me. I know."

Angela gasped, straining to rise. "You know?" Her eyes widened with fear. "Papa!" she cried out, her voice frantic.

Sam knew all too well what she thought. "He's alive, sweet angel. Even though I did have every intention of giving him a slow, torturous death."

The door slammed against the far wall. Alexi's powerful body was framed in the doorway, light from behind him casting an ominous glow around him.

"Alexi?" Angela said softly. "Let me talk to him, Papa. Please."

Reluctantly, Sam nodded his assent.

Angela touched her fingers to her father's hand then held her other hand out to Alexi. In two arrogant strides, he stood beside the bed, his eyes shimmering in the faint light.

Sam walked away, stepping outside the door and closing it behind him. Angela watched her father go, knowing it had been hard for him to leave her alone with Alexi. He didn't back down easily.

Alexi held her hand in his. His fingers were large and callused. With him beside her she felt fragile, delicate, a feeling at odds with her character and the life she had led.

The rain beat a steady crescendo on the rooftop, and embers from the fire spit and popped. She didn't know what to say; she only knew that with Alexi by her side she felt at ease, comfortable. He held her heart in the palm of his hand.

Angela watched his hardened features soften, his cold eyes warm until they smoldered with... what? Love? Probably not. All he'd ever felt for her was desire.

She brought his hand to her cheek, stroked his fingers lovingly. His flesh was warm against her own. Her lips touched his hand. She held on tight to his hand, now letting it rest on the bed. Silence seemed to engulf them.

"Are you all right?" His voice broke through the tension and the solitude she'd needed to find for a few moments before they were at odds once more.

"Yes," she said. His eyes told her he didn't believe her. "I just need to rest. I can't go with you right now."

Anger flared in the deep brown eyes that stared at her. A ferocity she'd never seen in him before glimmered darkly.' 'I'm very tired," she added, suddenly afraid of the fury she saw in him.

"I see," His tone was brisk. He rose, striding to the fire.

Not moving for many minutes, Angela wondered at his stiff composure. A silence that only minutes ago felt comfortable was now fraught with tension. Angela stared at his back for a few seconds, trying to concentrate, trying to compose her thoughts into a reasonable argument she could explain to him. Her efforts were useless.

His head now bowed, he appeared to pray. Then he turned his expression enigmatic. "How long?"

"I don't know. I feel stronger today than yesterday. Perhaps tomorrow I--"

"Do you prefer to stay here? With Stephan?" he asked the pain in his voice obvious to her.

She didn't understand. "Stay with Stephan?" she asked, puzzled by his question.

"Don't make me ask again."

"No," she said, beginning to understand. "Stephan doesn't want me here. He wants money."

"Stephen will get all the blood money he wants." Alexi's voice had grown threatening. "He won't have you."

"I don't understand."

"Stephan would take you, if you'd let him. He'd keep you to get to me, to show me he doesn't need the things I have to gain something I desire. That being a prince means nothing."

She moved over. There was plenty of room on the bed for Alexi, and right now she needed him, his warmth, his touch. She wanted him close to her.

"Hold me," she said. "Please."

She watched a shudder sweep through him as he assimilated her words. His hesitancy alarmed her. His reluctance brought tears to her eyes.

"I won't hurt you?" he asked, and once more his voice was filled with concern.

She shook her head. "No."

In seconds he had joined her on the bed, gathering her in his arms, the heat from him flowing into her, giving her strength and the courage to follow her father. His strong hands tenderly caressed the length of her back, pulling her closer.

She wanted to be part of him. Only him.

"If your father walked in on us now, I might be well and truly killed."

"Tortured."

"Would you save me?"

"He would not dare act the enraged father," she whispered, feeling for the first time in so long the security he represented to her. "And yes, I would brave any elements to save you."

She loved him beyond words.

His chuckle warmed her. "Perhaps not," he said. "Because I will not do anything to compromise you further. You must rest. If holding you is all I can have for now, so be it. Rest, little angel and soon I will take you down the mountain to my home. Then and only then will you have to make decisions. Do not let your father tell you what to do."

With that, she kissed him lovingly and fell asleep in his arms.

It was an unlikely party that made its way up the tree-lined road to Alexi's home the next day. Stephan had accompanied Angela, who rode on a travois fashioned by Sam and Alexi.

Angela had wanted to tell Alexi she wasn't going to be staying with him, but when the moment had arrived she lost her courage. He'd looked so frightened for her, so sincere.

She didn't want to hurt him any more than she already had. By running away she'd broken the promise she'd given him, and even though he didn't bring it up, she knew he remembered. Openly he'd forgiven her because he understood she'd had no choice. Deep in his heart, she knew he'd lost faith in her.

They were still at the same miserable impasse, both immovable in their convictions, both stubborn to a fault. Now that she knew she loved him so desperately, she could never live as his mistress. To Angela it would be better to spend the rest of her life with her few memories than to watch their love die a slow, torturous death at the hands of a cruel society that would never accept her.

High in the Rocky Mountains, listening to the wind and the crystal-clear streams, she would find peace. She would go home with her father, a place where she could hold her head high, not having to swallow her pride every time she saw someone she knew.

She would miss Alexi terribly; his devilish smile, the way his eyes smoldered with desire when he looked at her.

Leaving him was a small price to pay for her self-respect.

The travois pulled by Jabbar stopped at the front steps to Alexi's home. He dismounted. Before she could voice a protest, he swept her into his arms, holding her close, cherishing her. His broad shoulders protected her from the piercing gaze of the people who had come out to watch the return of their master. She closed her eyes, turning her head into his chest, relishing the feel of his strength, the scent of the man --at the same time knowing what these people thought of her. She was their master's whore, nothing more.

Shame filled her heart and her soul. It cut deeply. She had wavered too many times in her convictions.

Inwardly, she cried for her lost love, for her broken heart and the child who would never know his father. She had changed, matured in countless ways, and she knew her mind.

They walked up the steps and into the house. She remembered another tune when Misha had escorted her up the same front steps and then up the winding staircase to the upper bedchambers, pointing out the one she was to occupy.

Her world had been different then, her hopes and dreams still innocent and golden, filled with visions of a life with her dark warrior.

She had thought she could change him, change the world.

She couldn't. She accepted that now.

"Grandmother." Alexi's voice penetrated her murky thoughts. Angela opened her eyes, staring thoughtfully at a woman dressed completely in black. Her silver-gray hair was pulled back into a neat bun, her face creased with lines of weariness, her warm smile and outstretched arms beckoning her grandson home.

"Alexi," she said. The pride in the woman's voice reverberated clearly. "I'm so glad you received my letter. I prayed every day--every night--for your safe return. Now that you're here, where you belong, my heart can rest. You will settle down, marry, have children."

Natasha directed her gaze toward Stephan, whom she'd always considered family. "It has been so many years since we last saw each other. Will you be staying with us?"

"No, Grandmother. I have come with Alexi and Angela to be sure of their safety. I have a cause to fight for. I will not return for a very long time, if ever."

"You will stay the night."

Stephan nodded, and Natasha turned her attention back to her other grandson.

"I came as soon as I could. I had many lose ends to tie up. Traveling across America took more time than I thought it would." Alexi looked pointedly at Angela. "There were complications. I have come to some decisions. We will speak of this later." With Angela still in his arms, he hugged Natasha then placed a warm kiss on his grandmother's weathered cheek.

"Who is she?" Natasha asked, looking at Angela.

"My--" Alexi stopped suddenly, looking chagrined. "A friend," he finished. "A dear friend."

"Does she have a name?" Natasha queried, her tone stern yet gentle.

"My name is Angela Chamberlain," Angela answered for Alexi. "I met Alexi in the States. In Denver. I'll be returning soon with my father. We have a cabin near Denver." She was babbling, her nerves frayed. "You don't need to worry that I will marry your grandson and sully the family name."

Alexi's arms around her tightened perceptibly. He said nothing, his eyes once more growing cold and fathomless. The creases around his face deepened.

"I've enjoyed meeting you." Angela's words continued to pour out in a rush. "I'm sure Alexi will find a suitable bride and make you very proud, give you many wonderful great grandchildren." She prayed she'd finish before Alexi said what she knew must be on his mind. She expected a vehement, "You're going nowhere," but Alexi said nothing on the subject. His lack of concern hit her hard.

Instead he said, "She needs to rest. I'm sure you heard what happened to her. Stephan found her and took care of her. She has had a rough time the last few days." He paused, and it seemed to Angela he was at a lack for words. "Ivan is still here with Feodora?" he questioned, and every inch of his body seemed primed and ready to explode.

A sudden rash of jealousy swept through Angela at Feodora's name. "Ivan thought it would be best for them to leave once we received word you and the girl were all right. He feared for Najjar's sanity." Natasha laughed, a tender, knowing look in her deep brown eyes, eyes that matched Alexi's. "Ivan said the poor man has waited too long for a wife, and Feodora needed a man to look after her so she would find no more trouble. He said you'd understand."

Alexi nodded, and a dangerously hard smile formed on his lips then quickly vanished. "Ivan was wise to leave. He knew I would have punished Feodora for her actions. We will talk later," he said, continuing up the steps, Angela still held possessively in his arms.

~ * ~

Alexi walked past the door to the room he'd instructed Misha to give Angela and straight to his own room. He kicked the door open and stalked through it before pushing it shut then deposited Angela unceremoniously on his huge bed. "You are not going anywhere until we've had time to discuss this. You are mine."

She tried to move from the bed. His body blocked hers.

"You can't keep me against my will. You cannot force me to stay here. "Angela's lips trembled, her hair in disarray. Alexi did not want to talk. He wanted to make love to his little hellion, to convince her in every way he could find to bind her to him. He sensed that the only way to do that was to make love to her.

Loneliness pervaded his every heartbeat. Suddenly a lifetime without her looked very bleak indeed. He meant to test her, to know the truth. "Can you look at me and say that you are leaving?"

"Yes," she said, her small chin pointed determinedly into the air.

"Prove it." He spoke slowly, every nerve ending on edge, waiting for her to rise to the challenge.

"You can't ..." Her words were vehement.

"I can't what, angel? What can't I do?"

"Force me to stay here."

~ * ~

He stood over her, a devil in black, a brooding expression on his face that did not bode well for Angela. He thought he might lock her in the room if she meant to leave him.

"You can't keep me here," she said once more, almost breathlessly, her anger flaring even while the heat of desire raced like a demon-wind inside her. "I cannot be your mistress." The single word *mistress* was a soft hiss.

Still, he said nothing, his silence provoking her, intimidating her. She wanted to retaliate, to yell at him.

He needed to understand.

He would never understand.

"Can I get her anything?" Natasha asked, poking her head through the door sheepishly.

Angela lay back on the bed, waiting for Alexi to answer in his impervious way, always giving orders.

"Alexi?" Natasha asked again. "Is there anything wrong here? You look angry."

"Nothing is wrong," he said through gritted teeth, his gaze upon Angela turning tender. "Everything is wrong," he whispered so softly only Angela could hear. Then, "Angel? Is there anything my grandmother can get you?"

He was asking her? Suddenly Angela realized her rudeness. "A bath, perhaps. I'd love a nice, long, hot bath." *In steaming hot water scented with jasmine.*

"I will send someone up." Natasha slipped from the room, a wide smile flashing at Angela just before the door closed.

Angela's heart raced with anticipation. Alexi sat by the bed, watching her in the strangest way. He held one of her hands in his, his eyes closed. She heard the soft murmur of his voice.

"Heaven help me, I don't want you to leave. Please stay. I don't think I can live without you."

Moisture rose to her eyes, and a lone tear slid down her cheek. "I can't stay," she said. "I cannot live with you under these circumstances. I'd die a little bit each day until there was nothing left of me. I won't let you rob me of my self-esteem and my integrity."

"I see." His voice was a hoarse whisper in the airless room. "It is decided then."

She couldn't breathe. He was but a shadow of himself, his eyes dark and cold; it seemed as if his soul had left him.

"I don't think you do," she whispered slowly, reaching out to him then withdrawing her hand at the sad look he gave her.

"There is nothing more to be said. As soon as you're well you can return home with your father. I release you from any promises you have made to me."

He walked from the room. Her own energy and stamina drained from her. With a desperate moan of self-pity, she rolled to her side. Seeing nothing but a blur of blue flowers on the wall, she let the tears run down her cheeks until she finally slept.

Chapter Nineteen

Morning light stole across the land.

Hands folded in front of her, a heavy weight on her heart, Natasha watched the young woman who seemed to have stolen her grandson's heart. And she felt terrible for the ordeal Angela had gone through in her home.

Angela Chamberlain slept peacefully on the huge bed in Alexi's chamber. She was a beautiful woman, and if the stories she'd heard about Angela were true, she was courageous and headstrong, too. The two of them, Alexi and Angela, suited each other--except in one thing.

Angela was of common stock. The other nobles would never accept her. But the country was changing, on the verge of a revolution, and soon nothing would be the same. Anyone with half a brain could see the inevitable outcome. In a few years' time there might very well be no more nobles, and then what would the status of Angela's family matter?

Soon it would make little difference who married whom.

Natasha had needed her grandson home to put to rights all that her daughter's first husband had ruined. Now she felt guilt-ridden. She was a vain, selfish old woman, clinging to the past. Alexi's future had never been in this land. It still wasn't, but his heart was loyal and true. If she asked him, he would stay here. If she asked it of Alexi, he'd watch Angela walk away from him. He'd watch her because he could not admit he was in love with her.

Yet it was Stephan who belonged here, who thought of Russia as Ms home. He loved the land and the people fiercely, with all his heart and soul.

Alexi was deeply in love too. Any fool could see by the way he looked at Angela how much he loved her.

Natasha wondered at that. She had never thought of her grandson as a man who would not love. And his love for Angela should not come as a surprise because he'd always loved too deeply, all-consumingly.

She'd feared for him and his future.

Now all her fears were about to come true. If Angela left, he would never find love.

Angela stirred, pushing the covers away. As Natasha looked at Angela, it was not hard to see the physical beauty that drew Alexi to her. Her wheat blond hair flowed like a silken mantle across the pillows. And she had more integrity in her little finger than Feodora had in her entire body.

Angela was a tiny little thing with a huge heart.

Alexi would feel protective to a fault. Angela could tangle with any man and come out the winner. She had heart, courage and loyalty that knew no bounds.

"How is she?" Sam suddenly appeared by the bed, a brooding expression on his face.

"Fine." Natasha had not heard him enter. Sam always surprised her. He moved too silently and too quickly, unnerving her every time he mysteriously appeared at her side.

"We will leave in two days. Alexi arranged everything, including the use of his ship, the *Mystic*. His father will ensure our safe passage."

"When did Alexi leave?" Natasha asked. She'd seen her grandson's face when he'd left the room a few hours ago, and knew he would not return until Sam and Angela were gone. She knew his heart had shattered at the news. She'd felt his pain to the very core of her heart.

Sam walked to the window overlooking the stables. "This very moment," he said, running his hands through his hair. "If it would do any good, I'd go after the boy, beg him to return and work this out. I don't know the whole story, but I wish I did."

"He can't marry her," Natasha interjected quickly. "You and I both know the only other option is entirely unsuitable for you and for her. She is far too precious to live the life of a mistress. Alexi will come to terms with this situation. He has to. So much is at stake here."

"I would kill him," Sam gritted out, his hands fisted tightly at his sides. "If he's hurt her in any way, I will find him, hunt him down and make sure he pays for any crimes against her."

My Angel

Natasha smiled grimly. "You could try. You would not succeed."

"One of us would die," Sam went on. "I would have to defend her honor."

"If either of you died, it would make her life even lonelier than it will be now. She loves him."

"She wouldn't have gone with him otherwise," Sam agreed, his voice shaking with emotion.

"I have a suitable heiress in mind for him. I vowed I would not interfere, but I have. In time..." Natasha paused long enough to wipe a tear from her cheek. "In time they will both forget." Natasha knew those words for what they were--lies.

She had once loved like that: a love so enduring and so intense she felt it still when she thought of the man who had stolen her heart so many years ago--then married another. She would never forget that, nor could the emptiness inside her ever be filled.

"What will she do?" Natasha asked, realizing Alexi would want to know.

The question was entirely unsuitable, and Natasha knew it. What Angela would do when she returned to America was none of her business.

"I would like her to go to school, but I'm afraid she won't have anything to do with finishing school now. She's been on her own, had her adventure..."

"She is a willful lady."

"Yes, she is. Stubborn to a fault."

Natasha moved to the door, tired of speaking in hushed whispers. "Would you like some tea?" she asked, moisture filling her eyes, sadness filling her soul. She suddenly wished for a different ending to all this, a way to make Alexi happy, a way to heal his broken heart.

He would be devastated when Angela left, when he returned to a home that no longer sheltered his lover. He'd ridden off understanding that Angela would be gone when he returned. Alexi had thought his leaving until then was for the best.

Perhaps it was.

Natasha had no doubt these two were lovers. She also had no doubt that Angela carried Alexi's child. There were signs that only a woman would recognize. Little things.

She would not be the one to tell Alexi.

If Alexi knew, he would never let Angela go.

Never.

He would search the earth for her and his child.

~ * ~

Jabbar was tireless. Alexi road hard and fast. Exhaustion would not claim him, nor did he receive solace from the grueling pace he set each day. Day after day he rode farther into the mountains, higher and higher until he could barely breathe the thinning air.

Summer rapidly turned into autumn, yet here in this land surrounded by the Black Sea, one could scarce tell. Sweat trickled down his back and between his shoulder blades.

Alexi felt the subtle changes in the air.

His life spun chaotically.

He wanted nothing more than to rid himself of Angela's image. He could not. She had become an integral part of him, and he didn't know how he would survive without her.

He could not sleep. When he closed his eyes he saw the wheat color of her hair, the sky blue of her eyes. He could feel the soft brush of her lips against his own, hear the throaty sounds she made deep in her throat when he pleasured her.

He could not eat. He prayed that if he pushed himself hard enough and long enough, he'd find respite.

That was days ago.

Now he knew there was no relief, understood nothing would ease the emptiness deep inside.

He had become a hollow shell of a man.

And still he rode. Jabbar's sides heaved with exhaustion, yet the stallion moved to his master's will, his loyalty beyond compare.

Deep in the mountains, he found little solace. Nothing he could think of would make his life easier. Proposing marriage would have solved one problem, but in the process would have created more.

She was right in leaving him. He could never give her what her heart desired, what she deserved.

Selfishness had pushed him to demand so much from her, and she'd given even more. He was a fool.

His gaze shifted to the ocean, toward the west. Without slowing his mount, he jumped from Jabbar's back. The horse slowed then stopped.

Alexi held his hand high, a gesture of farewell and resignation. He was well and truly alone. The light and the heart of his life had left on a morning tide, never to return.

Only yesterday he believed he could not hurt any more. He did.

The *Mystic* should have sailed days ago, should be slipping through the Sea of Marmara on its way to the Mediterranean. The sea would be a wondrous sky blue, nearly the color of her eyes. Dolphins would follow the ship, playing alongside, singing to and chatting with the sailors--and Angela.

Angela's laugh would float with the wind. He remembered all too well the light in her eyes when she had seen her first dolphins, the way she clapped her hands together in childish glee.

Allah, if he could stand to go home, he would. He would work his fingers to the bone if there was a chance in hell he could ease the pain.

Standing on the top of the mountain he could see for miles around him. The cliffs were rugged, yet not as formidable as the Rockies. The rivers were crystal clear, yet they were not as clean and fresh as the Colorado River. The sky was a polished blue that sometimes melded with the Black Sea, but it was not as beautiful as the sky over Denver.

He had become a hollow shell of a man.

This land of his, he no longer considered home. This land where he inherited a title was not his to rule. The title meant nothing to him. Others could command in his place. Stephan could have it all. Once she thought about Stephan inheriting the title as well as the land, Natasha would not mind. Stephan was as much a grandson to Natasha as he was. Perhaps more so because Stephan belonged in Russia, and was willing to fight for his country and its people.

Stephan would understand, would make an admirable leader.

He felt the wind blowing off the sea. Closing his eyes, he absorbed the sounds and smells of this country. He let his thoughts sweep throughout him until they took hold. Suddenly, on the winds of time, he let out a wild cry. It freed his heart and his soul.

Alexi Popov, alias Devil Blackmoor understood what he must do. For several more hours he stared out over this land that had once claimed him. Memorizing all he could see, he stored the sights away so he could someday tell his grandchildren of its beauty. He recalled the folktales his grandmother had told him and committed them to his memory.

He sat down cross-legged on the mountain grass and asked Allah for guidance and the patience needed to fulfill his dreams and conquer his fears.

When he finished, he mounted his horse and rode back to the estate. A serenity he'd never felt before gave credence to his actions. What he had in mind would take a few months to achieve, possibly more, but with patience and diligent work he would convince Stephan to take over for him, and he would teach Stephan how to keep the books, and run the vast estate. Then he'd return to America. And he would find his angel. Pray to Allah she would still be waiting for him.

~ * ~

Beneath a sky of hammered gold, the *Mystic* skimmed past the minarets of Constantinople. Through clouded, vacant eyes Angela watched the sun go down like a blinding ball of white light, dolphins jumping playfully out of the water. Yet she could not smile. The world seemed unreal, almost unnatural.

Had it really been less than three months since she'd left New York?

While she stood at the bow, looking forward, the ship sailed through the Sea of Marmara then into the Mediterranean away from Alexi. One hour passed into the next. Glittering stars filled the midnight sky, and a full moon slanted a shimmering swath of light on the water. She didn't know how long she stayed at the bow of the ship.

She didn't care.

A burnished sun rose in the east, sending much-needed warmth across Angela's back. The chill within did not ease. Tears that burned deep inside were not shed.

"Angela," Sam whispered. "You've got to come below."

259

She'd lost count of the times her father had come to her, asking her to sleep or to eat. She didn't have the heart for either.

His fingers settled on her shoulders, his intentions well meant. If only his strength could flow from him into her. She longed for the power to feel again.

"I can't," she said on a whispered sigh, her voice barely perceptible. She felt her father stiffen, felt the change in his deep, even breathing.

"Then drink this." Sam handed her a steaming cup of coffee loaded with cream and sugar.

For the first time since she'd boarded the clipper once again, she turned from her view of her future. She accepted the drink and sipped gingerly. She didn't want to hurt him.

"Drink it all," he said.

She nodded. "Thank you."

Nothing more was said between them. It seemed her father meant to stay with her, bringing her self-imposed isolation to an abrupt end. He leaned on the railing of the ship, silent, never taking his eyes from the waters in front of him.

She would not fight him, she determined. If she did, he would dig his heels in and she would never find another moment's peace. Already she sensed his frustration, his sadness.

Truly he had her best interests at heart. But she'd left her heart in a foreign land, in the hands of a man they'd labeled Devil Blackmoor out west.

Weariness washed through her, her eyes closing despite her commands to herself to stay awake. She felt her knees give way as strong arms encircled her and lifted her. Giving in to memories of her childhood, she let her father carry her to her room without protest.

The coverlet he pulled over her was warm and soft. He kissed her forehead. Then he pulled the curtain closed on the window, on the light and on the past. That was good. The brightness of day served only to remind her of all she'd lost in the name of survival.

"Good night, Angela," he whispered. "I'm sorry, but you wouldn't listen to reason."

I'm sorry ... you wouldn't listen to reason. For a long time those words whirled around in her head.

Finally there was only a black emptiness. And for the first time in her life, Angela didn't care if she ever woke up.

~ * ~

When she did wake, her father was in the room. He was eating. His plate was piled high with sausages, eggs, potatoes and bread.

A new sense of reality lightened her heart. The sight and the smell of the sausages and the fresh-baked bread made her mouth water and her stomach rumble hungrily.

Her dreams had been filled with a little boy, a child who looked just as Alexi must have looked. He had dark brown eyes that twinkled with mischief, a lopsided smile that melted her heart, and a tenderness about him that made her wonder at her selfishness.

She carried a child deep inside her. She had so very much to live for, because she wanted this child to be born healthy and happy. She meant to make his life as wonderful as she could.

It wouldn't matter that the boy would not know his father. There were plenty of men in her life, men who would make her son feel wanted. After all, she had Trey, Dakota and her father.

Angela pushed her hair from her eyes and gave Sam Chamberlain a well-deserved smile. "Thank you," she told him.

His grin widened. "I take it you're feeling better." He spoke softly, almost as if he was afraid he'd break her.

"Much better." She swung her legs off the bed and tried to rise. Instantly she sat back down.

Sam was beside her. "Stay in bed a little while longer," he said.

"What did you do?" Her words were accusatory.

"I gave you a little something to make sure you'd sleep peacefully."

"I should be very angry with you."

"But you're not. And if that smile on your face means anything, I have no regrets," he said.

"I was a fool," she said, her hand resting on her stomach.

His gaze was filled with love and admiration. "No, Angela. You were hurting. But given your condition I couldn't let you heal on your own or find your own solutions. I had to step in."

Shock ricocheted to her toes. "You know." She didn't need to ask him. She knew the answer.

He nodded, a strange sadness in his expression, but joy in his eyes. "Does Alexi?"

"If he did, do you think for one moment he would have let us leave?" Angela answered. She hadn't told him because she knew he would never have let her go if he'd known the truth. Guilt was not a pleasant emotion. Alexi should know about his child.

"You can write him. We will mail the letter in the next port. In any case, it will give him time to decide how much he cares about you."

"I don't want him to know, at least not yet."

Sam hesitated, his lips thinning to a grim line. "Care to tell me why?" he asked.

"If he comes to America again, I want to know he came for me." With that said Angela managed to stand without swaying and make her way to the plate of food her father had brought her. She ate until she couldn't stand the sight of the food left in front of her.

Chapter Twenty

Dressed from head to toe in black, his hat sitting low, Devil Blackmoor watched the babe pull himself up and on unsteady legs toddle toward its mother. He counted backward.

Allah, but they'd made love only once.

Pride filled him--then a blinding rage so strong the blood pounding in his head blurred his vision. He could have never foreseen this. Willing his shattered nerves to calm, he absorbed the scene before him.

In motherhood, Angela was even more beautiful than he remembered. She wore her buckskins and a white shirt. He held back the smile that threatened. Still, she courted rebellion. Her hair was braided in one single plait, and at the moment it lay over her shoulder. The knife she'd always kept handy was at her waist, a shotgun rested against the same tree trunk she leaned against, and she wore a pistol she had strapped to her leg.

The baby let out an excited little coo at some new discovery. Alexi smiled, and happiness seeped through him. The emptiness he'd felt for over a year now--almost a year and a half--seemed to be fading slowly, his heart swelling with unbound love.

His child.

At least, he thought, surely the little one must be his. He'd asked questions at the trading post only five miles away. He'd seen Dakota and Emma for a few hours before continuing his journey. No one had mentioned a child.

The baby was his.

His son plucked a small white daisy. Holding the flower in his grubby little fist, he proudly showed the small treasure to his mama. She laughed. Alexi's heart flipped over.

He wanted to race down the hill and claim his son. He yearned to sweep mother and child into his arms and race off into the sunset, never looking back.

Except there was no setting sun.

And the mama would put up one hell of a fight.

No, that wasn't the way to right all the wrongs he'd committed against his lady. Alexi nudged the horse into the shelter of a thick stand of aspen. He wanted to watch his son a little while longer, needed to look upon the child and the mother, until his racing heart calmed. He loved them both. Allah, but it had taken him a long time to realize his love.

Angela kissed the child's finger. The boy chortled in glee, losing his balance and falling on his well-padded rump. Alexi chuckled deep in his throat, enjoying the play, and the experience of watching his child.

The boy was now on his back, his legs whirling madly in the air, his arms following suit. She tickled him and kissed him, blowing on his tummy.

Alexi's heart lodged in his throat.

From a distance he could hear her croon soft words to the child. She put a diaper on the boy, still murmuring words that made no sense.

Mesmerized by the sight in front of him, he watched her undo her shirt and bare one swollen white breast, crested with a taut nipple. Alexi swallowed hard. His legs tightened around the horse. Jabbar, sensing his master's agitation, shifted. She brought the babe to nurse, and all of Alexi's composure vanished.

He had plans.

This was too soon.

He would not go to her.

He would not.

~ * ~

The fine hairs on the back of Angela's neck prickled. Methodically and with grim purpose, Angela's hand closed over her pistol. Her fingers tightened uneasily. The babe gave a frustrated little wail then latched back onto the nipple she offered him. The clearing was still empty, but her sixth sense had kicked in. Someone was out there, watching.

Perhaps coming to this secluded place had not been such a good idea after all. Her father had not objected, though. The winter had been unusually long, and she'd grown so very restless shut up in the cabin. This sunny day had beckoned her, and she'd decided to ride into the high pasture.

A movement in the distance made her nerves dance with apprehension. A tall, broad-shouldered man strode from the line of trees in front of her. She brought the gun up. His long, lanky stride was all too familiar.

"Devil," she whispered. Her heart set up a frantic pounding. The urge to run swept through her, yet she couldn't move. Her fingers tightened around the child in her arms. Her breath came in short, ragged pants.

Slowly she let the safety off the gun and pulled back the trigger. "Don't come one step closer," she said and prayed he couldn't hear the fear in her voice--and perhaps the desire.

She pointed the gun directly at Alexi's heart.

He stopped midstride. The sun directly behind him shaded his features. He was nothing like she remembered. Yet, he was exactly as she remembered.

Hard. Cold. Ruthless. Had he come back to squeeze the last bit of pride from her soul? If she let him, he could do that to her. His gaze focused on the child.

He'd seen the baby.

God, no! "Hold it right there." Her shakiness left, replaced by a mother's fear and determination. Instantly she knew he would do anything necessary to take his child. He would not let go easily.

"I don't mean you any harm." His hands were raised high.

He'd called her bluff. "Don't think I won't." Her voice quavered and her determination faltered.

"Not for a minute, angel." He was walking toward her, his hands away from his gun.

He knew she wouldn't shoot. Slowly she relaxed, the gun barrel now pointing at the grass in front of her. Tears she hadn't shed for over a year began to fall from her eyes.

"I hate you." *I love you.*

"With good reason." He stood by her, his arms outstretched, waiting.

Defeated, she sobbed. Another unearthly wail filled the air as she recognized her greatest fear: out of the blue, Alexi had come for his child.

Not her. Never her.

Her heart shattered into a thousand unmendable pieces. Fumbling with the buttons--and despite a loud howl of protest--she fastened her shirt.

Determined to see this through, she rose to meet him. Her son's tiny mouth nestled against her neck, still pursed and still sucking.

She could see Alexi's face now, his eyes.

Anger radiated from him in searing waves. Still, she stood her ground. He would have to come all the way if he wanted to hold the son he'd sired. She would not meet him halfway. She'd already done that.

He would not take the child from her.

He would not.

Alexi plucked the child from her arms as if she were nothing, as if he owned the child. The babe looked at the man with curiosity in his eyes, his finger reaching out to touch Alexi's chin.

He gurgled delightedly, almost as if he knew Devil was his father.

The smile that slanted crookedly across Devil's face softened his harsh features. Then he looked at her. His coldness returned like the frigid storms that had swept the Rockies this past winter.

"You will not keep the boy from me," he said, his voice tempered, yet so very hard. "He will live in my home. You can decide what you want to do. Either come or stay."

He challenged her, provoked her.

"He's not your son," she returned.

"Liar."

There was no shred of tenderness in the expression or the single word he shot to her--no caring or concern for her. Fear left a cold emptiness inside her.

Alexi would do everything he said. She could not live with him, knowing he wanted only his son. There was no choice.

The child looked dwarfed in his arms, so very small and fragile. Her baby's eyes were the same color as Alexi's own, and his hair the same blue-black. The lie was apparent from the start, and she thought Alexi knew why she'd issued the false statement, why she had lied to him again.

He thought she meant to deny him his child.

But, Lord, it wasn't true. She did not want to keep Alexi from seeing and knowing his child. She was just so very afraid he'd take him from her.

And because of her lies, he meant to do that very thing.

She closed her eyes, resigned to the fate now waiting for her, for them. For a moment she rested her head in her hands, wishing she could change the course her life had taken.

She could not.

Silence engulfed them. Only the soft breezes wrapping around them made any noise at all. It seemed that with her declaration and his counter, the world had stopped turning.

Nothing mattered but her child.

And then he laughed.

"Little liar," he said again. "You don't expect me to believe this child is not mine?" he asked, his tone incredulous. Stepping even closer to her, the child held protectively in his arms, he touched her cheek.

An answer eluded her. The ground she stood on whirled crazily beneath her feet. She swayed, suddenly overcome by the uproar within her. She should have had time to prepare for his arrival.

Unable to restrain herself, she lifted her arms for her child. He didn't move to give her what she wanted.

"Can we sit down and discuss this?" he asked. "He needs a mother and a father."

"You won't take him from me." She didn't know if that was a question or a command. It no longer mattered. She meant every word, and she would meet this challenge he forced on her.

"We need to talk," he told her.

She watched his strong fingers as they gently stroked the child's back, soothing him as he once had soothed her. Tremors ran the length of her spine.

There was nothing to talk about. She was at his mercy, and she understood he would have his way. Even her father would not deny that Alexi had a right to his own child. Sam had warned her time and again to write to Devil, to tell him the truth.

Fear had always stopped her.

"I won't hurt you," he said again. His voice just as tender and seducing as she remembered. "I want only to share what's mine and yours."

Nothing she could do would stop the horrid, wonderful sensations just the sight of him gave her.

Get down on your knees and beg my forgiveness. Please.

He settled his long form arrogantly on the tree stump she'd just been leaning against, their child nestled in his arms.

"Why did you run, knowing you were pregnant with my child?" he asked. "Why didn't you tell me?"

It was not an accusation. She heard the pain in his voice, the unspoken yearning.

Once again she had no answer. Cold sweat trickled between her breasts and down her back.

"You know the answer," she said, unable to look at him. What she'd done had been wrong. Refusing to let him know about the child had been a horrible betrayal. But what he'd wanted from her had been far worse.

How could she tell him the truth?

How could she tell him she loved him?

He would never believe her.

Alexi moved with a fluid grace. Even with a child in his arms, he managed to sleekly close the distance between them and sit cross-legged on the blanket next to her. The baby whimpered, nestling into Alexi's neck, looking for something Alexi didn't have.

"You interrupted his meal." Her eyes lowered, remembering the sight she'd greeted him with only a few moments ago...an eternity.

"Insatiable, are you?" Alexi said to the child, laughing.

Reluctantly he handed the child over to her. Beneath her lashes, she waited for him to turn away. He looked pointedly at her breasts, his eyes hungry.

Insatiable.

There had always been that between them. Desire. Lust.

Shifting her shoulders slightly and holding a small blanket across her breasts, she managed to undo the buttons of her shirt. The boy latched on eagerly.

Alexi laughed again, the smile on his face growing. "We think alike."

Her insides churned. Apprehension and fear were not conducive to nursing. Angela tried to relax.

"Here," he said, and pulled her between his legs so her back rested against his chest, his arms supporting her.

Her feeble protest went unnoticed.

Warmth from him radiated through the layers of clothing separating them. While the child nursed, he massaged her neck and her shoulders with clinical detachment.

"You look tired," he said.

"It goes with the territory," she countered.

The braid she'd plaited this morning unraveled slowly, his fingers shifting through its length. His hand brushed her gently, provocatively now.

"Jasmine." He breathed deeply. "You remembered."

"It was handy," she told him waspishly, then instantly regretted the words and the tone.

Against her back, she felt the deep, low rumbling of his chest.

"The babe's asleep."

Indeed, the blanket had slipped and her entire breast was bared to his view. Heat flared. Instantly she remedied the situation, covering herself, setting the child in a warm nest of blankets and disengaging herself from the intimate contact she could succumb to so easily that it terrified her.

At every turn he tested, challenged anew.

Casually, he leaned back on an elbow. He plucked a blade of grass and chewed on it, always watching her. His eyes were brooding, searching, studying. He delved deeper than she wanted him to see.

Chills spiraled through her.

She swallowed hard.

"You've buttoned your shirt wrong..."

Indeed, she had the whole thing askew. Fingers trembling, she fumbled with the tiny holes and little buttons until she made a disaster of her clothes.

Embarrassment should not have played havoc with her senses. Memories of another time and place lodged in her head. She continued to fumble awkwardly.

"Let me," he said, brushing her hands aside, grinning crookedly, heart-meltingly.

He could do that to her.

His knuckles warmed her flesh, his eyes roaming blatantly, possessively.

"No." Her protest was weak.

"Fine."

Once more he leaned back in a negligent, uncaring pose. Nothing seemed to shake the man or rattle his nerves. She finished the chore then covered the child with the blanket she'd draped over her shoulder.

"Does he have a name?"

"What?" Her mind snapped to attention.

"Does he have a name?"

Alexi's patience seemed to be abundant today. He waited for an answer with his head cocked to match his grin.

"Alexander," she whispered, wishing all the while she hadn't named him that.

"What?" His pose changed, no longer quite so arrogant.

For a moment she thought she saw a flash of warmth in his eyes.

It vanished.

"What?" he asked again.

Strength and power vibrated in the depth and tone of the single word. He demanded all.

It wasn't a question, and she knew it. It was a command, a confirmation that she'd lied to him about the child's parentage. He wanted nothing but her complete surrender.

He sounded so very smug in the knowledge she'd just placed in his lap.

"Alexander Samuel Chamberlain," she told him, her chin lifted slightly, her emphasis on the last name.

He flinched. She was determined not to let him know how vulnerable she was. How much she had loved him.

"Popov," he told her, his tone brooking no argument, his gaze shredding her nerves until she trembled.

But there was much to argue. He had never seen fit to offer his name to her. Now he made it sound as if the past were her fault.

Tears swam in her eyes. Once again she broke down in front of him, and she hated herself for her weakness. This time she didn't hold a gun on him, and this time she found herself in his arms, wrapped in the heat and the warmth of the man she'd always loved--but a man who would not return that love.

She had no quick replies to his probing questions. The tears she shed were useless tears and would solve nothing. Yet she couldn't seem to stop. Angrily she brushed them away, but more followed. Unstoppable rivers of pain and anguish pulsed from her, wetting his shirt.

His hands were soothing hands, his words calming words. There was nothing personal or intimate about his gestures. He touched her heart and her soul while she reminded herself he wanted nothing from her except the child that lay sleeping peacefully by her side. For so long she'd held her love for him deep inside.

She'd given herself over to the care and nurturing of Alexi's small son so the child would not be like his father--cold and so very hard.

Now Alexi was demanding her soul, her heart, her firstborn, and as surely as he'd broken her heart once before, he would break it again. She had no defense against him.

He was not begging her forgiveness.

Instead he demanded their child.

"What do you want from me?" Her words were muffled in his shirt. She put her hands on his broad chest and pushed away from him.' 'What do you want from me?" she demanded again. Still, he held her within the circle of his arms, his expression almost cruel.

"Everything you're willing to give. Your love. Your hand." His voice cracked, and for a moment she thought she saw the chill in his eyes warm to a heated glow.

She was mistaken.

"I've already given all that I can."

"It's not enough."

"No more, Alexi. Go home. Go back to your country, where nobility is more important than love, and leave the two of us in peace. This is no place for a man so drenched in the ideals of the aristocracy that he can't see beyond his long, elegant nose."

She wiped the tears from her cheeks with her arm.

"Go home," she whispered.

"When you agree to come with me."

"Never."

"What? You've had your fill of adventure?"

His tone of voice, filled with scorn, the look in his eyes, suffused with pity, took their toll.

She rose, meaning to scoop the child into her arms. Too late she saw he'd read her mind and had little Alexi in his arms.

He rose.

"Not this time," he said with a slow drawl. He whistled for Jabbar. The horse wasted no time in coming to Alexi's side.

"You can't do this," she told him. "He needs to eat. He--"

"Wet nurses are not hard to find."

"What?" Her astonishment echoed in the small glade.

Jabbar nickered softly, nuzzling his master's arm. With little effort, the babe tucked against his chest, Alexi mounted his stallion.

"Are you coming or staying?" he inquired politely.

Chapter Twenty-one

Watching Devil Blackmoor ride toward the high pasture made Sam realize how much he loved Angela and wanted what was best for her. What was best for Angela was to be alone with Devil so they could work out their differences, and the next best thing for Angela was a speedy marriage.

A shotgun wedding, if necessary.

White Flower stood by Sam's side, his wife, Angela's mother.

"Go get the preacher," White Flower said, her small hand gently squeezing his own. "I'll pack her things. Devil will want to start for home as soon as it's done."

For a long moment Sam didn't move, couldn't. His heart pounded against his ribs. "You're sure?" he asked. "I don't want to be called a meddling old fool tomorrow. I gave Devil my word I'd give him time to convince her."

"I'm sure, and so are you. The only way she'll back down and marry him is if she has to. She's as stubborn as her daddy."

"Stubborn as her mama, you mean."

White Flower smiled. "You were of the same mind. Hard-headed. Determined to have your own way."

She ran her hands up his chest and kissed him. Sam grunted and took the woman into his arms, her fingers winding around his neck and feathering into his hair. He loved her so much, and he wanted Angela to be happy with her man.

White Flower pulled away. Their gazes locked, a wealth of unspoken knowledge flowing between the two of them. They understood each other, understood how sometimes two stubborn fools might have to be pushed together by those a little older and a great deal wiser.

Whether Sam liked it or not, Devil was Angela's man, and the arrogant aristocrat needed to be put in his place. Sam had seen how Devil had looked at Angela, saw the naked yearning, the love brimming hi his eyes.

Angela would have never gotten into this fix if she didn't love Devil.

How the hell the man had let her go was beyond anything Sam could understand. He understood duty. He understood loyalty and honor, too.

But Devil had crossed an ocean for Angela, given up his birthright, and Sam wasn't about to let all that effort go to waste. He wanted to see his daughter married and happy, and he wanted his grandson to have a strong last name, a name that wouldn't label the child a bastard.

Breathless from his kiss, White Flower could barely speak. "The preacher headed south from the trading post two days ago. On that lazy mule he couldn't have gotten too far. My bet is that he's stayed the night with the Johnson's. She's the best cook in these parts, and he has a hankering for good meals."

White Flower's hands had slid down his back, and now she was kneading the seat of his denims. "You got something else on your mind, woman?" he asked, his voice low and throaty. Unable to withstand her silent invitation, he groaned and pulled her into his arms for another heart-stopping kiss.

Everything he'd ever wanted, Sam found in this woman's arms. He didn't want to go anywhere but time wasn't standing still. He pulled away. "Now you keep that thought, woman," he said in a growl after giving her a warm smile. "I'm awful hungry."

"Hurry," she whispered, her subtle invitation hanging on the air between them like a potent aphrodisiac.

"South, you say?"

She nodded.

"Keep those two headstrong youngsters here--with the shotgun if you have to."

"Don't you worry," she told him.

He knew he didn't have to. White Flower would do what needed to be done. "Meddlin' fools," he mumbled to himself as he swung his leg over his fastest horse and set off down the mountain. He'd sure rather be riding White Flower right now and listening to her soft little sighs of pleasure.

Digging in his heels, he knew the quickest way to get what he wanted was to find that preacher and get him back here fast.

Halfway down the mountain, the entourage traveling his way made him pull up on the reins.

The man in front of him, he'd recognize anywhere. Ivan Civanovich rode a pure white stallion, and he blocked the trail. Three mules, carrying an assortment of packages, followed behind and further down the trail, he could hear the panting and muttering of another man as he hurried along.

"Best you move aside son. I've got business to attend to." Sam's voice, meant to be stern, echoed through the mountains.

The horse shifted. "I've already seen to it," Ivan countered, a wry grin spreading across his lips.

Sam pushed his Stetson back on his brow. "Now, that's real neighborly of you but I don't believe you understand what I'm getting at. You and I couldn't possibly be thinking along the same path," he said, even though he wanted Ivan to be seeing things his way. His mind shot back to White Flower and the way her breasts had felt nestled against his chest just a few minutes ago.

Ivan's smile was grim. "You wanted a preacher?" One dark brow quirked skyward. "I've saved you the trouble of riding for one."

Sam's horse sidestepped. Sam grunted.

Beyond Ivan, Sam could just make out the rattled rumblings of the preacher. He glanced quickly back at Ivan. "This your doing?"

Ivan nodded, then leaning on the horn of his saddle, he said, *' Alexi doesn't know. About time one of his people took matters into his own hands. If you know what I'm getting at."

Sam cocked his head to one side, assessing Ivan. "Good. Then you can take the brunt of his anger. Wouldn't want to lose anything important over this tiny matter." Ivan's laugh was full and hearty. "He's been meaner than a grizzly and twice as ornery ever since she left. Decided it was about time I got a good night's sleep for a change."

"Might as well warn you now, the two of them aren't going to like this."

"Too bad."

Huffing loudly, the preacher atop his mule pulled up alongside Ivan.

"Where's this wedding? And where's the bride and groom?"

"My house. Think you can make it a little bit farther? I'm sure White Flower will have something to appease your hunger." *She was surely cooking up something real nice when I left.*

"It's about time. This giant of a fellow hauled me from the dinner table without a by-your-leave. I can still smell Mrs. Johnson's sweet apple pie. Never got to finish the fried chicken."

"After the wedding you can order up whatever you want." Sam was suddenly feeling relieved that he wouldn't have to explain his part in all this. If Ivan didn't take full blame, at least it could be shared.

"Who's getting married?" the preacher asked again.

"Angela," Sam said.

"Alexi," Ivan said.

Ivan and Sam's gazes met and held. It seemed they had only the welfare of Angela and Alexi in mind. Working together they would see them married and happy.

It was about time.

~ * ~

Seeing Angela's stiff spine in front of him made Alexi more than aware that he'd gone about this reunion in exactly the way he'd planned not to.

She was all stubborn courage and raffled woman.

He'd challenged her and tested her in ways he shouldn't have.

Little Alexi squirmed in his arms, his full, pink lips puckering softly then sucking air. He'd be wanting his mother soon.

Hungry little devil.

Alexi groaned inwardly, remembering the challenge he'd tossed out to Angela. He'd never meant to delude her into thinking he would keep their child from her. How on earth had he managed to completely intimidate the woman he loved?

Sam had already given him permission to marry Angela, with the one stipulation that Angela agree. Now that he knew about his son, he didn't mean to give his sweet angel a choice--or to take the time to seduce her into compliance.

He no longer had the time to court her properly.

The babe let out a howl that would do any Sioux warrior proud--any clashing Tatar's, too.

Suddenly Angela was beside him, their knees touching, one arm outstretched, her eyes pleading. They had less than a mile to go before they'd reach Sam's house.

Ah, hell.

Slipping from the saddle, the babe in his arms, did not prove as big a challenge as handing him over to his mother. He didn't want to let go of his son, ever.

To top it all off, he didn't trust her to stay.

When she shifted sideways to hide herself from him, she had the look of a cornered animal, all wide-eyed and frightened. He sidestepped around her so he could watch, justifying the action by telling himself she'd be his wife soon then he'd see more than one beautifully shaped breast tipped with a taut, puckered rosebud.

Lowered lashes, a soft, rounded globe and a little boy nursing at his soon-to-be wife's breast all sent a surge of protective yearning sweeping through him bone-deep. Crouching down beside her, he touched the downy softness of his child's cheek. His knuckles brushed against feminine curves.

She inhaled, swift and deep.

He didn't acknowledge the touch, but it was all he could do to keep from smiling.

She wasn't immune to him.

The little gasp she'd emitted sent his heart racing. The stiffening of her spine he knew to be a defensive action against her emotions. Despite her show of bravado, she wanted him--perhaps as much as he wanted her.

If she didn't love him, he'd make do with desire until he could turn her around to his way of thinking. He sat back and crossed his arms over his chest, drinking in the scene.

He nearly reached out and took what was his when she shifted the child to the other breast. Her awkwardness and the gentle sway of her breasts had him rock-hard instantly. Long seconds passed before the child latched onto the other nipple; then, with trembling fingers, she covered herself.

He didn't know what he'd do if she looked at him with her passion-filled eyes again.

The last rays of the sun were dropping behind the mountains by the time she finished. The thought of moving on didn't appeal to him, nor did the thought of spending the night in Sam's house in separate bedrooms. He had food and a bedroll with an extra blanket.

They could stay here, talk, get to know each other again. He could cuddle his child without fear that she'd run out on him. There was little he liked better than a blazing campfire, the scent of wood smoke and a warm woman.

Caution was slipping fast. He wanted her in his arms and in his bed, tucked up snug against his heart. He needed to feel the steady beat of her heart, the rise and fall of her breasts.

The babe slept peacefully. It was now or never, he told himself, reaching out to slip the child from her arms. Alexi placed the child on a makeshift bed. Then he turned his attentions to his woman, his lady. He had abused her terribly, and he meant to make it up to her. He meant to show her that lovemaking was pleasurable for both parties. He meant to convince her he loved her more than life itself.

"Come here." His voice was husky with need.

She watched him with wide, beguiling eyes--and fear. She shook her head even while she swayed toward him. Buttoning her shirt seemed to take up most of her energy. He wanted to tell her to leave the fastenings be, that they'd be undone in a few seconds anyway.

"Please." he extended his hand. She wavered, then placed her trembling fingers in his.

Her small hand within his felt so good. He prayed she could not feel his fear. Rejection now was not what he wanted. His thumb traced a lazy circle on the inside of her delicately feminine wrist.

"I can't do this," she said, her voice trembling.

"You want to." He saw desire in her eyes. Jasmine filled his senses.

"That doesn't make it right."

Allah, but he needed to make it right. Where she was concerned he had too many regrets. The night in the hotel. His abduction of her. The times he never told her how much he loved her. The way he hurt her when he wanted to turn her into his mistress.

She'd been right to deny him. She did deserve better than his callous treatment of her. He had meant to put her on a pedestal, but in a place where he could keep her locked away from life.

He would make amends, if she'd only let him.

"You wouldn't fight me?" He was asking, he realized.

"I don't want you to do this," she said weakly, her voice a ragged sigh.

The words knifed his heart. She didn't want him to make love to her, but if he kissed her, if he seduced her, she wouldn't tell him no. "I understand," he said. But his patience was at an end. All he wanted was a kiss--one of her soft soul-shattering kisses--and he'd leave her alone until she understood he meant to do right by her.

He wouldn't compromise her.

This time they would do it all her way.

The right way.

~ * ~

She'd never felt so unsure of herself in her life. Devil had appeared out of nowhere and stolen her heart. How many times had he already done that?

Too many to count.

Fool.

Still, when he pulled her close, when he lifted her chin gently so that his mouth could cover hers, she let him. His tongue exploring, teasing her lips apart, warmed her soul, touched a part of her that had been dead for so long. His powerful, hard shoulders were beneath her fingertips, and she didn't want to let him go. Not now. Not ever.

She explored.

Need blossomed within her. She ran her hands up his thighs, resting them on the seat of his denims, then up his long back until they sifted through his hair.

A whimper of desire pulsed in the back of her throat. She opened to him, accepting his kisses and the yearning she felt inside. His hands were exploring her, resting for a moment on her hips and then moving along her sides until his thumbs touched the undersides of her breasts. Her blouse fell open, and she felt the fabric of his shirt against her tender, swollen nipples.

"Alexi." His name on her lips made him groan his desire, his hands roaming over her breasts. His tongue was deep inside her mouth, plundering.

All she could think was that it had been so long, so very long. She wanted his touch, yearned for his kisses, but she knew she had to have his love first.

That thought--along with his mouth descending to cover a nipple-- was like a splash of frigid water on her senses. She gasped a soft "no" and pulled away. Her face heated with embarrassment, desire and anger.

How dared he come here and start what was supposed to be dead and gone? There could be nothing between them. He would only trample her fragile emotions into the dirt.

Frantically pulling her shut together, she bent down to retrieve the sleeping child. Once again he was faster, scooping little Alexi into his arms, a wistful look on his implacable features.

"I won't be your mistress," she told him. "I won't!" This time her words took on a new strength and determination.

"I thought you knew the offer was rescinded a long time ago," he said, his voice husky with need, his eyes reflecting a deep sorrow.

"Don't touch me again," she told him, her arms outstretched for the child he wouldn't hand over.

His look was filled with the pain of rejection, but his determination never ceased to amaze her. "I will have you, angel. Don't ever doubt it. You're mine. I thought you understood."

"Never."

The lines of his face deepened, and his eyes lost the warmth of the passion they'd just shared. "Never is a long time." His words were soft and deadly.

"You can't seduce me." She shot out the challenge before she had a chance to think of the consequences.

His smile was roguish. He had been walking toward the horses, but he stopped midstride, his chin tucked neatly into his shoulder as he looked back to her, his eyes all she could see. Everything about him was cool assessment and arrogant command.

She balked.

He could seduce her with that look, and he knew it. She melted with a word of love, with a touch. Only a few seconds ago she'd been sweet and hot and wanting him more than life itself.

She stiffened and moved to the horse.

"I think it's time we moved on," she said.

"Perhaps it is," he said, his words a sultry promise, taking on a meaning all their own. "It seems we have company."

~ * ~

"Hello, there." The voice echoed between the mountains.

"Ivan." Alexi strode forward, the babe still tucked neatly in one arm. Ivan stared at the child, then at the boy's mother, and a look of tender amusement twinkled in his eyes.

Sam rode from the protective cover of the stand of aspens.

"Papa."

Foreboding gripped Alexi. He didn't like the look on Sam's face. For that matter, he didn't like the knowing grin plastered on Ivan's smug countenance.

The two of them had put their heads together, and he didn't think he would like what they had come up with.

"What do you want?" One-handed, Alexi helped Angela into the saddle then mounted Jabbar. The babe chortled and cooed delightedly.

"To escort the two of you to a wedding."

Ivan's voice was soft and cajoling. Alexi had never heard his friend sound so insincere in his life.

"Whose?" Angela's voice trembled with what sounded to Alexi like indignation.

He knew her father was behind this, because even as she asked the question, Sam pointed the shotgun at Alexi's heart.

"Yours and Devil's," Sam said with an irritating calm that rocked Alexi to his soul. When he'd talked to Sam earlier, the man had promised to stay out of this and let him mend the broken fences between them.

Alexi could have strangled Angela's father without a thought. All the steps he'd taken--the care he meant to woo Angela with--had now gone up in smoke, because they were being forced to wed by her father.

"No." She bristled like a little wildcat caught between two grizzlies.

He didn't like her answer at all.

"Would you rather he shot me?" The moment the question left his lips, he was sure he'd regret the answer.

She took long enough to form a reply. And with eyes wide and clear she said, "Yes, Papa. Shoot him."

Sam looked stunned. Ivan appeared ready to throw himself in front of the shotgun, even though he'd been an integral part of all this chaos.

"Not until you have his name all nice and legal, Angela. Then I'd be happy to oblige you."

Chapter Twenty-two

Helpless would sum up all the feelings that churned inside Alexi when he stopped in front of the log cabin and saw White Flower standing beside the door, a shotgun in her hand and a cartful of suitcases and boxes next to her.

Then all sense of control left him when the preacher stepped out of the house, Bible in hand. He could feel Angela stiffen. All the arguments she'd fired at Sam on the way down from the meadow had bounced off Sam's thick skull.

In a few minutes Angela would be his wife.

It was what he'd wanted for over a year now.

She'd be a little hellcat in his arms until he could wrestle with her feelings and convince her he wasn't all bad. That thought sent myriad sensations storming through him like a Texas twister.

Too little, too late, kept popping up in his head. He was over a year too late in marrying her, and he hadn't even had a chance to propose. What woman wouldn't have a bee in her bonnet?

He needed to pull her aside and find out what she was thinking. But he wasn't sure she'd tell him.

She'd had lots of time to succumb to his charms, and it seemed she still wanted to make a point--that point being that he was a low-down, dirty polecat.

He couldn't argue with her there.

But he meant to spend a lifetime making it up to her, if she'd let him.

"Dearly beloved..."

That snapped him to attention. He'd only half concentrated on the unfolding events. He wasn't even sure when he'd dismounted. Angela stood beside him, a nosegay of wildflowers in her hand and tears staining her cheeks.

This wasn't supposed to be happening this way. This hadn't been the bargain he'd struck with Sam. He'd wanted a willing bride.

Words of protest began then lodged in his throat with one warning look from Sam.

Before he could breathe deeply they were married, White Flower hustling them off to the wagon.

A kiss for Angela on both damp cheeks from her mother.

A boost into the wagon from Sam before White Flower handed Angela the sleeping child.

Jabbar and Kangee were tied behind them. Sam gave the horse pulling the wagon a slap, and they started down the trail.

Heavy silence fell between Alexi and Angela, enshrouding them like a cloak of death.

Alexi cleared his throat to speak, then thought better of it and snapped the reins. A cold chill settled in his heart.

The right words wouldn't come to mind. Allah, for this situation there were no right words. The horse plodded on, minutes changing to hours.

What did a man say to an unwilling bride?

The trail wound about the mountain. It would be hours before they reached the trading post. If he had the courage, he'd stop and make camp. He'd never felt so weak-kneed in his life.

Angela swayed, her head nodding.

Alexi knew an instant of panic. Then, the decision made, he called out to the horses, "Whoa."

The horses slowed and stopped. He jumped from the seat and helped a sleepy-eyed and exhausted Angela down from the wagon.

"We'll make camp here," he said, wondering how on earth he was going to sleep next to her and not make love to her--to his wife.

The brief contact he'd just had with her brought an instant hardening to his body, every muscle stiff with tension and a devastating need. Her breasts had pushed up against his chest, and his fingers had found purchase around her waist. The smell of jasmine filled the air around him, reminding him how long it had been.

Little Alexander let out a loud wail of discontent.

~ * ~

While Alexi started the fire and made dinner, Angela fed the baby. Through lowered lashes, she watched Alexi work his magic on everything he touched. She didn't want to give in to him. It shouldn't be so easy for him to waltz back into her life and take up where they'd left off. There should have been some kind of penance for his misdeeds.

Watching him stride down the hill toward her this afternoon had been her undoing. She'd wanted to run to him with arms open wide, yet she held back--held back because she wanted him on his knees and begging her forgiveness.

True, he believed his child should have his name. So did she. He desired her. Beyond that, she yearned for his love.

Perhaps in time.

There was so much that needed to be said. *We have to talk.*

She couldn't keep those words from her mind. Talking. How much talk could clear up all their problems? An eternity wouldn't be long enough.

He stood over her, a coffee cup in hand. She reached for it. Little Alexander now slept soundly in a shelter Alexi had made for them. It had been a busy day for the child, too. After all, she thought as she looked into the fire, a cacophony of thoughts clattering around in her head, it isn't every day your mommy marries your daddy.

Holding the cup with both hands, she let the heat emanating from the liquid warm her, sipping gingerly while she thought about the events of the day. Alexi settled down next to her, one leg stretched out, the other knee bent, his arm resting on it, his own cup of coffee sitting on a rock nearby.

"I didn't mean for this to happen."

She turned to him, stricken.

"I mean"--he ran his long, callused fingers through his hair--"I didn't want you to be forced to marry me. The minute I saw the baby, I--"

"I know," she told him, a forced smile on her face. "You had to give the child a name. I appreciate all that you've done." She watched her toes curl, feeling helpless and at a loss for words.

He took the cup from her hands, warming her cold fingers with his own. "If you'll let me, I want to do more. I would make a real life for you and our child. Cherish you both."

It seemed he waited for her to look at him. She couldn't bring herself to meet his gaze; the fear she felt was too powerful. His finger gently touched her chin.

"Angel," he said softly. "How can I make this right? Tell me."

If you have to ask ... "Just be here for him. Don't forget he's your son."

She heard him inhale, a softness to the sound that belied the harsh reality of their circumstances. The bridge separating them was too wide to cross this night. It might take years, even a lifetime. That dismal thought left her quaking.

"I want to make this right for you," he said. He lifted her chin, holding her still so their eyes would meet. His were warm and caring. She shuddered. "What can I do?" he asked again.

Hold me. Love me. Tears filled her eyes. It seemed all she'd done since he'd ridden back into her life was cry. Where had her determination and courage flown?

He pulled her into his arms, his strength comforting. Her head nestled against his chest, and she could hear the power of his heart, feel the steel that exemplified the man. She ran her fingers across his arms and shoulders, wondering if they would ever straighten this out.

To tell him the truth would mean unraveling her heart and soul for his inspection. She'd done that once before. She wasn't sure she could do it again.

For the sake of their child she had to try.

"What do you want from me?" she asked, pulling away from him slightly. The distance between them felt cold and dark. The need to be in the safe shelter of his arms filled her.

"A wife, a mother." He paused to smooth her hair back then to run his finger along the line of her jaw.

It was a tender gesture, a lover's caress. She grew bolder, daring now to blurt out the truth. "I love you," she said.

He looked startled by her words--at a loss. "Do you truly?" he asked.

A sharp retort came to mind. Instead, she said, "Yes," into the palm of his hand. But the question was and always would be, *Do you love me?* She was too afraid of the answer to ask.

She kissed his palm and she heard his indrawn breath. Disappointment welled inside her. Living without the words said would be no different now than it had been over the last year. If he didn't love her, at least he'd married her and accepted the child. She would do all she could to make him happy.

"Say it again," he whispered, his teeth nibbling where his ringers had traced. His warm breath sent rivers of heat through her.

"What?" she asked, unsure of him and his motives; but then, realizing what he wanted, she meant to deny the words. She couldn't. The first confession opened a chasm that needed to be closed. "I love you," she said softly into his mouth, which was now ravaging hers and demanding she accompany her words with action.

"Show me." He rained kisses on her face. "Show me, angel, just how much you love me."

Her heart turned over. Angela's fingers speared into his black hair, holding his head hard while her other palm rubbed quickly, greedily up his arm and over his shoulder and chest. She exulted in the familiar feel of him. "I love you," she said again into his mouth.

Angela moved an inch away so she could look into his eyes, but Alexi leaned into her, the movement too poignant for her to ignore. She wanted so much to hear the same words from him. As if it would entice a response, she wanted to say the words over and over again until he reciprocated the feelings.

He didn't. He seized her face between his palms and claimed her lips with a deep, possessing kiss, one she thought she would surely feel forever. Then he broke from her and, without another glance, strode toward the shelter where the bedrolls were laid out and ready.

She found herself shaking her head and pushing back against the log behind her. This was too soon. Too much, too soon. Despite the hot kisses and her revelation of love, she wasn't ready to let him make love to her.

"Alexi..." Her voice wobbled.

He tossed her a wicked, lopsided smile, his eyes twinkling devilishly in the light of the fire. Long, lanky strides brought him to her.

"Angela." The one word was as smooth as the finest Kentucky whiskey.

Suddenly he was on bended knee, her hand held gently in his own. "Will you do me the honor of becoming my wife?"

She felt wide-eyed and bashful under the onslaught of his gaze. After the fact, he didn't have to ask. But he did.

"Yes," she told him, wishing for more, yet knowing this was all she would get.

"Can you find in your heart a way to forgive me?" he asked.

Before she could do anything but nod and try to hide her shock, he scooped her into his arms. The bed was a few steps away. He stole a kiss as he strode toward the welcoming embrace of the blankets and the soft bed he'd sculpted out of fabric remnants from the box her mother had deposited in the wagon.

For a few seconds she did nothing more than close her eyes and listen to the wind rustle the pine needles and the sounds of the night animals singing their songs. When he set her down on the blankets, she opened her eyes, drinking in the sight of him and thinking it had been too long. Her gaze traveled over him in fascination, lingering on his mouth, his hands, his long legs. A potent feeling rose strong and hot in her. The first time she hadn't felt quite this way. Now the sensations were stronger, more intense, and much more heartrending. She wanted to do what he'd asked.

Show him.

She didn't want to ask him how.

His body gave a sudden jerk of surprise when she took his hand in hers and pulled him down beside her. His smile was rakish.

Her hands roamed restlessly over his face and shoulders, exploring. She pressed his mouth open to delve deeply inside, stroking wetly along its roof, over his tongue, across his teeth. Her manner was aggressive, with a singleness of purpose. She felt as if they were involved in a contest she was determined to win.

"I want this time to be different." His voice sounded raspy.

Reminded of the hated accusations that stood between them, she stiffened, waiting for his words proclaiming her a harlot. They didn't come, and he looked suddenly as if he knew what she feared.

"I believe in you," he told her. "And I want you to trust in me."

He'd read her mind and answered her question without speaking of the incident.

~ * ~

Inwardly he cursed himself. He'd learned from Stephan's mother that her virtue should not have been questioned, that sometimes women didn't carry inside them proof of their chastity. He should have listened to Angela. She had been so innocent and so trusting. His instincts had homed in on her lack of experience, but he'd been too blind to realize it. He watched and was enthralled with her.

Her eyelids fell to a sultry half-mast, beneath which passion glittered like hot jewels. "I do trust you."

Having been so long away from her, he didn't know what to think of her words. It should have been enough, but he wasn't exactly in a clear-thinking frame of mind. He was drawn back to her soft, sultry lips again and again.

He wanted to know if she wanted him as badly as he did her. Without knowing his question, she answered him.

"I want to see you. All of you," she murmured into his kiss. "Take off your clothes."

Part of him reacted with shock. For all his experience, he had always led and expected the female to follow. No one had ever demanded anything of him before. But another part of him responded to the strange urgency in her voice and had him tearing at the buttons of his shirt. She was touching and kissing each portion he uncovered, worshiping him with innocent appreciation until he stood sleek and dark before her. The palms of her hands rubbed up from the flat of his belly and over the swell of his chest to sweep over his shoulders, her gaze heated and admiring.

"You're beautiful. My dark warlord." She moved closer, so that her face nuzzled the center of his chest. She inhaled deeply, the scent of him filling her, touching her heart, and making her think it had been too long.

Her praise was an aphrodisiac. Needing the same closeness, his hands moved up the front of her shirt, seeking the small fastenings. He paused. "I would see you the same way."

She nodded, still pressed against him. He felt her smile.

He worked down the row of buttons until fabric parted, and he pushed the material from her shoulders. She wore nothing beneath.

"You're just as I remember you," he murmured as his hands skimmed over smooth skin.

He lifted her and helped her slip her denims off. Even as he sank into her upraised arms, she was melting with him. She was aggressive, bold in her desire, and he knew he'd always remember the moment. She was like no other.

Her boldness meant only one thing to him: she trusted him and believed in him. There was no reason to hold back. With one swift move he was sheathed inside her.

"Let's forget the past," she said breathlessly against his ear. She wanted him to believe in her and trust her. "I want to create something new and beautiful."

And so he meant to, with hard, fevered thrusts that had her arching up for more, crying out in soft little pleas until her body responded to his, guiding him to a fulfillment that defied time.

He pulled the covers around them, kissing her gently about the face and throat and breasts. She shifted languidly beneath him, holding his head, her eyes closed. She was so beautiful; she'd given herself so completely, he wanted to weep with the fullness of his love for her.

"I don't ever want you to regret this, Angela." He meant forever.

"I don't." She trembled. Then she shifted so they were side by side, and she nestled against him with soft little purring sounds of contentment. He was lost.

"I love you, angel," he said.

But she was already asleep.

~ * ~

Alexi didn't sleep. He was awake all night, knowing he still had to convince Angela that his reasons for coming back for her revolved around her alone, that until he had ridden into the clearing he didn't even know he had a child.

Words alone wouldn't be enough.

There would be no easy way. But when he looked down at the sleeping woman snuggled next to him, he knew in the end the struggle would be worth all his efforts. If he had to, he meant to bury his pride.

He'd always had everything he'd ever wanted--until Angela had walked out on him. Those months had been the hardest of his entire life, living without her, wondering if she'd ever forgive him. He should have fallen down on his knees and begged her forgiveness the moment he saw her. But he'd been too awed by the child even to think of begging. Then he'd been angry and hurt.

Now he could make up for the hurt he'd inflicted upon her. He would make sure that from this moment on she'd have everything she wanted. He'd die for her. He'd go down on his knees for her. She was his world. He'd tried so desperately to put her in a place where she couldn't touch his heart, because he'd always known there would come a time when he could no longer live without her. That time was now.

Toward dawn he finally drifted off into a light sleep, only to be awakened by the gliding of Angela's fingertips, swirling over his abdomen, playing about his navel. He was instantly alert, firm and pulsing eagerly in anticipation of her touch.

Without so much as a "good morning," she slid over him, engulfing him with her snug heat, accepting him again and again without reservation, until their hard, driving motion had them gasping in unison, straining for the reward they both knew awaited. With Alexi's hands on her hips to direct the rhythm, their climax grew nearer. He lifted his upper body to fasten his mouth upon the taut peak of one breast, sucking hard, biting down without gentleness, and she went wild above him, her body bucking, dissolving into a series of frantic quakes that pulled him over the edge of expectation into ecstasy.

After that she stretched over him, sighing lazily as he tried to prevent his total collapse. They needed to talk, and he couldn't afford to let this companionable time between them pass.

"Angela?"

"Hmm..."

"I've bought land in Wyoming. Cattle, too. My people are starting to build a ranch house. Ivan came with me, as well as some of his people who were left homeless and uprooted." He wanted her to like the arrangement. "All that was left in Ivan's homeland was pain and sorrow. I convinced him that America was heaven on earth."

She smiled up at the lightening sky overhead. "Anything else?"

"Do you have a problem with all those people underfoot while we're honeymooning?"

"We can go to higher ground, or perhaps to Trey's cabin in the Black Hills," came her firm reply.

He smiled. "I'd like that."

"Which?" She raked her fingers through his hair.

"Either one--both. If we take long enough, the house might be finished by the time we get back."

"You won't miss your home land?"

He shook his head. "This is my home."

"If you dare take a mistress, I'll take her to the top of the highest peak and leave her there."

"One woman is more than enough challenge for me."

He reached to draw out one of the sapphire earrings she wore then did the same with the diamond he wore. For a long moment he held them in his hand; then he exchanged earrings, slipping hers into his ear and the diamond into hers. The morning light caught the prisms of color. The sapphire stood out against his swarthy coloring as he came up on his elbow above her. It gave him a wild look, a dangerous air. She liked it.

"I love you, Angela. Wear my earring, and I will wear yours, so our hearts will always be united and we'll never forget all we mean to each other."

And under the clear Colorado sky, they spent the rest of the morning as lovers would, sharing their hopes and dreams and building a life together that would endure forever.

ABOUT THE AUTHOR

Born in Medford, Oregon, novelist Christine Young has lived in Oregon all of her life. After graduating from Oregon State University with a BS in science, she spent another year at Southern Oregon State University working on her teaching certificate, and a few years later received her Master's degree in secondary education and counseling. Now the long, hot days of summer provide the perfect setting for creating romance. She sold her first book, *Dakota's Bride*, the summer of 1998 and her second book, *My Angel* to Kensington. Each fall, Christine returns to the classroom-and the pool-as a math teacher and high school swimming coach. Her teaching and writing careers have intertwined with raising three children. Yet summer still seems to be lucky for romance. Awe-struck e-books released another of Christine's historical romances *Allura* in April 2009. *My Angel* is being re-released by Rogue Phoenix Press, as was *Dakota's Bride* earlier in 2010.

www.ingramcontent.com/pod-product-compliance
Lightning Source LLC
Chambersburg PA
CBHW061943170626
46813CB00006B/2510